Praise for *Caribbean Paradise*
by readers

"I loved this book! The Lord used it to remind me of so many things and encourage my heart! I have laughed and cried. I could totally see and hear the characters. I don't like to read, but I couldn't put this book down." G.C.

"I loved it! It brought back lots of memories of growing up in the D.R." S.B.

"Great book! It made me want to go to the Dominican Republic. Can't wait to read the next book!" M.H.

"I feel like I have been in the Caribbean, and thoroughly enjoyed my trip! I was reminded to 'trust' the Lord in the midst of the storms. Continue to write as the Lord gives it to you. I'm already looking forward to your next book!" B.S.

"I LOVED it! AWESOME! You did a WONDERFUL job! I am ready for the next one... :)" E.Y.

"What a great story! Thank you for sharing your heart and your very special characters with me. There are so many things I loved about it. I loved the use of history and great pictures of the places you've visited and researched. I really liked the way I was drawn into Hanna's and Jake's dialogues with God -- and how He is leading them. I loved the picture of Hanna's insecurities -- how they keep popping up and she has to trust God. (The book) left me feeling hopeful and refreshed -- affirming truths God has been working in my life." J.H.

"I loved it! Having worked on a foreign field as a missionary, I completely understood many of the battles (Hanna) faced. I caught myself laughing out loud at one point, and wanting to weep at others. It both convicted my heart, which wasn't so pleasant, and blessed me. Can't wait to read the next one!" J.C.

TERI METTS

Caribbean Paradise

Island Legacy Novel - *Book One*

Caribbean Paradise

TERI METTS

Caribbean Paradise

Copyright © 2010 by Teri Metts

All rights reserved. The reproduction or utilization of this work in whole or in part in any form or by any means is forbidden, except for brief quotations in printed reviews, without written permission of Teri Metts, Simple Life Ministry, P.O. Box 250, D'Lo, MS 39062.

This is a work of fiction. Names, characters, and incidents are either the product of the author's imagination or are used fictitiously, and any resemblance to actual persons, living or dead, business establishments, or events is entirely coincidental.

All Scripture quotations are taken from *The Holy Bible,* New American Standard Bible®, Copyright © 1960, 1962, 1963, 1971, 1972, 1973, 1975, 1977, 1995 by The Lockman Foundation. Used by permission. www.Lockman.org.

ISBN: 1453707220
EAN – 13: 9781453707227

*In loving memory of my mother,
Truly Hanna Lorch*

Before I was conceived, she dedicated me to the Lord for missionary service. I pray this book honors the sacrifice she made.

*"For this child I prayed, and the Lord has given me my petition which I asked of Him. So I have also dedicated (her) to the Lord; as long as (she) lives (she) is dedicated to the Lord."
I Samuel 1:27-28*

Acknowledgements

First of all I want to thank my heavenly Father for entrusting the writing of this story into my hands. If it had not been for His leading, help and counsel, I know it would have never been written.

I also want to thank my husband, Joe, for encouraging me every step of the way, and for the encouragement he continues to give on a daily basis. Because he believes in me, he helps me believe in myself – especially on those days when I'm tempted to give up and quit.

And many thanks go out to a special group of ladies who were the first to read my novel (when it was still in an embarrassing rough stage), and yet they were so gracious in their comments. For their help in catching mistakes in grammar, punctuation, and spelling – I am most grateful! A big thank-you to GiGi Creel, Ann Beauchamp, Jane Wilson, Melinda Hand, Sarah Black, and Jo Hebert, who shared her song, *Rhythms of Grace*, with me.

Finally, I want to say how thankful I am for family and friends who so often encourage and pray for me, and who believe in me as a writer. You'll never know how often your words of encouragement help keep me going! I love you all!!

Chapter One

Sweat poured down Hanna's back, pooling around the top of her shorts; her bright red t-shirt clung to her damp skin. She would not have thought it possible, but the heat and humidity of that mid-summer day rivaled what she and her mother had left behind in Alabama. If only there'd been a breeze, it would have helped. But not even a ripple stirred the sultry air as they stood at the base of a rut-riddled cobblestone path winding steadily up the mountainside.

Their journey had begun an hour earlier in the garbage strewn, traffic clogged streets of Cap Haitien, Haiti, transporting them over poorly constructed, unpaved mountain roads and dumping them in the small hamlet of Milot. Hanna was still trying to figure out why this side trip to the poverty stricken, politically unstable country of Haiti had been included in their Caribbean excursion.

Using her hand, she shaded her eyes against the glare of the sun while listening to their tour guide – a lanky, ebony-skinned Haitian named Jean-Claude, who lived in one of the weathered clapboard huts near the base of the mountain trail. He spoke English with a heavy accent and was a self-proclaimed local historian bubbling forth with a wealth of information. Hanna shifted her gaze, looking in the general direction of their destination: La Citadelle Laferriere – a massive stone fortress built between 1805 and 1820 as a part of fortifications designed to keep the newly independent nation of Haiti safe from possible French incursions – attacks, which ironically never materialized. With dramatic flare, Jean-Claude informed them La Citadelle, sitting atop the 3000 foot Bonnet a L'Eveque mountain, provided a view of the city of Cap Haitien as well as the Atlantic Ocean. He claimed that on a clear day even the eastern coast of Cuba – ninety miles away – could be seen.

At sixteen, Hanna felt certain she could walk the five-mile trail to the top of the mountain, but others in their group, mostly middle aged and older, opted for riding on the bony, undersized animals Jean-Claude called horses. Hanna thought they looked more like a pitiful mutation of pony, mule and donkey. Most appeared half-starved, many sickly. How any of the spindly, malnourished beasts successfully made the trek up the steep incline while carrying mostly overweight tourists in the hot, tropical climate of Haiti was beyond her. They'd been on the trail about thirty minutes when a guide repeatedly whacked the sluggish animal upon which Hanna rode with a stick. Her heart beat in time to the *clop-clop-clop* of hooves as she debated what to do. She dismounted the horse minutes later, claiming a need to stretch her legs.

Gravel crunched beneath the soles of her tennis shoes as she surveyed the rows of houses scattered along the mountain trail. For reasons she couldn't explain, Hanna felt drawn to the women and children standing in many of the doorways. Most of the children's dirty feet were bare, their baggy clothes stained and tattered. The women, dressed in thin, faded dresses or mismatched blouses and skirts, their flip-flop clad feet calloused and covered in dust, stared at the caravan of tourist as they plodded past their homes. The cracker box dwellings, no bigger than most laundry rooms in an average American house, were constructed of concrete blocks or rough-hewn clapboard and painted varying shades of blue, yellow or red. The roofs were made of corrugated tin; some floors were concrete, while others appeared to be dirt. The only men Hanna saw, other than Jean-Claude and the other "tour guides" helping lead *and* push the horses up the cobbled pathway, labored in open fields, laying out coffee to dry.

A woman squatting in front of a cook fire farther up the trail, her head bound in a colorful turban, glanced up as Hanna passed, her deeply lined, coal black face expressionless. A younger woman stood beside her, a scrawny child on her hip. The little one's gaunt face and bloated belly told a story Hanna didn't want to hear. A ditch, emitting a strong stench of urine and human waste, ran along side their house. Hanna swallowed back the bile that rose in her throat, distraught at the sight of children playing along the water's edge. Their laughter seemed out of keeping with their surroundings. She wondered how it was possible this sea of poor, hungry humanity lived along a path frequently traveled by well-fed, well-dressed foreigners, who individually paid more money to visit this one tourist attraction than most of the locals would see in six months. The scene reminded her of one of those commercials displaying pictures of starving children, which always seemed to come on whenever she and her parents were eating supper in front of the television. Only problem, there was no remote and no way to change channels.

Hanna glanced around at the others in her group, but no one else seemed to have noticed the squalid conditions and pervasive smell. Or maybe they simply chose not to. But how could they ignore the haunting eyes of the people? She knew she couldn't. In fact, as strange as it may have sounded, she felt a tugging on her heart, a desperate urge to find a way to bring a ray of hope into what appeared to be a bleak and dismal existence.

Once at the top, while everyone else oohed and awed over what Jean-Claude referred to as a breathtaking panorama of unfolding mountains, river pierced valleys and the deep blue waters of the Atlantic Ocean, Hanna gazed back down the mountainside – an inescapable longing in her heart.

"Lord God," she prayed. "If You'll let me, I want to come back to Haiti one day, not as a tourist, but . . . as a missionary."

Chapter Two

With hands clasped like a tight fist in her lap, Hanna Truly gazed out the window of the airplane as they neared the coast of the Dominican Republic, watching with nervous expectation for her first glimpse of the country where she would soon be living. Although not a hint of land was in sight, she knew somewhere in the vast expanse of turquoise-tinted ocean dotted with whitecaps sat the island of Hispaniola – home to the countries of the Dominican Republic and Haiti. Calling to mind maps she had studied, she could almost see the mountainous land mass sandwiched between the Caribbean Sea to the south and the Atlantic Ocean to the north, with Jamaica and Cuba like garnish to the west and Puerto Rico to the east. She had never been to the Dominican Republic, but had visited Haiti twelve years earlier – the summer before her senior year in high school.

"Excuse me, Miss."

Hanna shifted her attention to a smiling flight attendant, who drew two papers from a stack she held in the crook of her arm. "These need to be completed before you will be allowed to proceed through immigration and customs once we land in Santo Domingo," the woman said. "If you have any questions, let me know."

After filling out the forms, Hanna leaned her head against the seat and closed her eyes. The two young girls sitting behind her talked in hushed tones, their whispers a potpourri of Spanish. Farther back, a fussy baby whimpered. Unable to rest, Hanna peered through the window again. Faded peach and apricot splatters added a touch of color to the dusty blue sky. Below, the cobalt waters of the Atlantic Ocean splashed against sandy beaches bordering a mountainous terrain. She assumed it was the northern shore of the

Dominican Republic.

Minutes later the intercom crackled to life as the pilot announced – first in English, then Spanish – they were nearing their destination along the southern coast of the country. Hanna kept her eyes glued to the window, only vaguely aware of the flight attendants moving through the aisles collecting empty cups and wrappers. When one of the young women asked the man in front of her to fasten his seatbelt, Hanna ran a hand across her lap, making sure she was still buckled in. As the darkness of night engulfed the airplane, lights twinkled across the landscape below; but even as they made their final descent, she saw nothing indicating the presence of a city boasting more than three million people, which she had been told was the population of Santo Domingo.

When the plane touched down on the tarmac, lights flickered on overhead and the passengers erupted in applause, filling the cabin with a thunderous rumble. If she had not been buckled in, Hanna would have come out of her seat. An elderly, dark-skinned woman seated across the aisle looked at her and smiled, laugh lines crinkling at the corners of her eyes. "It's okay," she said. "It's only our way of saying we're thankful to have landed safely."

Hanna nodded. She hoped all the color had not drained from her face.

Once the aircraft came to a complete stop, she waited with mixed emotions as those in front and back of her crowded into the aisle, retrieving duffle bags and small pieces of luggage from overhead compartments. She was in no hurry to be the first off the plane. While she was looking forward to seeing her new home, fears of the unknown still clamored for attention. As the last of the passengers filed past where she was seated, she stood and stepped into the aisle. After double-checking to make sure she had everything, she walked toward the exit. Once inside the terminal, the *click-click-click* of small wheels rolling along the floor filled the corridor as she and at least a dozen more people pulled their carry-on behind them. She followed the others into a large room where immigration officials sat behind booths enclosed by glass, and disembarked passengers waited their turn to approach one of the windows.

Hanna made her way to what appeared to be the shortest line. As each of the four people ahead of her walked to the immigration window, she watched closely, hoping to see and hear a little of what to expect once it was her turn. Silently she practiced her Spanish as she tried to anticipate the appropriate responses to the questions the official might ask. Instead of calming her rising anxiety, her efforts only made matters worse.

Her Spanish was deplorable. Who did she think she was fooling?

When the official motioned for her to step forward, Hanna approached the window, placing her passport and papers on the counter with what she hoped was an air of indifference, as if going through immigration were a part of her regular routine.

Without saying a word, the man picked up the documents and sorted through them. Seconds later he looked at her through narrowed eyes. "¿Tarjeta de turista?" he said, each word cracking like a whip.

Hanna stared at him. His accent was thick and unfamiliar, nothing like anything she'd heard in Costa Rica. She ran a sweaty palm down the side of her skirt as she attempted to make sense of what he'd said. There was no use pretending – her fears had swept away any possibility of translating his words into something she understood. She swallowed around the metallic tasting lump in her throat. "No entiendo," she said.

The man's brow furrowed. "You have tourist card?" he asked in broken English.

She felt her face flush. Nothing mild – she knew it was bright red. Tourist Card? What was he talking about? "No entien – "

"He wants your tourist card. You can't get through immigration without it."

The voice had come from behind her. When Hanna turned around, the man next in line gave her a quick nod. She looked back at the immigration official. "I don't have one. No tengo."

He shuffled her documents together and placed them on the counter with more force than she thought necessary. "You need tourist card," he said, pointing to several booths located along the wall at the side of the room.

Hot tears welled in Hanna's eyes as she gathered her papers. She blinked several times in an effort to keep them at bay. The man who had spoken earlier pushed his way to the immigration window before she had time to collect her thoughts and step to the side.

Was it only her imagination or was everyone a bit impatient?

She grabbed the handle to her carry-on and walked to the middle of the room. Her fears were already being realized, and she hadn't even made it past immigration. "Oh Father God, please help me," she whispered.

She tried to reassure herself there was no need to panic but couldn't shake the trepidation threatening to crush what little confidence she had left. If only she had not allowed her foolish ego to keep her from practicing Spanish with the nationals during the year she'd spent in language study in San José, Costa Rica. Unfortunately, she'd realized too late that pride plus perfection did not equal success when trying to speak a new language. Now she feared her inadequate language skills might destroy her twelve-year dream of being a missionary before it had a chance to become a viable reality.

While trying to work up enough courage to approach one the men selling tourist cards, Hanna remembered the last letter she had received from Maleah Anderson, the mother of three of the four children she would be teaching in Paraíso – a small fishing village located along the southwest coastal highway of the Dominican Republic. Because the letter contained information about what to expect once she arrived in Santo Domingo, she had put it in her purse with the intentions of reading it again while on the airplane.

Of course, she'd forgotten.

She retrieved the three-page letter from the depths of her handbag and scanned it for instructions. Flipping to the second page, she found what she was looking for: *Don't forget to buy a tourist card before going through immigration.* The advice that followed was almost as important: *Be sure you have exactly ten dollars in cash in order to purchase your card. They don't make change.*

People milled all around her – some a little too close for Hanna's comfort. She opened her wallet to see if she had anything smaller than a twenty-dollar bill, while keeping an eye out for possible pickpockets. If someone were to make off with her debit card and all her cash, that would just make her day. As she pulled out two five-dollar bills, a man bumped her arm. Clutching her wallet to her chest, she glanced over her shoulder. The man mumbled something in Spanish and kept walking.

Hanna wondered if returning to Miami were an option.

After purchasing a tourist card, she finally cleared immigration and made her way to the baggage claim area – a dimly lit section of the terminal located on the backside of customs. Taking her cue from the other passengers, she secured a metal cart before proceeding to the luggage carousel. Although she had been forewarned there might be a long wait once she reached this leg of her journey, because of the delay at immigration, her luggage was already circling the carousel by the time she arrived.

She held the cart with her foot in an effort to keep it from rolling away and reached for one of her two footlockers as it passed, managing to slide it from the carousel onto the cart. She grabbed a suitcase and laid it on top of the footlocker. As the remaining footlocker and suitcase circled in her direction, she snatched one and then the other off the revolving conveyor belt and placed them on the floor. She squared her shoulders as she prayed for strength to stack the two on top of the others. Her foot ached from trying to hold the cart in place. She wiggled her toes. A pair of tennis shoes would have been a lot more serviceable than the thin sandals she was wearing.

Once she had all four pieces of luggage in place, Hanna breathed a sigh of relief, put her hands in the small of her back and stretched. She could feel sweat trickling down her spine. When had it gotten so warm? It felt like she was back home in Alabama on a hot July afternoon. Lifting her hair off her neck, she wished she'd put a scrunchie in her purse. A ponytail would be nice. She wiped the moisture off her forehead while watching the flurry of activity in the room. As Spanish chatter filled her ears, a dull, throbbing pain threatened to settle just about her eyes. She took a deep breath and maneuvered her cart toward the nearest customs line with hopes of making it that far without one of her carefully placed pieces of luggage sliding off.

Caribbean Paradise

~~~~~

Jake shifted from one foot to the other, his hands stuffed in the pockets of his favorite pair of blue jeans, which he realized that morning had seen better days. Although it had only been fifty or fifty-five minutes, it seemed like he and Isabela had been waiting outside of customs at the airport in Santo Domingo for hours. He was beginning to think the young woman they were supposed to be meeting had missed the plane in Miami. He'd heard the arrival of her flight being announced as they walked up almost an hour earlier, which should have been enough time for her to make it through immigration and clear customs.

He turned his attention to his six-year-old daughter, who was using the guardrail behind them as her personal jungle gym. Earlier she had tried to push her way through the throng of people gathered near the exit doors, but had made little progress. Within the last five minutes she had begun to slow down – showing signs of fatigue or boredom or both.

The last time either one of them had been to the airport in Santo Domingo was a little over a year ago when they returned to the Dominican Republic after a year and a half back in the States. Nothing much had changed. Family and friends still waited outside in the heat and humidity for arriving passengers, and an endless supply of solicitors offered taxi and hotel services – even at ten o'clock at night. Although he should have been used to the noise by now, the constant roar of people talking, baggage carriers shouting, and car horns honking as taxi drivers jockeyed for a parking place closest to the customs exit, set Jake's nerves on edge. When he took a deep breath, the pungent smell of fried food from the nearby open-air food court threatened to clog his arteries. He could almost see the greasy vapors as a muggy breeze managed to weave its way through the crowded waiting area.

"Where is she, Daddy?" Isabela asked for what must have been the tenth time in the last ten minutes.

He wondered the same thing. "I don't know, sweetheart. I'm sure she'll be walking through those doors any minute now." He hoped speaking the words would make it true.

"I want to see her picture again." Anticipation reflected in the child's blue eyes. "I don't want to miss her when she comes out."

Jake pulled a wallet-size photo out of his shirt pocket and handed it to her. The child had looked at it so many times it was worn around the edges. Her fascination with the young woman coming to teach her and the Anderson children was puzzling, even a little disturbing. He hoped she wasn't going to be disappointed. She'd talked of nothing else for days and had insisted they come to the airport to pick her up. Otherwise, he'd be back at the hotel – probably sound asleep by now, and Conner Anderson would be the one keeping this late night vigil.

While his daughter studied the photograph, Jake continued to watch the customs' exit. At her prompting, he'd already looked at the picture numerous times, permanently etching the young woman's smiling face in his memory: Straight, dark brown hair, oval face, olive complexion and what appeared to be forest-green eyes framed by thick lashes.

"I think she's pretty. Don't you, Daddy?"

He didn't have to look at the picture again. He knew Isabela was right. Even so, the affectionate manner in which she spoke of the young woman struck a defensive nerve. He swallowed back the urge to snap at the child. "If she looks like her picture, I think I would have to agree with you," he said.

A big smile spread across Isabela's cherub-like face, revealing deep dimples on either side of her mouth, her hair framing her face in Shirley Temple ringlets. Still holding the snapshot in her hand, she began expectantly watching the exit doors again.

Her eyes are the color of the Caribbean Sea. He'd heard it so many times he'd lost count. *And those dimples . . . just like her mother.*

Jake turned away. He needed to get a grip. Now was not the time to let his emotions get the best of him.

~~~~~

Once in line at customs, Hanna looked around the room as she waited her turn. As best she could tell, most of the people were a good representation of what her research said made up the general population of the Dominican Republic: mulatto – a mix of African, Caucasian and Taíno, which was the name of the prominent people group living on the island of Hispaniola when Christopher Columbus arrived. The vast array of skin tones and colors reminded her of the various shades of chocolate. Hanna glanced at her own arms, the skin tanned a golden brown by the Costa Rican sun. She could almost pass for one of the lighter skinned Dominicans – until she opened her mouth. It would be impossible for a national to mutilate the language like she could.

"Señorita."

Hanna jerked her head up. With the wave of a hand the man standing behind her motioned for her to move forward. Taking slow, deliberate steps, she pushed her cart toward the customs' table. After a brawny young Dominican transferred her suitcases and footlockers onto the conveyer belt, she held her breath while the official – a light skinned middle-aged woman – checked her passport and papers.

"Is this all your luggage?" The woman spoke English and offered her a friendly smile.

Hanna cleared her throat. "It is," she said, hoping her voice sounded calmer than she felt.

"Is this the first time you are visiting our country?"

"It is." She did not offer any additional information.

The woman placed the disembarkation form, along with the infamous tourist card, inside Hanna's passport and handed it to her. "I hope you enjoy your stay."

"Thank you."

Hanna's relief turned to panic when she realized a young man on the other end of the table was loading her luggage onto a baggage cart. His grin stretched from ear to ear as he jabbered at her in rapid-fire Spanish. Before she could object, he began pushing her luggage toward double doors located about thirty feet down on the left. She hastened to keep up.

After an older gentleman checked to make sure the numbers on her luggage matched her ticket stubs, she followed the younger man through the metal doors, where a grease-laden gust of hot air and a loud rumble greeted her. The sound of honking horns ricocheted off the roof and only added to the throbbing pain above her eyes. A sea of Dominicans congregated beyond a guardrail, bombarding her with unintelligible words of Spanish. She surveyed the group, wondering if any of them were waiting for her? She didn't have time to give it much thought. The young Dominican, already at the bottom of the ramp with her footlockers and suitcases, was talking to a man with skin the color of dark chocolate. Remembering she had been warned luggage theft was common, she hurried after him. When the second Dominican saw her, his face lit up like a floodlight.

"Buena noche, Señorita," he said. "Need a taxi?"

Hanna looked around, still trying to get her bearings. "I certainly hope not," she said, more to herself than to the man.

Still grinning, he said, "La Señorita, no need taxi?"

She shook her head. "No, I don't need a taxi."

The man's grin began to fade. "You sure, no taxi?"

His persistence was getting on her nerves. "I'm sure."

She turned her back on him, only to find herself face to face with the young man who still had her luggage. Even his cheerful grin looked wilted. She knew exactly how he felt. If her language skills were better, she could ask him to stack her baggage along the wall behind where they were standing, but that wouldn't work anyway. He was going to want a tip, and all she had was U.S. dollars. She'd seen places inside the terminal where she could have exchanged some of her dollars for pesos, but Maleah had told her it would be best if she waited and let them help her get her money exchanged.

Tears stung Hanna's eyes. Now what?

Looking around, she hoped to see someone who might be waiting for her. A tall, dark headed man, his hand resting on the shoulder of a little girl, caught her eye. The man seemed to be absorbed in thought, but the child, her hair falling in bouncy curls around her face, pointed in her direction. At the child's insistence, the man looked up. When he saw Hanna, he made his way toward her, the little girl dragging him along like an eager puppy on a walk with her owner. Although his expression remained pensive, the child appeared to be thrilled to see her.

"Are you Hanna Truly?" he asked once he was close enough

for her to hear him.

His deep blue eyes held hers. "I am," she answered.

A faint smile replaced the somber expression as he extended his hand. "Glad to meet you. I'm Jake Mason, and this is my daughter, Isabela."

Forcing herself to break eye contact, Hanna looked at the little girl and smiled. "Glad to meet you."

He pointed at the luggage on the cart beside her. "Are those your things?"

"They are. I was trying to figure out how to tell the man to leave them here when I saw you heading my way. I wasn't sure what to do about a tip."

"I'll take care of it." He turned and spoke to the man in what sounded to Hanna like fluent Spanish.

"I'm going to get him to leave your luggage on the curb," Jake said over his shoulder as he and the Dominican walked toward the street. "You and Isabela can wait with it while I get the van."

After the young man removed the footlockers and suitcases from his cart and placed them on the ground, Jake paid him in pesos for his services. Immediately the Dominican began chattering away in Spanish. First he pointed at Hanna then at the luggage then to the money in his hand. Hanna understood only bits and pieces of what he was saying, but she didn't have to understand it all; she knew somehow she was to blame for the scene he was creating.

When Jake only shook his head, the young Dominican turned to Hanna and began his demonstration all over again – spitting the words out faster than before. All she understood out of his tirade this time was "Señorita."

She looked at Jake. "Sorry, I don't understand what he's saying," she said.

Isabela giggled. "He's mad because Daddy paid him in pesos. He thought you would give him some American dollars. He asked you to give him more money – in dollars."

"Oh," was all Hanna could say. Embarrassment scorched her cheeks. Wasn't it humiliating enough this stranger was handling the situation for her without a child doing the translating? Chagrinned, she watched as Jake entered into another heated Spanish dialogue with the man, who finally tromped off in a huff, making sure he gave her one last disgusting scowl as he walked away.

"Don't worry about it," Jake said. "You two wait here. I'll be back in a minute with the van."

Hanna thought he sounded perturbed. With whom was he irritated? Her – the man – or both? Exhaustion joined forces with shame – together they engulfed her. If only there were a hole nearby she could sink into. Disappearing sounded like a good idea. Her eyes came to rest on Jake's daughter. She took a deep breath before speaking. "So . . . it's Isabela. Right?"

"Isabela Claire Mason," the child answered. "I was named after the Spanish queen who sent Christopher Columbus to America. He discovered the Dominican Republic, you know?"

"I did know that, but I didn't know the queen who sent him was named Isabela."

"She was. You know what else?"

"What?"

"Christopher Columbus named a town in the Dominican Republic after the queen. Nothing's left but some broken walls and stuff like that, but it used to be a town and it had my name. Daddy told me it's one of the most historical places in *all* the Americas."

"How about that."

"That's not all. Christopher Columbus' brother, Bartholo . . . Barthlo – "

"Bartholomew?" Hanna felt a laugh inching its way up her throat. The child's enthusiasm was contagious, her dimpled smile hard to resist.

"That's it. He started another town near where Santo Domingo is today and he named it Nueva Isabela. Nueva – that means *new*, you know?"

Hanna grinned. "Two towns . . . Wow! Guess that makes your name pretty special, doesn't it?"

"Sure does. You know what else?"

"What?" Hanna asked. She wondered if the child ever took a breath.

"Today's my birthday." The little girl placed her hands on her hips, her smile reaching from ear to ear.

"Really? You were born on April fourth?"

"Uh-huh. When's your birthday?"

"September twenty-sixth," Hanna answered.

"Hum . . . Are you as old as my daddy?"

Hanna bit her lower lip to keep from laughing. "I don't know. I'm twenty-eight."

"My daddy's thirty-five," Isabela said, raising narrowed eyes skyward as if she was doing the math. "That means he's older." Her eyes rested on Hanna again. "But that's not too old, is it?"

The persistent laugh escaped Hanna's lips. "That's not old at all," she said. "How old are you?"

"Six years old!" The words practically exploded from the child's mouth. "We had a party with cake and ice cream and presents. And you know what made it really exciting?"

Hanna bit back another laugh. She was finding Isabela Claire Mason to be an exceptionally delightful child. She just hoped she would be able to keep up with her. "What's that?" she asked.

"We had my party in Santo Domingo and I was born in Santo Domingo. Sophie too."

"Who's Sophie?" Hanna asked, thinking she'd heard the name somewhere before.

"Sophie Anderson. You're going to be teaching her too. Her birthday is March eleventh. She's six, like me." Isabela folded her arms across her chest. "Pretty neat, huh?"

"Sounds pretty neat to me."

A plain white van pulled to the curb. Jake jumped out and jogged around to where Hanna waited with Isabela. After sliding the side door open, he lifted her footlockers and suitcases one by one, placing them inside with such ease you would have thought they only weighed a few pounds each. She wanted to ask where he had been when she was wrestling them off the luggage carousel and onto that cart.

After picking Isabela up, he hugged the child and then put her inside the van. "Buckle up," he said, sliding the door closed. Before Hanna could make a move, he opened the passenger side door and offered his hand. When she placed her hand in his, her fingers tingled with subtle warmth. She stepped up, scooting onto the seat. Jake closed the door. Seconds later, he hoisted himself into the driver's seat.

Hanna stared straight ahead as Jake maneuvered the van into the flow of traffic outside the airport. Once they were cruising down what she guessed to be the main highway, he nodded toward the driver's side window. "That's the Caribbean." His deep voice rose above the noise of the air-conditioner. "I realize it's hard to see at night, but as your tour guide it's my responsibility to make you aware of these things."

She studied the view outside his window. A three-quarter moon peeked through a thin, willowy patch of cloud, and she could see water gently lapping the palm-studded coastline. Jake ran his hand along the stubble of his five o'clock shadow, and she shifted her gaze. In profile, his almost black hair looked as if he'd used his fingers for a comb. When he glanced her way, she turned her head, feigning interest in the passing scenery on the right side of the vehicle.

"Is this Santo Domingo?" she asked as they passed a grouping of small concrete houses.

"No. We're still on the outskirts of the city."

Hanna adjusted her air-conditioner vent, grateful to have cool air blowing directly on her face. "Is it always this hot and humid?"

"Only during spring, summer and fall. Winters can be quite pleasant."

"And by winter, you mean?"

"Oh, mid-December until early March. The daytime temps are in the mid-eighties and at night it may even drop into the low-seventies. Best thing about winter is the low humidity. You just missed it."

She noticed a slight rise at the corners of his mouth. "Just my luck," she said, glancing in the backseat to check on Isabela. The child hadn't said a word since they left the airport. She wasn't surprised to discover she had fallen asleep. "I think the birthday girl finally gave it up."

"I'm sure she's tired. She's been going since early this morning." His eyes darted in Hanna's direction. "How did you know it was her birthday?"

"She told me while we waited for you to bring the van around. She also told me how she got her name and that she and Sophie were both born in Santo Domingo."

"What else did she tell you?" Hanna thought he sounded defensive.

"That's about it," she said.

There was no response. Was it her imagination or had an unexpected cold front just swept through?

Chapter Three

For more than twenty minutes Hanna alternated between watching the minutes tick by on the clock above the van's radio and trying to discern which of the dark, shadowy structures they were streaking past were homes and which were businesses. On occasion she caught a glimpse of a flickering candle through an open door, while a deafening Latin beat rumbled from the depths of several of the buildings. With no help from Jake, she surmised the establishments were either nightclubs or bars. As for her *tour guide* – he had not offered any further information since apprising her of the fact she'd just missed the most pleasant season of the year. She wasn't sure which cave he had crawled into or why, but as they approached a massive concrete building that seemed out of place compared to what she'd seen so far, she decided to break the silence. "What's that?" she asked, pointing toward the peculiar superstructure.

"The Faro a Colón," Jake answered, his eyes still anchored on the road in front of them.

Hanna sighed. She loved a man of few words. "Translation, please."

"Sorry," he said, honoring her with a glance in her direction. "In English it's called the Columbus Lighthouse. It was built to commemorate the 500th anniversary of Columbus' arrival in the New World."

"A bit of an overstatement, wouldn't you say?"

"You'd really think so if you saw it lit up."

Hanna tented her hands in her lap. Not an overly stimulating conversation, but at least the man was talking. "Lit up?" she said, tapping her fingertips. "What do you mean?"

"It's equipped with high-powered lasers that project a vertical-shaped cross into the sky." He slanted his eyes at her. "Impressive, but it uses so much electricity half the city of Santo Domingo goes dark whenever they light it up."

"Did you say a cross?" she asked as she turned to get one last look at the mammoth building.

"Ironic, isn't it? The first time I saw it, my immediate response was – *The Light shines in the darkness, but the darkness does not comprehend it.*"

"Interesting," Hanna said, shifting in her seat to face him. "I've heard the spiritual darkness here is considerable."

Jake nodded. "Because of the voodoo influence from Haiti, I would say it's worse than in a lot of places. While most Dominicans know about Jesus Christ, they are clueless when it comes to grasping the fact that He died on the cross in order to save them. And yet – they spent millions of dollars to design a powerful light that illuminates the night sky in the shape of a cross." He shook his head. "It still amazes me every time I think about it."

"Hum . . . Guess that's why we're here."

He studied her for a moment without commenting, and then turned his attention back to the road. The clunky sound of tires hitting uneven pavement echoed in the silence.

Hanna feared she'd said something wrong and another icy blast might be in the forecast. "What's inside the building?" she asked, hoping a change of subject would keep him talking.

Jake cleared his throat. "It's more of a who . . . than a what," he said.

"What?"

"What I meant is, you should have asked who's in the Lighthouse, not what?"

"Okay . . . " Hanna fixed her gaze on the man. "Who's inside the Lighthouse?"

"Christopher Columbus."

A smile teased the corners of Hanna's mouth. She could see Jake grinning. "Tell me more . . . " she said.

"There's not much to tell other than there's a marble mausoleum in the center of the building that supposedly holds Columbus' remains."

"Supposedly?"

"Yeah, well . . . Spain and Italy both insist they have him. And in fact, I read recently that even Columbus, Ohio claims to have the old boy's remains."

She laughed. "Now you're just being cute."

"No, really. I read that somewhere." When he looked at her and smiled, Hanna's heart did a flip-flop. She wanted to tell him he had a nice smile, but decided that might be a taboo subject.

"Who do *you* think has the real Christopher Columbus?"

He shrugged. "Who knows? Ironically, I'm not sure too many Dominicans would be upset if they discovered it wasn't them. Those who might suffer loss from the tourist industry probably care, but the average Dominican – no."

"Why do you say that?"

"Columbus is not real popular around here. When he and his men arrived on the island they forced the Taíno – the natives who were living here – into hard labor. Eventually the work, as well as the diseases brought in by the early explorers, killed them all."

"I've heard that before. Is it true there are no Taíno left?"

"In terms of full blooded Taíno – it's true. You will come across people who are of Taíno and African descent or Taíno and Spanish or a combination of all three, but no pure Taíno."

"Wow . . . How sad."

"I would have to agree."

Hanna was glad to know they agreed on something.

~~~~~

It was almost midnight when they pulled into the parking lot of a small hotel in Santo Domingo. Hanna looked around as she stepped out of the vehicle, but it was hard to tell much in the dark.

"It's nothing fancy, but the rooms aren't bad, and it's affordable," Jake said, sliding the side door of the van open. "There's a nice courtyard in the middle where we can eat breakfast in the morning. We'll need to take your luggage in with us. It's never a good idea to leave anything of value overnight in a vehicle, especially in Santo Domingo. After I get Isabela settled in bed, if you'll stay with her, I'll get a luggage cart from the lobby and take your things to your room. It's next door to ours."

"I'm assuming the Andersons have already gone to bed," Hanna said as she walked beside Jake, who carried Isabela draped over his arms like a limp ragdoll, down the first floor hall of the hotel.

"I'm guessing they have. Maleah said she wanted to wait up to meet you, but it's gotten so late, I doubt she did."

"I wouldn't blame her." They spoke in hushed tones, like two kids sneaking in the house after curfew. The soles of their shoes made a faint squishing noise on the worn carpet. Hanna fought hard not to grin.

Jake stopped in front of a door and leaned his head to the right. "Would you mind getting the key out of my hand? I'm afraid if I try to open the door, I'll wake Isabela."

"Oh sure," Hanna said. As she reached around to take the key, her fingers lightly brushed his hand. She drew in her breath as a ripple of warmth crept up her arm.

Once inside the room, she watched as he laid Isabela on one of the double beds. After removing the child's sandals and covering her with the sheet and bedspread, he planted a soft kiss on her cheek. The little girl mumbled something unintelligible, then rolled on her side, once again fast asleep.

"I'll be right back," he said as he walked past where Hanna stood.

After he was gone, she sat on the end of the other bed. It had been a full and stimulating day. She puzzled over the fact that Jake and Isabela were the ones who met her at the airport. When she accepted the position in Paraíso, she was told she would be teaching the three Anderson children. While in language school, she received word another missionary – a widower who had previously served in a different location in the Dominican Republic – had been reassigned to Paraíso. His five-year-old daughter was being added to her school roster.

Her gaze fell on the sleeping child. Isabela's eyelashes looked like thick black feathers against her cheeks. She had her father's eyes. Hanna had not given much thought to what the widowed missionary would look like, but even if she had, she was confident the man she'd met tonight would not have been what she was expecting. With his dark tan, mussed-up hair and striking blue eyes, she could better envision Jake walking toward the water's edge at the beach, surfboard under his arm – looking out to sea as he anticipated catching the next big wave.

"Ya!"

Hanna's shoulders jerked as Jake's deep voice brought her back to reality. She felt the heat creeping up her neck and prayed it would not reach her face.

"Sorry. I didn't mean to startle you," he said.

She refused to let her eyes meet his. "That's okay. I think I had almost fallen asleep." There was no way she was going to tell him the truth.

"That's understandable," he said. "I put your luggage in your room, so you're all set. Here's the key."

Hanna picked up her purse and stood, then reached for the key, being careful not to touch his fingers as she withdrew it from his hand. She walked toward the door. "Thanks. See you in the morning."

~~~~~

The next morning Jake was trying, without much success, to do something with Isabela's hair. There was no getting a brush through the thick ringlets, but the comb he was using didn't seem to be doing much good either. His job probably would be easier if she would at least be still.

"Where's Hanna?" she asked, jumping up and down while he tried to work the comb through the back of her hair.

He gave up and tossed the comb on the nightstand. "I guess she's still in her room, but don't you think it would be better if you called her Miss Hanna?"

"What about Aunt Hanna? You know, like I do with Aunt

Maleah."

"That might work."

The child squealed as she swirled around and hugged his knees. "Is it okay if I go see if she's up?"

"I guess so, but you need to ask her if it's okay for you to call her Aunt Hanna."

"I'll ask, but I'm sure she won't mind." Isabela practically flew out the door, her words trailing behind her.

"You might want to see if the Andersons are up too," Jake called after her. He sighed as he sat down on the edge of the bed.

Aunt Hanna . . . An image of the young woman flashed before his eyes. Her thick, dark hair was longer than it had been in the wallet-size photo Isabela had worn thin, falling well below her shoulders. Her height had surprised him; he guessed she was at least 5'10. At 6'4" it was not often he met a woman who came anywhere close to his own height. He massaged the bridge of his nose. What did it matter?

Although it was customary for missionary kids to call adult missionaries *aunt* or *uncle,* his gut knotted at the thought of Isabela calling the young woman *aunt*. Like a runaway train, he feared if he didn't do something soon this whole situation was going to get out of hand. He'd tossed and turned all night as he tried to escape the uninvited emotions that started churning the moment he'd seen Hanna standing outside of customs. The few times he managed to drift off, her face had even invaded his dreams.

He stood and began throwing his and Isabela's things into a small suitcase.

When he walked outside ten minutes later, he found Hanna and Isabela seated at a table next to a trickling fountain, waiting for their breakfast to arrive. The tropical foliage of the hotel courtyard surrounded them, and the balmy air smelled of yeast bread and a sweet, syrupy fragrance – similar to honeysuckle.

Dressed in a jade-colored sundress, dotted with small yellow flowers, Hanna looked as if she'd chosen her outfit with the garden in mind. Her hair was pulled up in a ponytail, exposing the delicate lines of her neck. It disturbed Jake that he noticed.

"Hey Daddy," Isabela said. "Aunt Maleah and Uncle Conner

said they would be out soon."

"That's fine. I think I'll go put our suitcase in the van." Before his eyes had a chance to betray him further, Jake headed for the lobby door.

"What about Aunt Hanna's stuff?"

He stopped mid-step. "I'm sorry. I forgot." He did an about face, tightening his jaw as he looked at Hanna. He refused to allow his heart to override his will. "Are you ready to have your luggage loaded?"

She rose and walked toward him. "It's still sitting by the door where you left it last night." She held out her hand. "Here's my key, but I can help if you would like."

His fingers grazed the palm of her hand as he took the key, and a warm sensation raced up his arm. Like a fire alarm, a warning went off in his head. "No, that's okay. I can get them." He turned and walked away before anything else could be said.

~~~~~

Hanna glanced over her shoulder as she returned to the table. *No good morning or good to see you again. Wonder if he's always this friendly? It probably wouldn't be a good idea to ask Isabela if her father was moody. Maybe he was tired.* They *had* gotten in late the night before.

She slid into her seat at the table. Despite her little pep talk, she had an uneasy feeling his sullenness had something to do with her. She looked up when the lobby door flew open, but it wasn't Jake. Disappointment crashed over her like the rolling waves of the ocean. *Why did she care?*

Three children, two boys and a girl, bounded outside – all three redheads, with varying degrees of freckles sprinkled across their noses and cheeks.

Isabela sprang from her chair, ran over and grabbed the little girl by the hand, practically dragging her to the table. "Aunt Hanna, this is Sophie," she said with a big dimpled smile as she draped her arm around the other child's shoulders, creating a portrait in contrasts: dark ringlets and blue eyes against strawberry blonde pigtails and eyes the color of copper. Sophie's timid smile revealed a space where her two front teeth were supposed to be. Hanna resisted the urge to hum *all I want for Christmas is my two front teeth.*

"Glad to meet you, Sophie," she said.

The boys stepped forward, both grinning like the Cheshire cat. "This is Daniel and Caleb," Isabela said. "They're Sophie's big brothers."

"I'm pleased to meet both of you," Hanna said. If she remembered correctly, Daniel was the oldest, and they were only fifteen months apart in age, nine and eight respectively.

Quite a racket ensued as the children pulled chairs up to the table. When the waiter appeared to take their orders, Hanna listened in amazement as all three Anderson children told the man what they wanted to eat. Their fluent command of the language reminded her once again of her woeful inadequacies. That was twice already today, and it wasn't even eight-thirty. Earlier Isabela had been pleased to order breakfast for them, but having the child speak on her behalf had been a blow to Hanna's ego, not to mention her confidence. It was only a matter of time before she would have ample opportunity to make a fool of herself in front of Jake and the Andersons.

The banter among the four children soon became an amusing distraction. Like the swan in the story of the ugly duckling, Isabela was oblivious to the fact she was not a duckling . . . or in this case – an Anderson. When the child jumped from her chair, Hanna turned to see where she was headed, feeling disconcerted when she realized she was still hoping Jake would return.

"Hey Uncle Conner. Hey Aunt Maleah," Isabela cried as she ran toward a couple who were a composite of the three children sitting at the table.

"We apologize for taking so long," Maleah said, her smile warm in a densely freckled face, reminding Hanna of Caleb. "After we got the kids dressed and out the door, it took more time than we thought to get everything together and in the car. We brought enough stuff to last a week."

"That's okay," Hanna said. "I've enjoyed having some time to get to know them."

"You're too kind," Maleah said, her rich auburn hair brushing against her shoulders as she shook her head. "I'm sure you didn't expect to have full responsibility of all four rug rats your first day in the country."

Isabela and Sophie giggled. "Mommy, what's a rug rat?" Sophie asked.

Maleah walked to the table and gave one of her daughter's pigtails a jerk. Her hands were as freckled as her face. "You are."

"Where's my daddy?" Isabela asked, looking toward the door.

"He was sitting in the lobby reading a newspaper when we walked through," Conner said. With his reddish brown hair and dark chocolate eyes, the man was an older version of Daniel, even down to the slight gap between his top front teeth.

Isabela's bottom lip protruded. "Oh. Isn't he going to eat breakfast?"

Maleah patted the child on the head while turning hazel eyes in Hanna's direction. "Don't know, but I am. Did you leave anything for me?"

The look had been more curious than accusatory. Hanna didn't think she was justified in feeling paranoid, but she wondered if one reason the Andersons had been late was because they got caught up in a conversation with Jake about her. What had she done that would make him want to avoid her, even if it meant skipping breakfast?

Chapter Four

After leaving the hotel, the group headed for the Colonial City of Santo Domingo. Hanna thought it odd Jake insisted on all the children riding with him. He said it was so Maleah and Conner could share some of the history of the city with her without constantly being interrupted. She suspected he had other reasons, but kept her opinion to herself.

By noon her head was spinning. The whirlwind tour had included the Alcázar de Colón – a palace built in the early 1500's for Christopher Columbus' son, Diego; the Cathedral Santa María, where the *supposed* remains of Christopher Columbus had been housed before being transferred to the Faro a Colón; and El Conde – a pedestrian-only street, which Hanna discovered to her delight was bustling with places to shop and eat. Maleah assured her they would return when they came to Santo Domingo in early December to do their Christmas shopping.

Before stopping for lunch, Conner was adamant they visit the Fortaleza Ozama, which he explained was the oldest military fortress in the Americas.

"I apologize," Maleah said, looking up at Hanna from beneath a wide-brimmed straw hat, beads of perspiration dotting her freckled face. "I know you must be hungry, but this place is Conner's favorite." The sound of their shoes thudding against cobblestones echoed down the narrow street leading to the fort.

The truth was, Hanna felt like a sizzling piece of meat someone had slapped on the outside grill. Although something to eat sounded good, a cool place to rest and a cold drink sounded even better, especially when compared to the thought of traipsing around an old garrison. But not wanting to sound whiney, she kept that tidbit of information to herself. "I'm fine. Don't worry about it," she replied, hoping her smile didn't look too limp.

As they entered the fortress, Conner picked up a brochure, and then led them into a well-worn brick courtyard surrounded by a sprawling carpet of grass. "My ladies, for you I make deal," he said, his fake accent reminding Hanna of the young Dominican who had earlier that day offered to be their tour guide. "Let me show you fort. I charge you nothing." He laid his arm across Maleah's shoulders and pulled her to him. "Maybe you I let pay later."

After giving him a shove, Maleah took the floppy hat off her head and swung at him. "Conner Anderson, I can't believe you."

As a teenager, Hanna loved watching reruns of the old sitcom M*A*S*H. Conner reminded her of Hawkeye's best friend, BJ Honeycut – one of her favorite characters on the show. She pressed her fingertips to her lips and suppressed a laugh. When she glanced at Jake, she caught him smiling. It was the first time that day.

"Daddy, tell Aunt Hanna about the pirates," Daniel said as he ran up to his father.

Conner placed his hand on the child's head, ruffling his reddish brown hair. "You tell her."

The boy offered her a bashful grin. "You see that tower over there?" he asked, pointing toward a stout, medieval structure.

"I do," Hanna said, nodding.

"Did you know it was built as a look-out so the people who lived here could see the pirates whenever they tried to sail up the river?"

"No, I didn't. Pirates – Wow! Sounds exciting."

Caleb looked at his dad. "May we go inside the tower?" he asked. "I want Aunt Hanna to see the circle stairs."

"You need to ask her if that is something she would like to do," Conner said.

The child turned red-fringed, hazel eyes in her direction. "Aunt Hanna, would'ya like to do that?" he asked, his voice so soft she almost couldn't hear him.

"I would love to," she said, "and I think once we start school I'm going to let you and Daniel teach when we study the history of the Dominican Republic."

The boys exchanged freckled smiles.

"Daniel, Caleb – lead the way," Conner said, waving his hand in front of them.

As they entered the tower, Hanna pushed her sunglasses on top of her head. It took her eyes a few seconds to adjust. The inside of the stone structure felt damp and at least ten degrees cooler. It smelled of mildew – like the basement in her grandmother's old house. She followed Conner, Maleah and the children as they climbed a circular stairwell. Jake stood at the bottom. She wondered if he was going to join them or wait below. When Caleb looked down at her from his position several rungs farther up, she waved. Her reward was a wide toothy grin.

Once they reached the top, she could see the strategic placement of the fortress better. It reminded her of an old military war hero, standing sentry at the mouth of the Río Ozama, which had been one of the earliest harbors of the new world. A gentle breeze blew wisps of hair away from her face as she stopped and gazed across the river. She could almost taste the salt water of the Caribbean Sea only a short distance away, and the faint smell of sea life peppered the air. Conner and Maleah came and stood beside her.

"It must be the pastor in me," Conner said, "but whenever we visit this place I'm reminded of all those times David referred to God as his fortress." He ran his hand over the rough stone of a nearby wall. "The early settlers built this fort because they thought it would protect them from their enemies, but there were no guarantees. I'm thankful God's word assures us that when we make Him our fortress, our trust is not misplaced."

Maleah planted a hand on top of her hat as a welcomed gust of wind blew in from the ocean. "That's because *He* is our protection against the enemy," she said, stepping up to peer through one of the numerous embrasures. "The wall of this fort was built as a barrier against enemy artillery, but we have something even better – Our faith, which the Bible tells us extinguishes *all* the fiery darts of the evil one."

"What a promise," Hanna said as she turned at the sound of running feet.

Isabela slid to a halt in the loose gravel beside her. "Aunt Hanna – look!" The child's breath came in gulps as she pointed across the river. "You can see the old church, or . . ." She looked over her shoulder at Jake, who had only minutes earlier emerged from inside the tower. "What is it called, Daddy? A catha – "

Standing several yards away, Jake scuffed the ground with the toe of his sandal. "A cathedral," he answered, not bothering to look up.

"Yeah, a cathedral," Isabela said, turning back to Hanna. "You see . . . that's where Nueva Isabela was. Remember I told you about the two towns named after me . . ." The child giggled as she gave Hanna a sheepish look. "Well, not me – after the queen, but . . . you know, they still have my name."

Hanna could see Jake out of the corner of her eye. He appeared to have lost interest in whatever he had been studying in the dirt and was now watching her and Isabela. "I do remember," she said as she knelt down and draped her arm around the little girl's shoulders. Using the child's arm and finger as a sight, she looked across the river to a small cathedral on the other side.

~~~~~

After finishing the fortress excursion, the group returned to their vehicles where a discussion arose as to what they were going to do about lunch, who was going to ride with whom and what the plans were for the rest of the day. Hanna found it interesting that while everyone joined in, including the children, Jake remained detached. If she hadn't known better, she would have thought he didn't know the Andersons very well. But she knew that wasn't true. During their correspondence while Hanna was in language school, Maleah shared with her that she and Conner had been close friends with Jake and his wife, Katie. Hanna couldn't imagine why, but had no choice but to once again conclude his aloofness had something to do with her.

The jagged edge in Maleah's voice drew Hanna back to the

present debate. "I will if I have to, but I would prefer not to drive until we get well out of Santo Domingo. Trying to navigate through the nightmare they call traffic here unnerves me to no end."

Hanna could certainly understand why. The traffic they had encountered that morning as they drove from the hotel to the Colonial City rivaled anything she'd ever seen. She had only thought it was bad in San José, Costa Rica. Traffic there was a walk in the park compared to Santo Domingo. In the brief time she'd been in the city there were a number of constants she'd already noted: people pulling in and out, cutting others off without a backwards glance, making lanes where there were none, squeezing in between cars to make a fourth or even fifth lane as they sat waiting at traffic lights, while the pieces of scrap metal they called motorcycles buzzed by, weaving in and out so they could get to the front of the line, only to slow everyone down as they putt-putted away once the light turned green. Not to mention the constant horn honking, which she felt certain had already damaged her hearing.

"We could let Hanna drive," Conner said.

In stunned silence, Hanna shook her head.

Mischief danced in Conner's eyes. "What's wrong?" he asked.

"There's *no way* I'm driving."

"Ignore him. He just wanted to see how you'd react," Maleah said.

Hanna shifted her focus from Conner to Jake. Leaning against the van, with his arms folded across his chest, he appeared to be caught up in his own self-absorbed world. Did he even know what they were talking about?

Conner turned around. He must have seen where her thoughts had wandered. "Hey Jake, got any ideas?" he asked.

When Jake jumped, Hanna bit back a smile. "Doesn't matter," he said, quickly regaining his composure. "Why don't you let the kids ride with me? I really don't mind."

Guess he *was* listening.

"Are you sure?" Maleah asked. "They can get rowdy, especially when they are all together. I don't want them becoming too much of a distraction for you."

"We'll be fine. Won't we, gang?"

How was it the man could appear joyless one minute and upbeat the next?

Isabela put on a long face. "But I want Aunt Hanna to ride with us."

"Me too," Sophie chimed in.

Jake eyed Hanna and shrugged. "Whatever. But I think she would prefer to ride with Maleah and Conner."

Why didn't he say what he really meant? *He* would prefer she ride with Maleah and Conner.

Isabela grabbed her hand and pulled her in Jake's direction. "You want to ride with us, don't you, Aunt Hanna?"

Hanna cut her eyes at Jake. He still leaned against the van, but had shifted his hands to his pockets. His body language said he didn't care what she did. She doubted his body language was telling the truth.

She looked over her shoulder at Maleah and mouthed, "What do I do?"

Maleah appeared unruffled. "I tell you what – You girls may ride with Jake, Hanna too, until we get to wherever it is we're going to eat," she said. "If we choose someplace on the outskirts of Santo Domingo, I can manage from there, and we'll divide up – guys in one vehicle, girls in the other."

Isabela dropped Hanna's hand, latched on to Sophie's and started jumping up and down. "Yeah! Yeah!"

Jake opened the side door of the van. "So where are we going to eat?"

"There's a McDonald's on the road heading toward San Cristóbal," Conner said. "You kids want to eat there?"

Daniel and Caleb joined Isabela and Sophie in their chorus of "Yeah! Yeah!"

Hanna laughed. They looked like out of control jumping beans.

"McDonald's it is," Jake said as he helped the girls in, drawing the door closed behind them. He opened Hanna's door, then held out his hand.

Déjà vu.

Without making eye contact, she placed her hand in his, and then held her breath, anticipating the electric shock waves. She was not to be disappointed. What was it about the man that caused her to react that way?

After sliding into the passenger seat, she turned and looked at the girls, grasping for a diversion. "All buckled up?" she asked as Jake slipped into the drivers' seat.

"Yes, ma'am," they answered in unison.

Isabela lifted a baby doll, swaddled in a pink blanket. "See what I got for my birthday."

"I got one just like it for my birthday," Sophie said as she held up another swaddled baby.

"Don't you think your babies might get a little warm wrapped up like that?" Hanna asked. A sweaty stream snaked its way down her back, and her damp dress clung to her legs. Even the insides of her shoes squished. When Jake looked at her, a smile inched its way across his face. Hanna only thought she was warm a few seconds earlier.

"What?" she asked as she pulled her sunglasses down over her eyes.

"You think it's hot?"

"You might say that. Back home in south Alabama we take pride in believing we've cornered the market on stifling heat and humidity." She lifted her ponytail and leaned closer to the air-conditioner vent. "But it's been a long time since I experienced anything quite like this."

"South Alabama . . ." Jake said. His grin reached from ear to ear. "I never would have guessed."

If her accent kept him smiling, she'd keep talking. "Yep, born and raised . . ." She pushed her sunglasses down on the end of her nose, and peered at him over the top. "Or maybe that's reared . . . on the south side of Mobile Bay."

His laugh, like his voice, was deep and mellow. "The Gulf Coast, huh?" he said. "Well, the good news is – because Paraíso is in the mountains, for the most part it's a little cooler than Santo Domingo. But don't get your hopes up. It can still be unpleasant, especially since our houses aren't air-conditioned."

"So the rumor's true?"

"Unfortunately. Fans help, as long as there's power. If the electricity goes off before bedtime, we crank up the generators. Otherwise, we generally try and tough it out. But don't worry, after a while you get used to it."

"I sure hope so."

His smile lingered.

"You're getting a kick out of seeing me squirm, aren't you?"

"What makes you say that?" he asked.

"It's written all over your face."

~~~~~

Against his better judgment, Jake watched Hanna as she lifted her ponytail once again. The elegant contours of her face and neck captivated him. He feared desires he'd thought dead were fighting to live again. The depth of his emotional numbness had been so abysmal lately he hadn't thought it possible.

After he'd fallen in love with Katie, he'd had no reason to look at other women. Since her death, he'd not allowed himself the pleasure. He wasn't sure he was ready now, or if he would ever be ready, to care for another woman the way he had cared for his wife. His loss had taught him a painful lesson. The wounds of his heart were still tender, maybe even raw in spots. How could he risk loving again? Wouldn't that only increase his chances of getting hurt? The pain of another loss was something he didn't think he could bear. But it would seem his heart was threatening to betray him. He needed a plan, and soon . . .

Chapter Five

Racing heart, cottony mouth, difficulty breathing – Hanna felt the debilitating tentacles of a panic attack spreading through her body as they walked into McDonald's. It had started the moment she realized she might have to place her own order.

How could such a simple task reduce her to a yellow-bellied chicken? When had she allowed her fears to get so out of hand? She was discovering pride was a horrible taskmaster.

Possible solutions flitted through her thoughts: She could pretend she wasn't hungry – if only that were true. She could hang back, wait until everyone else had ordered and stepped away from the counter – might work, but too risky. She looked at the menu. On a number of occasions she had ordered a meal at the McDonald's in San José. The Spanish words for hamburger, French fries and soft drink were elementary. How hard could it be? No one would be paying any attention to her anyway.

Isabela walked over and stood beside her. "Aunt Hanna, what are you going to get?" she asked.

Hanna pretended to study the menu board. "I'm not sure. What are you getting?"

"A Happy Meal with chicken nuggets, French fries and a Sprite."

"That sounds good," Hanna said, covering her rising anxiety with a smile. This was getting ridiculous. Maybe it was time to 'fess up and admit the idea of testing her Spanish skills in front of everyone made her nervous. Okay . . . terrified her might be closer to the truth. She knew no one expected her to be fluent in the language after only twelve months of study, but she also knew that with practice she could have been speaking more fluently than what would come out of her mouth if she opened it and tried. No doubt her attempts would sound like baby talk compared to everyone else's command of the language, even the children's. Of course, the fear of what others would think was what had gotten her in this predicament in the first place.

Jake stepped up from behind her, his eyes fixed on the menu board. "What would you like to eat?" he asked. "It's on me."

Did that mean he planned on ordering for her? "You don't have to do that," she said, trying to be polite while hoping he insisted.

"No big deal. What's another Big Mac . . . or whatever it is that you want?"

"A Big Mac. I haven't had one of those in a long time. That sounds good."

"Anything else?"

"How about an order of fries and a Coke."

"You've got it," he said as he walked to the counter.

Hanna breathed a sigh of relief.

"This is great," Isabela said.

Hanna looked down at the child. "What's that?"

"It's like I have a mommy again," the little girl said as a dreamy smile covered her face.

Hanna's mouth dropped open. Surely she'd misunderstood what the child said. Jake's head pivoted in their direction. His eyes had turned to blue ice. *Guess not.* A chill of apprehension coursed up Hanna's spine. She considered defending herself, but for what? She'd not said or done anything for which she should feel guilty. Whatever illusions Isabela had, she'd come up with them on her own.

Jake brushed past her with their food on a tray, speaking only to his daughter. "Come on, Isabela." He walked over to a table next to where the three Anderson children were already seated.

Isabela climbed into a chair. "I want Aunt Hanna to sit by me, Daddy."

Jake placed a Happy Meal in front of her. "I think Hanna

needs to sit with Aunt Maleah," he said.

"But Daddy . . . "

When Jake gave Hanna her food and drink, his eyes defied argument. He turned back to Isabela. "If you would like, Sophie can sit with us."

Isabela sighed. "O . . . kay. Anyway, I'm going to get to ride in the car with Aunt Maleah and Aunt Hanna on our way home."

Hanna shivered as Jake's eyes shot daggers of accusation her way. *Hey,* she wanted to say, *the travel arrangements weren't my idea.*

~~~~~

Jake sulked while he ate, not bothering to make conversation with anyone. Why in the world would Isabela say such a thing? She'd never acted like it bothered her that it was just the two of them. She'd never mentioned wishing she had a mother. Why now? Why Hanna? She'd only met the young woman yesterday, but it was as if she had already bonded with her. But . . . why?

He focused on the wall several feet away as he considered the awkwardness of Isabela's comment. More than anything it made him mad. It seemed lately he was reacting all too often to people and situations with an unexplained anger. Where was it coming from? While Isabela's innocent observation may not have been reason for anger, one thing he knew for sure: He was not going to allow Hanna to take Katie's place in his daughter's heart.

Jake's hand shook as he took a bite of hamburger. The meat and bread lodged in his throat. He tossed the uneaten portion back on the tray. Watching Isabela as she handed Sophie one of her chicken nuggets, he wondered how often the child thought about her mother. When Katie first died, she'd asked for her often, even waking up at night – crying and wanting her mommy. Come to think of it, that had not happened in a long time. Not that he wanted Isabela to still grieve over the loss of her mother, he simply didn't want her to forget.

His jaw tightened. As soon as he could get Isabela alone he was going to have a talk with her. She needed to understand Hanna was there to teach her – nothing more. Maybe he should insist she call her Miss Hanna, or even Miss Truly. He should have put his foot down first thing that morning and told her she couldn't call her Aunt Hanna. The term obviously conjured up more affection than the child needed to be feeling for the young woman. Maybe he also needed to talk to Hanna or have Maleah talk to her. Whichever – Something needed to be done . . . and soon.

~~~~~

Hanna forced herself to act lighthearted and join in the conversation with Conner and Maleah as they discussed plans for the trip back to Paraíso. It appeared they had not heard Isabela's comment or seen Jake's reaction.

Conner leaned back in his chair and glanced at his watch. "It's almost one-thirty now. If the traffic isn't too bad, and if we can make it without any more stops, we should be home by five-thirty, más o menos . . . give or take fifteen minutes or so."

Maleah wiped her hands on a napkin. "I had wanted to stop by the caverns at Pomier and let Hanna see some of the Taíno pictographs, but I guess we'd better save that for another time."

"Personally, I think everyone's about ready to head back," Conner said. He looked at Hanna. "Would it be okay with you if we came back another time to visit the caverns?"

She shrugged. "Fine with me. Since I don't know what you're talking about, I guess I won't know what it is I'm missing."

Maleah and Conner both laughed. "Guess it can wait, then," Maleah said.

Conner pushed his chair back and stood as Maleah began gathering empty cups and wrappers to be thrown away. "I'll tell you about the Taíno pictographs on our drive home," she said. "We'll make a trip back someday so you can actually see them."

"Sounds good," Hanna said, watching Jake out of the corner of her eye as he placed the empties from their table on a tray. She wondered what he was going to do about Isabela once they started loading up the vehicles for the drive to Paraíso. She imagined the child would make quite a scene if he changed his mind and wouldn't let her ride with her and Maleah.

"Last call for a bathroom break," Conner announced as he headed toward the door. "I don't want to get down the road a ways and hear, *I gotta go*. Remember – public restrooms are hard to find between here and Barahona."

Hanna took one last sip of her Coke, then stood. "How far is Barahona?" she asked.

"About three to three and a half hours," Maleah said. "Hopefully we can make it home without someone needing to go to the bathroom. We'll see . . . "

Hanna was the last to exit the restaurant. As she stepped outside, she used her hand to shade her eyes against the blinding sunlight and watched as Isabela and Sophie headed toward the Andersons' mustard colored Jeep Wagoneer, cradling swaddled baby dolls in their arms.

Guess that answered that question.

Maleah helped the girls into the car. "Jake, I'm going to be following you," she called over her shoulder. "Don't forget we're back here."

Jake walked toward the driver's side of the van. "We won't forget you," he said. Opening the door, he looked at Hanna. When she matched the intensity of his gaze, he averted his eyes and climbed into the van.

"What was that all about?" she muttered under her breath as she slid in on the passenger side of the Jeep.

While Maleah hugged the back bumper of Jake's white van and worked her way into the flow of traffic, Hanna contemplated asking about the man's peculiar behavior. Whispers drifting from the back seat reminded her that little girls often have big ears. She decided on a safer subject – the Taíno caverns.

"So, what are these caves you were wanting me to see?" she asked.

Maleah kept her eyes fastened on the road ahead. "You know who the Taíno people were, don't you?"

Hanna thought back on the conversation she'd had with Jake during the ride into Santo Domingo from the airport. "They were living on the island of Hispaniola when Columbus arrived."

45

"That's right. In fact, they were the largest people group on the island at that time. Depending on the source, it is believed there were anywhere from 500,000 to 1,000,000 Taíno living here when the first group of explorers arrived from Spain."

Hanna turned around when Isabela called her name. The girls huddled behind one of the baby blankets. "What are y'all doing?" she asked.

Isabela stuck her head out. "This is our house. Don't ya like it?"

Hanna nodded. "Looks like fun." She shifted her attention back to Maleah. "Sorry," she said.

"No problem. Trust me – I'm used to being interrupted."

Hanna laughed. "One of the blessings of motherhood, I suppose?"

A smile brightened Maleah's freckled face. "Yeah, if you say so."

"I know. You can tell I'm not a mother."

Maleah chuckled.

"Moving right along," Hanna said. "What is the connection between the Taíno and the caverns you were talking about?"

Maleah flashed her another smile. "Well . . . archaeologists have discovered caves across the island that contain drawings – many are painted, others etched onto stone. Some of the carvings date back two thousand years, and it's believed they are the work of the Taíno."

"That's incredible," Hanna said, shaking her head. "If it's true, that means Taíno lived here during the time Christ walked on the earth."

"Amazing, isn't it?"

Hanna jumped at the sound of a car horn. A black SUV flew by. "Do you ever get used to that?" she asked.

"Yes and no. Depends on how frayed your nerves are."

"I'm afraid if I tried to drive, my nerves would always be frayed."

"Paraíso is quieter. Nothing like the traffic here."

"Good. Ooo - kay, back to the Taíno – these drawings – they are of what?"

Maleah glanced over her left shoulder as she changed lanes. "Various things," she said, "although it's believed most represent spiritual beings, and that the Taíno considered the caves to be sacred entrances to the spirit world. Other drawings and carvings represent food. Interestingly, human heads are a common feature."

Hanna shuddered. "You're talking about drawings of human heads, not actual skulls . . . right?"

"Just drawings," Maleah said, laughing. "Many are represented by two dots for eyes and a half circle for the mouth – kind of like an ancient version of our modern day smiley face."

Hanna's skin crawled at the thought of ancient 'smiley faces' staring at her.

Maleah must have read her mind. "Kind of creepy, isn't it?" she said.

"Kind of . . . What do the children think of these places?"

"They like them – especially the boys. You know how kids are. They think being inside a cave is an exciting adventure."

"Speaking of children, our two have gotten awfully quiet," Hanna said, looking toward the backseat. Both girls were asleep, their babies safe in the crooks of their arms. She nodded in their direction. "They're so cute."

"I can see them in the rearview mirror. They're quite a pair."

Hanna inhaled. Maybe now would be a good time to ask a few questions. She slowly exhaled. "I guess they've been friends almost since birth," she said.

"To hear them tell the story they've been *sisters* since birth. However, I'm not sure how much either of them remembers up until Jake and Isabela moved to Paraíso last March."

"How old was Isabela when her mother died?"

"A little over three. Jake and Isabela stayed in Kansas for about a year and a half after Katie died. We visited them once during that time while we were on assignment in the States, but the girls were only four."

"So . . . " Hanna hesitated as she pondered how far she could go in exploring this topic without appearing nosey. "Would you say Isabela has adjusted well? I mean . . . you know . . . losing her mother at such a young age and all."

Maleah cleared her throat and cut her eyes toward the rearview mirror. The heavy breathing of the sleeping children mingled with the rhythmic pounding of Hanna's heart. She hoped she'd not overstepped the boundaries. Several tense seconds passed before Maleah finally spoke. "Isabela appears to be adjusting well," she said. "It's Jake I'm worried about."

Hanna gulped. That was a door she wouldn't have to force open. "Yeah, I've been wondering if he was always so – "

"Distant – detached – aloof."

Hanna jerked her head in Maleah's direction. "Well, yeah."

A smile crept across her freckled face. "You look surprised."

"I guess I am. I was beginning to wonder if it was me."

"Today . . . some of it may *have been* because of you."

"But what ha – "

Maleah reached her hand toward her. "Wait – let me finish. Jake's been melancholy since they returned – understandable. Lately he's seemed more irritable . . . on edge. Conner and I've seen a side of him we didn't know existed. But . . . today, I don't know. There was something else bothering him."

"And you think it might have something to do with me?"

"Maybe . . . "

"Any ideas why?"

Maleah's eyes narrowed. "I'm still working on it."

Hanna looked out the passenger side window. She could feel her Big Mac churning in her stomach. "When you figure it out, would you let me know?"

"I will. I promise."

Chapter Six

Over the next three hours they traveled on roads that were not nearly as bad as Hanna had feared. After leaving San Cristóbal they followed Highway 2 – Carretera Sánchez as it is known by the locals – along the foothills of the Cordillera Central. Maleah served as tour guide, pointing north where the mountains began their slow ascent skyward.

"The Cordillera Central is the most rugged mountain range in the country," she said. "From north to south it covers a large portion of the central part of the Dominican Republic."

Hanna's eyes lingered on the forest-covered ridge spreading outward and upward along the horizon. "With each passing minute, I'm more and more amazed at the beauty," she said. "I don't know why, but I was expecting the mountains to be nothing more than rolling hills."

"They're certainly much more than that," Maleah said, chuckling. "Pico Duarte – the highest peak in the Caribbean – is located only a few hours from here, and many of the locals refer to the Cordillera Central as the Dominican Alps."

"Sounds inviting?"

"It does, doesn't it? Compared to the rest of the country, the temperatures in the higher elevations are almost always refreshing. In fact, during the winter months it's not unusual for the nighttime temps to drop near the freezing mark."

"I'm assuming that doesn't ever happen in Paraíso."

"No," Maleah said, sounding amused. "The lowest it ever gets in Paraíso during the winter is around seventy, and that's probably a stretch."

The landscape transformed into a coastal plain smothered in sugarcane fields near a town Maleah called Baní – A modest, crowded pueblo offering nothing of significance as far as Hanna could see that would entice her to come back. Silently she prayed Paraíso would prove to be more appealing.

Once through Baní, they continued following Jake's van along Highway 2 as they climbed a small mountain range where cliffs soared high above the winding road. About forty-five minutes later they passed through a town Maleah referred to as Azua – A small hamlet straddling the highway as it passed through. On a number of occasions Hanna had to use restraint to keep from gasping as pedestrians meandered perilously close to the road, seemingly oblivious to the swarm of traffic streaming by. It wasn't the first time that day she'd observed such precarious pedestrian activity. It appeared few Dominicans took safety issues seriously.

Several miles later the road divided, and Maleah followed Jake as he took the southwesterly route headed for Barahona. The drive had not been nearly as long as Hanna had expected.

"Over time you'll become well acquainted with Barahona," Maleah said as she maneuvered through the heaviest traffic they'd encountered since leaving the outskirts of Santo Domingo. "It's the largest town in the region, and since it's only thirty minutes from Paraíso, it's a nice place to come to whenever you need to get away."

On the last leg of their journey Hanna found herself holding her breath one minute and catching it the next as the roller coaster highway carried them through panoramic views she imagined could rival those of far greater renown anywhere in the world. For thirty minutes they passed one fishing village after another, each fringed by the teal-blue waters of the Caribbean, with palm-studded beaches pushing hard against rugged mountain cliffs. As the highway rose and fell, Hanna discovered each new setting was more breathtaking than the last.

"We're only a few minutes from Paraíso now," Maleah said as the road dipped to yet another small community. "This is San Rafael. There's a waterfall here that flows out of the mountainside and forms a balneario."

Mentally, Hanna flipped through her Spanish vocabulary Rolodex. The word Maleah just used was not there. "What's a balneario?" she asked.

"A good English translation would be *watering hole*," she said, glancing at Hanna. "It's what you might call a natural swimming pool. There's also one at Los Patos – located just on the other side of Paraíso. That one sits at the mouth of a river. Both are refreshing getaways on a hot summer day."

"Which is every day around here. Right?"

"Almost."

The road swung upward again, and they were soon on the outskirts of another small, idyllic seaside village – edged by ocean pounded cliffs and a majestic view of the Caribbean.

"Welcome to Paraíso," Maleah said.

Hanna swiveled her head in awe as they followed the highway around the upper portion of town. "I know you told me Paraíso was in the mountains, but I never dreamed it would be this beautiful," she said.

"Beautiful, but poverty stricken," Maleah replied. "Other than the beauty, there's not much here. The region remains largely undeveloped. With such gorgeous beaches, you would think someone would recognize the potential for tourism, but so far they haven't."

"I'm sure tourism would be a wonderful boost to the economy," Hanna said, "but tourists – and all that usually comes with them – generally mar the beauty of any landscape. Wouldn't you agree?"

"You're right, but this area of the country could sure use a good shot in the arm," Maleah said, cocking her head to the left. "After you've been here a while, you'll understand what I mean."

"Probably so."

Maleah stayed close behind Jake's van as he turned onto a dead-end street. Hanna noticed a scattering of houses, all concrete block and painted some shade of blue, green or pink, lined the sides of the narrow, paved road. Jake stopped in front of the second house on the right. Maleah swung around him and into the driveway. She turned off the engine and sighed. "Here we are."

Isabela bounced up and down in the back seat. "Our house is over there at the end of the street, right next to that basketball goal."

Hanna got out of the car and stretched while looking over the hood in the direction the child had pointed. She drew in her breath. The setting reminded her of a Thomas Kinkade painting – Caribbean style: a cozy home on a dead-end street, flanked by dense tropical vegetation and mountains sweeping down into the backyard. She turned to face the Andersons' home – a concrete block structure painted a pale blue. The flat terracotta roof stretched beyond the house and served as a covering for a one-car carport and a porch running across the front. A vast collection of bicycles, children's toys and sports equipment filled the open garage. Two rocking chairs sitting on the porch extended a warm welcome, and a hammock Hanna could hear whispering her name swung gently in the breeze. She turned back around just as Jake stepped out of the van.

"So, Hanna, what do you think?" Conner asked as he headed her way.

Hanna gazed toward the mountains reaching heavenward behind the house across the street. "I'm still in shock. I was just telling Maleah this wasn't quite what I'd expected when she told me Paraiso was in the mountains. It's gorgeous."

"I hope you still feel that way once you've been here a while," Conner said. "It is pretty, but not an easy place to live. The culture, the poverty, the power outages, the humidity – "

"Conner Anderson!" Maleah's hands went to her hips. "Let the girl enjoy it for a while. She can be a tourist for at least a few days." She turned to Hanna. "It really is a lovely place. Don't let him tell you otherwise."

"Yeah, it's paradise. That's why they call it Paraíso," Conner said with a wink.

"Why do you say that?" Hanna asked.

"Didn't you know Paraíso means paradise in Spanish?"

Hanna felt the warmth of embarrassment rising to her face. That was something she probably should have known. "Oh, yeah . . . I guess I hadn't put two and two together."

Jake burst out laughing, catching Hanna by surprise. "I doubt it was this hot and humid in the Garden of Eden," he said.

"Well, now . . . I don't know if I would be so quick to make that assumption if I were you," Conner said. "Maybe that's why they were nak – "

"Conner!" Maleah huffed while shaking her finger at him. Hanna felt laughter bubbling up in her throat, but held it in check when Maleah looked at her. "Okay, okay," the woman said, "I'd be lying if I told you there were no adjustments to be made. But you're right . . . it *is* gorgeous." She glared at Conner. "Try and remember that when all the other junk is threatening to pull you under."

Hanna decided she was going to enjoy working with the Andersons.

As for Jake – the verdict was still out.

~~~~~

As instructed, Hanna handed her plate to Maleah, who scraped the small amount of uneaten food into a bowl before adding the plate to the growing stack in front of her. She tapped the bowl with a fork. "Our dog loves leftovers," she said.

They had just finished eating a typical Dominican meal prepared earlier that day by a local woman who worked for the Andersons. Maleah looked at Hanna as she added the last plate to her stack. "What do you think of Dominican food so far?"

The small boneless chunks of fried chicken had been similar to what Hanna was used to back home, but the red beans and rice had a unique flavor that was new. "It was good," she said, "although I was surprised when I took my first bite of the beans and rice. I was expecting them to taste like what we eat in the south – more of a Louisiana Cajun style. But . . . " she shrugged, "they were good, just different."

"The difference is a blend of Spanish, African and Taíno seasoning," Maleah said. "It's called comida criolla."

Conner chuckled. "All that means is it's cooked with onion, green pepper, garlic, cilantro and a tomato-based sauce you can buy in any of the local grocery stores."

Maleah flashed her husband a stern look as she held up one of the leftover fried plantains. "Another staple – plátanos. Fried like this they're called tostones, but sometimes they're served sweet."

Conner smiled his boyish grin. "They're especially good when mashed and served with pork cracklings or for breakfast with fried eggs and cheese."

Hanna assumed he had not seen the look of warning Maleah sent his way a few seconds earlier. Either that or he didn't care. "Sounds interesting," she said, "but I think my stomach needs a little time to adapt before getting that adventuresome." She looked at Maleah. "Do you mostly cook Dominican style?"

"Me? No. I usually prepare American dishes. That way we don't get tired of Dominican food. We also still have our big meal in the evening, but you'll discover most Dominicans have their main meal in the early afternoon – around one-thirty or two."

"That's why Isabela and I often end up here for dinner." Hanna shifted in her chair and looked at Jake. He'd hardly spoken all evening. "Our Dominican helper is a great cook," he continued, "but sometimes I want something other than chicken with rice and beans, and I still prefer a lighter lunch and heavier dinner. Unfortunately, I'm not a very good cook, so Maleah is kind enough to make enough for us."

"Hey Jake," Maleah said, propping her elbows on the table and leaning forward. "You prefer a heavier dinner or supper?"

Jake shook his head as he sat back in his chair, resting his arms on the sides. "Dinner. You heard what I said."

"So, Hanna, what do you call the last meal of the day?" Conner asked.

Hanna chewed on her bottom lip as she glanced around the table. "Well, ah . . . let's see." She rested her eyes on Jake and scrunched her nose. "Supper . . . "

"You see, Jake," Maleah said.

"Why do I feel outnumbered?"

"Because you are."

"Only because I'm surrounded by a bunch of southerners." Jake focused on Hanna and grinned.

Conner tented his hands in front of his chest and tapped his chin with his fingers. "Now that we have that settled," he said, looking at Hanna, "we'd like to know a little more about you."

After Jake's teasing smile, Hanna's stomach had hardly had time to resettle. It felt like it had reached the wash cycle, and she could feel her supper – or maybe that was dinner – agitating. Did they actually think she'd be able to talk? "Like . . . what?" she asked.

"Oh, I don't know," Conner said, his expression serious. "We've read the biographical information the mission board sent when you first accepted the assignment, but we thought it would be nice if you could share a few things with us personally – like where you're from, something about your family, your call to missions – whatever you feel comfortable sharing."

Hanna studied her hands, which she held tightly clasped in her lap. What to tell? Her brain hummed with unanswered questions. How much did they really want to know? For that matter, how much would she feel comfortable sharing? Was there something specific they were looking for? She took a deep breath while scanning the faces around the table. All of her interactions with Conner and Maleah so far had been warm and accepting, but still . . . she didn't know these people. As for Jake . . . sheer vulnerability seemed out of the question.

"Well . . . for starters – I'm from Daphne, Alabama, which is located across the bay from Mobile . . ." She cleared her throat before continuing. "My parents are Peter and Kathy Truly, and I'm an only child. My mother teaches elementary school, and my father is in management. Seven years ago I graduated from the University of Alabama with a degree in elementary education. From there I went to seminary . . . " She looked at Conner and shrugged.

"We're you already considering missions at that time?" he asked.

"I was. I had made a public commitment to fulltime mission service during my junior year in high school."

"What prompted your decision?" Maleah asked.

Hanna met the woman's gaze. "Well . . . I've had a fascination with missions since I was eight or nine years old. In fact, some of my fondest memories are of visiting with missionaries during the missions fair our church hosted each year. Over time I began to sense God was calling me in that direction." She paused and took a sip of water, hoping to soothe the itch tickling her throat. "On the morning I made my decision public our pastor had been speaking directly to the young people in the church, challenging us to seek God's will for our futures. At the end of the service, I knew God was telling me it was time to share my calling with my church family."

All eyes were on her. Hanna felt like she was on the witness stand. "Anything else?" she asked.

Conner's brown eyes narrowed. "What about your decision to come to Paraíso? How did you know this was where God was calling you to serve?"

Why the interrogation? Hanna's insecurities rose like a flash flood after a heavy rain. She wrapped her arms around her midsection in a tight hug. Were they questioning whether she was the one God had called to teach their children? Did they have reason to think she wasn't qualified for the job? Was it possible they had already picked up on her inadequacies with the language? In a matter of seconds, her fears became ammunition for Satan as he bombarded her with the same accusations he'd been making against her for months: Who do you think you are? Why would God call *you* to the mission field? Do you really think you're good enough to be a missionary? You can't even speak the language; how do you expect to communicate? You're only fooling yourself if you think you're going to succeed.

Supper surged from her stomach to her throat. Could it be true? Was she only fooling herself?

Chapter Seven

"Are you okay?" The sound of Maleah's voice jarred Hanna out of her defeatist musings. A look of concern covered the woman's freckled face.

"Oh, yes. I'm sorry," Hanna replied. "I guess I'm just tired."

A smile replaced Conner's stoic expression. "I'm sure you are," he said. "Would you rather share some other time?"

"No, that's okay." Hanna breathed deeply. "You wanted to know how I knew God was calling me to Paraíso – Right?"

"I did," Conner said, still smiling. "I was just curious, but if you're too tired, it's no big deal."

"There's really not much to it," Hanna said, feeling somewhat reassured. She loosened the grip from around her waist, her hands falling once again to her lap. "After seminary I returned to Daphne and took a job teaching second grade in the local public school system. During that time my call to missions remained strong. A year later, I contacted the mission board and began the process for appointment. Naturally, with a degree in elementary education I was interested in a teaching assignment. Over the next few months they sent me a number of job descriptions. As I prayed about which one I should accept, God kept bringing me back to this one in Paraíso." She held her hands steady and lifted her shoulders. "No burning bushes or Damascus Road experiences, I simply felt this was where He wanted me to serve."

"Well, we're glad you're here," Maleah said, reaching over to give Hanna's arm a squeeze. "I can't tell you how much I'm looking forward to having some female companionship with another

American. I love my Dominican friends, but sometimes I get lonely for someone who speaks my language and understands my culture."

Hanna looked around the dining room table. *Was that it?* No one was questioning her calling or debating whether she was right for the job? Was it possible the opposite was true and she was actually wanted? As all her fatalistic speculations scurried away like roaches exposed to the light, she almost laughed. When was she going to learn to call Satan's bluff and stop falling for his lies and accusations?

"I second that," Conner said. "Ah, well, I mean the part about being glad you're here." His face flushed, blending with his freckles. "As for the female companionship," he cleared his throat and looked at Maleah with downcast eyes, "I think I have all of that I need."

Maleah pursed her lips, but her eyes danced with laughter. It was obvious she was having a hard time keeping a straight face. "You'd better be careful," she said. "You're about to get yourself in trouble." Her eyebrows lifted. "But . . . you have to admit you're glad I'll have someone else to gab with, aren't you?"

Jake pushed his chair back on two legs and folded his arms across his chest. "That sounds like a loaded question, if you ask me," he said.

Conner nodded. "I think you're right. I'd better stop while I'm ahead."

Jake grinned and lowered the front of his chair to the floor. "I'm not sure I would say you're ahead," he said as he stood, "but stopping is probably a good idea." He walked across the living room and stuck his head in the hallway. "Isabela, it's time to go."

Before Hanna could stand, Isabela bounded into the room and headed straight for her. "Good night, Aunt Hanna. I'm so glad you're finally here," she said.

Keeping an eye on Jake, Hanna gave the child a hug. "Thank-you, sweetie. I'm glad to be here." Although she wasn't sure how she would have described Jake's reaction, she was thankful it did not appear to be anger.

Minutes later she stood with Maleah and Conner on the front porch, watching as Jake walked and Isabela swirled down the

Caribbean Paradise

driveway. When they reached the street, Isabela waved and shouted, "Good-night." The corners of Hanna's mouth lifted as she listened to the sweet sound of little girl giggles being carried along on a gentle breeze.

~~~~

  Jake held Isabela's small, plump hand in his. It felt wet and sticky. The loose gravel crunched beneath their feet as he guided his daughter over the broken asphalt. Her steps were a mixture of skips and jumps. How could she have so much energy after such a long day? When the moon's rays highlighted her dark, bouncing curls, memories of Katie flooded his thoughts. With his free hand he ran his fingers through his own straight hair. Isabela had inherited her ringlets from her mother.

  Taking a deep breath, Jake began trying to process the myriad of emotions he had felt that day. For the most part, they were a muddled mess in the pit of his stomach as if someone had put them in a blender and pressed puree. Over the past few weeks he'd toyed with an expectation or two in terms of what the young teacher the mission board was sending would be like, but Hanna Truly definitely caught him off guard. From the moment he first saw her standing at the bottom of the exit ramp outside of customs, anxiously looking for someone to rescue her, he had battled emotions he'd not felt in a long time. He had to admit the unexpected stirrings were somewhat reassuring. He'd felt numb for so long, he had feared he might never feel again. His interactions with others had become a charade. He could smile or frown, laugh or cry – at all the right times, but he knew the truth: his broken heart lay limp and lifeless in his chest. It was as if a part of him died with Katie. If it had not been for Isabela, he believed he could have simply quit living.

  All of that had changed during the last twenty-four hours. Jake lifted his eyes toward the moonlit sky. Although his emotions had been tangled and unpredictable, at least he'd been feeling something. While at times it was anger, irritation or resentment, the two times he'd held Hanna's soft hand in his as he helped her into the van, he'd felt more alive than he had since Katie died.

But why did such feelings bring on a wave of guilt?

Why had Isabela's delight bothered him so much when she felt like a normal child ordering lunch with her parents at McDonalds?

Why had he treated Hanna so rudely? She had not done anything.

He unlocked the door to the house and ushered a more subdued Isabela inside.

Lord, he prayed silently, *I really need Your help on this one.* He wondered if anyone was listening. He hadn't exactly been on speaking terms with God since Katie's death. Like everything else, his numbness had affected his relationship with his heavenly Father. He would often go weeks without uttering a prayer or opening his Bible. To do either always threatened to surface emotions he didn't want to admit existed, much less wanted to deal with.

Jake led the now exhausted Isabela down the hall to her room. While helping her get ready for bed, his thoughts drifted back to Hanna. His response to the young woman both thrilled and scared him. The loneliness that engulfed him when Maleah talked of needing a female companion had been startling. For just a moment he wanted to echo her sentiments. While Conner may not need another woman in his life, was it possible he did? But thinking that way made him feel unfaithful . . . to Katie, to the vows they had made to one another, and even to Isabela and the memory he needed to protect where her mother was concerned.

Jake leaned over and kissed the child on the forehead. "Good night, sweetheart," he said. He turned off the light and headed down the hall to his own bedroom. Leaving the room in darkness, he laid down on top of the bedspread, still fully clothed.

Another wave of loneliness threatened to drown him.

"I think I may have preferred the numbness to this," he said out loud to the inky stillness as uninvited tears slipped from his eyes and ran down the sides of his face.

The ceiling fan, which had been providing a reprieve from the heat, stopped turning. Down the street a generator roared to life.

~~~~~

Hanna slipped through the barred breezeway that served as the laundry room for the Andersons' home into her own small apartment at the back of the house. Running her hand along the wall, she found the switch and gave it a flip. The room came alive with light, and two ceiling fans began stirring the muggy air. She shut the door and took several steps forward before being swallowed in darkness so black she couldn't see her hand in front of her face. She glanced over her shoulder as panic, like the prickly legs of a spider, crawled up her back.

She was tired. No . . . utterly exhausted better described how she felt. Everything was so new and so . . . foreign. What was going on? She took a couple of steps back and reached for the switch on the wall. She flipped it down and back up. Nothing. When the door creaked open, she screamed.

"I'm sorry," Maleah said. "I didn't mean to startle you."

Hanna spun around. Maleah stood in the doorway holding a lantern. Shadowy light danced along the walls and across the furniture. Hanna closed her eyes and willed her heart to stop racing. "That's okay," she said. "What's going on?"

"The electricity went off. Welcome to the Dominican Republic." Maleah offered her a feeble smile. "Actually, I'm pleased we made it this long."

"Does this happen every night?"

"Yes . . . no . . . who knows? There's no rhyme or reason to our power outages. Just about the time we think a pattern has been established, it changes. Most days, it goes off for several hours in the morning or afternoon, and then again in the evening. There are days it's off only six or eight hours. Other times it might be off ten or twelve – or more. Like I said, no rhyme or reason."

Hanna blew out her breath. "I know this is another one of those things you told me about in your letters, but it's certainly different experiencing it firsthand. Man, when it's dark around here – it's dark."

Maleah walked over to the sitting area of Hanna's apartment and set the lantern on top of a small desk. "In some ways it seems this country is full of darkness, both physically and spiritually," she said as she pulled a box of matches and a couple of stubby candles out of the pocket of her skirt and held them up for Hanna to see. "You are probably going to need these from time to time. For now, Conner is filling the generator with gas. We'll be up and going again with some lights in a few minutes. We'll let it run for about thirty minutes so we can get ready for bed, but then we'll need to turn it off." She laid the candles and matches on the desk. "Sorry. I know you probably wanted to get a few things unpacked. You can use the lantern if you like."

"No, that's okay. I'm pretty tired. I'll probably find a nightgown, get a quick shower and go on to bed."

Maleah cleared her throat. "Um . . . about that quick shower. There's no water pressure when the electricity is off, and we don't get it back with the generator. You might get a small trickle at the sink to wash your face, and there's some bottled water on the shelf above the toilet that you can use to brush your teeth. In fact, even when we have water pressure it's not a good idea to put any of the tap water in your mouth. We don't want you getting sick."

Hanna tried to smile, although her effort probably more resembled a grimace. She had been sweating since she got up; now she would have to go to bed without a shower. It was promising to be a rather miserable night. She heard the rumble of the generator moments before the lights and ceiling fans came back to life.

"That's better," Maleah said as she turned to leave. Just outside the door she paused and cleared her throat again. "One more thing. When the generator goes off, so will the fans. Like I said – Welcome to the DR."

"I think my miserable night just got more miserable," Hanna muttered under her breath as the door closed. A full-fledged pity party seemed appropriate.

After finding a lightweight cotton nightgown, she dressed for bed, shook her hair loose, splashed a tiny bit of water on her face and, as instructed, brushed her teeth using bottled water. Before getting in bed, she decided to crank the louvered glass windows in the sitting area open a little further, hoping for a better airflow in the tiny apartment. One of the windows looked out over the backyard while the other one faced a patio, which she had noticed earlier was more like an outside extension off the main living room. The smell of gasoline stung her nostrils, and the unsettling roar of the generator grated on her frazzled nerves. It appeared the gas-powdered energy source was housed somewhere near the end of the covered brick terrace.

Hanna returned to the other side of the room and pulled back the lightweight yellow and lavender flowered bedspread, along with the top sheet, folding them both at the foot of the bed. She doubted she would need either. As she lowered her head onto the pillow, she heard the generator slowly die, taking the lights and what little air that had been circulating with it. Although exhausted, she was convinced there was no way she would be able to sleep. The night air felt thick and balmy, her sweaty back, damp on the sheet below her. She turned on her side and stared into the darkness.

"Lord, I know You are the reason I'm here," she prayed, "but . . . I've got to be honest – I never dreamed it was going to be so hard, and I've only been here twenty-four hours. I feel so lonely . . . so far away from anyone and anything familiar. When Maleah wrote and told me about the heat and humidity, no air conditioning, the power outages, the crazy traffic – I remember thinking, *Oh, I can handle that*." She choked back a sob. How many times over the past year had she had similar conversations with God? It seemed He was determined to rid her of every ounce of self-reliance she'd ever had.

She'd often heard people talk about God moving them out of their comfort zone, but up until she arrived in Costa Rica, she'd not realized how comfortable she was. She sighed as the tears flowed. "Oh Lord, how I pray I didn't miss You on this one," she said. "But even if I got it right, and this is exactly where I'm supposed to be, I don't know . . . Oh, Lord Jesus, please help me."

After a while the tears slowed, then subsided altogether. Hanna welcomed the peace that settled over her. "Thank-you, Father," she whispered. Reflecting upon the events of the day, she hoped her mind and body would eventually give in to the overwhelming fatigue. Although she tried to think of other things and other people, the one face that kept invading her thoughts was that of Jake Mason. Something about the man stirred her emotions in ways she hadn't felt since her early college days when she started dating a young man she believed was going to be her husband.

Initially they seemed to be on the same track, but he turned out to be someone totally different from the strong, committed Christian he had presented himself to be. Once she realized he was not the one God had chosen for her to spend the rest of her life with, she'd broken up with him. She grieved for months, but in time God healed her wounded heart. She had hoped to meet someone in seminary who shared her passion for missions, someone to serve alongside her on the mission field. But it didn't happen. Ultimately she had no other choice but to trust her future into God's hands, believing there was a reason He wanted her to set out on this journey alone. Looking back, she realized that had been the beginning of the work God was in the process of doing in her life.

As for Jake, he appeared to be suffering from a broken heart, a heart more deeply damaged than hers had ever been. To lose a boyfriend of your own choosing was one thing; to lose your wife and the mother of your child . . . she could not imagine the pain he had suffered. It had been almost three years since Katie's death, yet Hanna felt certain she'd seen in Jake's eyes a lingering sorrow. Although she had just met him, she wondered if there was something she could do to help alleviate his pain. Then again, whom was she kidding? How could she help someone else when she seemed unable to help herself? She cringed even as the question trudged through her thoughts.

Off in the distance, Hanna heard a dog barking. She rolled to her back and stared at the darkened ceiling. God was the only one who knew about the battles she'd fought. She'd known she was in trouble when she first realized learning to speak another language required a healthy ability to laugh at oneself and keep going . . . something she'd never been able to do. As a result, her faltering attempts to speak Spanish frequently washed her in shame, until she had ultimately stopped trying to communicate. Instead, she poured herself into the study of the written language. But unfortunately, having a textbook knowledge of Spanish grammar and phonetics did not train her ears to understand the language when spoken – especially by nationals; nor did it give her the opportunity to practice speaking the words and sentence structures she was faithfully digesting.

Most troubling had been the realization her fears of being shamed stemmed from her childhood. Fresh tears streamed down her cheeks at the memory. Her father was a workaholic; her mother a perfectionist – Nothing but *the best* had always been expected of her. Both parents had been short on praise when she did well, but long on advice whenever she failed to perform to their level of expectation. Over time, she too had become a perfectionist and often her own worst critic. Up until the past year she'd spent her life striving for excellence. The operative word here being striving. Perhaps the hard lessons she was now being forced to learn would not have been necessary if she had realized a long time ago that when God said, *"Cease striving, and know that I am God,"* He meant it. She had breezed through college and seminary and had arrived in San José expecting language school to be no different. But in a matter of months all her confidence had crumbled – like a poorly constructed building during an earthquake. She faced fears of failure for the first time in her life and could only imagine the humiliation of having to return home – all because she couldn't master the Spanish language.

For years she'd told people God called her to be a missionary. How would she explain His failure to equip her for the task to which He'd commissioned her? For months this question haunted her, until finally her eyes had been opened to the truth: She had never asked God to equip her, but had thought of learning the language as something she could do – all on her own. During the past year she'd come face to face with her own weaknesses, manifested in her inability to do what she'd been called to do. It was proving to be a slow, painful process, but she now realized God was allowing her to taste failure because He wanted her to know success would not come as a result of her own efforts, but because of her dependence upon Him.

Considering all the junk in her own life that still needed to be unlearned and redirected, why in the world was she entertaining thoughts of helping someone else?

As if Jake would let her even if she could.

Chapter Eight

Hanna awoke sometime later to a bright light shining in her face. She placed her hand over her eyes, shielding them from the offensive intrusion. At first she couldn't remember where she was, but as the fog of sleep lifted, she realized she was in her new apartment in the Dominican Republic. Pushing up on her elbows, she looked around the room. She was alone, and the door was shut.

How strange. Who turned on the lights?

As she sat upright it occurred to her. She hadn't flipped the switch to off before getting in bed. The power must have come back on. She climbed out of bed, padded to the sitting room and extinguished the light with one jerk of the chain, while allowing the fan to continue rotating. Back in bed, she checked the battery-operated clock on the end table. Three-sixteen. After pulling the chain to the light over her head, she lay down. The current of air generated by the fans provided a welcome relief from the heat. A while later, she grabbed the top sheet from the end of the bed and covered up.

The next time Hanna awoke, rays of sunlight strolled through the louvered windows and frolicked on the braided sage-green rug in the sitting room. She could hear someone rattling plates in the kitchen on the other side of the laundry room outside of her apartment door. Through drowsy eyes she watched the swift movement of the fans, now circulating cooler air. It took her a few minutes to realize rotating fans meant the electricity was still on.

She could get a shower!

Hanna jumped out of bed, snatched a bar of soap and a bottle of shampoo from one of her suitcases, then headed for the tiny bathroom, which was separated from her bedroom by a pale green curtain suspended across the small opening between the two rooms.

Fifteen minutes later, she emerged from the bathroom, one towel wrapped around her body, another twisted turban-style on her head. Stepping in front of the mirror attached to a small dresser, she unwound the terrycloth turban. As she worked a brush through her hair, the heavy locks dispensed vanilla scented droplets down her back. She patted her shoulders dry while surveying the apartment, which wasn't much larger than a medium size bedroom. Conner had told her it was originally the maid's quarters and had consisted of a small bedroom and bath. A modest sitting area had been added and furnished with two white wicker chairs accented by cushions in a floral pattern of yellow, lavender and green, matching the bedspread now lying on the floor at the foot of the bed. A dark mahogany end table sat between the two chairs and supported a lamp. On the opposite wall stood the desk, also a dark mahogany, where Maleah had placed the lantern and candles the night before – a silent reminder of the frequent power outages.

After getting dressed, Hanna opened the armoire sitting next to the door. There were six drawers down one side and a place for hanging clothes on the other. Glancing around the room, she realized there was no closet. Her eyes fell on the suitcases and footlockers still sitting where they had been placed the night before – only one had been opened. When her stomach growled, she agreed she wasn't up to the challenge of finding a place for all of her stuff until after she had something to eat.

The smell of cinnamon greeted her as she walked into the kitchen, and she heard what sounded like a coffee cup clanging against a saucer in the combination dining and living room, followed by the deep intonation of Jake's voice. Her heart skipped a beat. How could just the sound of the man's voice cause such a stirring of her emotions? She poured a cup of coffee from a pot that was half empty, then lifted a cinnamon roll out of a pan sitting on the counter and placed it on a plate. As she entered the dining room, Conner and Jake both looked up. When Jake smiled, her heart skipped another beat.

A devious smirk crept across Conner's face. "Well, look what the cat dragged in," he said. He narrowed his eyes as if he were giving her a good once over. "Although I have to admit you look a lot better than the usual catches around here."

Hanna saw the corners of Jake's mouth twitch. "What exactly does that mean?" she asked as she put her coffee cup and plate on the table and pulled out a chair.

"Didn't Maleah tell you?" Conner asked. "We have rats in these parts that are bigger than most Chihuahuas in the U.S. That's why we have cats."

Hanna sat down hard. She was sure her face had turned white. "You're kidding. Right?"

Jake leaned back in his chair. "Oh no. He's not kidding. I've seen cat and rat skirmishes in the field beyond our house that could rival the best cocks fights in the country."

"You two stop it!" Maleah said as she entered the room from the other side of the house. "You're going to scare the poor girl to death."

"Well, honey, we don't want her to be uninformed," Conner said, his boyish grin reminding Hanna once again of B.J. Honeycut on M*A*S*H.

Hanna looked at Maleah. "Are they really serious?"

Maleah sighed. "I'm afraid there's a lot of truth to their tales. However, you need to know our cats are great mousers . . . or I guess that would be ratters. Anyway, they keep the rat population under control. We haven't seen a rat in the house in months."

Hanna looked back at the still smiling faces of the men. "I've about decided it takes a lot of guts to live in this place. Guts I'm not sure I have."

"Oh, come on . . . " Conner said a little more gently. "It's really not that bad. I promise."

A shadow passed over Jake's face. Had the thought that she might not stay bothered him? Surely not. She took a bite of cinnamon roll and watched as a large calico cat sauntered in from the patio and rubbed against Maleah's legs. The animal's purrs sounded like the engine of a well-maintained Model-T Ford.

"Speaking of our ratters, this is Angel – one of the best

ratters in all of Paraíso," Maleah said. "She was smaller than the rats when Conner first brought her home, but as you can see," she stooped and picked up the cat, "she's not hurting for nourishment these days."

Hanna's eyes widened. "Did she get that big eating rats?"

Maleah laughed. "No, I was teasing. She generally doesn't eat the rats she kills. More often than not she leaves them on the doorstep. You know . . . as a love offering to show how much she appreciates us."

Hanna gulped down her first swallow of coffee. She wondered how well she'd be able to sleep at night knowing there were rats around.

Conner placed his hands firmly on the arms of his chair. "Not meaning to change the subject," he said, "but what are the plans for the day? Surely we're not going to sit around all morning discussing the rat population of Paraíso."

"I thought we'd give Hanna a tour of the neighborhood this morning," Maleah said. "After lunch, maybe we could take a drive around town and even go to one of the beaches or watering holes." She looked at Hanna. "What do you think?"

"Whatever y'all want to do," Hanna said. "I still need to unpack, but that can wait. I'm looking forward to seeing more of Paraíso. Some of the views of the beaches as we came in yesterday were breathtaking. I would enjoy getting to see one up close." Conner pushed his chair back and stood. "Good. Sounds like a plan. Jake, do you want to go with us?"

Jake glanced for a fraction of a second at Hanna before answering. "I think I will," he said. "Are you taking the kids or leaving them here with Celia?"

"Probably taking them with us," Maleah said. "I'm sure they would enjoy showing their new teacher around town."

Jake looked at Hanna again, this time making eye contact. Was he thinking twice about his decision to go with them? "I'm sure Isabela would enjoy that too," he said. Hanna thought she heard a measure of resignation in his voice. "I'll go home and see if she's up. When I headed out this morning I told Rosalinda to let her sleep a while. She seemed rather tired last night."

"Our kids were worn out too," Maleah said, "but they are up and about now. I expect at any moment they'll be in here looking for something to eat. How about we meet in thirty minutes." She checked her watch. " Say . . . around nine. Would it be all right if we start our tour of the neighborhood at your house? Hanna might like to see where you and Isabela live."

Jake's eyes fell on Hanna one more time. How she wished she could tell what he was thinking.

An awkward silence filled the space between them.

Maleah cleared her throat. "If you would rather not, we can meet back here."

Jake emerged from the dazed glare he'd fixed on Hanna and looked at Maleah. "No . . . I'm sorry." His chair scraped across the terrazzo floor as he stood. "Guess I'm a little tired myself. Our house in thirty minutes. We'll be ready."

Hanna took a sip of coffee, peering over the top of the cup as he walked toward the door. Dressed in cotton khakis and a casual light blue and white pinstripe shirt, a pair of brown leather sandals on his feet, she still couldn't get over how he simply did not fit what she had always thought of as the "missionary type". Something wet and warm brushed across her hand, startling her out of her thoughts and almost out of her chair. The biggest Boxer she'd ever seen stood beside her. She rubbed the dog between the ears while speaking gently. She hoped the animal was friendly. "Hello there," she said. "What's your name? Did you enjoy your leftovers last night?"

"Greta. What are you doing in the house?" Maleah said as she walked into the dining room drying her hands on a kitchen towel. "You get back outside."

The dog's stubby tail thumped the floor. Hanna continued rubbing her head. "Hi, Greta. Nice to meet you."

"Come on, Greta," Maleah said as she stood next to the open double doors leading from the living room onto the back patio. "She knows she's not supposed to be in the house. Guess she saw someone new and thought she could get away with it."

"She's a beautiful dog. She scared me at first, but she seems friendly."

"Sometimes I wonder if she's not a little too friendly,"

Maleah said. "She's supposed to be a guard dog, but most of the time acts like an overgrown puppy. Although, we have noticed whenever the neighbor's gardener is trimming the trees in the backyard, Greta jumps at the wall, growling as if she would tear him to pieces if she could get to him. Not that I would want anyone to get hurt, but . . . I hope if someone did attempt to enter the house through the backyard, she would at least give them a good scare."

While Maleah led the dog back outside, Hanna rose from the table, and slipped into the kitchen. After taking one more swig of coffee, she placed her cup and plate in the sink next to the mug Jake had been using – Inevitably her thoughts drifted in his direction.

~~~~~

Walking down the street toward his house, Jake was once again mystified by the mixed emotions he battled every time he saw Hanna. Even now, feelings of being alive contrasted with guilt and betrayal. Earlier he was shamefully perplexed when Hanna walked into the Andersons' dining room dressed in a knee length dark purple skirt and a lavender pullover T-shirt, and the sight of her made him feel like he did the first time he saw Katie. For so long he'd felt empty, the void his wife left in his heart so vast he thought there would never be another woman who could have that kind of effect on him. The emotional stir Hanna caused both intrigued and unnerved him. He wasn't sure he was ready to go where his heart might be trying to lead him.

Katie had been the love of his life. When they got married, he had given his heart to her completely. Now that she was gone, he wasn't sure what he was supposed to do with the broken pieces of that heart. How could he offer even a small fragment to another woman without betraying the commitment he had made to his wife on their wedding day? Would it mean he no longer loved her or that he was being unfaithful? Surely it would be easier to remain as he was – protecting his heart. Although it had not factored into his decision to return to the DR, he had to admit one of the perks of leaving the States had been the distance it put between him and well-meaning family and friends who had been trying to play matchmaker. How ironic to think his own heart would take up where they'd left off.

He wasn't sure how he was going to do it, but he had to put an end to the feelings he was having for Hanna. God had called him to Paraíso to work, not waste his time on foolish schoolboy emotions. If only he could find something in Hanna to dislike, maybe it would be easier to put her out of his mind.

The sooner, the better.

Chapter Nine

Hanna returned to her apartment to brush her teeth. She stopped at the door on her way back out and pushed one of the footlockers with her foot. Surely there would be plenty of time to unpack later. She stepped into the laundry area and pulled the door shut behind her. Entering the living room of the main house, she could hear Maleah and Conner talking to the children, encouraging them to hurry up. She walked out the double doors through which Maleah had escorted Greta earlier, onto the large brick patio – the same one she could see from the window above the desk in her apartment. On the backside of the patio stood a waist high fence; beyond was the backyard, enclosed by a tall concrete wall painted the same light blue as the outside of the house. The yard, although not much wider than the width of the house, was deep, and hosted a flourishing bouquet of tropical plants and trees, most of which Hanna did not recognize. Greta lay on the other side of the short fence. A secured gate denied her access to the patio and house.

When Hanna felt a cat rubbing against the calves of her legs, she looked down expecting to see Angel, the large calico she had met earlier. Instead, a petite, light gray and white tabby greeted her with a soft *meow*. She picked the cat up. "Another good ratter, I hope. What's your name?"

"That's Sugar," Sophie said as she entered the living room. "She's my favorite because she's sweet, just like her name." The child grinned, displaying the empty space where her two front teeth used to be.

Hanna stepped back into the house. "She does seem sweet,"

she said as she stroked the cat, now cuddled up in her arms and purring softly. "Does she like to catch mice and rats?"

"Oh yeah! One time she caught a rat this big . . . " Sophie held her hands almost a foot apart.

A shiver ran up Hanna's spine. Surely the child was exaggerating – like a fish tale where the fish gets bigger and bigger each time the story is told.

"I think we're all ready," Maleah said as she walked into the room.

"Sounds good," Hanna replied. She thought she detected a touch of weariness in the woman's voice.

"I see you've made the acquaintance of the best ratter in all Paraíso."

Hanna nodded. "Sophie was just telling me about one of her big catches." She looked down at the child. "By any chance do you think Sugar would come to my apartment for a sleepover? You know, to help keep the rats away."

Sophie giggled. "Aunt Hanna, you're funny."

~~~~~

On the way to Jake and Isabela's house, Hanna found herself skipping over potholes with almost every step she took. She had to laugh when Conner called her *Grace.*

"Potholes are a Dominican trademark," he said.

"No kidding," she answered as she continued her *graceful* dance.

Maleah nodded in the direction of the worn basketball goal Isabela had pointed out the evening before. "Daniel and Caleb think it's great fun to come down here and play basketball with Jake and some of the other boys in the neighborhood," she said.

With its raveled net hanging on by only a few cords, Hanna thought it looked not only well used but also dearly loved.

"Jake's a natural born athlete," Conner added. "If it's not basketball, it's a game of baseball in the open field behind his house. He's a great coach, and all the kids love him. Most Dominican boys dream of playing big league sports, and watching Jake use his skills and their dreams as a platform for ministry has been a real blessing."

It was easy for Hanna to picture Jake as he played basketball with a group of dark-skinned Dominican boys. She could almost see him dribbling on the crumbled asphalt before vaulting toward the bent goal in a demonstration of just how easy it was to dunk the ball. A smile slowly lifted the corners of her mouth. "Are sports his primary ministry?" she asked.

"They are," Conner said. "In fact, that was a part of the lure we used to get him to come back to the Dominican Republic. We'd opened a community center about a year after Katie died in hopes of attracting many of the children who often play baseball and basketball in the streets and open fields around Paraíso. It's amazing how much these kids love to play ball. Even without proper equipment, they are fiercely determined and often have some real talent. Once the center opened, it didn't take me long to realize I had neither the time nor the skills to keep up with the demand."

Maleah smiled. "The kids came out of the woodwork, so when we heard Jake was thinking about returning, we used our need for a fulltime sports director as bait. It worked."

"It has certainly made my job easier," Conner said. "I was thankful to have the time once again to focus on evangelism."

They turned and walked up the driveway of an incandescent turquoise house that was similar in construction and style to the Andersons', only smaller. "I like the color," Hanna said. "Dominicans really like them bright, don't they?"

Conner nodded. "This is nothing compared to the vivid colors used by the Haitians. We'll make a trip to the border one day so you can see the difference for yourself."

"They're here! They're here!" Isabela yelled as she ran out the front door and headed straight for Hanna.

Realizing she was on a collision course with the child, Hanna decided she might withstand the impact better if she stood still and braced herself. Within seconds Isabela hit her at full speed. "Aunt Hanna, you're finally here," the little girl cried in delight as she wrapped her arms around her legs. "I couldn't wait to see you again."

Maleah stopped to witness the dramatic interaction, then

turned and looked at Conner. "Darling, I think we've been replaced."

Conner chuckled. "I believe you're right."

Isabela let go of Hanna's legs and ran to give Maleah a hug. "Aunt Maleah, I still love you and Uncle Conner, but . . . " she turned back to Hanna, "I love Aunt Hanna too, and I'm sure glad she came to live with us."

Moved by the child's innocent declaration, Hanna bent down to give her a hug. Standing back up, she saw Jake on the front porch, his arms folded across his chest. His welcome was not as warm as Isabela's. In fact, she was afraid even the mid-morning heat could not melt the cold stare he'd fixed on her.

"Good morning again," she said once she drew close enough to speak. "What a gorgeous location you have. How awesome it must be to have the mountains outside your back door."

"It's nice enough."

"Daddy, is it okay if I show Aunt Hanna my room?" Isabela asked, looking up at her father with wide eyes.

"That's fine, sweetheart," he said, resting his hand on top of her dark curls. "You may be our hostess and show her around. I'm going to talk to Uncle Conner."

Isabela grabbed Hanna's hand. "Come on," she said.

Along with Maleah and Sophie, they spent the next fifteen minutes touring the house. Isabela's room made up for what Hanna thought was an otherwise drab décor. There were stuffed animals and dolls scattered everywhere – in baby beds, cradles and strollers. A kitchen set sat along one wall, complete with oven, sink and refrigerator. Isabela's name – in large wooden letters painted hot pink – graced one wall. Above the bed hung a painting in brilliant reds, blues, yellows, and oranges, of what appeared to be a village, complete with men, women, children, houses and animals.

"I like the painting," Hanna said.

Isabela grinned. "It's Haitian. They always paint with really, really, REALLY bright colors. My mommy bought that picture the last time she went to Haiti. You know – the time she got sick."

"Oh, I see . . . " Although Isabela's observation sounded matter-of-fact, Hanna looked at Maleah for help.

Maleah nodded and smiled. "Katie loved the Haitian people.

She and Jake served in Pedernales, which is as far as you can go in the Dominican Republic before running into the Haitian border. They probably spent as much of their time working with Haitians as they did Dominicans."

"I love the Haitian people too," Isabela chimed in. "Just like my mommy. Sometimes we'll see Haitian women and children begging on the street corners when we go to Barahona and I make Daddy take me somewhere so we can buy them something to eat."

"Why do you buy them food instead of giving them money?" Hanna asked.

"Daddy says that's the best thing to do, because if we give them money someone might take it away from them. But if we give them food, they eat it right away."

Hanna placed her arm around the child's shoulders and gave her a hug. "I bet they look forward to when you come to town," she said.

"Yep, I think you're right, especially since I can talk to them in Creole. That's what they speak in Haiti you know."

"Do you really speak Creole?" she asked the child while looking at Maleah, who tipped her head, acknowledging the information was true.

"Sure do." Isabela looked up at her as if to say, "why is that so hard to believe?"

"Did your mommy teach you?"

Isabela shrugged. "Maybe some, but when I was little a girl from Haiti lived with us. She helped mommy take care of our house – cleaning, cooking and stuff like that. Mostly she's the one who taught me how to talk the way the Haitian people talk."

Once they returned to the living room, Hanna stopped to survey the backyard, which more closely resembled a baseball field than a yard. Although beautiful, the mountains rising majestically along the outer edge looked out of place. As with the basketball goal out front, she easily envisioned Jake playing with the local children, this time teaching them how to hit a home run or catch a fly ball. The friendly greeting of a small terrier-type dog brought her back to reality.

"This is Waggles," Isabela said as she squatted and gave the brown and black dog a hug. "And that's Socks." She pointed to a gray cat snoozing in the sun on top of the patio table. "She's one of Sugar's kittens." The child walked over and picked up the cat, not worried in the least that she was interrupting her morning nap. "We named her Socks because all her paws are white. See . . . " she said, holding the cat up for Hanna's inspection, "it looks like she has on socks. Pretty neat, don't you think?"

"Pretty neat," Hanna agreed. "Is Socks a good ratter like Sugar and Angel?"

Isabela wrinkled her nose. "Huh?"

"You know, is she good at catching rats?"

"Oh yeah! That's why we got her. Daddy said the rats were eating us out of house and home and we had to do something."

Maleah fell out laughing, but Hanna didn't find the child's comment funny. "Uh-huh, I see," she said, glancing at Maleah. "Something tells me whether I like it or not, it's inevitable that one day I'm going to come face to face with one of these lovely critters y'all keep telling me about."

"I'd say you're right," Maleah said as she wiped tears from beneath her eyes. "And unfortunately, it'll probably be when you least expect it."

"That's what I'm afraid of."

Conner chuckled. "Are we ready to move our tour to the streets?" he asked.

"I think so," Maleah answered.

"Then let's go," Conner said.

"May I walk with you, Aunt Hanna?" Isabela asked.

"Of course you may." Hanna took the child's hand while extending her other hand to Sophie, who looked as if she was feeling excluded. "And I want Sophie to walk with me too. If she would like, that is."

Sophie nodded as she slipped her hand in Hanna's, her look of dejection replaced by a big freckled smile.

With Isabela on one side and Sophie on the other, Hanna made her way toward the front door. She cast a look in Jake's direction for the first time since their earlier interactions. For a moment his eyes met hers. All Hanna's early childhood training in politeness told her she should thank him for allowing her to tour his home, but since he didn't seem to be in a hospitable mood, she decided to express her appreciation to Isabela instead.

"I really like your house, Isabela," she said. "Thank you for being such a good hostess and showing me around."

Isabela giggled. "You're welcome. With my mommy gone, Daddy says it's my job to be the lady of the house, and that's what ladies do – they are the hos . . . the hotess . . . whenever someone comes to visit." She turned her eyes up at Jake as he moved in behind them. "Isn't that right, Daddy?"

He patted the child's arm. "That's exactly right. And you have been a very nice *hostess* this morning."

Hanna breathed in the masculine scent of his cologne. He stood close enough for her to touch him. She rolled her shoulders, hoping to calm the rapid beating of her heart. When she dared to glance at him, he averted his eyes and reached back to pull the door closed. She'd caught him watching her.

Chapter Ten

The contagious sound of the girls' giggles started Hanna laughing as they made a game out of hopping over potholes on their way back up the street. Soon Maleah joined them, her floppy straw hat bouncing up and down on her head, causing Hanna to laugh so hard her sides hurt. When they reached the end of the street, she doubled over, wrapping her arms around her waist as she tried to catch her breath before plopping down on the curb beside Maleah.

Maleah pulled her hat off and used the sleeve of her shirt to wipe the sweat from her face. "I can't remember when I've had so much fun."

Hanna gulped for air. "It . . . *was* fun," she said while watching Isabela and Sophie run toward a group of children gathered in the street in front of the Andersons' home. "I wonder if they might loan us some of their energy?"

Maleah placed the straw hat back on her head. "That would be nice."

Hanna looked over her shoulder at the building behind them. "I hope we're not sitting in front of someone's house."

"It's okay. This is our local colmado."

Hanna squinted in the bright sunlight. "What's a colmado?"

"Kind of like a corner grocery store. There's one in almost every Dominican neighborhood. This one is owned by a family named García. Originally it was only a house, but they turned the front room into a store, which is *also* a common practice around here."

Hanna looked again at the small establishment Maleah called

a grocery store. "This isn't where you do all of your shopping, is it?"

"Oh no. There's a larger market in town, but we come here when we run out of something – like milk, eggs, bread . . . or if we just want a snack or a soft drink."

A soft drink – Hanna's mouth watered. Her throat felt parched. Something wet and cold sounded good. She stood and brushed dirt off her skirt. She could only imagine what she looked like. She could tell her ponytail was in dire need of a redo, but she didn't have a brush. *Oh well,* she thought as she looked toward the Andersons' where a game of kickball was in progress.

Conner stepped up beside Maleah, who still sat on the stoop in front of the colmado. "The older boy there is the Garcías' youngest son," he said to Hanna. "His parents own this colmado. They're nice people. Not as well off as the other families on the street, but definitely better off than many who live in Paraíso."

Hanna watched the young Domincan boy, who she guessed was around ten or eleven, kick the bouncy rubber ball Daniel had rolled toward him. His skin was a dark golden brown and his curly black hair appeared to be soft rather than wiry – unlike several of the other children who had joined the game. "The colmado must do a pretty good business," she said.

"They do okay, but Señora García and their oldest daughter, Giselle, also work for a couple of wealthy Dominican families who live near the Malecón – the road running along the beachfront. I'm sure the combined incomes help bring up their standard of living."

Hanna nodded as she turned her attention back to the game. Jake ran up and down the side of the street, his deep voice rising above the clamor of the screaming children. He seemed to be in his element.

Maleah stood. "While the men keep an eye on the children, why don't I take you inside to meet Señor García," she said.

"I'll go with you," Conner said. "I haven't had a chance to talk with Pedro in a while. This would be a good opportunity to visit without seeming pushy."

"Pushy? What do you mean?" Hanna asked.

"We've been trying to witness to them, but haven't gotten far," Conner said. "Like so many Dominicans, they are complacent about religion, believing their Catholic roots are enough to save them. I'm always looking for opportunities to build a relationship with them, and in the process I ultimately hope to earn their trust."

Hanna followed Conner and Maleah into the small store where Conner greeted a dark headed man standing behind the counter. "Buenos Días, Señor Pedro. ¿Cómo está?"

"Bien, bien." The man's response included a broad toothy smile, which appeared exceptionally white against his dark complexion.

Hanna thought he looked more Indian than African – perhaps Taíno. Age-wise, she would have guessed him to be fortyish. While he seemed friendly, she had difficulty deciphering the Spanish pouring from his mouth as he talked with Conner and Maleah. Instead of trying to keep up, she inspected the small store. Rows of primitive shelves hung from the walls and were stocked with a variety of canned goods, boxed non-perishable food items and household products. Behind the counter, which ran the full length of the room and held several glass jars filled with packaged cookies and wrapped candies, were more food-laden shelves. An antiquated refrigerated drink box sat in front, reminiscent of old country stores in the States. The compact market appeared to have a little bit of everything, including the oppressive heat Hanna had already discovered was the norm for Paraíso. A clunky cash register sat on one end of the counter, while a small oscillating fan perched on the far end rattled as it stirred the thick, sultry air, but provided little relief.

After giving the store a good once over, Hanna turned her attention back to the Andersons and Señor Pedro. Although she understood some of what was being said, she still struggled to get into the flow of the conversation. Fearing at any minute Conner or Maleah might try and draw her in, familiar waves of dread descended upon her. She wondered if it would be rude to slip outside. Of course, appearing rude beat the alternative: embarrassing herself in front of her new peers. She slowly backed up. A few steps into her attempted escape she bumped into someone standing in the doorway. Turning too quickly, she stumbled and lost her footing.

A firm hand grabbed her arm, steadying her before she could

fall. "Going somewhere?"

Hanna looked into Jake's sweat drenched face. She took a deep breath, inhaling a fusion of perspiration and cologne. "Ah, yeah . . . I . . . ah . . . I was." Her heart beat triple time. His hand lingered on her arm and a fiery jolt raced toward her cheeks. "I was just needing a breath of fresh air."

A slow smile graced his lips. "I understand. These cramped quarters can get a bit stuffy." He let go of her arm, but maintained his doorway watch.

She cleared her throat. "You're blocking the exit, you know."

"That I am." He made no effort to move. "Did you meet Señor Pedro?"

She glanced toward the conversing threesome and considered saying she had, but decided lying probably wasn't a good idea. "Ah, well . . . no . . . They got caught up in a conversation and I didn't want to interrupt."

"I'll interrupt for you." He placed his hand on her arm once again and guided her toward the counter. As they approached, three sets of eyes turned in their direction. Speaking Spanish, Jake addressed Conner and Maleah. "Don't you want to introduce Hanna to Señor Pedro?" he asked.

Hanna was able to follow the introductions Conner made, and even managed a feeble, "mucho gusto," at what she hoped was the appropriate time. After that, her ability to keep up went downhill, so she decided her best course of action was to simply nod and smile. Oddly enough her plan worked and soon she was forgotten. She inched her way toward the door and was moments away from making her getaway when a young woman stepped inside. Early twenties, dark curly hair, stunning hazel eyes in a creamy milk chocolate complexion – Hanna guessed she was a García.

"Bueno día," she said, dropping the 's' as Hanna had been warned Dominicans often did.

"Buenos días," Hanna barely whispered. Taking a step toward the door, she hoped she could still quietly slip outside.

"¿Cómo etá?" the girl continued.

"Bien." Hanna nodded and took another step.

"Me llamo Giselle. ¿Cómo se llama?"

Hanna drew a deep breath. The girl's name was Giselle and she was asking for her name. *You can do this*, Hanna silently reassured herself. But when she opened her mouth to reply, she realized all the other voices in the room had grown quiet and everyone was looking at her. She almost gagged on the cottony mass in her throat. Although she knew the right words to say, instead of uttering intelligible Spanish, what came out sounded like gibberish. Such a simple, basic reply; only three words, and one was her name. How could she have messed it up? Heat crept up her neck, and she wanted to run out the door, then keep running – all the way back to Alabama.

With her eyes she pleaded with Giselle, hoping against hopes she'd understood what she'd said. The perplexed look on the girl's face told her she had not.

Giselle turned to the others. "¿Ella no habla Español?"

Hanna saw Jake roll his eyes. She wanted so badly – in perfect Spanish – to answer Giselle's question with a resounding, "Yes! I do speak Spanish." But she didn't dare try. How was it possible to mentally say the words correctly only to have them come out so wrong? She stood glued to the floor, unable to will her legs to move. Hot tears pooled in the bottom of her eyes. She prayed they would not spill over.

Maleah must have realized how mortified she was, because she stepped to her side and assured Giselle she did speak Spanish, but was a little nervous. When she introduced them to each other, Hanna managed another "Mucho gusto" and, in an effort to camouflage her humiliation, pasted on a smile.

Giselle placed her right cheek next to Hanna's, kissing the air beside her face. It was the first time she'd been greeted with a "Latin kiss" since leaving Costa Rica. "Es un placer conocerla," Giselle said as she stepped back.

"Equalamente," Hanna mumbled, hoping the young woman understood she was glad to meet her too.

Chapter Eleven

For Hanna, the rest of the day passed in a blur. She tried without much success to press through the thick fog blanketing her thoughts as Conner and Maleah drove her around Paraíso. Soon after leaving the colmado, Jake had excused himself, saying he had work to do. But Hanna could tell her inability to carry on a simple conversation in Spanish had not set well with him. And while she wanted Conner and Maleah's approval and respect, for some reason it was Jake's she desired most of all. After the fiasco at the colmado, she knew she would never have it.

The smile she'd pasted on hours earlier remained in place, but it only masked the tangled emotions inside. Staring out the window at the blur of blue, green and pink clapboard houses, most in desperate need of repair, Hanna planned her next move. Once they returned to the house, she would pack what little she'd unpacked and then ask Conner to take her to the airport in Santo Domingo. If necessary, she was willing to wait in the terminal until she could catch the next available flight home – where English was spoken with a slow southern drawl and no one expected her to speak Spanish. When Conner asked if she would like to visit one of the beaches or watering holes, she declined, claiming she was tired and would probably enjoy it better if they waited until another day – one she knew would never come.

Maleah pointed at a two-story white building with Clínica Paraíso written across the front. "That's our local hospital," she said. "It's not much, but it's better than nothing. At least they have a doctor and nurse on twenty-four hour call."

Hanna only nodded. It didn't really matter; she wasn't

staying long enough to need them.

Maleah rolled down her window. "Gotta love the music," she said. "Quite lovely, don't you think?" She looked over her shoulder and grinned.

Hanna wasn't sure which was worse – the loud wailing Maleah referred to as music or the blast of heat that assaulted her when the window was lowered. Her eyes followed a small motorcycle as it putted past the window, the driver transporting a woman and two young children. "I still can't believe it's legal for three or four people to ride on a motorcycle like that," she said. "What was it y'all called them?"

"Motoconchos. Rural Dominican taxis," Maleah replied. "Nothing like them for getting around town."

"Not me," Hanna said. "I think I'd rather walk."

Maleah laughed. "I remember saying the same thing when we first moved here, but I have to admit there have been a few occasions when I needed to get somewhere quickly and I realized a motoconcho was my best option. Can't say I liked it, but it wasn't as bad as I thought it would be."

Hanna was thankful she wouldn't be around long enough to ever be that desperate.

"Here we are, home-sweet-home," Conner said as he pulled into their driveway. "I hope you're not on overload."

"Oh no. I'm fine," Hanna lied.

"Aunt Hanna! Aunt Hanna!" Isabela and Sophie plowed into her before she'd taken two steps away from the car.

After returning from the colmado that morning, it had been decided the tour around town would be more pleasant if the children stayed home, so they were left in the care of the Andersons' Dominican helper, Celia. Hanna had seen the girls playing with their dolls in the hammock on the front porch when they pulled up. As she walked toward the house with Isabela on one side and Sophie on the other, they filled her head with stories of the adventures they'd had while she was gone. She was tired of wearing her artificial smile, and the girls' shrill voices shredded what had to be her last nerve. Making matters worse – it felt like someone was operating a jackhammer just above her eyes. She should have hugged Maleah when she told the girls they needed to clean up Sophie's room before supper, but she didn't. Instead, Hanna headed straight for her apartment

After closing the door behind her, she sat on the bed, squeezing her eyes tight against the bitter sting of tears. The overhead fan rattled on high, attempting to give much-needed relief from the late afternoon heat and humidity. "At least the electricity is on," she whispered, as if some unseen force might overhear if she spoke too loudly and decide to turn it off. Letting her sandals fall to the floor, she pulled her feet up and reclined on the bed. She refused to push the replay button on the language ordeal that morning. As for her plan to return to Alabama – she was too tired. Maybe later . . .

Placing her hands behind her head, Hanna stared at the rhythmic motion of the fan. Soon her eyelids grew heavy and she drifted off to sleep. When she awoke, dusk filtered through the louvered windows, casting smoky shadows on the furniture, and she heard voices on the patio.

She walked to the bathroom sink and splashed cold water on her face, then ran a brush through her hair, pulling it back up in a ponytail. The voices on the terrace grew louder, wafting through a small window above the shower. She recognized Jake's Midwestern accent and Conner's north Florida drawl. The last thing she wanted was to have to face Jake, but maybe it would be better to get it over with. She turned to walk away but stopped short when she heard him say her name. As she tiptoed into the sitting area of her apartment, she told herself eavesdropping was a bad idea.

She was in no mood to heed good advice.

Except for a trickle of light from the patio, the room now sat in darkness. Hanna stood quietly and listened.

"I'm sorry," Conner said. "I really don't understand why this has you so upset. You're not even giving the girl a chance."

"It's not that I don't want to give her a chance," Jake said, his voice sounding impatient. "But I don't understand how someone could spend a year in language school and not be able to respond to a basic question in Spanish."

"You heard what Maleah said – She was nervous. I'm sure realizing we were all waiting to hear her answer had to have been intimidating. I can't believe you're being this petty."

"Petty? Come on . . . "

"Yes, petty. In fact, if I didn't know better, I would say you were looking for an excuse not to like her."

What? Hanna stopped herself before she spoke the question out loud. Why would he do that?

"That's ridiculous," Jake replied. He didn't sound too persuasive.

"You're denying it's true?"

Jake cleared his throat before answering. "Of course it's not true." Strangely enough, Hanna wasn't convinced.

"You're actually this bent out of shape because she had trouble telling Giselle her name?"

"Why do you find that so hard to believe? All she had to say was, *me llamo Hanna.* How difficult is that?"

Hanna took a deep breath, and then blew it out a little too loudly. She placed her hand over her mouth and waited, hoping they had not heard her.

"When you're new, it can be harder than you seem to remember," Conner said. "You've just forgotten what it was like."

"I don't think so. After a year in language school, Katie and I both could have carried on a fairly decent conversation. One thing I know for sure, we could have told someone our names."

"That's because you and Katie, Maleah too for that matter, didn't struggle with the language. It seemed to come naturally to you all. I struggled. You may not remember, but when we first arrived in the DR I was having a hard time. Now that I think about it, I remember feeling intimidated by all of you. I'd open my mouth to say something, and then realize you were listening, and it would be as if I forgot everything I'd ever learned. I'm sure that's what happened with Hanna today. You've gotta let up on her."

"I don't remember you having a hard time when we first got here."

"That's because I did my best to get out of speaking Spanish whenever you were around. Besides, we weren't together much in those days. Over time I settled in and it got better. That'll happen with Hanna too. I'm sure of it."

Caribbean Paradise

Hanna leaned against the desk. If she stayed, at least she'd have an ally in Conner. But one thing was certain, even if Jake moved beyond this, she'd still not have a chance – not if Katie was going to be the gauge by which he measured her.

"I'm not convinced," Jake said. "I know she's here first of all to teach the children, which obviously she will do in English. But I was hoping she'd be able to help with the work too. The way I see it, we don't have time to babysit someone who can't communicate with the nationals."

Hanna flinched at the sound of someone hitting the glass top of the patio table.

"Jake, honestly, I'm tired of this whole conversation," Conner said. "Hanna has only been in the country three days, and it's my opinion you're expecting way too much of her. It may not be easy but you need to try and think back . . . really try to remember what it felt like to be new here. You're way too calloused. I don't know what's come over you, but you're not the man we used to know. I know Katie's death had to be harder than anything I could ever imagine. Even so . . . as your friend, I've got to tell you – this isn't right."

A chair scraped against the brick. "As for *baby-sitting* Hanna – don't worry," Conner continued. "No one is asking you to help her adjust in any way. In fact, if you plan on continuing with the attitude you've had tonight, it'd probably be best if you stayed away until you can see fit to have a change of heart. I love you, I really do, but I'm not going to let you ruin Hanna's chance of making it here. Maleah and I will see to it she's taken care of. Trust me, you don't have to give her second thought."

Jake coughed, and another chair scraped across the bricks. "Look, I'm sorry," he said. "Maybe I did react a bit too harshly. I don't know . . . I just don't remember struggling, and Katie definitely didn't. By the time we arrived in Pedernales, it was as if she'd been speaking the language all her life. I'm not saying I don't want Hanna to make it. I don't know . . . honestly, I don't know what I expected. I'm sorry. I really am."

Conner said something else as the two men walked back in the house, but Hanna could no longer make out the words. Seconds later Jake called for Isabela.

Not sure what to do, Hanna stood frozen in front of the sitting room window. "Lord, this isn't turning out the way I thought it was going to," she said. "I honestly thought You had called me here, but I'm no longer sure. If You could see a way to get me out of this mess, I would certainly appreciate it. I don't think I can do this. I really don't."

She slid into one of the wicker chairs and leaned forward, placing her face in her hands. The dam broke, and the floodwaters flowed unhindered down her cheeks until her entire body shook.

~~~~~

Jake silently chastised himself as he and Isabela walked toward their house. Adding insult to injury, Isabela was pouting.

"But Daddy, I just wanted to tell Aunt Hanna good-bye. She'll think I don't like her."

It was the third time she'd said the same thing since leaving the Andersons'. Jake was losing his patience. "Isabela, I already told you . . . Aunt Hanna was tired. She went to her room to get some rest. She knows you like her. I promise I'll let you go see her first thing tomorrow morning."

The child resumed her pout, bottom lip protruding further than before. Like two whipped pups, they made their way up the driveway and into the house.

Isabela picked at her dinner, claiming she was too sad to eat, so Jake accompanied her to her room and helped her get ready for bed. As he tucked her in he promised *yet again* he would take her to visit Hanna the next morning. After kissing her goodnight, he walked out on the patio. Darkness clung to the mountains. He sat in a plastic lawn chair and placed his hands behind his neck. Leaning his head back, he stared into the sky where stars blinked like fireflies at twilight on a warm summer night. If he had been in a better mood, he would have tried to find the constellations, but his sour attitude kept him from enjoying the beauty God had set before him.

He considered praying, but he'd been such a jerk he was sure God wouldn't find him any better company than Conner had. Of course he knew better, or he *should* know better. As loving and patient as Conner was, he knew his heavenly Father was even more so. Truth was – he was not yet willing to completely admit he was wrong, so it was probably best if he kept his distance from God. Unfortunately, that seemed to be the way it was in their relationship anymore. It didn't used to be that way. There was a time when they shared an intimate friendship, but all of that changed when Katie died. Conner had called him calloused. Good description. He *had* become calloused. When you're calloused, you don't get hurt as easily. He'd been hurt enough to last a lifetime; he didn't plan on letting it happen again.

When Waggles yapped, Jake looked toward the yard. The dog had her nose to the ground, cutting tracks through the grass, obviously on the trail of some local vermin – probably a rat. Jake clamped his lips and refused to smile as memories of teasing Hanna earlier that day surfaced. He quickly refocused on his more recent assessment of her.

Maybe her ineptness that morning at the colmado was a result of nervousness or of feeling intimidated. Even so, how could someone complete a full year of language study and not be able to say one of the first sentences they taught you? Well . . . Conner was right, although he'd never own up to it publicly – he *had* been looking for an excuse to still his heart against the attraction he'd been feeling toward her. Now he'd found it. Granted, it wasn't as big a deal as he was trying to make it out to be, but it would have to do.

Had he not prayed he would find something that would keep him from feeling more for her than he should? Okay . . . Maybe prayed wasn't exactly what he'd done, but God knew his heart, and by letting him see her weakness had given him a good excuse to distance himself from her. Although she was pretty and personable, stirring up longings he'd thought dead, wouldn't it be hard for him to respect someone who couldn't hold her own with the language? After all, mastering the language was imperative to being able to effectively minister in a foreign country. Hard or not, he didn't have time to play nursemaid to someone who couldn't pull her own weight. If Isabela wanted to spend time with her, that was fine. He'd stay busy with his work and let Conner and Maleah take on the responsibility of training the new missionary.

Jake placed his hands on the arms of the chair, pushed himself up and walked back in the house.

Chapter Twelve

As the tears subsided, Hanna wiped them from her face with the backs of her hands, but Jake's words still weighed heavy on her heart. Knowing he didn't think she should be there would make it even more difficult for her to stay. The best thing to do was request Conner and Maleah's assistance in making whatever arrangements were needed in order for her to resign and get a flight back to Alabama. Maybe waiting at the terminal wasn't such a great idea, but she hoped the process would not take long.

A light tapping on the door interrupted her thoughts. She cleared her throat before responding. "Yes?"

She heard Maleah's muffled voice through the closed door. "Supper's ready if you're interested."

"No, thank you. I'm not hungry."

"Okay, but if you change your mind, help yourself to whatever you can find in the refrigerator."

"Thanks." Hanna was grateful Maleah had not opened the door and discovered her sitting in the dark. She needed some sleep before explaining her need to go home. Without rest she'd probably blubber her way through, crushing any prospect of avoiding further embarrassment.

She rose from the chair and turned on the light so she could see in order to get ready for bed. At least the power was still on. As she walked toward the bathroom, her eyes fell on her Bible, which she'd placed on the bedside table the night before. She did an about face, walked over and picked it up, clutching the book to her chest.

She knew exactly which passage of scripture she needed to read.

Hanna sat on the edge of the bed and turned to Ephesians 6:10-17, quietly reading the words out loud: "Finally, be strong in the Lord and in the strength of His might. Put on the full armor of God, so that you will be able to stand firm against the schemes of the devil. For our struggle is not against flesh and blood, but against the rulers, against the powers, against the world forces of this darkness, against the spiritual forces of wickedness in the heavenly places. Therefore, take up the full armor of God, so that you will be able to resist in the evil day, and having done everything, to stand firm. Stand firm, therefore, having girded your loins with truth, and having put on the breastplate of righteousness, and having shod your feet with the preparation of the gospel of peace; in addition to all, taking up the shield of faith with which you will be able to extinguish all the flaming arrows of the evil one. And take the helmet of salvation, and the sword of the Spirit, which is the word of God."

As God spoke to Hanna through His word, she recognized the present situation for what it was – another attack of the enemy. It wasn't time to give up in defeat, but instead a call to be diligent in faith, to stand firm against the one who would do anything in order to discourage her; the one who would find great pleasure in seeing her abandon a twelve-year call upon her life. How many times had she fought this same battle while studying in Costa Rica? How often had Satan taunted her with belittling accusations in regards to her inability to communicate in the Spanish language? She now understood her tendency toward relying upon her own abilities, as opposed to depending upon God, had resulted in a rather large crack in her spiritual armor.

Hanna flipped the pages of her Bible to another familiar passage – II Corinthians 12:7-10. Could it be God wanted to use this most recent attack in order that she might better know the sufficiency of His grace? In verse 7 Paul referred to his thorn in the flesh as a messenger of Satan God allowed in order to keep him from exalting himself. Ouch, that hurt. How often had she been guilty of thinking a little too highly of herself than she should? By placing her in circumstances where she was forced to trust in His power as it was perfected in her weakness, was God's intent to keep her from pride?

And if so, was she going to yield?

~~~~~

The next morning, instead of enlisting Maleah's assistance in helping her resign from her post, Hanna humbly explained the reason for her shortcomings in the language and asked Maleah if she would be willing to tutor her in Spanish. Several days later, Hanna approached Giselle García and asked if she would be willing to meet with her a couple of times a week so she could practice her communication skills with a national. The young Dominican woman was thrilled to help and wanted to know if Hanna would teach her English in return. They became fast friends, and their time together was often spent reeling in laughter as they attempted to communicate in each other's language. Practicing Spanish, while Giselle attempted to speak English, helped Hanna learn to laugh at herself as opposed to living in fear of what others might think of her. She also began sharing at least one meal a week with the García family, which provided her with learning opportunities, not only in the language but also in the culture, that she could have never gotten in a classroom.

During those initial weeks, Hanna saw very little of Jake. Isabela came to play with Sophie almost every day, but her father kept his distance. At first Hanna was disappointed, but God reminded her that what Jake Mason thought of her didn't really matter. She wasn't in Paraíso to impress a man; she was there to serve Him.

~~~~~

Late on a Tuesday afternoon, four weeks after she'd arrived in the country, Hanna returned to the Andersons' following a visit with Giselle, her head reeling from all she'd learned that day. As she stepped into the living room, she heard Jake's mellow bass voice before she saw him. He was sitting on the patio talking with Conner. They both looked up before she could steal by unnoticed. Conner lifted his hand and waved. Jake only nodded. Without asking permission, Hanna's heart rate accelerated. She returned the nod and slipped into the kitchen where she found Maleah preparing supper.

"Hi there. How are you?" Maleah asked.

Hanna swallowed around the thickening lump in her throat. "Fine. Do you need any help?"

Maleah swiped the back of a floured hand across her sweaty brow. "Would you mind feeding Greta? I forgot earlier today. She was whimpering a few minutes ago. I know she must be hungry."

"No, I don't mind."

Hanna opened the screen door leading into the breezeway where the dog food was kept in a large plastic garbage can. Greta stood on the other side of the barred gate, her brown eyes downcast in a reddish tan face.

"Hey there, girl," Hanna said, reaching through the bars and rubbing the dog on the white patch above her eyes. Greta lifted her head in grateful response, her stubby tail shooing a few gnats as it wiggled back and forth. "You wait there and I'll get your food."

Hanna stepped past the washer and dryer, glancing toward the decorative bricks, which served as a divider between the passageway and the patio located on the opposite side of the breezeway from where Greta waited for her supper. Sunlight and the sound of the men's voices seeped through the small openings. Without looking down, Hanna picked up the large scoop used to dish out the dry chunks of food and leaned toward the brick wall. As she strained in an effort to hear what was being said, tiny, prickly feet ran across her hand and up her arm. After flinging scoop and rat across the terrazzo floor, she flew back into the house, screams rising from deep in her throat. She'd only made it halfway through the kitchen before she collided with a firm surface and someone grabbed her by the shoulders.

Eyes closed, Hanna gasped for breath, getting ready to let go of another blood-curdling scream. A hand clamped over her mouth, and she caught a whiff of familiar cologne. "Rats . . . " she wailed as she shook free of Jake's hand and fell against his chest.

He slid his arms around her waist and pulled her to him. He was laughing so hard she could feel his body shaking.

"It's not funny," she sobbed into the collar of his shirt.

"I . . . know . . . " he said.

Hanna could still hear him snickering. She pressed her hand against his chest and gave him a shove. Conner was standing behind him, and Maleah stood by the sink, both trying to keep a straight face.

Hanna stomped her foot. "It's . . . not . . . funny!"

Jake's face sobered. "Of course it's not." Laughter danced in his eyes. "Where were they?"

She pointed toward the screen door. "In the dog food. One ran up my arm. I think there were a couple more in the trash can."

Conner pushed past Jake and walked into the breezeway.

"Jake, come here," he called seconds later. "You've got to see this."

Maleah followed Jake out the door; Hanna reluctantly traipsed after her. Conner had the garbage can tilted on its side. "There's at least a half dozen baby rats down in there," he said.

Hanna shivered and scurried back in the house.

After assisting with the disposal of the rats, Jake chuckled as he walked through the kitchen. Hanna picked up a dishtowel to throw at him, but he had already stepped into the living room and was calling for Isabela before she could take aim. A couple of minutes later he leaned his head back through the door. "See you," he said. His eyes still sparkled.

Maleah looked at Hanna and grinned. "Thanks for the help," she said.

Hanna glared at him. "Yeah, thanks."

~~~~~~

As Jake walked in the front door of his house, he released a heavy sigh. He couldn't help but smile at the memory of Hanna's hysterics over the rats, but the feel of her in his arms . . . *Whew!* What was he thinking? He shook his head. He didn't need to let that happen again.

Chapter Thirteen

Following the incident with the rats, Hanna hoped Jake would visit more often, but he didn't. She wondered if he ever thought about the brief moment he'd held her in his arms. She tried to put it out of her mind, but the memory often invaded her thoughts. If she had not been put out with him for laughing, she would have lingered a little longer. His arms around her waist, her head on his chest – It had been a perfect fit.

A couple of weeks later, Hanna returned from another practice session with Giselle and found Maleah sitting at the keyboard in a corner of the living room, her eyes closed, and face turned up in worship. The woman's soft alto voice washed over Hanna like a gentle spring rain. Not wanting to intrude, she tiptoed toward the kitchen. She'd only gotten halfway across the room when Maleah called her name.

Hanna turned around. "Sorry. I didn't mean to interrupt."

"You didn't. How was your visit with Giselle?"

"Fun, as always." Hanna smiled as she remembered the laughter they'd shared. "Giselle is such a sweetheart. Her family too."

"They are sweet people."

Hanna sat on the sofa. "Did you know there are ten people living in that house behind the colmado?" She counted them off: "Señor and Señora García, Giselle, two younger sisters – one has a three-year-old son, three younger brothers, and a grandmother – Señora García's mother."

Maleah nodded. "For Dominicans, that's not unusual."

"But they have only three bedrooms and one bath. Because the original dining and living room are now the colmado, the kitchen serves not only as their kitchen, but also as their dining room *and* living room."

"I know that seems like tight quarters to us," Maleah said, "but they actually have more room than a lot of families the same size."

"Giselle said the same thing. Just today she told me they consider themselves blessed because most families in Paraíso don't have nearly as much as they do."

"Just goes to show, it's all in what you're accustomed to. As Americans, we're spoiled, you know . . . "

"Tell me about it," Hanna said.

Maleah gazed off toward the patio. "I have no doubt God put you and Giselle together," she said. "There's nothing like having a Dominican friend to help you learn the language and make the cultural adjustments needed in order to be a successful missionary. I think that was one reason Katie Mason adjusted so quickly. While we both had an equal command of the language, Katie was much more outgoing. She was making friends right and left while I was pining away in self-pity."

Hanna sighed. Katie Mason might be gone, but her shadow remained. Was there anything the woman hadn't done well? "I can't imagine you pining away in self-pity," she said to Maleah.

"Oh, but I did. I tried to make excuses – like the fact that I had two toddlers to take care of. I constantly worried that if I let them play with the neighborhood children, they might get sick. Or if I took them to the market, they'd pick up germs."

"I can understand you're concerns."

"Having concerns is one thing, but giving way to fear is quite another. It took a while for me to realize God was big enough to protect my children. My mother came to help out when I had Sophie." Maleah chuckled. "Later, in a letter I wrote to a friend I'd made in language school, I said the best thing about my mom's visit was she felt sorrier for me than I did for myself."

Hanna smiled. "It's still hard for me to imagine you having difficulty making friends. You seem so at home here."

Maleah ran her hand across the top of the keyboard. "I am now, but those first couple of years we were here, this keyboard was the closest thing I had to a friend."

"Really? How's that?"

"The lonelier I got, the more often I found myself sitting right here. For some reason it seemed easier for me to pour out my pain *and* my complaints to God through music." A soft laugh escaped her lips. "At first I sang songs I already knew – like hymns and some contemporary praise and worship. Then one day I was reflecting on a passage of scripture God had used to speak to me during my quiet time that morning and the next thing I knew I had put the words to music."

"Had you written songs before?"

"No. I had never considered that was something I could do. What a sweet blessing it was to discover a God-given talent at the bottom of my pit."

"The song you were singing when I came in, did you write it during that time?"

Maleah shook her head. "That one I wrote more recently. But on days when I'm really struggling, I often go back to those earlier songs."

"Have you translated any of them into Spanish?"

"I have. In fact, some of the songs we sing during the services we hold here on Sundays and Wednesdays are ones I've written."

"Really." Hanna's thoughts turned to one of the talents God had given her. She wondered if she'd ever be able to use it on the mission field. When she first accepted the job in Paraíso, she'd felt confident she would. That was before she'd known how much of a battle she was going to have with the language. Now . . . she wasn't sure.

"What are you thinking?" Maleah asked.

Hanna gazed toward the front door. She wasn't sure if she was ready to share her dream with Maleah. What if she discouraged her or told her she didn't see how it would be possible? She wasn't ready to have her dream crushed, even if it did seem unachievable. "It really wasn't anything," she replied.

Caribbean Paradise

"Something is on your mind," Maleah said. "I can almost see the wheels turning behind those pretty green eyes of yours. Come on, you can tell me."

Hanna took a deep breath. "Okay . . . Do you remember me telling you about the Bible studies I've written?"

"I do. What about them?"

"Well . . . there was a time when I thought I would be able to use my writing skills on the mission field."

"I think that's wonderful. What's the problem?"

"What's the problem? Where have you been the last six weeks? Remember me? The one who spent a year in language school and is still having trouble with *¿cómo se llama?* I imagined you'd think the idea a bit farfetched."

Maleah's eyes narrowed. "I'm surprised at you," she said. "Why shouldn't you be able to translate your Bible studies into Spanish? I don't find the idea farfetched in the least. Didn't you tell me you feel you have a good grasp of the language when it comes to reading and writing?"

"I did, but that's my opinion. You may not agree."

"Then, let me be the judge. I'm giving you a homework assignment. I want you to pray about which one of your Bible studies God would have you translate into Spanish first. Once you've gotten it finished, I want to see it."

Hanna's jaw dropped and she stared at Maleah. "You're serious, aren't you?"

"You bet ya!" Maleah placed her fingers on the keyboard once again. "Do you want to hear the first song I wrote? It's from Matthew 11:28-30. I call it *Rhythms of Grace*."

As Maleah began to play and sing, Hanna realized God was speaking directly to her through the message of the song. Although she'd been doing better, she knew she still had much to learn when it came to resting in God and trusting Him to adequately equip her for the work He'd called her to do.

"Are you tired, worn out, burned out on religion? Then, come to Me, get away with Me, so you'll recover your life. I'll show you how to take a real rest. Just walk with Me and work with Me. Watch how I do it. Learn the unforced rhythms of grace and I won't

lay anything heavy or ill-fitting on you. Keep company with Me and you'll learn how to live freely and lightly. Isn't that what you need?

Oh, Jesus, can You really teach me how to live freely and lightly? Cause I'm tired, worn out, burned out on religion. And I come to you to get away with you so I'll recover my life. Can You show me how to take a real rest? I'll walk with You and work with You. I'll watch how you do it. I'll learn the unforced rhythms of grace. And, you won't lay anything heavy or ill-fitting on me. I'll keep company with You and I'll learn how to live freely and lightly, cause that's what I need. Oh, Jesus, You can really teach me how to live freely and lightly when I come..." *

~~~~~

Several days later, Hanna sat with Maleah on the front porch, watching Daniel, Caleb and Sophie play kick ball with some of the neighborhood children in front of the house. The familiar scene reminded her of that infamous day when they sat in front of the colmado and watched Jake coaching a game much like the one now in progress. Her eyes scanned the group of children, looking for Isabela's dark bouncy curls. She wasn't there. *How odd.*

Maleah pushed up out of the rocking chair. "Would you be interested in a cup of coffee or a bottle of water?" she asked as she turned toward the front door.

"Some water soun – "

"¡Señora Maleah! ¡Señora Maleah!"

A petite, dark-skinned woman hurried in their direction. When Hanna realized it was Rosalinda, Jake's Dominican helper, her breath caught in her throat. She followed Maleah as she jogged toward the street. Rosalinda spoke in starts and stops, gasping for breath. The bits and pieces of what Hanna understood were disturbing. Something about Isabela not feeling well, a high fever and vomiting.

"Por favor, Señora Maleah, venga a la casa." Tears coursed down the woman's weathered cheeks.

Maleah turned to Hanna. "Did you catch all that?"

"Most of it. Did she say Jake is in Barahona?"

Maleah nodded. "Yeah. He won't be back until late afternoon or early evening. I'm going with Rosalinda to check on Isabela. Please ask Celia to keep an eye on my kids, and then I want you to come down to Jake's. I may need you."

~~~~~

Hanna walked through the front door of Jake's house and made her way to Isabela's room where she found Maleah sitting on the side of the bed wiping the child's forehead with a wet washcloth.

Rosalinda exited the bedroom wringing her hands and shaking her head. Hanna heard a mumbled *tisk-tisk* as she walked by.

Isabela looked at her with sad eyes. "Aunt Hanna, I don't feel good." It was the same pitiful look Greta had given her the day she found the rats in the dog food.

Hanna sat on the opposite side of the bed from Maleah. "So I heard," she said, brushing dark curls away from the child's face. "How long have you been feeling sick?"

"I don't know." Isabela sounded so pathetic Hanna didn't know whether to laugh or cry. "I tried to eat some toast for breakfast, but it made my tummy hurt and I threw up."

Hanna placed her hand on the side of Isabela's face. "You feel a little warm." She looked at Maleah. "Have you taken her temperature?"

"Just before you came in. It was almost 103. I asked Rosalinda to get some children's Tylenol. That's where she was headed when you came in. She said Isabela has thrown up three times already this morning." She ran the washcloth across the child's forehead again. "It's probably a stomach virus."

Isabela's bottom lip quivered. "Is that as bad as dengue fever?"

"No, sweetheart." Maleah glanced in Hanna's direction. "A virus is just a bug – a bacteria that gets in your body sometimes and makes you sick. Usually it doesn't last more than twenty-four hours."

"How long is twenty-four hours?"

"Oh . . . about a day. You should be feeling better tonight.

By tomorrow chances are you'll be back to normal."

"I hope so. Daddy wouldn't like it if I had dengue fever." Tears glistened in the child's eyes.

Hanna looked at Maleah. She shook her head and scrunched her nose.

By the time Rosalinda returned with a couple of chewable children's Tylenol and a glass of water, Isabela had closed her eyes, her thick black lashes reminding Hanna of Jake. What was he going to think when he came home and discovered his daughter was sick?

Maleah took the tablets from Rosalinda. "Isabela, do you think you could chew these up for Aunt Maleah?" she said. "They'll help you feel better." Isabela nodded and opened her mouth. Maleah placed the two small pills on her tongue. "How about a couple sips of water?" she asked. Isabela pushed up on her elbows while Maleah held the glass to her lips. A few swallows later, she shook her head and lay back down.

Maleah stood and looked at Hanna, tilting her head in the direction of the door. When she started to get up, Isabela grabbed her hand. "Aunt Hanna, please don't leave."

Hanna cut her eyes at Maleah. "What do I do," she mouthed.

Maleah pushed a wayward curl off Isabela's forehead. "Aunt Hanna will be back in a minute," she said. "Rosalinda is here."

Isabela fixed her big blue eyes on Hanna. "I want *you* to stay with me."

"Okay, sweetheart, Aunt Hanna will stay with you," Maleah said. "I'm going to take her to the kitchen and show her where a few things are first. Do you think you'll be alright until she gets back?"

"Uh-huh," the child whimpered, closing her eyes again.

Hanna followed Maleah to the living room. "I really think it's only a virus," Maleah said. "My biggest concern is that we get her fever down and keep enough liquids in her to keep her from dehydrating."

"She seemed concerned it might be dengue fever. Any chance that's what she has?" Hanna asked.

Maleah shook her head. "No, I really don't think so. I'm sure since her mother died from complications of dengue, she fears that may be what's wrong. But her symptoms are more characteristic of a stomach bug."

"What are the symptoms of dengue fever?"

"High fever and severe body aches, later a rash. Although nausea and vomiting are possible, when I asked Isabela if her legs or arms hurt, she said no, just her tummy. If it was dengue, she'd be complaining of overall pain, not just her stomach."

"I see."

"I'm going to the colmado to get some 7-Up and popsicles," Maleah said. "Then I'll stop by our house and get Celia busy making some of her famous homemade chicken noodle soup. I had a virus one time and had gone days without keeping anything down. Only hours after Celia handfed me some of the broth from the soup she'd made, I felt much better. By this afternoon or evening it may be just what Isabela needs."

"I hope so." Hanna looked back in the direction of Isabela's room. "I've not been around sick children much. She looks so pitiful."

"I'm sure she feels pitiful but . . . she'll be okay."

"As a mother, I know you've had lots of experience in this area. Maybe you should sit with her and let me go to the colmado."

"I doesn't matter to me, but I think our patient specifically asked that you stay with her."

"I know she did but I haven't a clue why."

"Surely you've noticed how much the child enjoys being with you," Maleah said, a gentle smile lifting the corners of her mouth. "One day last week, I overheard her telling Sophie she wished you could be her mommy."

"You're kidding," Hanna said, shaking her head. "That's really sweet, but it's rather unlikely it'll ever happen. Jake hardly even acknowledges my existence."

"He's stubborn, that's for sure," Maleah said. She looked as if she were trying to stifle a laugh. "By the way, if Jake did acknowledge your existence, would you consider being Isabela's mommy?"

Hanna felt her face flush as she realized how what she had said must have sounded. "I didn't . . . I didn't mean it the way it came out."

Maleah patted her arm. "I know. I was teasing you. Even so, you never know what the future might hold."

"My guess is the future doesn't hold wedding bells for Jake and me. Except for the day I discovered the rats in the dog food, the man hasn't spoken more than a dozen words to me since that awful day when I made such a fool of myself at the colmado."

"That's his loss," Maleah said as she turned toward the front door. "I'll be back in a few minutes."

Chapter Fourteen

By late afternoon Isabela was fever free. Hanna had spent the day sitting by the child's side, periodically wiping her forehead with a wet washcloth and coaxing her to drink a little 7-Up. She'd also been successful in getting her to suck on a couple of cherry flavored popsicles – *her favorite* – according to Isabela. Once she started feeling better, the child asked Hanna to read to her. They spent over an hour reading through Isabela's library of children's books. Through it all, Waggles slept on the end of the bed, occasionally emitting a whimpering squeak.

"I think Waggles must be dreaming," Hanna said as she watched the brown and black terrier's body rapidly jerking as she slept.

Isabela looked at the dog. "What do you think she's dreaming about?"

Hanna placed her index finger on the tip of the child's nose. "I bet she's dreaming about you and how much fun you're going to have running and playing once you get better."

Isabela giggled. "Maybe I'll be well enough to play tomorrow."

"I bet you will." Hanna reached down and rubbed the dog's head. "How long have you had Waggles?"

"We got her for my birthday after we came back to the DR."

"Was she a puppy?"

"Uh-huh. She was so cute. Some people Daddy met at the Community Center brought her and her brothers by one day and asked if we wanted one. Daddy let me pick her out."

"Does she sleep with you?"

Isabela glanced at the dog and grinned. "Usually. At first Daddy didn't want her to, but when I asked nicely, he said okay."

~~~~~

Around six that evening Maleah brought over a pot of Celia's chicken noodle soup. The steaming aroma of chicken, onions and celery made Hanna's mouth water. She placed a bowlful, along with some crackers and a glass of 7-Up, on a tray and carried it to Isabela's room, setting it on the bedside table.

"Aunt Hanna, would you please feed me?" Isabela asked, her lower lip protruding. "I still don't feel so good."

Although she knew the child felt well enough to feed herself, Hanna couldn't resist the pathetic request. She imagined it was the same reason Waggles got to sleep with her. "Okay," she said. "I guess sick little girls need someone to feed them. I remember when I was your age and would get sick, sometimes my mother sat by my bed and fed me."

"Is your mommy still alive?"

Hanna slid a spoonful of soup into the child's mouth. "Why, yes," she said. "She and my dad live in Alabama. Do you know where that is?"

Deep furrows formed across Isabela's forehead. It looked as if she was trying to decide if she knew where Alabama was. "I don't think so," she finally said.

"I'll show you on a map sometime. When we start school that can be one of our geography lessons. Would that be okay with you?"

"Sure . . . " Isabela said, sighing deeply. "I guess when my mommy was still alive she took care of me whenever I was sick, like your mommy did when you were little." She shook her head. "But I don't remember."

Hanna offered the child another spoonful of the savory smelling soup. The direction in which the conversation had turned felt a little awkward. "I'm sure your mommy took real good care of you," she said.

"Yeah . . . I think so, but all I really remember about my mommy is what Daddy tells me." Isabela looked up at Hanna. "Did you know I look like her?" she asked.

"So I've heard. She must have been beautiful."

The child placed a sweaty hand on the side of Hanna's face. "I think you're beautiful," she said, "and I'm glad you were here to take care of me. It's kind of been like you are my mommy." Her voice dropped to barely above a whisper. "Can I tell you a secret?"

Awkward switched to uncomfortable. Hanna looked toward the window on the other side of the room. She felt Isabela touch her cheek again. "Aunt Hanna, did you hear me? I wanted to know if it was okay for me to tell you a secret?"

"A secret . . . well . . . sure."

"Good. I've been wanting to tell somebody." Isabela's blue eyes sparkled as she leaned closer. "I think one day you're going to be my mommy," she whispered loudly. "You see . . . I'd been asking God to send me a new mommy, and as soon as I saw you I knew He'd answered my prayer."

Hanna stared at the child in disbelief. When the sound of a man clearing his throat wafted across the room, she almost dropped the bowl of soup. She knew who it was before she turned around. "You about scared me to death," she said as she took a deep breath in an effort to calm her unsettled nerves.

Isabela reached her arms toward Jake. "Daddy, you're home. Did you know I've been sick?"

"What's she talking about?" he asked, his gazed fixed on Hanna. "Has she really been sick?"

"Uh . . . yes . . . a stomach virus. Rosalinda came down to the Andersons' around ten this morning and told us Isabela had a fever and had been throwing up, so Maleah and I came to check on her. She's much better now. She hasn't thrown up since around noon."

Jake reached down to Isabela's uplifted arms, easily lifting her off the bed. He placed his face next to hers. "She doesn't feel like she has fever now."

"No. It's been gone for a couple of hours. She was just eating some of Celia's homemade chicken soup." Hanna held the bowl up as if she needed evidence.

"I appreciate you sitting with her this afternoon, but I'm sure it wasn't necessary. Rosalinda could have taken care of her."

Isabela spoke before she could say anything. "I didn't want Rosalinda. I wanted Aunt Hanna. I asked her to stay with me." The pathetic pout was back.

Jake looked at Hanna. She nodded, feeling daunted by his intense scrutiny. "She did ask me to stay. It was no problem. Once she got to feeling better, we've been having a good time – reading books, talking . . . " Her words hung in the tense air.

Jake turned away from her before speaking. "Well . . . thank you," he said. "I'm sure I can handle it from here."

Hanna felt like a servant being dismissed by a disapproving master. "Yeah . . . sure . . . " she stuttered, irritated by the fact she was once again allowing him to make her feel inept. She set the bowl on the tray and stood to leave, then glanced back at Isabela. "Good-bye sweetie. I hope you continue to get better."

"I want to give you a hug," Isabela said as she reached out her arms.

Hanna cut her eyes at Jake. It would be impossible to hug the child without touching him. When he made no move to put Isabela down, Hanna leaned toward her. Her hand brushed across the collar of the man's red knit shirt as she hooked her arm around Isabela's neck. Placing her cheek next to the child's, her face came to within inches of Jake's uplifted chin. She closed her eyes and breathed in the light scent of his cologne.

"Good-night, sweetheart," she said to Isabela as she walked away. "I'll check on you tomorrow."

"I love you, Aunt Hanna."

Hanna chose not to look back.

~~~~~

Jake popped the tab on a Coke as he walked outside soon after getting Isabela in bed for the night. He stopped and looked toward the silhouette of the mountain nestled close to the edge of his property. A scattering of stars played hide-and-seek with billowing clouds drifting sluggishly through the sky. It hadn't rained in a while and, like the throat of a man languishing in the desert, the ground was parched. A good downpour would be a welcome relief.

Jake breathed deeply. His earlier interactions with Hanna had left him feeling disconcerted. Warmth crept up his neck as he remembered her breath caressing his chin as she hugged Isabela. He rolled his shoulders.

He had to admit he had been impressed when he discovered Hanna was spending a couple of afternoons a week practicing Spanish with Giselle García. Ironically, the fact that she was making progress disappointed him. As much as he hated to acknowledge the truth, he had hoped she would continue to struggle and ultimately decide to return stateside. Overhearing Isabela's secret only increased his disappointment.

After dropping his tired body into one of the four patio chairs, Jake propped his feet on an old plastic crate he often used as a footrest. Clouds now cloaked the flickering starlight. Sipping on his Coke, he stared into the darkness. He didn't know whether he felt angry or sad or both. Isabela's secret was so innocent. He realized the child meant the memory of her mother no harm. He knew she was missing out on much of what she would be getting if there were a mother in the home. No doubt, fantasizing over the possibility of one day having another mommy was probably normal for a child who had lost her mother at such a young age. And while Maleah served as a good substitute, he realized it was not the same.

So why did he feel the way he did toward Hanna? Resentment . . . anger . . . even jealousy. Jealousy? What was there for him to be jealous of? Were these feelings for himself . . . or Katie? Was it possible he not only feared Hanna would someday take Katie's place in Isabela's heart, but that over time she might actually intrude on the special bond he and his daughter shared? After all, for the past three years he had been both father and mother to the child. Was he afraid of losing some of the affection Isabela so lavishly poured on him? What kind of father was he if he would allow such selfish fears to interfere with his daughter's happiness?

Setting the empty can on the table beside him, Jake placed his elbows on the arms of the chair and lowered his face into his hands. If he were on talking terms with God, this would be a good time to ask for guidance. But his firm determination to stay away from Hanna – as well as his continued critical attitude toward her – had only served to widen the chasm he felt stood between him and the God he once walked with so closely.

What was it Isabela said? She'd been asking God to send her a new mommy, and she believed Hanna was the answer to her prayers. Really now . . . Wouldn't a new mother for Isabela mean a new wife for him? Jake raised his head. Large drops of rain pelted the metal patio awning. He took a deep breath. The humid night air smelled of wet sod. A new wife . . . Memories of holding Hanna a couple of weeks earlier teased his senses. *Don't go there.* Was it possible God would answer the child's prayers without first forewarning the father? Then again, who was to say He had not been trying to forewarn him? How could God speak to him if he wasn't listening?

When Jake glanced toward the mountains again, the familiar words of the psalmist came to mind: *"I will lift up my eyes to the mountains; from where shall my help come? My help comes from the Lord, who made heaven and earth."* He knew God would provide any guidance he needed. But he wasn't ready to admit he had been wrong; nor was he ready to face whatever unhealed hurts still lurked within his heart. Both would be painful. He'd had enough pain during the past three years; he didn't think he wanted any more. Staying busy helped focus his thoughts on other things. Keeping his distance from Hanna also seemed to be the right choice. Furthermore, if he were going to protect his daughter from future heartache, perhaps it would be best if he tightened up on her interactions with Hanna as well. Maybe Isabela had been spending an excessive amount of time at the Andersons' and needed to spend more time with him at the Community Center or on the ball fields. After all, he'd been neglecting her a little too much lately.

Chapter Fifteen

Hanna wiped sweat from her brow as she returned to the Masons' the following morning to check on Isabela. The day already promised to be a scorcher. Her thin cotton dress clung to her back while pieces of broken asphalt, which left the road pitted with potholes, pushed hard against the bottoms of her sandals. She stepped over one of the miniature craters and smiled at the memory of playing leap frog with Maleah and the girls the morning she toured Jake and Isabela's house. How quickly the storm clouds rumbled across the sky that day, obscuring sweet memories and eclipsing them with humiliation as she struggled in her attempt to talk with Giselle. Hanna pursed her lips. In some ways that seemed like a lifetime ago.

Rosalinda greeted her at the front door. Her woolly salt and pepper hair was pulled back at the nape of her neck, and she wore a tattered white apron over an orange button up blouse and ankle length brown paisley skirt. Hanna felt like a giant standing in front of the diminutive Dominican woman whose ancestry appeared to be mostly African.

"Buen día, señorita Hanna. ¿Cómo etá?" the woman said, a bright smile accenting the wrinkles on her weatherworn face.

"Bien. ¿Y usted?"

"Bien, gracia."

"¿Cómo está Isabela?" Hanna asked, still not comfortable with the local custom of dropping the 's' in most words.

"Ella etá mucho mejor. Ahora etá con su papá."

"Muy bien," Hanna said, thankful to hear Isabela was feeling better, but curious as to why Jake took her with him to the Community Center. She considered asking Rosalinda but thought better of it. "Gracias," she said instead. "Tenga un buen día."

"Equalamente."

Hanna walked down the driveway, pondering the information Rosalinda had shared with her. In all the time she'd been there, she didn't think Jake had ever taken Isabela to work with him. She shrugged. Maybe he wanted to be sure the child was completely well before leaving her with Rosalinda or at the Andersons'.

~~~~~

A week later, Hanna settled into a rocking chair next to Maleah on the Andersons' front porch, coffee cup in hand. She breathed deeply, allowing the aroma of fresh brewed Dominican café to invade her senses. The gentle swaying of the hammock caught her eye, and she glanced toward the tan canvas sling where Sophie played alone.

"Where's Isabela been lately?" Hanna asked Maleah. "She hasn't been over since the day before she got sick."

"I asked Jake the same question yesterday when I saw him at the Community Center. He told me he felt like he'd been neglecting her and they needed to be spending more time together."

"Sounds like a good excu – I mean reason . . . to me." Sipping cautiously, Hanna grinned at Maleah over the top of her coffee cup.

Maleah's laugh sounded more like a grunt. "Whatever you say. Truth is, I'm having a lot of trouble understanding Jake these days."

"Just remember, you promised that when you figured out what part my arrival has played in his strange behavior, you'd let me know."

Maleah grunted another laugh. "I will but don't hold your breath."

~~~~~

Almost another week passed and still no Isabela. Hanna was convinced the change of routine was a deliberate attempt on Jake's behalf to keep the child from interacting with her. What bothered her most was realizing his decision kept the girls apart. She mentioned it to Maleah one afternoon as they finished a tutoring session.

"I wouldn't worry about it," Maleah said. "Sophie has been playing with Perla and Pamela, the two little girls who live next door."

"Has she asked about Isabela?"

"A time or two the first week and maybe once since then, but that's all. Don't worry . . . she's fine." Maleah pushed her chair away from the table and stood. "By the way, how's that Bible study coming?"

Hanna grimaced. "I'm working on it."

"I want to see it when you're done." A furrow creased Maleah's brow. "Don't make me give you a bad grade for this six week term."

Hanna laughed as she stood. "Give me a few more days."

~~~~~

The next afternoon Hanna was on her way to visit Giselle when the sound of shouting children drew her attention in the opposite direction. A group of Dominican boys played basketball at the end of the street. She stopped in the middle of the Andersons' driveway and watched the game, halfway expecting Jake to appear at any moment. When several minutes passed and he didn't show, she walked across the road toward the colmado. In her hand she carried the Bible study Maleah had asked her to translate into Spanish. She wanted Giselle to proof it before showing it to Maleah. She was also praying God would use the content to speak to her Dominican friend about her need for a personal Savior. Stepping on the concrete stoop outside the door of the small market, she glanced down at the papers, silently asking for God's favor.

As she took a second step, she collided with someone exiting the store. When a hand gripped her arm, she jerked her head up. "Sor . . . compromi . . . " The words stuck in her throat. It was Jake.

"Unless you've had a lot of practice, walking and reading at the same time can be dangerous," he said. A smile teased the corners of his eyes.

Hanna's skin felt hot beneath his fingers. "I see that," she replied. "So how have you been?"

"Fine," he said, letting go of her arm. "And you?"

"Doing okay, but I've missed seeing Isabela. I'm assuming she's fully recovered."

The warmth in his eyes cooled. "She's a lot better," he said, stepping outside.

Hanna maintained eye contact. "Good to see you. Tell Isabela I asked about her."

He stepped onto the sidewalk. "See you later."

He had not said he was glad to see her, nor did he promise to tell Isabela she'd asked about her. She doubted he would mention her to the child at all.

As she watched Jake walk away, Hanna's heart slowed to its normal rhythm. At least she had not allowed the man to intimidate her this time. She slipped through the door of the colmado. As her eyes adjusted to the inside lighting, she realized the store was empty. She walked over to the counter where she could hear voices coming from the kitchen of the Garcías' home. "¡Hola!" she called.

Señor García appeared in the doorway, white teeth gleaming in his dark face. "Buen día, Hanna. ¿Como etá?"

"Bien, ¿y usted?"

"Bien, bien, gracia."

He escorted her to the kitchen, where she greeted Señora García and her mother before making her way to the bedroom Giselle shared with her grandmother, two sisters and three-year-old nephew. When the young woman saw her, she jumped up from the bed where she was sitting and greeted her with a light peck on the cheek. Soon they were chattering away in Spanish, catching up on what had happened since they had last been together.

Hanna relished the time she got to spend with Giselle. It had not taken her long to discover the young woman, with her creamy chocolate skin and dark hazel eyes, was beautiful both inside and out. It deeply burdened Hanna to realize her precious friend didn't have a personal relationship with Jesus Christ. She had begun praying on a daily basis for Giselle's heart to be tendered toward the One who had died to save her.

Once they'd gotten caught up, Hanna handed Giselle the Bible study she had written. She explained about the assignment Maleah gave her and asked her to read through the study, making corrections as needed. "¿Puede ayudarme?"

"¡Si!"

Once she finished reading the three-page study, Giselle looked at her. "You write this?"

"Si. Do you understand?" Hanna asked.

"Comprendo. I understand. Muy bien. Very good." She held up the pages. "You write. No help?"

Hanna laughed. "No help."

"Wow!" Giselle said, using an English exclamation she'd picked up from Hanna soon after they started studying together.

Hanna felt greatly relieved by her response, but wasn't sure what to think when the young woman grabbed her by the hand and pulled her toward the kitchen. Giselle's parents were still talking with her grandmother, a wiry Dominican woman with weathered skin the color of milk chocolate, black hair peppered with gray, and thick dark rimmed glasses. Her smile was always generous, although minus several teeth. Except for the missing teeth, Señora García favored her mother, who like Señor García appeared to have strong Taíno roots.

Hanna felt her cheeks flush when Giselle handed the Bible study to her mother and told her parents how good it was. Señor García stood behind his wife and read over her shoulder. Giselle pulled out a chair and motioned for Hanna to sit. Once seated, Hanna glanced around the room, taking in the quaint surroundings that were becoming more and more familiar. Two mismatched tables pushed together to make one filled the room to overflowing. Ten straight back chairs encircled it – none were the same color or style. A stove and sink stood to Hanna's right, with a few unadorned cabinets overhead. The refrigerator dominated the wall on the far end, a simple relic from a bygone era. Above it, a round battery operated clock told the time. It was almost four. Hanna looked at Giselle who sat to her left. She had not said a word since handing the papers to her parents. With wide-eyed wonder, the young woman watched them as they read. Hanna rested her forearms on the table and watched with her.

Señora García finished the last page, turned it over as if making sure there wasn't more, looked at her husband, then laid the papers down on the blue and white checkered table cloth. Hanna's head buzzed as they started talking at the same time, bombarding her with questions, which ironically had nothing to do with her ability to write a Bible study in Spanish but instead with their desire to understand the meaning of the content. Although she had prayed what she'd written would help Giselle grasp the gospel message, she never dreamed God was going to use it to speak to her parents as well. For the next thirty minutes she answered their questions as best as her language skills would allow. Once she realized she might be in a little over her head in terms of accurately communicating the truth of God's word in Spanish, she asked if they would be willing to come to the Andersons' for church the following Sunday and talk with Conner. When the entire family showed up and gave their lives to Christ, she was awed beyond words.

"Where is this Bible study Pedro was talking about?" Conner asked Hanna over lunch later that day.

"I guess they still have it." She lowered her head, but raised her eyes to look at Maleah. "It was the one I had translated into Spanish as a part of my homework."

Maleah arched an eyebrow. "Why didn't I ever get to see it?"

"Because I took it with me on Thursday to see if Giselle would help make corrections before I let you read it."

"And did she?" Maleah asked.

"No. After she read it, she showed it to her parents. Nothing was ever said about how well it was or wasn't written. They wanted me to help them better understand how they could have a personal relationship with Jesus Christ."

"Pedro told me they could tell there was much more to your belief in God than anything they'd ever known," Conner said. "It seems they had been discussing some of the things you were sharing during your weekly visits with them. Whatever you wrote in that Bible study convinced them it was time to make a decision."

"Rather amazing," Maleah said.

"Amazing indeed," Conner added, folding his arms across his chest. "I want a copy. It appears whatever you wrote explained so clearly the way of salvation, the whole family was able to understand. That's something Maleah and I have failed to accomplish in the two years we've been witnessing to them."

Hanna shifted in her chair. She felt unworthy of all the praise. "Please don't give me credit where credit isn't due," she said. "Any understanding they got from reading that Bible study had to have been the work of the Holy Spirit. Besides, I'm sure what I had written only confirmed what you two have been telling them. Lots of seeds have been planted. I'm just honored God has allowed me to be a part of the harvest."

~~~~~

Two weeks later, the small group of believers that met regularly at the Andersons' for Bible study and worship gathered at Playa Los Patos for a baptism. A celebration dinner was set to follow. Hanna was thrilled to witness her first outside baptism. While it wasn't the Jordan River, she felt the Dominican balneario was an excellent substitute. The natural fresh water swimming hole, sitting at the mouth of a river, framed on one side by a scraggy mangrove swamp and the other by a rugged mountainside, presented a memorable backdrop for the symbolic act of obedience. Hanna stood barefooted at the water's edge, the white-pebbled beach uneven and jagged beneath her feet, watching in awed reverence as Conner baptized the nine oldest members of the García family. Once Giselle's three-year-old nephew was old enough to make a personal decision to accept Jesus Christ as his Lord and Savior, Hanna felt certain he too would join his family as a member of the body of Christ.

With the addition of ten people to the group of eighteen already meeting at the Andersons' home on Sundays and Wednesdays, the living room now burst at the seams. Conner and

Maleah asked the small congregation to join them in praying about the possibility of building a church facility on a piece of property the mission owned next to the Community Center. A little over a week later Conner submitted a request for a volunteer team from the States to come and help with the construction of a building.

"How does that work?" Hanna asked Maleah that afternoon as they prepared lunch.

"Once the board receives a request, they usually check to see if there are any volunteer groups that have asked for an assignment in this area," Maleah said over her shoulder as she pulled mayonnaise and sandwich meat from the refrigerator. "If there are, it may only be a matter of a month or two before a group arrives. If there are no teams waiting on the sidelines, it'll take longer."

"So you've had volunteer teams come and help you before?" Hanna asked as she poured sweet tea into glasses.

"Several, actually," Maleah said. "In fact, the Community Center was built with the help of a team from Texas. For the most part, Conner and I believe making a request is kind of like putting out a fleece. If God is the one leading us to build, in His time He will provide a team."

After lunch Hanna retired to her room for a short siesta. As she drifted in and out of a light slumber, she dreamed she was talking to Jake. When she awoke, she lay in bed for several minutes while remnants of the dream as well as a few cobwebs dissipated. Her back was soaking wet and the overhead fans had stopped turning. The power must have gone off while she slept. She pushed herself into a sitting position and swung her legs over the side of the bed. As she stood, the sound of a familiar bass voice floated in from the patio. No wonder she'd been dreaming about Jake. When she heard Conner mention her name, she padded toward the window above the desk in the sitting area.

Jake cleared his throat. "I don't know," he said. "I'm afraid she would get in the way and slow us down. She knows nothing about the area, and with her weak language skills, don't you think she'd be more of a hindrance than a help?"

Hanna rolled her eyes. She didn't have to guess to whom he was referring. She pulled out the desk chair. When it creaked as she sat down, she held her breath, not letting it out again until Conner started talking.

"My thoughts were that making the trip would allow her the opportunity to see more of the country and get some exposure to the people and work we're involved with along the Haitian border," Conner said. "As for being a hindrance, I disagree. She has been a terrific help to Maleah and me. I see no reason why the same would not be true with the work in Pedernales and Anse-a-Pitres."

Hanna heard Jake sigh. "I'm not sure she's been here long enough," he said. "I suppose one day she might be a help with the work on the border but . . . I don't know." Hanna's breath caught in her throat as she waited for him to continue – she knew what was coming. "I don't mean to keep harping on this, but still . . . her poor language skills are a major concern."

"You don't have clue what you're talking about," Conner said. "What do you *even* know about her language skills? When was the last time you heard her speaking Spanish?"

"Ah . . . let's see . . . I guess it was that day at the colmado."

"Do you know how long ago that was?"

"A month? No . . . maybe two."

"Try closer to three." Conner sounded peeved. "And while you've been busy with your work and keeping to yourself and whatever else it is you've been doing, Hanna has been trying harder than anyone I've ever known. If you would give her half a chance, my guess is you'd be surprised at how her language skills have improved. By the way, did you know every member of the García family – all but the littlest one – has professed faith in Christ? In fact, we baptized them just a couple of weeks ago."

"No . . . I didn't know that," Jake responded. "That's great news . . . but what does it have to do with Hanna's language skills?"

"A lot." The tone of Conner's voice had pitched upward an octave. "Maleah and I had been trying for almost two years to reach that family, with no results. Then Hanna started going over there a couple of times a week, and while she was working on her language skills, she also took the time to share her faith with them. Next thing we know they all show up one Sunday for church asking questions about what it means to have a personal relationship with Jesus

Christ."

Conner took a deep breath before continuing. "When I asked why the sudden change of heart, they pointed at Hanna. Turns out she had written a Bible study in Spanish and shared it with several members of the family, asking for their help in editing or critiquing or something like that. Smart girl. The focal verses of the Bible study were John 1:1-14, John 3:16 and John 14:6. While they thought they were helping her with a paper, they were introduced to the Word who became flesh, the only begotten Son of God, who is the way, the truth and the life – the only way to God the Father."

Sweat trickled down both sides of Hanna's face. Without the fans, her small apartment felt like an oven set on high broil. Barely breathing, she listened for Jake's response.

"And you're saying the study was written well enough that they were able to understand it?"

If squeezing through the louvered windows had been a possibility, Hanna would have strangled the man.

"You amaze me! You really do!" It sounded like Conner might do the job for her. "Why do you have it out for Hanna? I don't get it. Yes! It was written well enough that they were able to understand it. I dare say it was written better than you or I could have done. It seems our young teacher arrived with a much better command of the written language than the spoken. I thought we could even take a few copies with us to give to Pastor Jeremías in Pedernales."

"Maybe . . . " Jake said, sounding unconvinced. "Do you mind if I take a look at it before making a decision?"

"Not at all," Conner said. "And, back to our original conversation. I want Hanna to go with us on the trip to the border."

"If you feel that strongly, what can I say? It'll complicate matters, you know. We'll have to get two hotel rooms. But if you want to take her . . . she can go."

Hanna heard chairs scraping against the brick patio floor. "I appreciate it," Conner said. "I think if you would lighten up, you'd really like her." His voice grew fainter as they walked back into the house.

Hanna stood and stared out the window. She wished she

could have seen the look on Jake's face after Conner's last comment.

Chapter Sixteen

Jake tried to read Hanna's Bible study as he walked home. When he stumbled over a pothole, he was reminded of his encounter with her three or four weeks earlier at the colmado. It would seem neither one of them had had a lot of practice reading while walking. He hated to admit how pleased he'd been to see her that day. What would Conner say if he knew the reason he was being so hard on her was because he feared if he did lighten up, he might like her a little too much? He raked his fingers through his hair. Why had he allowed Conner to talk him into letting her make the trip to Pedernales with them? Three or four days in close proximity was going to put a serious kink in his vow to keep his distance. Maybe he should try again to convince Conner her going wasn't such a good idea, but somehow he imagined it wasn't going to work. He'd probably be better off saving his breath.

Stepping into the living room of his house, Jake saw the message light on the answering machine blinking. He laid Hanna's Bible study on the coffee table before pressing the play button. His gut twisted at the sound of Katie's mother's voice. He hadn't realized until after Katie was gone how much she sounded like her mother.

"Hi Jake. I've got some time off from work coming up in a few weeks. If possible, I would love to come and visit you and Isabela. Give me a call. Love you."

Jake had not seen Katie's parents since the day they stood teary-eyed at the airport in Wichita, Kansas, waving good-bye as he and Isabela made their way through the security check-point on the first leg of their journey back to the Dominican Republic. Although Isabela talked on the phone with her grandmother on a regular basis, it had been over a year since she'd seen her.

Katie inherited her dimples from her father, but the Shirley Temple ringlets had been passed down from her mother. Now in her late fifties, Susan Williamson's curls were more salt than pepper. She and Katie's father, Roger, had last been in the Dominican Republic only weeks before their daughter's death. They had been a part of the volunteer team that came from Kansas to help in the aftermath of a hurricane, which hit the island early in the season that year, leaving hundreds dead along the southern border between the Dominican Republic and Haiti and thousands more homeless. As a nurse, Susan proved an invaluable asset as they administered medical assistance in Anse-a-Pitres, Haiti.

Usually disease-carrying mosquitoes are not as much of a problem in the dry arid terrain in southeast Haiti as they are in other parts of the country, but the torrential rain and assaulting waves of the storm had left the area soggy for weeks afterwards. The countryside, usually cracked and dry, was pockmarked with pools of stagnant water, providing ideal breeding grounds for mosquitoes. An outbreak of dengue fever hit the small border town of Anse-a-Pitres only days before the volunteer team arrived. Although they'd practically clothed themselves in insect repellent and had worn long pants and long sleeve shirts, somehow at least one persistent, disease bearing mosquito broke through the protective barrier, not only infecting Jake's precious wife, but eventually taking her life.

After talking with his mother-in-law, Jake sat on the sofa and stared at Hanna's Bible study still laying where he'd dropped it on the coffee table. Susan was arriving in less than three weeks, four days before he and Conner planned on leaving for Pedernales. He'd offered to delay their trip, but she insisted on his going, maintaining it would give her and Isabela some quality grandmother/granddaughter time. She'd said if she needed anything, Maleah would be right down the street, and Isabela could serve as her translator with Rosalinda.

"We'll be fine. It'll be great fun." Jake could still hear Susan's words of assurance.

He picked up the Bible study and then let the pages float back down onto the table. He wondered what Susan would think of Hanna, especially when she realized the attractive young woman was making the trip to the border with him and Conner. He stood and headed for Isabela's room. The child would be thrilled at the news her grandmother was coming. He only hoped with the time spent away from Hanna, she'd forgotten about her "secret." What *would* Susan think if her granddaughter shared her fantasy with her?

~~~~~

A week after Hanna overheard Jake and Conner discussing the trip to Pedernales, Conner invited her to go with them. She accepted the invitation, never letting on she knew about Jake's reluctance to let her go. She'd dreamed of returning to Haiti since the trip she made with her mother twelve years earlier. Now that she had the opportunity, she was determined not to allow Jake's opinion to prevent her from going.

Two days later she returned from a study session with Giselle and found Jake sitting in the Andersons' living room talking with Conner and Maleah. All three of them looked at her when she walked in the door, their expressions reminding her of children who had been caught with their hands in the cookie jar.

Maleah cleared her throat. "Ah, Hanna . . . We were just talking about you."

Hanna bit back a sarcastic, "you could have fooled me," as she offered the threesome a thin smile. "Really? No wonder my ears were burning," she replied.

"It's all good," Maleah said, patting the sofa cushion beside her. "Come join us."

Hanna perched on the edge of the sofa, both feet planted firmly in front of her. Maleah laid a freckled hand on top of hers. "We were talking about the trip to Pedernales."

Hanna looked at Conner and then Jake. Conner was smiling as if to say, "Yep, that's right." Jake had his right ankle resting on top of his left knee and was examining the toe of his tennis shoe. She suspected she wasn't going to get the whole truth out of any of them. "Yeah . . . well, I'm looking forward to going," she said.

Maleah was all smiles. "Did you know Isabela's grandmother is coming for a visit? She's going to stay with Isabela while you all are gone."

Hanna shifted her eyes from Maleah to Jake. He had placed his foot on the floor and was looking at her. "I'm sure Isabela is excited about that," she said.

He nodded, a faint smile lifting the corners of his mouth. "She is. They've not seen each other since we came back to the Dominican Republic."

Maleah squeezed Hanna's hand. "This is Katie's mother. She's a nurse. She and Katie's father live in Wichita where her dad pastors a church."

Hanna chewed on her bottom lip and looked back at Jake. Why did she sense they were hiding something from her? The tension in the room was thicker than the oppressive afternoon heat. "I will look forward to meeting her," she said.

Jake slapped his hands on his thighs and stood. "Guess I need to get home. Rosalinda should have dinner ready, and Isabela will be looking for me."

Conner rose and walked him to the door. Hanna glanced at Maleah. She wanted to ask what was going on but decided she might rather not know. If Maleah wanted to tell her, she would. If not . . . she'd let it go.

~~~~~

The day after Jake and Isabela made the trip to Santo Domingo to pick up Katie's mother, the three of them showed up at the Andersons' soon after lunch. Hanna was in the kitchen grabbing another glass of sweet tea when she heard a light tapping on the doorframe of the front door, which was usually left open during the day. She set her glass on the counter and walked into the living room. When she saw who was standing at the door, she almost panicked and considered yelling for Maleah, but decided against appearing impolite in front of Katie's mother. By the time she reached them, her heart was beating three times its normal rate.

A tall, slender woman with soft silver curls and piercing blue eyes stood between Jake and Isabela. Obviously the child had gotten her beautiful eyes from both sides of the family.

What a striking couple Jake and Katie must have made.

Isabela's dimpled face beamed. "Aunt Hanna, this is my grammie. She came all the way from Kansas to see me."

The woman smiled and extended her right hand. "Glad to meet you, Hanna. Isabela talked about you almost non-stop on our trip from Santo Domingo to Paraíso."

Hanna darted her eyes at Jake as she shook the woman's hand. "Nice to meet you too. It's Mrs. Williamson, right?"

"Susan to you."

Hanna stepped out of the doorway. "I'm sorry. Won't y'all come in?"

"Jake tells me you're from Alabama," Susan said as they moved toward the living room.

"You mean Jake *and* my accent."

The woman tipped her head back and laughed. "That too."

Hanna spent the next hour sitting awkwardly on one end of the sofa with Maleah in the middle and Jake's mother-in-law on the other end. Conner and Jake sat in chairs across from them. While on occasion Maleah or Conner would say something to try and draw her into the conversation, for the most part Hanna felt out of place. Jake refused to make eye contact, but Katie's mother periodically leaned forward and looked in her direction.

As they got ready to leave, Susan approached her. "I was wondering if you could come to the house and visit with me for a little while tomorrow," she said.

Hanna glanced at Jake who stared at his mother-in-law, his eyes unblinking and mouth slightly open. She swallowed back a giggle.

Susan patted him on the arm. "I believe Jake has work to do at the Community Center, so I thought maybe you could bring Sophie over to play with Isabela and you and I could get better acquainted."

Hanna cast a look in Maleah's direction. Before she could speak, Susan continued. "Of course Maleah is welcome to come too, but she and I will have lots of time to visit after you leave for the border with Jake and Conner."

Maleah nodded. "I appreciate the invitation, but I do have some things I need to get done here." She smiled at Hanna, who wondered if there was some kind of silent communication going on between the two women. "But I'm sure Hanna would enjoy the visit."

Although Jake had by now fixed his eyes on Hanna, she found his expression hard to read. She felt certain he would prefer she say no. She looked at Susan. "I appreciate the offer," she replied. "What time would you like for us to be there?"

"How about in the morning around ten?"

Hanna took a deep breath. "We'll be there."

Susan slipped an arm around her shoulders, giving her a quick hug. "Good. I'll look forward to it."

~~~~~

Hanna arrived at the Masons' promptly at ten the following morning, Sophie at her side. Before she could tap on the doorframe, Isabela came sliding in their direction, her sock feet slippery on the terrazzo floors. "Grammie," she called over her shoulder, "Aunt Hanna and Sophie are here." She flung her arms around Hanna's legs. "I've been missing you so much," she said.

Hanna lifted her eyes just in time to see a bewildered look flash across Susan's face. She stooped to hug Isabela. "I've been missing you too, sweetheart." She reached over and pulled Sophie into the hug. "I bet you and Sophie will enjoy playing together this morning."

The girls beamed at each other. Isabela reached her hand out and took Sophie's. "Come on. Let's go to my room," she said.

Hanna stood and smiled at Susan. "Good morning. How are you today?"

"I'm fine," the woman said as her right brow lifted. "So tell me . . . what was that all about?"

Hanna shrugged. "We haven't gotten to spend a lot time together lately, that's all."

"Come on in and let's get something to drink, then we can visit. Something tells me there's more to the story than that and I want to hear it."

With coffee cups in hand, Hanna followed Susan onto the patio. "I hope this is okay with you," the woman said. "I love the view."

Hanna surveyed the picturesque scene on display before them. As the sun's rays frolicked across the bumps and crevices of the mountainside, playing hide-and-seek in the dense tropical foliage, she was reminded of the English translation of the word *paraíso*. To the early explorers, the lush mountain terrain – bordered by magnificent beaches and teal blue waters – must have looked like they thought paradise should look. If it were not for the stifling heat and humidity, Hanna probably would have agreed. She took a sip of coffee and turned her eyes toward the attractive older woman sitting beside her. "I guess you don't have mountains in Wichita, do you?" she said.

Susan shook her head. "No, but it has its own beauty. On a clear summer day the sky looks bigger than life – miles and miles of blue stretching on for what seems like forever."

"Sounds nice."

Susan held her coffee cup to her lips and blew, her eyes fixed on the mountains. "So . . . tell me . . . Why haven't you and Isabela gotten to spend much time together lately?"

Hanna's stomach churned – the butterflies were restless today.

Susan turned and peered at her over the top of her cup. "You can tell me the truth," she said.

"Is there a reason you want to know?"

Susan leaned back in her chair, propping her feet on an old crate sitting in front of her. A deep furrow formed across her forehead. "In recent months, every time I've talked to Jake I could tell something was bothering him," she said. "He's been fighting some kind of battle, but I was having trouble putting my finger on it until the last couple of days. On the trip to Paraíso from Santo Domingo, as Isabela babbled incessantly about you, I noticed Jake was awfully quiet. When I asked him about his relationship with you, he shrugged his shoulders and said, 'what relationship?' But his body language screamed something totally different." She smiled at Hanna. "As we visited yesterday afternoon at the Andersons', I watched the two of you. I've been a pastor's wife for over thirty-five years, and God has graciously gifted me with a fair amount of discernment." She placed her hand on top of Hanna's. "The emotional energy passing between you and Jake was so intense I think even if the power had gone off we would have still had electricity."

Hanna felt the heat creeping toward her face and her chin trembled as she attempted a smile. "But . . . you had to have misread something. Jake . . . " Her throat constricted and a tear slid down her cheek. "He doesn't care much for me."

"No . . . " Susan patted her hand, "I didn't misread anything. Jake wants to believe he doesn't care for you, and I don't know what he's been doing, but whatever it is – if he's hurt you, it's because he's trying to keep from caring too much."

Several more tears trickled down Hanna's cheeks. Giving up on her coffee, she placed the cup on a small table beside her chair, and then brushed the tears away with her hand before slanting watery eyes at Susan. "Why are you talking to me about this?" she asked with a sniff. "I mean . . . you're Katie's mother. If it were true, although it isn't, but if it were – wouldn't it bother you to know Jake was interested in someone?"

"Jake is thirty-five years old," Susan said, resting her coffee cup on the arm of her chair. "How selfish would it be if I expected him to stay single for the rest of his life? How selfish for me to not want him to love again." She turned her blue eyes in Hanna's direction. "As for my granddaughter – the child was only three when her mother died. As she grows older, shouldn't I want her to have a mother in her life?"

Hanna blew out a puff of air. "Wow! I don't know. I would think it would take a lot of letting go to allow another woman to step into that role in Isabela's life. What if this new wife and mother were jealous and didn't want you in their lives?"

Susan laughed softly. "So . . . would you push me out?"

"Me?" Hanna blinked her eyes. "Of course not, but it's

unlikely I'm the one you're going to be dealing with. Like I told you, Jake doesn't care much for me. Except for the first few days I was in the country, he's hardly spoken more than a couple dozen words to me."

"Seriously?"

"Oh, seriously. You would think I've got the plague the way he acts around me. For six weeks or so he allowed Isabela to spend time with me, but more recently he's even put a stop to that."

"Then that's the reason Isabela said she's been missing you?"

Hanna nodded.

"And why did he cut off the interactions between the two of you?"

Hanna gazed toward the mountains. "My guess is he was afraid she was becoming a little too fond of me."

"Why do you say that? Is it because he found out Isabela thinks God brought you here to be her new mommy?"

The woman's question recaptured Hanna's attention. Susan looked at her with sober eyes, but appeared to be holding a smile in check. "How did you know that?"

"Because Isabela told me."

"When?"

Susan's smile escaped and burst forth in laughter. "On the trip from Santo Domingo to Paraíso."

"You're kidding. Did Jake hear her?"

"Oh yes, but he didn't say anything. I let his silence pass while Isabela continued telling me all about you. By the time we got here, I couldn't wait to meet you."

Hanna shifted in her chair so she could see the woman better. "But surely you've been able to tell how Jake feels about me."

"That I have, and I've already told you what I think." Susan's eyebrows rose significantly. "I've also been able to tell how you feel about him."

A fresh wave of warmth rushed up Hanna's neck to her face. "Whatever it is I feel for him," she said, blinking back more tears, "doesn't matter if he won't give me the time of day." She flinched when she heard Jake cough. She and Susan turned their heads simultaneously. He was walking toward them, but Hanna didn't think he'd been close enough to hear what she'd said.

Susan rose from her chair. "Jake, I didn't expect you back so soon."

Hanna stood and brushed at the wrinkles in her skirt with sweaty palms. She could feel Jake's eyes on her.

"I did what I needed to do at the Community Center," he said, "then decided I should come home and get a few things done around here since we're leaving day after tomorrow for Pedernales."

Susan slipped her arm through Hanna's. "Well, Hanna and I've had a nice visit. I know she's looking forward to making the trip with you and Conner."

Hanna glanced at her watch. "Guess I need to get home," she said. "I'll probably pack sometime this afternoon myself. With church and all, tomorrow will be a full day."

Susan wrapped her arm around Hanna's waist and gave her a warm motherly hug. "Why don't you let Sophie stay and play? I'll walk her home in a little while."

"I'm sure she'd like that," Hanna replied. As she walked past Jake, she offered him a guarded smile.

"See you Monday," he said.

She nodded. "See ya . . ."

Chapter Seventeen

Hanna rose early Monday morning. As usual, she'd not needed an alarm clock. The reliable crowing of the neighbor's rooster woke her long before the sun peeked over the horizon. For the first day of their journey she chose an ankle-length, sage green skirt with a cream-colored, button-up blouse – both made of cool cotton, and a pair of flat, slip-on sandals the color of eggnog. After learning skirts and dresses were the more culturally acceptable attire for Christian women in the southwest part of the Dominican Republic, she had restocked her wardrobe with an assortment of skirts, blouses, multicolored T-shirts and sundresses before leaving the States for Costa Rica. She had feared she would miss her blue jeans and suffer withdrawals, but since arriving in Paraíso had realized a loose fitting skirt or sundress was significantly cooler than pants anyway. At least *that* cultural adjustment had been relatively painless.

Standing in front of the mirror, she brushed her hair into a ponytail and checked her make-up. Anxious doubts shimmered in the dark green eyes staring back at her. She walked over and laid her brush and make-up bag on the bed, then picked up her Bible, opening it to Psalm 56. Before facing Jake for a full three days she needed the spiritual fortitude only God's word could provide. She read verses three and four out loud. "When I am afraid, I will put my trust in You. In God, whose word I praise. In God I have put my trust; I shall not be afraid. What can mere man do to me?"

She laid her Bible along with the brush and make-up bag inside the small suitcase she'd packed for the trip, whispering a prayer as she zipped it shut. "Dear Lord, today I place my trust in

You; therefore, I will not be afraid of Jake's words or attitude toward me. Please help me remember I am here because You have called me. I am Your beloved daughter, and You love me with an everlasting love. I praise You Father that Your acceptance of me is not based on how well I speak or do not speak the language; nor is it based on Jake Mason's opinion of me. Please fill me with Your Holy Spirit so I can walk in Your love, Your joy and Your peace."

It was only seven-thirty, but the humidity was already pushing the limit. Hanna stopped in front of an oscillating fan, savoring the moment as a refreshing breeze gently blew tendrils of hair loose from her ponytail. She was afraid to imagine what it was going to feel like once they drew closer to the southwest corner of the country where she was told temperatures often topped one hundred.

She stepped outside and placed her suitcase near the edge of the front porch before sitting in a rocking chair to wait for Jake and Conner. She gazed toward the mountains rising behind the house across the street, reminding her of the conversation she'd had a couple of days earlier with Susan Williamson. Never in her wildest dreams would she have thought Katie's mother would turn out to be an advocate. Even so, she doubted the woman's sentiments were going to make much of a difference in the way Jake felt about her.

Maleah appeared a few minutes later. After setting a small cooler beside Hanna's suitcase, she turned and smiled. Tiny sweat beads glistened on her forehead. "You know me," she said, "I couldn't send you on your way without a snack and something to drink. There are bottles of water and several cans of Coke in the cooler." She handed Hanna a Ziplock bag full of warm chocolate chip cookies. "And I thought you might enjoy these."

Hanna breathed deeply as she held the bag up for inspection. Vanilla and chocolate – the delectable aroma teased her taste buds. She thought she'd smelled something baking as she passed through the kitchen. It was just like Maleah to have gotten up earlier than usual so they could have fresh cookies for the trip. The words *thank-you* lodged in her throat when she saw Jake's van turn into the driveway.

As if reading Hanna's anxious thoughts, Maleah reached

over and patted her shoulder. "I've been praying for you," she said. "It's going to be okay. No . . . it's going to be better than okay. You just wait and see."

Hanna frowned at her freckle-faced friend, wondering how she could be so confident everything was going to turn out all right. She didn't have time to ask. She stood as Jake, dressed in a pair of khakis and a three-button pullover knit shirt the color of robins' eggs, walked toward them. His eyes cast hues mimicking the various shades of the Caribbean. Hanna glanced away as a wave of insecurity rolled down her spine. She had spent the last fifteen minutes trying to convince herself his opinion of her wasn't important. In a matter of seconds, all her resolve melted like a block of ice exposed to the hot Dominican sun.

It was going to be a long three days.

Hanna waved goodbye to Maleah as they pulled away from the house. Conner had offered to let her ride up front, but knowing Jake objected to her making the trip in the first place, she opted to forego the awkwardness sitting across from him would have created. She chose to sit behind him instead, with hopes of enjoying the ride without being distracted.

As they passed the colmado, Conner glanced at the clock on the dashboard. "It's eight o'clock now, which means we should get to Pedernales sometime between nine-thirty and ten – provided we don't encounter any unforeseen detours."

"Sounds good," Jake said. Hanna was surprised when he turned the conversation in her direction. "I hope someone told you pit stops are few and far between for the next couple of hours," he said.

Hanna gritted her teeth. He was already thinking of ways she might prove to be a nuisance. Why hadn't she stayed with Maleah? Turning her face away from the window, she caught his reflection in the rearview mirror. He was grinning – at her! She allowed the corners of her mouth to ease into a smile. "Maleah told me, so I passed on my usual cup of coffee," she said. "I may sleep all the way there, but hopefully I won't need a potty break."

When Jake laughed, she jumped. Her nerves were strung much too tight. She took a deep breath and told herself to relax.

Caribbean Paradise

"Sounds like she's smarter than the two us," Jake said, looking at Conner. "Of course, I had to have my coffee this morning. Wouldn't be a good idea for the driver to fall asleep."

"*Not* a good idea," Conner replied with a smile. "By the way, Hanna, did anyone tell you the place where we're staying only has cold water?"

"No . . ." She could see Jake watching her reaction in the rearview mirror. "I don't think that was mentioned. However, since Maleah did tell me that it is usually hotter and even more humid in Pedernales than in Paraíso, maybe I won't mind taking a few cold showers. I'm guessing Pedernales isn't exactly resort quality, huh?"

"Not exactly," Conner said, "although the hotel where we're staying is one of the more popular choices in Pedernales. It's small, only a dozen or so rooms."

"The rooms are clean, which isn't always the case with hotels in these smaller towns," Jake added. "And there's a gazebo where they serve breakfast. We'll eat there tomorrow morning."

"Sounds quaint," Hanna said.

Jake nodded. "Even without hot water, I think you'll like it. We'll check in as soon as we get to town, and then we're taking you to the Haitian market. Every Monday and Friday Haitians from Anse-a-Pitres set up market along the border. It's a touch of local culture you don't want to miss."

Conner looked at her and smiled. "Who knows, you may even find a something you can't live without."

"What do they sell?"

"Fruit, vegetables, chickens, fish . . . and lots of clothing and household items," Conner said. "Any chance you are in need of a good pair of counterfeit designer jeans or tennis shoes?"

Hanna studied Conner's expression, trying to determine whether he was serious or teasing. "Do they actually sell counterfeit clothing and shoes?" she asked.

"The best genuine counterfeit in all of the Dominican Republic can be found at the Haitian markets, and at rock bottom prices too," Jake said. "Most of their customers are Dominican wholesalers."

Conner extended his hand toward Hanna. "Hand me those

cookies. All this talk about shopping has made me hungry."

Hanna shook her head and passed the bag up front.

"Get a whiff of that," Conner said, waving the opened bag around until the delectable smell filled the van.

Hanna's mouth watered, but she didn't dare eat anything. The nervous juices in her stomach didn't need company.

While the guys munched on cookies, she leaned her head against the window and closed her eyes. The sound of Jake clearing his throat startled her out of a light slumber. Barely opening her eyes, she glanced toward the front. She sat up straighter when she realized he was looking at her once again in the rearview mirror.

"Were you asleep?" he asked with a sheepish grin.

A few cobwebs lingered, and she stared for a moment at his reflection, offering him a weak smile. "Almost."

"You awake now?" His grin stretched to the corners of his eyes.

"I think so. Why?" she asked, hoping the expression on her face did not expose the confusion in her mind. What in the world was he up to?

"I wanted to let you know I read the Bible study you wrote. It was really good. Conner told me about the impact it had on the García family. Just curious, what prompted you to write it?"

Hanna hesitated. While he seemed genuinely interested, lessons learned made her fear he might be setting her up for the kill. She looked at Conner, hoping to get a cue from him, but he was gazing out the passenger side window. She drew her eyes back to Jake's rearview mirror reflection. If this kept up, she'd need to move to the other side. "It was a homework assignment," she said. "Maleah has been tutoring me in Spanish. When I told her I hoped to one day translate some of the Bible studies I've written into Spanish, she –"

Jake interrupted her. "You've written other Bible studies – in English?"

"Well . . . yes. I've been writing Bible studies since I was in college. Even as a child I loved to write, so when I couldn't find the right study for a group I was leading in my dorm, I decided to write something myself. Since then I've written about twenty-five short studies."

"I see." Jake said. "And Maleah had you translate one into Spanish?"

"Yeah. I was hesitant at first because I felt my Spanish skills weren't good enough, but Maleah felt the time spent translating would help me gain a better grasp of the language."

"Why did you choose that particular study?"

Hanna undid her seat belt and slid to the other side. Jake glanced at her and smiled. "That's better," he said.

"I thought it would probably be safer if you weren't constantly looking in the rearview mirror."

"Oh yeah," Conner piped in. "Now he'll just be turning his head to look at you. Sounds a lot safer to me."

Jake glanced at Hanna again, this time winking. "You know Conner, you may be right," he said. "Those green eyes could easily become a distraction."

Hanna struggled to keep her mouth from falling open. "If you'd like, I could move back to the other side." She felt her face flush as soon as the words left her lips. What a stupid thing to say.

Jake laughed. "No. You're fine right where you are. I have no objections to be able to see you better," he said. "So . . . where were we? Oh yeah . . . I wanted to know why you chose to translate that particular Bible study."

"I was hopeful I could use it as a witnessing tool with Giselle," Hanna said. "We've been meeting a couple of times a week. She helps me practice Spanish and I've been teaching her English. Once the Bible study was translated, I asked her to check it for errors before I gave a copy to Maleah."

"So, did she help you with the editing?"

"Well, no. After she finished reading it, she showed it to her parents and grandmother. Before I knew what had happened, they were asking me questions about what it meant to have a personal relationship with Christ. I did my best to share with them the plan of salvation, then asked if they would come to church at the Andersons' the following Sunday. They said they would. After Conner talked with them, they all accepted Jesus as their Savior. I was blown away."

"I can see why. That's a powerful story."

"Guess my written Spanish skills are better than my spoken." The words slipped out before she realized what she'd said.

"I haven't heard you speak Spanish lately," Jake said, "but if that Bible study is any indication of your ability to write in the language, I'm impressed. God has blessed you with an awesome gift, and I hope you plan on doing more translations." He punched Conner in the arm. "Wouldn't you agree?"

"Absolutely," Conner responded, looking over his shoulder at Hanna and giving her a warm B.J. Honeycutt smile. "I would even like to use some of what she's written during our weekly Bible studies."

"Really?" Hanna said.

"Really. In fact, I would like for you to pray about leading the Bible study sometime."

Hanna gasped. "Oh, no . . . no Conner, I couldn't ever do that."

"Haven't you taught the studies in the past?" Jake asked. Hanna jerked her head in his direction. Did he actually think she could teach in Spanish?

"Yes . . . yes, of course," she stammered in reply. "But . . . that was in English. There's no way I could teach a Bible study in Spanish."

Conner laughed. "That's the way I felt when I first felt God calling me into the ministry. I thought there was no way I would be able to stand in front of people and talk, much more teach or preach. As a child and teenager I was painfully shy. I couldn't imagine how I was ever going accomplish what I felt God was calling me to do, but once I surrendered to His will, the most amazing thing happened. Whenever I would start to teach or preach, peace would rise up within me and the words would simply flow. I knew it had to be God because on my own I couldn't do what I was doing."

"I understand," Hanna said, "but what you're talking about was in English."

"Then – yes. But remember, now I preach and teach in Spanish too. I'll let you pray about it first, but if God has gifted you to write and teach Bible studies, He will give you the skills you need, whether it's in English *or* Spanish."

Hanna still wasn't convinced. "I know that, but . . . I came here to teach the children – *in English.*"

"I'm sensing God brought you here for much more than that," Conner said. "Let's pray about it and see where He leads."

Trying to sort through her thoughts, Hanna stared at the rugged terrain passing by on the right side of the vehicle. Conner's suggestion that she pray about teaching in Spanish one day was unnerving, but her fiercest emotional battle had to do with the sudden change in Jake's attitude toward her. Over the past three months he had avoided her and, as a result of overhearing his conversations with Conner, she knew he questioned whether she should even be on the mission field. The Jake who'd been interacting with her this morning was someone she didn't recognize at all. She certainly was willing to allow for the possibility God was at work and the one responsible for his sudden change of heart; even so, it was probably wise not to let down her guard too quickly.

"What do you think of this part of the country so far?" Conner asked, drawing her from her private reverie.

"Ah, well . . . " Although she'd been gazing out the window, she hated to admit she had observed very little about the passing countryside.

The corner of Jake's mouth lifted slightly. "I think she's been sleeping with her eyes open."

"And missed the southern tip of the Pedernales Peninsula," Conner said.

"Guess that means you've fallen down on your job as tour guide," Jake replied.

"It looks like a green desert," Hanna interjected.

"Good description," Conner said. "The road we're on now forms the northern boundary of Parque National Jaraqua."

"I've heard of that park," Hanna said, focusing her attention on the landscape as it slipped by. "It's a wildlife reserve of some sort, isn't it?"

"See, she doesn't need a tour guide," Conner said.

Hanna grinned when she saw Jake roll his eyes. "You would probably enjoy the Laguna de Oviedo," he said, glancing at her again. "We passed the turn a little while back. It's a six-mile-long saltwater lagoon made up of a dozen small islands, which create a natural habitat for birds and turtles, including a year round population of flamingos. It's considered the top bird watching locale in the country."

"Flamingos? Really? That I would like to see."

"We'll come back sometime," Jake said. "Make a day of it."

Hanna resisted the temptation to look around as if she were trying to figure out who had just spoken. She was starting to wonder if the man driving the van was an imposter. And if so, what had he done with the real Jake Mason?

Ten minutes later, they entered the outskirts of a small town. "Here we are," Jake said. "It's basically a primitive fishing village on the back side of nowhere, but I guess I'll always have a soft spot in my heart for this place."

From what Hanna could tell, Pedernales wasn't significantly different from the other towns she'd seen dotting the southwest region of the country. Tree lined streets with brightly colored houses and an ample supply of the ever-popular motoconchos appeared to be the norm. A gust of hot, humid air assaulted her when Jake opened his door and got out of the van in front the small establishment he referred to as their hotel. She watched as he walked toward what she assumed was the office. Personally, she wasn't sure she was ready to leave the comfortable climate-controlled environment of the van.

Conner turned in his seat and smiled at her. On a whim she decided to ask his opinion of Jake's behavior. "I know we only have a couple of minutes before Jake comes back," she said, "but do you have any idea why he has suddenly decided to be so nice to me?"

Conner glanced toward the door through which Jake had only a few seconds earlier disappeared. "First and foremost, answered prayer, although Maleah and I did talk to him a week or so ago. Remember the afternoon you came in and we were all in the living room?"

"And looking really guilty. Yeah, I remember. I wondered what was going on."

Conner laughed. "Maleah and I have been trying to figure

out why he has reacted so negatively toward you. This may sound crazy, but we finally decided he was afraid he could possibly like you too much, so he either consciously – or subconsciously – decided not to like you. Does that make sense?"

Hanna nodded. "You think he's been trying to sabotage the relationship with me because he's not ready to get *involved* – for a lack of a better way to say it – with someone." Memories of her conversation with Katie's mother surfaced.

"I couldn't have said it better myself."

Hanna unbuckled her seatbelt and scooted to the middle of the seat. "Interesting. So what did you and Maleah say to him?"

"We told him how much help you were to us and about the way God was using you in the lives of the García family, and then asked if he would pray about his attitude toward you. Maleah pointed out that this trip would be a lot more pleasant if he would try to be a little kinder."

"How did he respond?"

"Considering the way he'd been acting recently, I was surprised when he responded positively. He told Maleah she was right and promised to be nice. Since we'd been praying, guess I shouldn't have been surprised, but I was."

"Do you think that's the only reason he's being nice?"

Conner looked at her and smiled. "Why? Because God answered our prayers?"

"No . . . I meant because Maleah asked him to try and be nice."

"I knew what you meant. But honestly," Conner lowered his voice as the office door swung open, "I think it's because he likes you."

Hanna slid back to the right side of the seat and re-buckled. Jake opened the driver side door and stuck his head in. "Hot enough for you guys?"

"I'm comfortable," Hanna answered, "but I'm guessing that's getting ready to change." She watched as he pulled himself back in the van. Did she dare believe he actually enjoyed her company? Was it conceivable he had been acting as he did toward her in an effort to protect his heart? Up until the last couple of days, she'd not considered that a possibility, but as strange as it sounded, it made sense. If that were the case, could she trust him? After all, he wasn't the only one who wanted to protect their heart.

Chapter Eighteen

After grabbing a bite to eat, Jake and Conner took Hanna around town, introducing her to some of the locals. When she realized other than acknowledging introductions she was not going to be expected to engage in any of the conversations, she relaxed and enjoyed the excursion. Although she knew her language skills were considerably better than the last time Jake heard her speak, she was not ready to try her hand at communicating in front of him. The wounds from that dreadful day at the colmado still had not healed completely.

For Hanna, visiting the Haitian Market proved to be a long awaited opportunity to once again touch and taste a bit of the Haitian culture. Initially, even the stench of raw seafood baking in the late afternoon heat could not ruin the experience for her. The open air stands along the Dominican and Haitian border – populated with dozens of merchants peddling all manner of foods, household goods and various items of clothing – were a fascinating sample of a uniquely different world. When she stopped and gazed toward the outskirts of the town of Anse-a-Pitres, Haiti, tears of joy filled her eyes. It was hard to believe for the first time in twelve years she was standing within walking distance of a Haitian village.

Jake stepped up beside her. "Every time I come back to Pedernales it feels in some ways as if I never left."

"Is it much the same now as it was when you and Katie first arrived?" she asked.

"The town of Pedernales hasn't changed much, but the border looks noticeably different." He pointed toward a tall chain link fence. "That fence, for example," he said. "When we first moved here, there was nothing but a knee-high chain, and Haitians freely circulated back and forth to work in Pedernales. Now Dominican military makes regular round-ups and if they find any illegal Haitians on Dominican soil, they transport them back across the border."

"I remember reading somewhere that tension between the two countries is common," Hanna said.

"Unfortunately, that's true. Different languages, cultures, backgrounds – Problems between the Dominican Republic and Haiti historically go back two or three centuries. Although economically both countries fall somewhere near the bottom, Haitians are often viewed with distain by many Dominicans."

"Do you think living in Pedernales is harder than in Paraíso?"

"In some ways. Mostly because it's a long, hard drive to a city of any size or significance . . . But most of my memories of living here are good." Jake looked at Conner. "Do you remember those first few years in the country?"

Conner's laugh sounded more like a *humph*. "Do I ever. There were times I wasn't sure we were going to make it."

Jake's eyes appeared to register a memory. "Those *were* some faith building days. At first Katie and I were encouraged because the people were friendly and seemed to accept us, but it didn't take long to discover they were more interested in being friends with Americans than in having a personal relationship with Jesus Christ. It didn't make sense to us, but everyone seemed satisfied with their halfhearted version of Catholicism, which many combined with what appeared to us to be rather bizarre religious practices. Most didn't see any reason to change. We later learned people often refer to this fusion of beliefs as vudu dominicana."

Hanna watched a group of Haitian women, their heads covered in wide brimmed straw hats or wrapped in brightly colored turbans, selling their wares only a few yards from where they were standing. "What is vudu dominicana?" she asked, drawing closer to Jake's side as the throng of merchants and shoppers pressing in from all directions sent a sudden surge of uneasiness threw her veins.

"Voodoo – or as the Haitians call it – Vodou. It's a type of spirit worship that was introduced into the country by African slaves," he responded, apparently not bothered by the claustrophobic surroundings. "What is seen today is a mixture of African religious beliefs and ceremonies, with residual rituals taken from Catholicism and Taíno worship. Many Catholic Dominicans practice some form of voodoo, but it's worse in Haiti where it seems they have their own distinct blend of the religion."

Hanna took a deep breath, and then wished she hadn't. Large metal bowls filled with the entails of some kind of animal sat only a few feet away, spoiling in the hot sun. The pungent smell accosted her before she realized what had happened. "I guess that's one of the reasons the spiritual darkness on this island seems so thick," she replied, hoping her voice didn't sound as unsettled as her stomach felt.

"Most definitely. Back in the States there are those who may question whether demons really exist, but you don't have to be here very long before you realize they're real."

"How long were you here before you had any kind of breakthrough in terms of sharing your faith?"

Jake turned his back to the market. "Why don't we head to the van," he said.

Hanna wondered if he hadn't heard her or was avoiding the question altogether. She matched his stride as they walked away from the crowded stalls, thankful for the reprieve. Conner followed only a few steps behind.

"It was about two years," Jake said seconds later. Hanna kept her eyes focused on the ground as he continued talking. "I'll never forget how excited we were the night we held the first Bible study in our home. When we finally baptized a couple of people, we were thankful we had hung in there. Knowing lives had been changed for eternity made it worth all we'd had to go through. After a couple of years, we had a small group of young believers that met in our home for Bible study, much like the group that's meeting at Conner and Maleah's."

"What happened to them when you left?"

The corners of Jake's mouth slowly lifted. "Praise the Lord, they kept meeting. In fact, that's the reason we've started periodically making these trips. The group has grown. There are about twenty-five or thirty men, women and children who meet on a regular basis. A young Dominican I had the honor of leading to Christ and then discipling, serves as their pastor. We'll be attending a Bible study at his house tomorrow night."

Jake puckered his lips as he raised his chin, jutting it forward, pointing toward the border Dominican style. "There's also a small Haitian congregation in Anse-a-Pitres we try to visit and encourage. Their pastor is the father of a young woman who worked for Katie and me. She was a great help, especially after Isabela came along. She loved Isabela and Isabela loved her. I think when we had to leave so suddenly, her heart was doubly broken . . . " His voice caught as he continued. "I know it was hard on her losing Katie and Isabela at the same time. I hope we'll get to see her while we're here."

~~~~~

"You guys hungry?" Jake asked on the way back to the hotel. "I know a place that serves fresh fish and conch. Anybody interested?"

"Sounds good to me," Conner said. "How about it, Hanna?"

"Do they get their seafood from the Haitian market?" she asked.

A look of puzzlement skirted across Jake's face. "What?"

"Most of what we saw at the market smelled a bit . . . rancid," she replied, wrinkling her nose. "I was just wondering where this restaurant you're talking about gets their fish and conch."

"The smell got to you, huh?"

"Well, yeah . . . a little," she said, hoping Jake didn't see her admission of the truth as another weakness to use against her.

Jake looked at Conner, and then glanced at Hanna, a smirk clearly visible on his tanned face. "Not to worry, this restaurant buys their seafood right off the boats. It's fresh."

"Oh. Hey listen, I'm sorry," Hanna said. "I'm really not trying to be difficult."

Conner shifted in his seat, peering at her over his shoulder.

"Hanna, it's okay. We wouldn't eat seafood bought at the market either."

Jake fell out laughing. "Not unless we had a death wish."

The restaurant turned out to be another unique sampling of the local culture, with meals served under a large bohío – a circular thatched-roof hut similar to the ones the Taínos would have used. Ceiling fans dispersed the aroma of seafood simmering in a union of familiar spices and seasonings. The "chef's special" was fish or lambí (conch) served three ways: ajillo – in garlic sauce, criolla – in tomato sauce, or vinagre – in vinegar. Hanna chose ajillo and was thankful Jake did too since it meant her garlic breath would be canceled out by his. Lively music, a distinct mix of Latin and Caribbean flavor, added character to the overall eating experience. Several times during the meal Hanna found herself either swaying to the beat or tapping her foot on the concrete floor.

"So what are the plans for tomorrow?" Conner asked after swallowing his last bite of lambí criolla.

Jake pushed his empty plate aside, propped an elbow on the table and rested his darkly stubbled chin in his hand. "I thought we would eat breakfast at the hotel, and then go across the border to check on Pastor Hennrick." He looked at Hanna. "We'll have to park the van and walk, so you'll probably want to wear tennis shoes. Also, don't forget to bring your passport along with some other personal identification, like your driver's license."

"Okay . . . " Hanna drummed her fingers on the arm of her chair. "Just curious, is getting across the border difficult?"

"No, not really, especially since most of the border guards know me. Foreigners don't often use this crossing, but I've made enough trips back and forth I generally don't encounter any problems. The most important thing is remembering to head back before the border closes, otherwise you may end up spending the night in Anse-a-Pitres, which you really wouldn't want to do. But we're only going over for a couple of hours and will be back long before the gate is locked for the night." Jake released his chin and placed his hand on top of hers. She caught herself before she flinched. "Nothing to worry about," he said. "The exit and entrance taxes you have to pay are the worst part about crossing the border."

Hanna nodded and smiled. She didn't dare try to speak. She only hoped the shock wave coursing through her body did not show on her face. When he squeezed her hand before letting go, she realized she was fighting a losing battle. The heat rose from her neck to her cheeks – he'd have to be blind not to notice.

Conner pushed his chair back and stood. "I suggest we head to the hotel. I don't know about the two of you, but I'm rather tired. All this talk about the walking we're going to do tomorrow has only made it worse."

"I agree," Jake said, placing both hands on the table and pushing his tall lanky body to a standing position.

When Hanna stood, Jake stepped back and, with the sweep of his hand, motioned for her to go ahead of him. As she followed Conner, she felt Jake lightly place his hand on the small of her back. Once outside the restaurant, he fell in stride beside her.

"I'm really glad you came with us," he said. "You've been a bright spot in our trip." He cocked his head toward Conner. "Ole Conner there isn't much to look at."

"That's all a matter of opinion," Conner said, flashing them a toothy grin. "It just so happens Maleah thinks I'm rather nice to look at."

Jake gave him a friendly shove. "She's in love with you. And you know what they say – *love is blind*. Since I'm not blinded by my love for you, why don't you let Hanna ride up front on the way back to the hotel?"

"Works for me," Conner said, winking at Hanna.

Jake hurried over to open the door for her. When he offered to help her up, she placed her hand in his. His long fingers encircled hers. By the time he closed the door, she could feel her heart thumping erratically in her chest.

Back at the hotel, Conner said goodnight, leaving Hanna and Jake alone. As they approached the door to her room, she pulled the key out of a pocket in her skirt. Jake took it from her, his fingers lingering for a moment on the palm of her hand. His smile was as warm as his touch. He opened the door and stuck his head inside. "I know it's a bit rough, but it's one of the best deals in Pedernales. At least there's a ceiling fan, which hopefully will provide a little relief from the heat . . . unless – "

"The electricity goes off," Hanna said. "Does this place have a generator?"

"Probably, but my guess is they only use it when absolutely necessary. The good news is Pedernales doesn't experience power outages as frequently as the rest of the country."

She stepped inside, surveying the room. "Any chance I'll have critters sharing my room with me?" she asked.

He leaned against the doorframe and laughed. "Hopefully only a lizard or two. They're pretty harmless."

"That depends," she said. "The small reptiles we call lizards in Alabama – yeah, but some of the ones I've seen around here could cart you off in the night."

"Unless one of the big ones slipped by while we've been standing here talking, the only lizards you might find would be of the smaller variety. But if it would help you rest easier, I'll do a room check for you."

Hanna knew her fears probably seemed silly to Jake. She suspected Katie had not been afraid of the local wildlife. Even so, she would most likely sleep better if he looked around. "I know you must think I'm acting like a little kid, afraid there's a monster in the closet . . . But if you don't mind, I would appreciate it."

"No problem," he said, stepping inside.

Hanna stood beside the door while Jake checked the bathroom, a space reserved for luggage, around and under the bed, dresser and a small desk. The room reminded her of one the individual units that made up what people in the States often referred to as motor inns. Although most of them had either deteriorated with age or been destroyed by hurricanes, a scattering could still be found along the Alabama coast and Florida panhandle.

"Nothing. Guess you're safe for the night," Jake said as he walked back toward her with his hands held out, palms up.

"Thank you."

He stopped and leaned to within a couple of inches of her face. "No problema."

By the time he backed away, Hanna's heart was pounding so hard she could barely breathe.

Stepping through the threshold, he glanced back at her. "By the way, don't let the bedbugs bite." He reached behind him and pulled the door closed.

Chapter Nineteen

Hanna shifted from one foot to the other as she watched Jake and Conner walk toward where she waited for them at the hotel gazebo the following morning. The palms of her hands felt sweaty, and her throat dry. The change in Jake's attitude and actions the previous day had far surpassed anything she could have hoped for. But it was a new day.

"Good morning," Conner said, his smile bright and cheery. "How'd you sleep?"

"Not too bad, considering – "

"We didn't have power half the night," Jake finished for her, a noticeable glint in his eyes. "It did get a little warm, didn't it?"

"It was uncomfortable for a while," Hanna admitted, "but I was pretty tired, so I managed to get some sleep." The scent of Jake's cologne was slightly intoxicating. If it had been anyone else, she would have said he was standing close enough to invade her personal space. But under the circumstances, she wasn't complaining.

He leaned in even closer, a hint of mischief now dancing in his eyes. "No boogie men, bed bugs or critters to bother you?"

A tingling sensation fluttered through Hanna's veins. "No. Thanks to you, as far as I know, I had no company last night."

Conner shook his head, but Hanna could tell he approved. "Enough talk about ghoulies and ghosties and long legged beasties and things that go bump in the night," he said. "Let's get some breakfast, then head for the border."

Hanna and Jake exchanged bewildered looks as they

followed him to a table.

~~~~~

Hanna walked between Jake and Conner on the sun-baked road to Anse-a-Pitres, watching the little puffs of dirt that rose with every step they took. Whenever a motorcycle putted past, the dust swirled around them, coating their sweaty arms and faces with a thin layer of grime. By the time they reached the outskirts of town, her throat was parched and sand crunched between her teeth. The sun steadily ascended at their backs, beating down with such intensity she was afraid to think what it was going to be like when they returned to Pedernales a couple of hours later. Even so, she was overwhelmed with emotion. She'd dreamed of this day for twelve years. It was hard to believe she was actually back in Haiti. Although ravaged by poverty, the country still held a fascination Hanna could not shake.

"Do you know what Haiti was once called by the French?" Jake asked as they walked past a flimsy shack made of corrugated tin and palm branches.

Hanna shook her head. "No. What?"

"Le Perle des Antilles."

When she dipped her chin, eyeing him with a stern squint, he reached over and gently jerked her ponytail. Was he flirting with her? The new Jake had her baffled. She never would have imagined the man she'd known up until a couple of days ago could be so charming, even if he did have sweat trickling down the sides of his face, leaving streaks in the dusty film.

"What's the matter? Don't you speak French?" he asked.

She rolled her eyes. "I'm still working on Spanish, I'll tackle French some other time. In the meanwhile, would you mind speaking English? That is, if it wouldn't be too much trouble."

"If you insist," he said with an exaggerated huff. "In plain English, the early French explorers . . . " He stopped and grinned at her. "You do realize they wouldn't have spoken English, don't you?"

"I should slap you," she said, glaring at him.

He raised his hand as if to protect his face. "A bit testy, aren't we?"

"Hot and sweaty too." She willed herself not to smile.

"I see. Well . . . *if* they had spoken English, they would have called this part of the island *The Pearl of the Caribbean.*"

Hanna studied the deplorable shanties lining the rut-riddled, dirt packed street on which they were walking. "You're kidding. Why?"

Jake's eyes followed the same path as hers. "Haiti's landscape was once vastly different from what it is today," he said. "I've heard that when the *French-speaking* explorers first arrived," he glanced at her and smiled, "the island was covered with fruit bearing trees and the forests were full of mahogany. Over the years France became wealthy off the sugar and coffee produced here. Supposedly there was a time when Haiti was considered the most valuable colony in the world."

She swept the area with her eyes. "What happened?"

His expression grew solemn. "She's been ravaged by the selfishness and greed of man, who stole all her natural resources, then like a discarded lover left her wounded and bleeding while they moved on to more youthful and fertile lands."

Hanna maintained a straight face, but could feel one corner of her lip twitching in amusement. "*What* was that all about?" she asked.

Conner leaned his head back and laughed. "Treasure this moment. The man doesn't wax poetic often."

"Oh, but it's nice to know I can when circumstances call for it." A smile swept across Jake's face, sending goose bumps up Hanna's spine. "You have to admit my description of what happened was right on target," he said.

"You're right," Hanna said as she glanced around. In a matter of seconds the stark reality surrounding them settled upon her shoulders like a heavy, cumbersome burden. It was easy to understand why Jake called Anse-a-Pitres a forgotten no-man's land in the southeast corner of Haiti. Taking in the sights and sounds of the small rural village, she quickly realized she was not adequately prepared for the sensory overload that confronted her.

Weatherworn people dressed in tattered clothes filled the dirt streets. Those who wore shoes had on ratty flip-flops, sandals or tennis shoes with no shoelaces. Many of the houses were poorly constructed one room hovels made of everything from pieces of wood haphazardly fitted together to cardboard, rags, straw or banana leaves, while others were of cement block or rough-hewn clapboard with corrugated tin roofs, reminding Hanna of the houses she'd seen as a sixteen year old traveling a cobblestone trail up the mountain to the Citadel near Milot, Haiti. A couple of chickens pecked in the dirt in front of warped plywood house to their right while a goat wandered aimlessly ahead of them. Women, many with their heads wrapped in brightly colored turbans, sat on squatty chairs, tending cook fires. How they could stand the additional heat, Hanna could not imagine. They passed a group of children playing with a pig in a muddy ditch, which she feared was actually a cesspool of human waste; the scene once again reminiscent of her visit to Haiti twelve years earlier. There was a smell so foul she prayed for the grace to keep her breakfast from coming back up. Burning mounds of trash filled the air, already so hot it was suffocating, with a smoky acrid haze.

Jake's deep voice penetrated her thoughts. "You okay?" he asked, slipping a damp gritty hand in hers. If she hadn't been okay before, she certainly wasn't now.

She swallowed hard, hoping to settle her stomach. "I guess I wasn't prepared for how bad it was going to be."

His grip tightened. "Do we need to go back to Pedernales?"

She blew out her breath. "Oh no, no . . . I want to be here. I want to do this. I'll be okay."

"Don't feel bad," Conner said. "My stomach does flip-flops every time we come here. The seeing is bad enough, but the smells can about do you in."

"This may be a stupid question," she said, trying hard not to let the distaste she was feeling show on her face, "but . . . what *is* that smell?"

"You sure you want to know?" Jake asked.

"I think so." She hoped she wouldn't be sorry.

He looked around. "The worst of it is raw sewage. Then, there's the garbage, which sits for weeks rotting in the heat before being burned. The outcome – the nauseating smell being emitted by these smoldering mounds. They do the best they can, but with no running water, sewage system, electricity or place to dump their garbage . . . Well, you get the picture."

"All too vividly. Is it always this dry?"

"This part of the country is for the most part arid. *Although*, in a matter of weeks as tropical storms begin building up in the Atlantic, there's always the possibility the area will be hit with torrential rain. When that happens, it's not unusual to find pools of stagnant water – breeding grounds for mosquitoes and the diseases they carry – like malaria and dengue fever. With little access to medical help, there are times when the situation becomes critical. That was what had happened when Katie and I brought the medical team over just before she got sick . . ."

Tears glistened in Jake's eyes as a fragile silence hovered between them.

"Sorry," he said seconds later, his voice thick with emotion. "It's getting better, but sometimes the memories are still painful."

Hanna squeezed his hand. "It's okay. I can't imagine what you've been through."

Conner must have noticed the awkwardness of the moment because he moved in a little closer. Hanna was thankful for his discernment. "Katie loved these people," he said. "You would be surprised how many in this little town knew her. Because of her witness for Christ, I'm sure she lives on in the lives of many in Anse-a-Pitres."

Hanna caught sight of a young man walking in their direction. His coal black eyes were fixed on Jake, and his smile, pearly white in a deep mahogany face, reached from ear to ear. Although his pants and shirt were faded and threadbare, he carried himself with a humble dignity.

After conversing with the man for several minutes in Creole, Jake switched to Spanish and introduced him to Hanna as a member of Pastor Hennrick's church.

"Is it common for people around here to speak Spanish?" Hanna asked as the young man walked away.

"Many do," Jake answered, "especially those who do business at the Haitian market. You can be assured for the most part

Dominicans are not going to lower themselves and speak Creole, so it's not unusual to find Haitians who have acquired at least a working knowledge of Spanish. When you realize so few can read or write, and yet they speak Creole and Spanish and sometimes French, it's rather amazing. "

"Really helps boost my ego," Hanna said.

"Yeah," Jake said, "seems like God is always looking for ways to help keep me humble. He frequently uses these trips to Anse-a-Pitres to remind me of how often I'm guilty of grumbling or complaining about the littlest things, when in reality I'm blessed beyond comparison."

"Like the power outages we have to put up with," Conner interjected. "If the people of Anse-a-Pitres had what we have, they would consider themselves blessed."

"It's impossible for me to comprehend living totally without electricity," Hanna said, glancing around at the crowded street. "How many people live here?"

Conner looked at Jake and shrugged. "I'm not sure exactly,"

"Seems like someone once told me it's around 20,000," Jake answered.

A sea of people crowded the dirt street on which they walked. Hanna thought perhaps all 20,000 inhabitants had somehow managed to congregate in that one location. "Besides the Haitian market, what do these people do for a living?" she asked.

"Many of the men are fishermen," Jake said, "but with outdated boats and equipment they don't make much of a living. There was a time when it was easier for them to get across the border, and some found work in Pedernales, like Bijou – Pastor's Hennrick's daughter, who worked for us."

"Does she still live in Pedernales?" Hanna asked.

"No. She moved back home with her family when we left. That's where we're headed now. Conner and I wanted to check with her father and see how things are going with the church here."

~~~~~

A couple of hours later, Hanna juggled mixed emotions

when they crossed the border onto Dominican soil. Exhausted physically, her energy sapped by the relentless heat of the sun, she was more than ready to sit under a fan with a refreshing bottle of water. Running a hand over one of her arms, she felt several layers of sweaty dirt. No doubt she stunk, but she knew Jake and Conner couldn't smell any better. A cold shower sounded inviting. Emotionally, she felt like a tightly strung guitar. Her senses were on overload. It would probably take several days to process all she had seen and heard. A part of her already wanted to go back; another part was afraid she might spend months recovering.

Pastor Hennrick and his wife had been delightful. Jake had told her the Haitian woman's given name was Chante, but that culturally, married women were known by their husband's first name – thus Pastor Hennrick's wife was introduced to her as Madame Hennrick. Bijou, the couple's oldest daughter who had worked for the Masons, was away visiting family in another town. Hanna could tell Jake was disappointed.

The hospitality the pastor and his wife offered had been sweeter than any Hanna had ever encountered. She and Madame Hennrick tried with little success to communicate, but even without the verbal interaction, as sisters in Christ – they bonded. Most of the conversation had been in Creole, although occasionally Jake translated into Spanish. When they got ready to leave, Madame Hennrick stood between them, taking Hanna's hand with her left and Jake's with her right. A look of motherly concern covered her charcoal face as she spoke first to Jake, and then kissed Hanna on the right cheek while whispering something in Creole. Hanna didn't know what had been said, but was touched by the kind gesture.

As they had walked down the dusty road toward the border, Jake and Conner had talked enthusiastically about the promise they made Pastor Hennrick to return in three or four months in order to hold a weeklong seminar for a group of people in the church who wanted some in depth biblical training. Since only a few could read, most of the teaching would be done using a method of Bible study called Chronological Bible Storying, which, as Jake had explained to Hanna, presents the Bible as oral literature in a narrative format that is easier for people who are illiterate to understand.

While they talked, Hanna entertained the possibility she might be allowed to come back with them. Maybe she could work with the children. Perhaps Isabela could come too and serve as her translator. Surely the idea wasn't completely inconceivable. She would pray about it for a while and, if she felt led, ask Maleah her opinion before broaching the subject with Jake. But for now, she wasn't ready to make herself that vulnerable with him. His attitude toward her so far had been significantly better; she didn't want to change the mood of the trip by asking something he might think ridiculous.

Chapter Twenty

That evening Jake suggested they stop by another local restaurant for dinner before going to the home of Pastor Jeremías for Bible study. Hanna ordered what she already knew to be a Dominican staple: rice, beans, chicken and tostones. As far as Dominican food goes, it wasn't too bad.

Fearful of finding herself in a situation where her language skills might fail her, Hanna battled anxiety as Jake drove them to the young pastor's house. Although she had made tremendous progress, she knew her ability to speak the language still would not be considered fluent. Her stomach churned as memories of Jake's critical attitude evoked feelings of intimidation. She wrapped her arms tightly around her waist and prayed he couldn't hear the gurgling symphony.

Once at Pastor Jeremías' home, she discovered her fears had been unfounded. The members of the Pedernales church were lovingly patient when her language skills faltered. Several even found great delight in practicing their English with her. For the most part, Jake was too busy getting caught up to notice how well she was or was not doing. On occasion he caught her eye from across the room and flashed her an amiable smile. Each time, the gesture caused mild warmth to ripple across her cheeks.

They traveled back to the hotel on darkened streets still swarming with people. Most doors to the houses they passed were open, and often the occupants sat out front – many of them playing dominoes. The colmados appeared to be favorite gathering spots; the doorways blocked by at least two or three men downing bottles of beer while engaged in loud, animated conversation. The scene reminded Hanna of Paraíso.

As soon as Jake stopped the van in front of their cozy motor inn, Conner slid the side door open and jumped out. "I don't mean to be rude," he said, "but I don't feel well. See y'all in the morning."

Jake turned to Hanna as he pulled the key out of the ignition. "Sounds like Montezuma's revenge to me. Hope neither one of us gets it."

"Do you think it's as bad as that?" she asked as she placed her hand on her stomach, hoping it was only the power of suggestion causing it to rumble.

Jake grinned and opened his door. "Probably not. Conner has to be careful what he eats. I'm sure something didn't agree with him." He pointed toward the gazebo. "Would you like to sit and talk a while?"

"Sure." The rumbling in her stomach switched to fluttering.

As they settled at one of the tables under the lighted thatched roof pavilion, a gust of wind blew across Hanna's face. She lifted her ponytail, allowing the refreshing breeze to cool the back of her neck. Out of the corner of her eye she could see Jake studying her, his elbows resting on the arms of the chair and his hands tented.

"What do you think of Pedernales and Anse-a-Pitres?" he asked.

"I'm really glad you let me tag along," she said. "I'm sure living here is not easy, but I can see where the work would be extremely rewarding."

He lifted his right foot and placed it on the knee of his left leg. "Really?" he said with a smile. "I wasn't sure you'd get it."

"Get what?"

"I wasn't sure you would understand why I like this part of the country so much." He tapped his fingertips together in a rhythmic beat. "You're right – living here is hard, possibly harder than anywhere else in the Dominican Republic, but something about the place still tugs on my heart."

Hanna wondered why he cared one way or another whether she would *get it*. "I guess if that's what you mean, I do get it," she replied. "I've definitely felt that pull on my own heart." She lifted her face to welcome another breeze. "Would you mind telling me a little about what it was like when you and Katie lived here?"

A shadow fell across Jake's face and his eyes clouded. Hanna feared she'd gone too far. But just as quickly as the gray fog had fallen, it lifted. His grave expression softened into a smile. "It was not a whole lot different than what you've seen the last couple of days," he said. "It's hard to believe that when we arrived we were two twenty-eight year olds who up until a year earlier had never lived more than a few hours from where we grew up. We didn't have a clue what we were doing." His eyes rested on Hanna. "Thinking back on those early days, I know it had to have been God who called us – Otherwise I doubt we'd have made it more than a few months. Our faith in His calling was what kept us going."

Hanna shifted in her chair. "I can certainly relate there," she said, "but I can't imagine coming straight from language school – just the two of you – to what you have referred to as the back side of no-where."

"Katie often called it the jumping off place," he said, gazing off into the darkness. "I suppose our greatest blessing was that we both had a decent command of the language. As for Katie, she was one of those people who never met a stranger. Although the work in terms of starting a church was slow, in a relatively short period of time we had at least begun making friends."

"How long had you been living here when you met Pastor Hennrick?"

"Oh, let's see . . . " His eyes narrowed in thought as he lifted his chin. "About six months. We decided to hire Bijou when Katie was three or four months pregnant with Isabela. The heat and humidity had begun to slow her down. Having a maid seemed foreign to us, but once we realized we'd be providing a job for a young woman who desperately needed one, we felt at peace about the decision."

"I've wondered about that too," Hanna said. "In the States, having a fulltime maid is a luxury, but here it seems to be rather common. Maleah told me much the same thing as you just shared. Did Bijou live with you?"

"She did. Although it was easier in those days to get back

and forth across the border, Haitians who lived in Anse-a-Pitres and worked in Pedernales were often harassed. She was only seventeen when she started working for us, but we immediately realized we shared a kindred spirit, which in time – once we muddled our way through the language barrier – we discovered was our faith in God. "

Hanna leaned forward and placed her elbows on the table, cradling her chin in her hands. "So her dad was already a pastor?"

Jake nodded. "His family is from Thiotte, a town a couple of hours north of Anse-a-Pitres. That's where Bijou is now. At one time there was a missionary couple living there, and Pastor Hennrick's family all came to Christ through their ministry. The man discipled Hennrick and helped train him as a pastor. Later Pastor Hennrick and his family moved to Anse-a-Pitres for the sole purpose of starting a church."

"What an awesome story. Where is this missionary couple now?"

"They returned to the States several months before Hennrick and Chante moved to Anse-a-Pitres. That's one reason we formed such a close friendship. They missed their missionary friends and we were able to help fill the void. Of course, the relationship has worked both ways. They were such a blessing to Katie and me during the time we lived here." His eyes drifted once again toward the darkness beyond the gazebo. Off in the distance a radio blared some rendition of Latin music.

"Did you and Katie grow up together?"

When Jake spoke, his words were slow and deliberate. "No, we met in college." His eyes rested on Hanna. "We both grew up in small towns near Wichita. Katie attended a junior college her freshman year and then transferred to Friends University, where I was a student, our sophomore year. We met in late October while attending a meeting for students interested in participating in a mission trip to Mexico over the Christmas holidays. I walked her back to her dorm that night." He shrugged. "And . . . I guess the rest is history."

"History for you, but not me. What happened?"

A perplexed look flitted across his face. "You sure you want to hear all this?"

"I wouldn't have asked if I hadn't wanted to know."

He stretched his long legs out in front, leaned his head back and stared at the top of the gazebo. "Let's see . . . I asked her out that night, and neither one of us dated anyone else after that. By the time we got back from the mission trip that Christmas we knew we were supposed to be together. We got married the summer between our junior and senior years in college." He looked at her. "You're *really* sure you want to hear all this?"

She smiled and nodded.

"Well, okay . . ." he said, rubbing his hand across the stubble of his five o'clock shadow. "After graduation we moved to Kansas City, where I attended seminary and Katie taught tenth grade English. When I finished seminary, we moved to Hays, Kansas, where I served as pastor of a small church until we were appointed as missionaries. Like you, we went to Costa Rica for a year of language school before coming to the Dominican Republic. Isabella was born a little over a year after we arrived in Pedernales. When she was a year old we returned to the States for a six-month furlough. We had been back in the DR a year and a half when Katie got sick . . ."

He stared at the table, not saying anything else. His expression gave no hint of what he was thinking.

Hanna brushed imaginary crumbs off her dress, trying to decide what to say next. "I guess trips like this bring back a lot of memories," she finally said.

"They do," he said, sitting up straighter, "but I was just thinking . . . this has been the first trip I've made since Katie died when the memories have been more sweet than sad. It's been good." A smile lifted the corners of his mouth as he hit the arm of his chair with the palm of his hand. "Guess you and I need to get to bed," he said. "We're heading out early in the morning."

Hanna stood, placed her hands in the small of her back and stretched. "I am a bit tired now that you mention it. We did a lot of walking today." She turned toward him.

"That we did, and if we can make it a few steps farther," he slipped his hand in hers, "I'll walk you to your door."

As they stood in front of Hanna's room, Jake reached out as he'd done the night before and took the key from her hand. Once the door was opened, he motioned for her to step inside, then stood in the doorway inspecting the room. "I don't see any boogie men," he said. "Think you'll be okay?"

She tried to keep a straight face, but laughed instead. "I'm sure I will be."

"In that case . . . " he stepped toward her, "I will say goodnight."

He was invading her personal space again. As his eyes tenderly examined her face, she thought he might kiss her. When he lifted a hand and pushed a stray strand of hair behind her ear, she drew in her breath.

"It's okay. I don't bite," he said with a grin. "I just wanted to say thanks."

"For what?" she asked, her voice barely a whisper.

"Oh, for listening. For caring. For being you . . . " He turned and walked out the door. "By the way . . . " He glanced at her over his shoulder. "Madame Hennrick really likes you. She told me I'd better not let you get away." He pulled the door closed behind him.

Caribbean Paradise

Chapter Twenty-One

On the trip back to Paraíso Hanna accepted Conner's offer to let her sit up front, partly because she wanted to, and partly because Jake insisted. She was astonished at the difference three days had made. Obviously God had been working in Jake's heart before they left on Monday for Pedernales; even so, she would never have dreamed his attitude toward her could take such a drastic turn for the better in such a short period of time.

From the beginning, when Jake met her at the airport, it had been apparent he knew how to be a gentleman. Yet until three days ago, the man she'd known had for the most part been somber and moody. Discovering he was capable of being not only polite, but also charming, had been an unexpected delight. Hanna couldn't wait to get home and tell Maleah she'd finally met the real Jake Mason. But before she could say a word, Maleah pounced upon them with her own good news. The mission board had approved the request for a volunteer team, and one was due to arrive in a little over three weeks. The group's original project in Mexico had been cancelled at the last minute, which meant they were available and ready, but with no place to go. The Paraíso request was a perfect match.

Early the following day, Jake and Isabela left to take Katie's mother to the airport in Santo Domingo. She would be flying home later that afternoon. Hanna grabbed a few minutes to share with Susan about the trip to the border and how differently Jake had treated her. The woman seemed genuinely pleased and promised to keep in touch.

Over the next three weeks, Hanna discovered preparing for the arrival of a volunteer team was in itself a lot of work. There were trips to Barahona to buy supplies that could not be found in Paraíso; followed by the compilation of a list of materials that could not be found in Barahona that would need to be purchased in Santo Domingo when Conner and Jake went to pick the group up at the airport. Sleeping arrangements needed to be made, dividing the eight team members evenly between the Andersons' home and Jake and Isabela's. Daily menus, which involved providing not only three meals a day, but also mid-morning and afternoon snacks, had to be planned, and the necessary food items found and purchased.

Although Hanna enjoyed seeing Jake on a daily basis, as he was often in and out of the Andersons' home as they prepared for the team's arrival, the sudden flurry of activity did not allow much opportunity for them to spend in one-on-one interactions. The evening before the group was due to arrive, she was sitting in one of the rocking chairs on the front porch when he stopped by to pick up Isabela. He had spent the day making last minute preparations with Conner at the worksite and would be leaving early the next morning for Santo Domingo. Hanna had been working alongside Maleah, Celia and Rosalinda since eight o'clock that morning getting the two houses ready for the arrival of their guests. The following day would be spent in food preparation, cooking ahead of time that which could be frozen and reheated later. It promised to be a hot, sweltering day.

She felt her heart flutter as she watched Jake walking up the driveway wearing a pair of faded, worn blue jeans with frayed holes in the knees and a dirty white T-shirt. She wondered if the sight of him would always take her breath away. He stepped onto the porch and leaned against a nearby post. The masculine scent of sweat and sun-baked skin permeated her senses as the warmth in his blue eyes greeted her affectionately. Hanna sensed the look conveyed something more than friendship. She hoped so because as hard as she had tried to fight it, she feared she was falling in love.

"A little muggy tonight, isn't it?" he said.

"A little," she agreed, thankful her voice did not quiver when she spoke. "I came out here hoping there might be a breeze. The main house feels like a sauna. My apartment is even worse." She lifted her eyes upward. "Of course, I'm not sure this is much better. That ceiling fan feels like a hair dryer set on high."

"Yeah, while Conner and I were working today I was wondering what kind of effect this heat was going to have on the volunteer team," he said as he eased his lanky body into the chair next to Hanna's. "We'll need to be sure they're drinking plenty of water. I'd hate for someone to get dehydrated."

She drew her feet up to the cross bar of the rocking chair and laced her fingers around her knees. "At least they'll be able to tell the folks back home how bad it was suffering for Jesus on a Caribbean island," she said.

He threw his head back and laughed. "It can be both comical and exasperating watching the raised eyebrows you get when you tell people where you're serving. I don't know how many times I've heard: *I'm sure it's got to be hard living in the Caribbean, but I guess somebody's got to do it.*" He stretched his legs out and crossed his ankles. "If they only knew."

"Probably most of the people who think that way wouldn't make it more than a day or two before deciding they weren't the right *somebody*."

Jake's smile faded, and a flicker of concern dimmed his eyes. "I know living here isn't easy," he said, "but I hope you've decided you *are* one of those somebodies."

"I think so," Hanna said, her eyes meeting his. "I have to admit the last four and a half months have been a much greater challenge than I ever thought they would be. But I'm thankful to be here and I think I'll stay."

"Good. I like having you around."

"Thanks."

He placed both hands on the arms of the rocking chair and pushed himself up. "Guess I need to get Isabela and head to the house. Conner and I will be leaving at six o'clock tomorrow morning. It's going to be a long day."

"I suppose I'll venture back into the sauna," she said.

He held out his hand and pulled her up, then slipped his arm around her waist, drawing her to his side.

She returned the hug. "I know you'll be tired by the time you get back tomorrow night."

"I'm sure we will be," he replied as he placed his hand in the small of her back and guided her toward the front door.

After stepping through the threshold, Hanna stopped, turning to look at him. "Guess I'll see you tomorrow evening."

He touched the side of her face with his fingertips. "Yeah, see you when we get back."

"Daddy, Daddy," Isabela cried as she bounded around the corner.

"Hi sweetheart," Jake said as he swung the child up in his arms and gave her a squeeze.

Hanna placed her hand on the cheek he had caressed and quietly slipped away.

~~~~~

Jake leaned against the metal guardrail outside of customs. He could feel sweat beading across his forehead and forming rivulets down his spine. Typical of late summer afternoons in Santo Domingo, the muggy air was oppressive, even hotter than it had been the evening he and Isabela waited in the same spot for Hanna to arrive. While Conner watched for the volunteer team, Jake reflected on that night almost five months earlier.

Although he had not wanted to admit it, he'd been attracted to Hanna from the moment he first saw her frantically searching the crowd with those darkly fringed, forest green eyes. Without an adequate command of the language, no wonder she'd been in a state of panic. The memory brought a smile to his face. Now he could laugh about it, but back then he was looking for any excuse not to like her.

He was grateful Conner forced his hand in making the decision to take her with them on the trip to Pedernales and the Haitian border. For the first time since Katie's death, he'd been able to see that area of the country with different eyes. Instead of painful memories, he'd envisioned the possibilities he once dreamed for the work there. He knew sharing the experience with Hanna significantly affected his overall attitude. Even so, he still struggled with twinges of guilt, wondering if allowing himself to care for Hanna – even as a friend – was not in some way being unfaithful to Katie.

In recent weeks he'd asked himself the same questions over and over again: If he threw caution to the wind, allowing his feelings for Hanna to have free reign, what would ultimately happen to the love he had for Katie? Was it possible to hold on to a love you once had for someone who is now gone and also love someone else? And, what about Isabela? He fluctuated between not wanting the child to forget her mother and realizing for the most part her memories of Katie were sketchy at best. But what would happen if he allowed another woman to fill that void in her life? Would she forget what few memories she had of her mother? And yet, in reality, did he actually think he was going to be able to preserve that memory forever in Isabela's heart? He wanted to let go and see where the relationship with Hanna might take them, but –

Conner tugged on his arm, jolting him out of his thoughts. "I think that's them," he yelled over the rumble of voices, shouting taxi drivers and honking horns.

"Where?" Jake asked, his eyes searching the crowd of people exiting customs.

"There." He pointed toward a group of Americans making their way down the ramp on the opposite side from where they were standing.

Jake kept pace with Conner as they made a path through the throng of people still waiting for family and friends to walk through the double metal doors. When they reached the group of volunteers, the looks of panic on their faces reminded Jake of Hanna. Except one – a woman, conversing in Spanish with the men who had helped them out with their luggage. He couldn't remember when he'd heard an American speak the language so fluently. While Conner approached several of the male volunteers, Jake stood a few feet away, watching her. Confident – Poised – Self-assured. Something about her reminded him of someone, but whom?

Her movements were animated, gesturing with her hands as she talked, and periodically slinging her reddish-blond hair over her shoulders. Her eyes reminded him of emeralds, almost catlike. A scattering of freckles graced her nose and cheeks. Tall. Slender. Elegant. Dressed in a pair of white slacks, a dark yellow top and a pair of low heel sandals, she looked more like she'd just stepped out of the pages of a fashion magazine than off an airplane in the Dominican Republic. Her age was elusive – early thirties – a little older perhaps. He couldn't be sure.

As he studied her more closely, he was startled when he felt his heart do a flip-flop. Who *was* this woman? Surely he'd never met her before, but she looked so . . . familiar. Like someone . . . someone he'd known well. But who was she?

A few minutes later, the woman turned her attention from the Dominican men who stood waiting for instructions on where they needed to take the mound of luggage piled high on their carts and glanced first at Conner and then at Jake. She made eye contact, smiled, looked away, and then did a double take. Jake realized who she was about the same time it apparently registered with her who he was.

"Jake Mason . . . " she said.

"Shelby? Shelby Wilson. Land sakes! How long has it been?"

When the woman tilted her head back and smiled, delicate laugh lines crinkled the corners of her eyes. "I can't believe it," she said. "It really is you. How long *has it* been? Too long, I'd say. How have you been?" She looked around at the congested reception area and scrunched her nose. "And what are you doing here?"

"I'm a missionary," Jake answered. "I live here."

"I'm not surprised to hear that," the woman said, giving him a once over with her catlike eyes. "But . . . I'll have to say – you don't look much like any missionary I've ever met. You're still as handsome as you were back in high school."

He could feel the heat rising to his cheeks. Suddenly he felt like he *was* back in high school. The memories rolled over him like water flowing down a mountainside. Physically, his senses were set on edge. It took a few seconds for him to find his voice. "You haven't changed much yourself," he said. "In fact, I'd say the years have been good to you. You look great."

"You two know each other?" Conner asked, working his way toward them.

"Yeah," Jake answered. "We went to high school together."

He felt Shelby sidling up to him just before she hooked her arm through his. The scent of her perfume was alarmingly enticing. "He makes it all sound so innocent," she said, leaning toward Conner. "We didn't *just* go to high school together. We were sweethearts."

As she rubbed her free hand up and down his arm, Shelby's words landed on Jake's ears like a purring kitten, throwing his emotions into a tug of war. On one hand he loved the way it felt to have her arm in his. On the other hand, he wasn't sure he ought to be feeling this way at all – wasn't sure he *wanted* to feel this way. Her actions were a bit unsettling. What if he were married? What if his wife were standing off to the side watching? Shelby didn't seem to care. Shouldn't her unbridled flirtatious actions be a concern to him? Even though he knew he should be backing away, he felt himself leaning a little closer.

"Sweethearts. How about that," Conner said as he extended his hand in Shelby's direction. "I'm Conner Anderson. My wife Maleah and I work with Jake in Paraíso."

Shelby untangled her arm from Jake's and shook Conner's outstretched hand. "Shelby Wilson. Glad to meet you. Is your wife with you? What about your wife, Jake?" she asked, looking down at his left hand, where the gold of his wedding band glinted in the sunlight. Her look of disappointment reminded him of a pouty schoolgirl. He wasn't sure whether it pleased or bothered him. Man, he needed to get his act together – *and* soon!

Conner cleared his throat. "Uh . . . hum . . . no . . . Maleah is back at the house with the children. As for Jake's wife, I'll let him tell you on the way back to Paraíso. We need to get going. We have at least a five-hour drive ahead of us. Plenty of time to talk and get caught up."

Jake bristled when a disapproving scowl furrowed Conner's forehead. "What was that all about," he muttered under his breath he as they corralled team members and luggage toward the waiting vehicles. He looked at Shelby and smiled. He was a grown man. He didn't need Conner's input or approval.

Chapter Twenty-Two

After helping load the baggage into the trailer attached to the Andersons' jeep, Jake stepped away from the vehicle while Conner told the eight members of the volunteer team what to expect for the rest of the afternoon and evening. Shelby stayed close to Jake's side, frequently cutting her eyes at him. When he dared to look in her direction, a coy smile ruffled her lips. He jerked his attention back to Conner.

"It's three-thirty now," Conner said. "From here we will go to San Cristóbal, a town located on the other side of Santo Domingo. It's about an hour and a half to two-hour drive – depending on traffic. Since I'm pulling a trailer, we may have to take it a little slower than usual. We will stop there for supper . . . or dinner," he glanced at Jake and smiled, "whatever you call it. If you are hungry now, there are snacks in the van and jeep." He looked at Jake again. "Did I leave out anything?"

He shook his head. "I think you covered it."

"Anyone have any questions?" Conner asked, his eyes scanning the group.

The team members looked at each other, several shaking their heads.

Conner clapped his hands. "Okay then. Let's get on the road. I can take three in the jeep with me. Five of you can ride with Jake."

Shelby and four of the men followed Jake to his van. Shelby claimed the front passenger seat before anyone else had a chance. While she sat waiting, Jake spoke to each of the men, introducing himself as they climbed into the second and third seats through the sliding side door. He hoped he would be able to remember their names later.

Once in the driver's seat, he worked his way through traffic, following Conner as they began the long drive back to Paraíso. He could hear the four men talking quietly among themselves. Shelby sat next to him, her long legs crossed, acting as if she arrived in a hot, humid, foreign country on a regular basis. While Jake's sweaty shirt stuck to the vinyl upholstery, and perspiration clung to his upper lip, she looked as if she'd been relaxing in an air-conditioned lounge for the past hour. Trying to keep his eyes on the road, he couldn't help but notice once again how great she looked. Was it really possible the woman sitting across from him was thirty-four years old?

He turned onto the main highway, the Caribbean clearly in view on the driver's side of the van. In his peripheral vision he could see Shelby watching him. After several minutes of quiet observation, she spoke.

"So, Jake. Tell me about this wife of yours."

His appreciation of her beauty came to a screeching halt. He opened his mouth, but his thoughts were so filled with anger, he could not draw enough breath to speak. How could she ask about his wife so flippantly? He clenched his teeth; resisting the urge to say something he'd probably regret later. And then he realized she wasn't being disrespectful. She didn't know Katie was dead. As he tried to determine the best way to answer her question, he noticed her eyebrows were drawn together, her face conveying a look of bewilderment.

"You *are* married, aren't you?" she asked.

"Well, no . . . I'm a widower," he said, rapping the steering wheel with the heel of his hand. "My wife – Katie, died three years ago."

He wasn't sure how he would have described the expression on Shelby's face as his announcement registered with her. Probably it was a mixture of surprise and maybe a little sadness, but somewhere in the mix was relief, which she quickly tried to mask with concern. He realized the truth. While she was grieved to hear his wife had died, she was glad to know he was single.

"I'm so sorry," she said. The faint smile on her lips did not escape his notice. "Did you come here after she died?"

"No . . . " He was finding it harder than he thought it would be to tell her about Katie. Since the trip to Pedernales, the pain had not been as deep. It had been rather easy when Hanna asked questions, but he regarded Shelby's interest as an invasion of his privacy. He felt a large lump forming in his throat, but when he tried to clear it, the cottony mass refused to be dislodged. It took several attempts to get the words out. "We were both missionaries here. She contracted dengue fever while we were working in Haiti. By the time I realized how bad it was, it was too late."

Shelby's reaction appeared to be one of genuine concern. "Jake, really – I'm sorry. I'm sure that must have been hard on you. I'm surprised you stayed."

"Actually, I didn't. We went back to the States for a year and a half, then returned a little more than a year ago. At first I wasn't sure I could come back, but after time away realized this was where we needed to be." His jaw twitched. "So . . . we came back."

A ridge formed across Shelby's forehead. "We?"

Jake smiled. "My daughter, Isabela, and I. She's the joy of my life."

"Isabela, what a pretty name." Shelby looked toward the palm-studded beach. "Don't we have Queen Isabela to thank for sending Columbus on his travels when he discovered the Americas?"

"You obviously know your history," he said. "Once you meet my daughter, she'll probably tell you all about how she was named for Queen Isabela."

"Was she?"

"No . . . not really," he said, tilting his head to the side. When he heard his neck pop, the tension significantly decreased. "Katie and I just thought it was a pretty name. But once Isabela was old enough to realize there had been a Queen Isabela, and that a couple of small settlements in the Dominican Republic were christened La Isabela, she likes to tell people she was named after the famous queen."

"She sounds delightful."

"Who?" Jake couldn't resist flashing her a teasing smile.

"The queen or my daughter?"

Shelby gently punched his arm. "Your daughter, silly. How old is she? And no, I don't mean the queen, I mean your daughter."

"Isabela – my daughter, not the queen," he winked at her, "is six years old, going on eighteen."

"I can't wait to meet her."

Jake cast a discreet glance at the Faro a Colón as they passed. Memories of making the same trip with Hanna paraded before him. He cleared his throat. "How about a change of subject. Are you still living in Kansas?"

"I am."

"You know, I don't remember seeing anything in the information we received from the mission board that said you guys were from Kansas. Maybe it was there, but I think Conner and Maleah must not have noticed either. Otherwise, I feel certain they would have mentioned it." He turned the air-conditioner down a notch. "So . . . how is it you ended up coming on the trip?"

Shelby peered over the headrest at the other team members. From what Jake could see and hear they weren't paying them any attention. Apparently convinced no one was listening, she looked back at him. "I've gotten involved with the singles group at the church I'm attending in Wichita. When they started talking about needing a translator for the mission trip they were making to Mexico, I signed up. When the plans changed, I decided I could use my Spanish in the Dominican Republic as well as I could have in Mexico."

"I heard you speaking Spanish at the airport. Where did you learn to speak the language so well?"

She shifted in her seat, her reddish blond hair moving with her before settling loosely across her shoulders. "I don't know that you would remember, but I took Spanish in high school. The summer before my senior year I went to Spain with my parents and fell in love with the country. After that I started toying with the idea of majoring in Spanish. When I told my dad what I was thinking about doing, he made arrangements for me to live with some friends of the family in Madrid the summer after I graduated. He thought it would give me the opportunity to make sure I really wanted to make

Spanish my major."

"I'm guessing the summer in Spain solidified your decision."

Shelby pursed her lips and nodded. "It did. In fact, if my parents had let me, I would probably have moved to Madrid and studied there, but they thought it was a better idea for me to get my education in Kansas."

"What have you been doing with your major?" Jake asked as he checked the side view mirror before changing lanes behind Conner.

"After graduating from college I traveled around Spain for a year. For a while I thought I was in love with a young man there. I even dreamed of getting married and settling down in Madrid." A smile fluttered across her face as her shoulders rose and fell. "But . . . as often happens with young love, it didn't work out. So I moved to Wichita and got a job teaching high school Spanish."

"Are you still teaching?"

"I am, but who knows . . . " She swept a hand in front of her. "Maybe while I'm here, I'll discover God is calling me to be a missionary in the Dominican Republic." She reached over and squeezed Jake's arm. "Wouldn't that be the funniest thing if after all these years God brought us back together like that?"

Jake propped his elbow on the ledge below the window, steering the van with his left hand, while threading the fingers of his right hand through his hair. He wasn't sure he was ready for Shelby to move in on his turf – not now, not ever. Remembering the last time he'd talked with her, he was surprised to see her on a mission trip at all. The thought of her being a fulltime missionary was a little hard for him to visualize. But . . . *With God, all things are possible.* "Well, maybe," he said, hoping the tone of his voice didn't reflect his thoughts. "Who knows what God might do? I have a few questions, though. As I remember, when we parted ways, you didn't have much interest in God. What brought about the change of heart? Don't get me wrong. I'm thrilled to hear you talking this way. I'm just curious as to how God finally got your attention."

Shelby studied her hands. "It's kind of long story," she said. "You sure you want to hear it?"

The *click-click-click* of the turn signal echoed in the silence.

"I really would," Jake said after changing lanes again. "But if it's going to take a while, why don't you save it until after dinner. We'll be stopping soon."

"How much longer will we be on the road after we leave San Cristóbal?"

"About three and a half hours. Will that give you enough time?"

She laughed. "It should. I'll give you the condensed version."

Jake chuckled. He hoped she was being funny.

~~~~~

When they stopped to eat, Jake tried to mingle, but every time he turned around Shelby was on his heels. The volunteer team included only two women: Shelby, and an attractive brunette named Karen. If asked, Jake would have guessed Karen was in her late thirties or early forties. The six men were of varying heights and weights, with ages ranging probably from late twenties to mid-forties. While they ate, Jake sat at a table with Shelby and two of the men who were riding with them in his van. Jeff was tall and brawny with thick sandy blond hair and dark brown eyes. Mike was shorter, but compact and muscular. His dark hair was streaked with gray, his eyes blue. He appeared to be the oldest in the group. Both men had been on numerous mission trips and were well acquainted with construction work. Jake liked them immediately.

After dinner, Shelby scurried toward the front passenger side door of the van as if she were afraid one of the men might try to take her prized seat away from her. Jake found her actions a bit disturbing. Perhaps her confident façade had a few nicks and cracks after all. Once on the road, he waited for her to speak first. If she wanted to tell him her story, fine. If not, that was okay too. For a while she silently gazed out the window, which seemed odd to him considering how talkative she'd been earlier.

After about fifteen or twenty minutes, she shifted in her seat. Although her eyes rested on him, she remained mute. With raised eyebrows, he dashed a look in her direction. "Well . . ."

"Do you still want to hear how God finally got my attention?" she asked.

Jake shrugged. "Sure."

"The long or condensed version?" Her voice lacked its previous luster.

"Whichever. Surely even the long version won't take more than three hours to tell." He forced a smile and hoped the inflection in his voice didn't resonant with the irritation that was starting to build.

When several seconds passed and she still hadn't said anything, he looked at her and dipped his chin. "You don't have to tell me if you don't want to," he said. "I was just surprised at the change and was curious as to what had brought it about. That's all."

"I understand," she said. "When we were in high school, I was pretty critical of your faith. I have to admit there have been times I wished I'd listened to you. Things may have turned out differently. Who knows . . . we may have gotten married and wouldn't even be having this conversation right now."

Jake saw the longing in her eyes. He could not imagine what it would have been like if he'd missed out on his life with Katie, but he wasn't going to tell Shelby he was glad it hadn't worked out between them. He chose his words carefully. "I guess that's the way life is. We never know what our lives might have been like if we had chosen different paths."

"That's for sure," she said, staring straight ahead. Her expression gave no hint of what she was thinking. She took a deep breath. "Anyway . . . After spending the summer in Spain, I returned home and majored in Spanish at Kansas State. Although I'm certainly not proud of it, I have to confess the partying lifestyle I had developed my last two years in high school only moved into overdrive at K-State. I dated around, had a couple of short-lived relationships, and did a lot of stuff I'm ashamed to admit."

She pursed her lips and cast a sideways glance at Jake. "Go ahead," he said.

"When I arrived in Spain soon after graduating, I went looking for the party crowd and met the guy I mentioned earlier at a club." She hesitated, tapping a manicured fingernail against the console. "A few weeks later I moved in with him. I was naive enough to believe we would eventually get married, but about ten months into the relationship he met someone else and it was adios Shelby. That's when I decided to return to Kansas, where I got a teaching position in Wichita. About a year after I started teaching, the school's football coach asked me out for a date. We got married six months later. He liked his booze and was as much a partier as I was in those days. For a while it seemed a match made in heaven." She cut her eyes at Jake. "Ah . . . well, sorry about that. You know what I mean."

Jake couldn't help but smile. "I do," he said, "although I'm guessing in time you discovered it really wasn't."

"No, I'm afraid not. He was a nice guy when he was sober, but when he got drunk, he was often abusive. For three years I endured the verbal assaults, but the night he hauled off and hit me, I knew I'd had enough. I left him and filed for a divorce. It was awkward at first. I was thankful when he accepted a coaching position at another school. A year later I took back my maiden name."

"I'm assuming you never had any children?"

Out of the corner of his eye, Jake saw her flinch, and she seemed momentarily lost in a memory. "No, something for which I'm grateful, I guess . . . " As she'd done earlier, she peered over the seat back, obviously making sure no one else was listening. When she spoke again, her voice was barely above a whisper. "Because of some bad choices I made – once in high school, once in college and then again while living in Spain – I can't have children." When she paused, he thought he heard her sniff. "I have scar tissue the doctor says will probably keep me from ever getting pregnant again."

Jake concentrated on his driving. The rhythmic *ka-thump – ka-thump – ka-thump* of tires hitting pavement pulsated in his ears. It took a few seconds to process the implications of what she had just shared. Before he could say anything, she continued. "I know. You don't have to say it. I should have listened to you."

He shook his head. "I wasn't thinking that at all. I certainly wasn't going to say *I told you so.*"

"Well, you should." Her voice sounded raspy. "Remember

the time we went to that youth conference and they talked to us about saving ourselves for marriage? You told me then one of the reasons God's word says we should not become sexually involved outside of marriage is to save us from a lot of heartache. I thought you were crazy. I realize now you knew what you were talking about. My decisions have certainly caused me a whole lot of heartache."

"I'm really sorry to hear that," Jake said, resisting the urge to lay a reassuring hand upon hers. He needed to be careful not to give her any false encouragement. "But I'm guessing somewhere along the way you made peace with God, and I hope you have allowed Him to heal your pain."

"I have, but sometimes the memories still hurt." She choked on a sob.

"I understand – for different reasons. But I've certainly had my struggles in allowing God to heal my hurts."

Shelby leaned toward him on the console, lowering her eyes and pouting her lips. "I'm sorry, Jake. Here I am talking and talking about me, when I can't imagine the pain you've suffered."

"That's okay," he said. He was in no mood to get into a discussion about his own battles. "I did ask, you know. I'm still waiting to hear how you finally got your relationship with God straight."

"Oh, well . . . " She cast him a look he assumed was supposed to appear innocent. "I did tell you it was a long story. Are you sure you want to hear the rest?"

"Why not?" he said. What else could he say?

Shelby's sandals slid off her feet and she pulled her left leg under her before turning sideways in her seat. "After my divorce was final and I was all alone, I tried the partying scene again – hanging out at bars and nightclubs. Ultimately it all left me feeling that much more lonely. I remember waking up one day and thinking that if there wasn't more to life than what I was experiencing, I didn't want to live anymore." She smiled at him from under heavy lashes. "It really is funny that God has caused our paths to cross again, because during those long, solitary days I began thinking about the year you and I dated and the time spent hanging out with the group from your church. I started wondering if there might have been something to what you guys kept trying to tell me. I remembered making a decision for Christ at a fall bonfire. Do you remember that night?"

Jake nodded as he allowed his thoughts to drift back to an earlier time, the fall of his junior year in high school. "I do remember. In fact, although I had noticed you before that night, I wouldn't have considered asking you out if you hadn't been a Christian. After you made a decision for Christ, I decided it would be okay."

She laughed. "Guess the joke was on you. I don't believe my decision was real. Of course, I think after a while you figured that out."

"I did, but at first I hoped you were just a young Christian and needed time to grow. It really hurt when I realized it wasn't going to work out between us."

She ran the tips of her fingers down his arm. Her touch felt silky soft against his skin. He almost cringed, but caught himself.

"Ah, Jake . . . what a sweet thing to say." Her hand lingered on his forearm. "You know – I thought there was something wrong with you. What seventeen-year-old guy breaks up with a girl because she doesn't want to save herself for marriage? I thought you'd lost your mind. Now I realize I was the one who was messed up, not you."

He quietly blew out his breath when she drew her hand back to her lap. "What happened next?" he asked. He was ready to move on with the conversation. "After you started considering the possibility there'd been something to what we'd been saying, what did you do?"

"I decided it was time I tried church again. I didn't know what I was doing, but I thought it certainly was worth a try. After all, nothing else I'd done up until then had worked. I started attending a church near where I live. It didn't take me long to realize I'd never actually given my life to Christ. Once I did, it made a big difference. I still struggle at times because of all the poor choices I've made, but I know I'm forgiven and God has wiped the slate clean."

"That's an awesome testimony," he said. "Since your language skills are so strong, I think I'll talk with Conner and see if you can share one night with the church group in Paraíso. That is, if you would be comfortable doing so."

"Maybe," she said.

"I think you should pray about it. Who knows? God might use your past to help draw someone to Him."

"You really think He could?"

"Of course I do."

Chapter Twenty-Three

Hanna's heart began a slow ascent the minute she saw Jake helping the pretty strawberry blonde out of the front seat of his van. When he shut the door and the woman slipped her arm in his, it reached her throat and settled there, threatening to choke her. She thought Jake looked a little uncomfortable, but he made no effort to free his arm. She watched in stunned silence as the two of them walked arm in arm to the back of the trailer where Conner and the other team members were removing suitcases and duffle bags. Jake pulled away from the woman's grasp as he began helping sort through the mound of luggage already sitting on the ground.

When Maleah stepped up beside her, Hanna whispered, "Do you know that woman standing by Jake?"

Maleah squinted as she looked toward the van, already shrouded in the muddy gray shadows of dusk. "I can't see her very well," she said, "but I don't think so. Why?"

"She's acting awfully friendly with Jake." The words caught in Hanna's throat as she tried to swallow around the pulsating heart-shaped lump.

"Really?" Maleah squinted again.

"Really."

Hanna studied the tall, attractive blonde now strolling up the driveway beside Jake, who carried a suitcase in each hand. The woman kept touching his arm as she talked, her body language emitting familiarity.

"Humm . . . I hate to say it, but I don't like the looks of this," Maleah said as the two drew closer.

Hanna gulped, but her heart still refused to budge. Hot tears burned her eyes. "Do you know her?" she asked again, blinking several times in an effort to keep the tears at bay.

Maleah sighed loud enough to be heard several houses down. "No, but it appears she knows Jake."

As the couple stepped onto the porch, Jake looked up, briefly meeting Hanna's gaze before focusing on Maleah.

"Maleah . . . Hanna . . . I would like for you to meet Shelby Wilson," he said with a slight tremor in his voice. "She and I went to high school together." His smile failed to reach his eyes. "Small world, isn't it?"

Hanna's heart dropped from her throat to the pit of her stomach, where it rumbled in protest. She forced herself to smile as Jake finished the introductions. "Shelby, this is Maleah Anderson and Hanna Truly."

Shelby confidently extended her hand to Maleah first. "Nice to meet you. You're Conner's wife, right?"

"That's right . . ." Maleah answered, taking the woman's hand. "It's nice to meet you too."

Shelby stretched her hand toward Hanna, but her eyes were on Jake. "Hanna . . . I don't think I remember Jake mentioning you."

Hanna flashed her eyes at Jake. His face flushed red, and she was surprised when he stuttered as he tried to explain. "No . . . I . . . gu . . . guess I forgot to mention Hanna." The firm line of his jaw twitched. "We got busy catching up and talking about old times." He seized Hanna's eyes with his, looking as if he wanted to say something else, but he didn't.

Shelby's eyes never left his face. Out of the corner of her eye, Hanna could see her looking at him, her brow creased with fine lines. After dropping Hanna's hand, she cleared her throat, recapturing Jake's attention. Having obviously gotten what she wanted, she turned to Hanna, her lips chiseled in a tight smile. "So, Hanna, are you Conner's other wife?"

Hanna stared at her, not bothering to keep what she knew was a look of derision off her face. Was the woman's comment meant to be cute or deliberately sarcastic?

Maleah snorted. "I'm sure Conner would be the first to tell

you he has his hands full with just one wife," she said. "Hanna works with us here in Paraíso. She helps with the church and teaches our children."

"I see," Shelby said, fixing her eyes on Jake again. "Very convenient, I'm sure."

Jake shifted his weight from one foot to the other as his smile faded. Hanna felt certain the tension among them was thicker than the muggy air around them.

When Maleah spoke again, her voice carried traces of restrained annoyance. "Shelby, we're glad to have you with us. Let me show you where you'll be staying. I'm sure the men could use Jake's help in getting the rest of the team and luggage where they need to go."

As the three walked past Hanna into the house, Jake looked at her and smiled. It seemed a feeble effort. She stood unmoving on the porch, watching Conner walk up the driveway with a short, dark headed woman and two men, both with sandy blond hair. She barely acknowledged the introductions. After Conner led the three inside, she stepped off the porch and into the yard, gazing toward the silhouette of the mountains across the street. Seconds later Jake came back outside, Isabela in tow. He must have deposited Shelby's bags in Sophie's room, where she and the other lady from the team would be staying, then quickly made his exit.

As soon as Isabela saw her, she ran over to say goodnight. Hanna squatted beside her, the dry grass tickling her knees. The child threw her arms around her neck and planted a moist, warm kiss on her cheek. When Hanna stood back up, Jake was standing in front of her. She wished she had enough nerve to ask if he planned on giving her a goodnight kiss too. That would show that Shelby whatever her name was.

"Guess I'll see you tomorrow," she said.

"Si Dios quiere."

She tried to smile at the common Dominican reply, but when she realized she didn't have the energy, she abandoned the attempt. "Yeah, if God wills it," she said.

His eyes held hers as he brushed several stray wisps of hair away from her face. Despite the humid night air, Hanna felt a shiver run up her spine. "See you in the morning," he said. Taking Isabela's hand, he guided the child toward the van where four of the male team members sat waiting to be transported to his house.

Once she was settled in the front seat of the vehicle, Isabela leaned out the window and yelled, "Good night, Aunt Hanna. I love you." With dramatic flare she blew her a kiss.

Hanna lifted her hand to her lips and returned the gesture. "I love you too, sweetheart. See you tomorrow."

When she turned toward the house, she wasn't surprised to find Shelby standing in the doorway. Maybe it was wrong, but she felt a measure of satisfaction knowing the woman had witnessed her interactions with Jake and Isabela. She hoped she would realize Jake was off limits, but something told her Shelby Wilson was not the type to be stopped so easily. When Hanna reached the door, she blocked her way inside.

Shelby tipped her head toward the van as it rolled down the street. "Adorable child, isn't she?"

"Yes, she is."

The woman looked at her through intense green eyes. "What did she call you?"

"Aunt Hanna."

"Are you her aunt?"

"No. It's customary for missionary children to call all missionary adults *aunt* or *uncle*."

Shelby's eyes never left Hanna's face. "I see. She seems quite fond of you."

"She's fond of Maleah too."

Shelby shifted her gaze, peering over Hanna's shoulder in the direction of Jake's house. "So, what's your relationship with Jake?"

Hanna scrutinized the woman, trying to decide if she was even going to answer her question. Who *did* she think she was anyway? "We're friends. Good friends," she finally said, hoping to end the conversation.

"Uh-huh. You know, Jake left out something when he introduced us tonight."

Hanna balled her fingers in fists so tight her nails felt as if they might pierce the palms of her hands. "I'm waiting."

"We didn't *just* go to high school together." Shelby's expertly shaped eyebrows arched as she stepped aside. "We dated the better part of a year."

Hanna brushed past her. She was too tired to engage in a battle of words with the woman. Without looking back, she headed toward the kitchen. "You'll have to excuse me," she said. "I'm rather tired, and we'll be getting an early start in the morning. Good night."

~~~~~

As Hanna stood at the kitchen counter the following morning helping Maleah and Celia get breakfast ready for the team, she heard the squeak of rubber soles against tile and glanced over her shoulder. It was Shelby, dressed in red Capri pants and a white button up blouse. Her hair flowed casually over her shoulders, and her make up looked like something you'd see in an ad for a cosmetic brochure. If Hanna hadn't known better, she would have guessed she'd just stepped out of the pages of a photo shoot. At least she had on tennis shoes instead of heeled sandals.

Hanna glanced at her own less-than-perfect attire – a pair of old faded jeans, a light blue T-shirt that would make a good dust rag, and a pair of tennis shoes with holes in them. She'd pulled her hair up in a ponytail and hadn't bothered with make-up. For goodness sakes, they were going to be working a construction site during one of the hottest and most humid months of the year, not drinking lemonade under a palm tree at the beach.

Although she knew she should be the first to say hello, Hanna let Shelby have the honor and did well to grumble, "Good morning," in reply to the woman's cheerful, "Good morning ladies or . . . should I say, Buenos Dias?"

Maleah turned from the stove, where she was scrambling eggs, and looked in Shelby's direction. Hanna almost laughed out loud when she turned back around and rolled her eyes before returning the woman's greeting. "Good morning, Shelby," she said. "My, don't we look pretty?"

"Why, thank you."

Shelby had taken Maleah's comment as a compliment, but Hanna knew better – her freckled-faced friend had little patience for pretense.

A few minutes later, Hanna heard the sound of Jake's voice coming from the living room and realized the group staying at his house had arrived. Obviously, Shelby did too. When she abruptly left the kitchen, Hanna felt a wave of jealousy roll over her. "This is going to be a long week," she said through gritted teeth.

"You can say that again," Maleah said as she scooped eggs into a big bowl.

Hanna picked up a platter of fruit and followed her into the dining room, giving the living room a quick once over as they entered. Shelby had already sidled up to Jake. Hanna willed herself not to look in their direction again. She refused to give the woman the pleasure of knowing she cared.

Once all the food was in place, Conner called the group together and said the blessing. Hanna stood in the threshold of the kitchen while team members made their way down either side of the dining room table, filling their plates with food. She could see Jake and Shelby in her peripheral vision. Jake leaned against the wall, his hands in the pockets of a pair of worn blue jeans, watching as people made their way through the food line and occasionally nodding in response to something Shelby said. When the last person approached the dining room table, he spoke for the first time since Hanna had entered the room. "Shelby, don't you want something to eat?" he asked.

She perused the food from a distance, and then turned her mouth down in a sneer. You would have thought he'd offered her pig slop. "Oh no. I'm not a breakfast eater," she said. "I'll pass."

He pushed himself away from the wall, standing erect. "Okay then. I think I'm going to get something before it's all gone. It's a long time until lunch, and we've got a lot of work to do. I'm sure I'll need something to keep me going." He walked off without looking back. Minutes later, his plate full, he passed in front of Hanna, stepped to her side and stopped. "Good morning," he said.

"Good morning," she replied.

"Like your outfit." His jaw twitched as if he were trying hard not to smile.

She couldn't help but laugh. "Every group needs a smart-aleck," she said.

"I wasn't trying to be a smart-aleck. I think you look cute."

"Yeah, right. If I look cute, what do you think of Miss Fashion Plate over there?"

Jake glanced in Shelby's direction before bringing his eyes back to Hanna. "Personally, I think she's going to look foolish out in the middle of a construction site." He lifted a forkful of egg off his plate. "But since she came as a translator and not a worker, maybe she thinks her outfit fits the job." He slid the food in his mouth.

Hanna felt her throat constrict. "Translator? What do you mean?"

"Shelby's fluent in Spanish. The original assignment in Mexico included a request for a translator. I guess they didn't realize we wouldn't need one here."

"I see . . . " Hanna felt her stomach twisting in knots as she watched Shelby walking toward them. Something told her time alone with Jake was going to be rare over the next seven days. She imagined Shelby would see to it.

Caribbean Paradise

Chapter Twenty-Four

Hanna was pleasantly surprised when, for the most part, the first day at the worksite passed rather smoothly. On occasion she noticed Shelby trying to sidle up to Jake, but he didn't allow her to distract him for very long. Hanna stayed busy helping Maleah run errands and trying to make sure everyone drank enough water. As best she could tell, Shelby did a lot of walking around and very little work. The biggest irritation of the day transpired minutes after Shelby introduced a Dominican construction worker to a thirty-something male team member named Peter.

Hanna watched the Dominican man walk away and then cringed when Shelby slung her strawberry-blond hair over her shoulder while flashing Peter an unnaturally white smile. "Did you know the Spanish translation of your name is Pedro?" she asked.

"No, I didn't." Peter's laugh sounded self-conscious. Hanna felt sorry for him. Although she would have no trouble describing Shelby's actions as flirtatious, she doubted the woman cared for the man in the least. "How do you say your name in Spanish?" he asked.

"Well, you know . . . Shelby doesn't translate well into Spanish," she answered in her know-it-all fashion.

If the poor man didn't speak Spanish, Hanna wondered how in the world she expected him to know her name was difficult to translate.

"So, what name are you using?" Peter asked.

"My middle name is Marie, so whenever I'm in a Spanish speaking country I go by Maria." She flashed him another bright smile. "I like to make it easier for the nationals by using a name they already know."

Hanna resisted the urge to stick her finger down her throat and gag. She couldn't help but wonder how often Shelby visited Spanish-speaking countries. She talked as if it was something she did on a regular basis. Maybe that explained why she knew the language so well. Intimidating thoughts clouded Hanna's thinking as she walked away. It was bad enough Shelby was attractive, self-confident and interested in Jake – Did she also have to be fluent in Spanish?

~~~~~

Before leaving the worksite late Saturday afternoon, Hanna helped Jake, Conner and the volunteer team members arrange fifty folding metal chairs on the concrete slab that was to be the foundation for the new church facility. They, along with the group of believers who met regularly at the Andersons' on Sunday morning, were going to gather at the construction site the following morning for Bible study and worship.

The power went off Saturday night around ten-thirty and did not come back on until six o'clock the following morning. It had been a hot, miserable night. When Hanna entered the kitchen Sunday morning, it was almost seven-thirty. She had gotten up as soon as the power came on and taken a quick shower. She was already dressed for church in a knee length black skirt and a hot pink blouse. She'd left her hair loose and it flowed gently over her shoulders and down her back. While not cosmetic brochure quality, she'd taken special care with her make-up. As bad as she hated to admit it, she felt like someone had entered her in a competition with Shelby for Jake's affections. While she knew she couldn't compete with the woman in the language, when it came to physical beauty – with some effort, she hoped she could at least hold her own.

The kitchen was empty, and silence reigned in the combination living and dining room. Hanna pulled a mug out of the cabinet next to the sink and poured herself a cup of coffee. Maleah obviously had been there earlier.

"How can you even think of drinking something hot after the night we just had?"

Hanna started at the sound of Shelby's voice, causing coffee to slosh back and forth in the lime green mug. She was thankful she'd not filled it to the top; otherwise the dark liquid would have probably spilled over and down the front of her blouse. She turned to face the woman. When she saw she was wearing tan slacks with a burnt orange blouse, Hanna resisted the temptation to tell her that pants were inappropriate church attire for women in rural areas of the country. But since Shelby was only going to be there one Sunday, she decided it probably didn't matter. No need to be catty.

"After a while you get used to it," Hanna said, breathing in the rich coffee aroma. "I guess my need for a caffeine fix is greater than my desire to stay cool."

Shelby huffed as she opened the refrigerator. "Is there any juice?"

"Should be."

The woman pulled out a large carton of orange juice and set it on the counter. Hanna handed her a glass. Shelby flashed emerald eyes in her direction. "How frequently do you have nights without electricity around here?"

"At least three or four times a week, sometimes more. Occasionally we'll have an entire week when it goes off every night for at least a few hours."

Shelby glared at her. "You mean we could have more nights like the one we just had?"

"I can almost promise we will," Hanna said, reining in a smirk.

Shelby picked up her glass of juice and stormed out of the kitchen. Hanna lifted her coffee mug. "Here's to you," she said. She knew she was being ugly, but had no desire to exercise proper restraint.

Jake and Isabela did not come to the service held on the new church site, but maintained their regular Sunday morning routine at the Community Center where Jake often mixed Bible study with a game called Bible baseball. A friend of his had come up with the idea – combining the game of baseball with Bible trivia. The local kids loved it. Hanna heard them yelling as she walked with the Andersons and the volunteer team members past the center on their way to the construction site. Shelby had not been informed that Jake would not be in attendance at their service until it was too late for her to run next door and join him. Hanna felt a smug satisfaction when Maleah gave her the news.

Because Jake's Sunday activities included lunch, he and Isabela did not show up at the Andersons' until late that afternoon. Shelby was at his side almost immediately, but he didn't seem to notice. Of course, Hanna had to admit he didn't spend much time with her either. A lot needed to be accomplished over the next five days, therefore, most of the discussion that evening centered on plans for the rest of the week. The hope was there would be a completed structure by the time the group left on Saturday. It was a tall order, but with help from men in the church and several hired professionals from the community, it was achievable.

~~~~~

Monday passed uneventfully, and Hanna began to relax. Although Shelby relentlessly sought out opportunities to interact with Jake, Hanna could tell he was too busy to care one way or another. One thing she'd discovered about Jake, when it came to work, he took what he was doing seriously.

That evening, after everyone had retired for the night, Hanna noticed the patio light was still on. When she looked out the window of her apartment, she saw Shelby sitting alone at the table, Angel purring softly at her feet.

"No wonder she's not tired," Hanna grumbled as she walked away. "She's the only one not doing any work. Unless you call walking around looking cute and chit chatting with the Dominicans, *work*." She got in bed and turned off the lamp, expecting to fall asleep before her head hit the pillow, but instead of visions of sugarplums dancing in her head, images of Shelby sitting alone on the patio passed before her eyes. Her conscience began to bother her. She knew the Holy Spirit was trying to get her attention, but she chose to allow the groaning of the fan as it stirred the thick air to drown out the voice of conviction.

The following morning, Hanna was delighted when Jake spent even less time talking with Shelby than he had the previous days, and more time interacting with her. During a mid-morning break he asked Hanna if she would like to go for a walk. It gave her great pleasure to see the look on Shelby's face as they left the construction site together. Secretly, Hanna turned her nose up at the woman and said, *so there!* Ignoring the nudge of the Holy Spirit was harder than it had been the night before. Even so, her feelings of smug satisfaction were becoming intoxicating. She should have known better. After the fact, she realized God's word says *pride goes before a fall* for good reason.

Hanna was still savoring the sweet taste of triumph in the game she had unwittingly begun to play with Shelby when Giselle stopped by the worksite to see how she was doing. While they talked, Shelby approached them, looking cocky and self-assured as always. In her flawless Spanish, she asked Hanna if she would introduce her to her friend. Although Hanna understood what she was asking, her brain shifted into panic mode. Intimidation washed over her like a tidal wave. She tried to think of the proper way to make the introduction, but she knew even her best Spanish would sound amateurish to Shelby. Giselle must have read her thoughts, because she smiled politely at the woman and introduced herself.

Shelby gave Hanna a contemptuous look, her eyes hardening in disapproval. "You do speak Spanish, don't you?" she asked.

Hanna stuffed her hands in the pockets of her jeans and shifted self-consciously. "I do, just not well."

Using her own version of Spanglish, Giselle came to her defense. "Ella speak good Español."

"She's just being nice," Hanna said as the heat of shame rose to her face. "I've made some progress, but still have a ways to go."

"With practice, you'll get there," Shelby said in a patronizing tone while patting Hanna on the arm. It might as well have been her head.

Hanna wanted to find a hole somewhere to crawl into. This was all she needed – Shelby armed with ammunition to use against her. She didn't have to wait long before the woman fired up her guns.

~~~~~

That evening Hanna returned to her apartment in order to change her dirty, sweat-drenched shirt before dinner. After slipping her arms through the sleeves of a clean royal blue T-shirt, she stopped in front of the dresser mirror to redo her ponytail. The sound of a familiar bass voice drifted through one of the sitting room windows. Against her better judgment, she stepped closer and listened.

"How long has she been here?" Shelby asked.

"Almost five months now, I think."

"He thinks . . ." Hanna mouthed.

"Really? Is that all? For some reason I'd gotten the impression she'd been here a while. How long has she been studying Spanish?"

Hanna cringed. *Here goes* . . .

She heard Jake take a deep breath. His response was slow in coming. "About a year and half. She studied for a year in Costa Rica before coming here."

"A year and a half." Shelby's response dripped with sarcastic surprise.

"Why do you want to know?"

"It's nothing really, but this afternoon when I asked her to introduce me to a young Dominican woman who came by the worksite, Hanna didn't understand."

"What do you mean she didn't understand?"

"She just stood there with this blank look on her face. I don't think she'd understood a word I'd said."

What? Hanna couldn't believe her ears.

"Had you asked in Spanish for her to introduce you to the woman?"

"I did. I had no idea Hanna couldn't speak Spanish. Otherwise, I would have asked in English. I've been watching her. She seems kind of . . . out of place, not a good fit for the work here, especially if she's having trouble with the language. Wouldn't you agree?"

Hanna stood frozen in place as she waited for Jake's reply. All she needed was for Shelby to remind him of her inadequacies. He'd only just recently started treating her with respect. How much prompting from an old girlfriend would it take for him to digress in his opinion of her? Truth was – she didn't trust Jake anymore than she trusted Shelby.

When someone knocked, Hanna jerked her head toward the apartment door. Before she could move, the door opened and Maleah stuck her head in. "There you are. I wondered where you'd gone."

Frustrated, Hanna drew in her breath and then quietly expelled it. Unless she called Maleah's attention to the fact she'd been eavesdropping, there was no way she was going to hear Jake's response to Shelby's question. She'd have to let it go. She picked up the brush and finished redoing her ponytail. "My shirt was soaking wet, so I decided to change before supper." She looked at Maleah. "Did you need me to help you do something?"

"If you don't mind, would you put some ice in the glasses? I think everyone is ready to eat."

"I'd be glad to," Hanna said, forcing her lips into a smile.

Chapter Twenty-Five

Hanna filled the glasses with ice and carried them into the dining room, placing the tray on a card table that had been set in the corner for drinks. Jake and Shelby were still on the patio talking. She wanted it not to matter, but it did. She watched them out of the corner of her eye as she helped arrange food on the dining room table. Jake leaned against the wall of the house with one tennis shoe clad foot crossed over the other. She imagined his arms were folded across his chest, but couldn't see the upper part of his body. Shelby stood between them with her back toward the double doors leading into the living room. Hanna got the impression she was either trying to block Jake's line of vision, block his way should he try to come inside, or both. She wouldn't put anything past the woman. Shelby had made her intentions clear: she wanted Jake Mason. And from what Hanna had observed so far, what Shelby Wilson wanted she probably got. Greta sat on the other side of the short fence that bordered the patio. Jake and Shelby appeared not to notice. The Boxer's big brown eyes drooped. She looked sad and forgotten. Hanna could relate.

By the time Jake and Shelby ambled inside, everyone else had been served. Close to fifteen minutes had passed since Hanna heard Shelby asking Jake if he thought she seemed out of place in Paraíso. She wondered what had been said after she stopped listening. Had they spent the entire time discussing her woeful inadequacies in the language? Had Shelby managed to convince Jake she was a much better candidate for missionary? After all, she spoke the language like a national. And other than the meltdown Sunday morning, she had not wilted as badly as Hanna first thought she would. The more Hanna thought about what all might have been said, the worse she felt. She had been making progress in the language, and felt she was becoming an asset to the work of the mission, yet she knew she still had a long way to go before anyone would consider her a successful missionary. This certainly could prove to be a major speed bump in her journey toward renewed confidence. Maybe she'd only been kidding herself, especially if she thought she would ever measure up to Jake's expectations.

After the dinner dishes had been washed and put away, Hanna poured herself another glass of sweet tea and returned to the dining room. She pulled out a chair next to Maleah, but chose to sit with her back to the living room. All the team members except Shelby had retired for the evening. Shelby, on the other hand, sat next to Jake on the sofa, talking to Conner about the possibility of sharing her testimony with some of the church members.

Maleah patted Hanna's hand. "It's going to be okay," she whispered. Hanna tried to smile, but she knew the end result was flimsy. Maleah turned her attention back to the conversation between Conner and Shelby.

While tuning her ears to listen, Hanna watched drops of condensation streaking down the sides of her glass of tea.

"I appreciate your desire to share your testimony," Conner said, "but with all we've got to do in order to get the building finished, making arrangements to have the kind of gathering you're talking about would only slow us down and possibly keep us from completing the project before the team leaves on Saturday."

"I was thinking Maleah and Hanna could make the arrangements while you guys worked," Shelby said.

Maleah's eyes widened, and her freckled cheeks flushed red. The woman shook her head with such force Hanna could hear her hair swishing against her shoulders.

"Excuse me," Maleah said, the two words snapping like a firecracker. Hanna felt certain three sets of eyes had looked in their direction. "I'm not exactly sure what you all are talking about, but I don't have time to add anything to my workload." She placed her hand on top of Hanna's. "Furthermore, Hanna doesn't have the time either." Maleah glared at the threesome, dark embers smoldering in her hazel eyes. "We're both already on overload."

Now that her name had been dragged into the discussion, Hanna turned her chair around and faced the living room – just in time to see Conner raise his hands in mock surrender. "Whoa! Hold up!" he said. "You and Hanna are not being asked to do anything else." He looked at Jake and Shelby. "I learned a long time ago you don't want to ruffle the feathers of an Irish woman."

"I didn't mean to upset anyone," Shelby said, flashing Maleah what Hanna assumed was meant to be an innocent smile. "It's just . . . after hearing how God finally got my attention and helped me straighten out my life, Jake said he thought it would be a good idea if some of the church members and their friends could hear my story." She slipped her arm through Jake's. "Isn't that right?"

Hanna felt a knot forming in the pit of her stomach. Listening to this conversation had been bad enough, but watching Shelby snuggle up to Jake was almost more than she could handle. He stared at the floor, making it difficult for her to read his reaction. While she wouldn't have said he looked comfortable, he didn't appear to be as rattled as he had the night they arrived from the airport. Obviously Shelby's little speech out on the patio had hit its mark.

When he didn't say anything, Shelby slid her arm down, entwining her fingers in his. "Jake, darling, that is what you said, isn't it? You know I wouldn't have suggested it otherwise."

Jake cleared his throat, glanced at Maleah, avoided making eye contact with Hanna, and then rested his eyes on Conner. "I did make the suggestion," he said, "but I have to admit I didn't take into consideration the work involved in pulling something like that together."

Like a flash of lightening, Shelby's face registered both disappointment and indignation. If Hanna had not been watching her closely, she would have missed it. She guessed everyone else did. The woman seemed to quickly recover her composure. "No big deal," she said, lifting her shoulders in an unruffled shrug. "If it's too much work, we can do it next time." She squeezed Jake's hand and smiled. "Now that I know Jake's here," her laugh sounded schoolgirl giddy, "you guys will be seeing a lot of me in the future."

Having made her declaration, Shelby looked at Hanna in triumph. Hot tears surfaced, overflowing before Hanna had a chance to stop them. She dipped her chin as several unwelcome drops splashed in her lap. She heard Maleah's chair scrape against the floor as she stood; a second later she felt her hand on her shoulder. "If you don't mind, I could use your help in the kitchen," she said. "There are a few things I'd like to get ready tonight so we don't have as much to do in the morning."

Hanna followed Maleah into the kitchen and then continued walking toward her apartment. "Thanks," she said as she passed.

"It's going to be – "

"I know . . . it's going to be okay. See you in the morning."

~~~~~

The following morning, Hanna stepped into the kitchen a few minutes before seven to help Maleah and Celia get breakfast ready for the team. Not even the savory smell of frying bacon could pull her out of the pit she'd fallen into. When Shelby entered the room a few seconds later, Hanna slipped several feet farther into the cavernous abyss.

"Buenos Dias!" Shelby said.

Hanna clenched her teeth. The woman's cheerful greeting resounded in her ears like fingernails scraping across a chalkboard. Dressed in khaki Capris and a bright red blouse with matching sandals, not a hair out of place, her makeup perfect – she looked, as usual, like a fashion model.

"How does the woman do it in this heat and humidity?" Hanna muttered under her breath while running her hand over her own hair, where wispy strands had already broken loose from the ponytail she had hastily brushed into place minutes earlier. Once again, she hadn't bothered with make up. What was the use? She would sweat it off within the hour.

When neither Hanna nor Maleah said anything, Shelby engaged Celia in conversation. Hanna shuddered. She suspected the friendly Spanish chit-chat was nothing more than a performance on Shelby's part for her benefit – A means of intimidation, giving her the opportunity to flaunt her superior command of the language. If that was her plan, it was working. Hanna kept her back turned, plunking chunks of pineapple, papaya, mango and banana on a platter Maleah had handed her earlier. The last piece of fruit in place, she snatched up the finished product and brushed past Shelby as she exited the kitchen on her way to the dining room.

"Excuse me," she mumbled.

~~~~~

Jake did not appear at the Andersons' for breakfast. When Hanna arrived at the construction site an hour later, he was already busy at work, his *faithful assistant* at his side. Attempting to act indifferent, she approached one of the volunteers, a sandy headed, brown-eyed young man named Scott. "Do you need any help?" she asked, flashing him what she felt was a friendly smile.

Scott returned her smile and appeared pleased she'd offered to help. "Sure," he replied. "I was getting ready to prime this wall. With your help, we can probably finish it in half the time it would take me to do it alone."

Hanna chatted with Scott as they began the process of priming the interior wall at the back of the room. A couple of times she glanced over her shoulder, hoping Jake had noticed he wasn't the only one who could fraternize with the team members. But . . . he didn't seem to be paying her any attention. He was too busy listening to Shelby. Hanna tried to stay focused on her own work, but her heart wasn't in it. Once the priming job was finished, she excused herself and stepped outside. She felt guilty for attempting to use her interactions with Scott as a means of making Jake jealous. She rubbed her temples with her fingertips as tears burned her eyes. How had she allowed herself to get pulled into the game it seemed she was now playing?

She kept her back to the worksite as she stood on the sidewalk, arms folded across her mid-section. The buildings surrounding what was fast becoming the new church facility were made of either concrete block or clapboard and painted one of the traditional blues, greens or pinks. Most were faded and peeling. Traffic was noontime heavy, but would soon be much quieter as the locals headed home for their afternoon meal and siesta. A radio blared from inside the corner colmado, and several giggling children sat on the front stoop, sharing a bottled orange soda. Men and women dressed in clean, but worn shirts, skirts or pants, crowded the sidewalks bordering both sides of the street.

After greeting several people as they walked past, Hanna turned around. She could see Jake and Shelby through one of the church's unfinished windows. Although Shelby was doing most of the talking, Jake appeared to be enjoying her company. Hanna drew a deep breath, her shoulders lifted then fell, and a soft sigh escaped her lips. Had it only been five days ago she had felt hopeful things might work out between her and Jake? Placing one leaded foot in front of the other, she began the mile and a half walk to the Andersons'. Maleah and Celia would need her help as they prepared lunch. A motoconcho sped by, and she considered hailing the young driver, but he was gone before she could get his attention. The late morning sun beat hot upon her head, and a blanket of despair weighed heavy upon her back. She took short shallow breaths, hoping to avoid a full-fledged panic attack. The last time her heart hurt this bad was during her junior year in college. She frowned at the memory, her chin quivering. Was she destined to get involved in relationships with men who could not be trusted?

Hanna's spirits dropped even lower when Jake and Shelby arrived at the Andersons' a little while later, Shelby's arm draped loosely through his. After fixing their sandwiches, they sat alone at the patio table, where Shelby repeatedly reached over and caressed Jake's arm. From where Hanna sat at the dining room table it would have been impossible not to notice. "How cozy," she mumbled as she rearranged the food on her plate for the third time since sitting down.

"Daddy, Daddy." Hanna jerked her head up as Isabela ran out the double doors toward her father, holding a piece of paper in her hands. "Look at the picture I drew for you."

Jake took the paper from the child. Shelby leaned over,

joining him as he studied whatever it was she had drawn. "That's so pretty," Shelby said, slipping her arm around Isabela's waist and pulling her close. Jake draped his arm over his daughter's shoulders, drawing the three of them into a tight hug. At the sound of Isabela's laughter, Hanna swallowed against the lump forming in her throat and turned back to her lunch, but she couldn't eat. Hurt, disappointment, jealousy – all three emotions caused her stomach to rumble in protest every time she tried to take a bite. Finally she gave up, threw everything in the trash and retreated to the kitchen to help Celia.

Once he finished eating, Scott invited Hanna to walk with him back to the church facility and help prime another wall. Although tempted, she declined. Hoping to make Jake jealous was not a good reason to accept the young man's invitation. Scott was a nice guy, and she refused to do anything that might eventually complicate matters even further. She delayed returning for as long as she could, but by one-thirty knew it would not be long before she was missed and someone came looking for her.

Chapter Twenty-Six

Back at the construction site, Hanna volunteered to help with the distribution of supplies. A makeshift workstation in the shape of a square had been created using three six-foot tables positioned along one wall of the building. With so many people rummaging through the materials, the tables were in a sad state of disarray.

As much as possible, Hanna kept her back to the room. Staring at a blank wall trumped watching Jake and Shelby working together. As she made her way through a box of sandpaper, sorting the different sheets according to grades, her concentration was interrupted by an annoying *click-click-click*. When she turned around, she found Shelby standing in front of her, tapping long fingernails on the table, her lips parted in a flashy display of incredibly even, white teeth.

"Why Hanna, when did they put you in charge of supplies?" she asked. "I thought you were helping Scott prime the walls." Her hair floated across her shoulders as she glanced toward where the young man was working. "He's such a great guy. I was pleased to see the two of you had paired up earlier today."

Hanna gritted her teeth, combating a strong desire to wipe Shelby's smile of victory right off her face. "Was there something you needed?" she asked.

"A bit testy, aren't we?"

"Just trying to do my job."

"In that case, Jake sent me over here to get a dozen two inch nails."

After counting out a dozen nails, Hanna embedded them in

the palm of Shelby's outstretched hand. "Anything else?"

"I think that's all," Shelby said with a smirk. "I would stay and chit-chat, but Jake needs my help." Her cat green eyes spoke volumes, declaring her the winner of the competition she and Hanna had entered five days earlier. She turned and sashayed away.

As a well of emotions gurgled in her throat, Hanna knelt behind the supply tables and pretended to sort boxes stored underneath. It seemed a safe place in case Shelby staged some kind of mini-drama once she reached Jake. If she did, Hanna wanted a good excuse for not being a part of the audience.

That evening she wasn't as successful.

Shelby stood by Jake's side in the Andersons' living room as she conversed with three of the other volunteer team members. Her voice carried throughout the room, and Hanna imagined her theatrics, at least in part, were for her benefit.

"I'm really enjoying the work here," Shelby said. "In fact, I'm beginning to think the reason I felt compelled to study Spanish in high school and college was because God wanted me prepared when He called me to the mission field."

Karen, the only other woman on the volunteer team, pinned her with a baffled squint. "I didn't realize you were interested in missions when you were in college," she said.

Hanna saw Shelby flinch and her jaw tighten. Something about the tone of Karen's voice made her suspect she, unlike a number of the men on the team, was not fooled by Shelby's sudden interest in missions.

Shelby glared at the woman. "Well, I wasn't," she said. "You've heard my testimony. I wasn't even a Christian when I was in college, but that doesn't mean God wasn't working in my life."

Karen's dark eyebrows fused in a frown. "So now you believe the reason you majored in Spanish was because God's ultimate plan was for you to be a missionary?"

"Isn't that what I said?" Shelby snapped as she slipped her arm in Jake's. "It's all become clearer over the last few days."

Karen rolled her lips while shaking her head. "Were you already feeling called to missions before you came on this trip?" she asked.

Hanna grinned when Shelby grabbed the woman with a look that could kill. "Does it bother you that I feel God may be calling me to be a missionary?" The words spewed from her mouth like steam from an overheated radiator.

"Not at all." It looked as if Karen was trying hard not to smile. "It's just taken me a little by surprise, since up until today I've never heard you mention it."

"Well, if she feels God is calling her to be a missionary, I think that's awesome," said a short, stocky team member. Hanna couldn't remember the man's name. "I'm sure already knowing the language should be a great asset."

"Sure it would." Shelby cast a triumphant look at Karen. "If I got an assignment in Paraíso, I could by-pass language school in Costa Rica and be back here in a matter of months." She tiptoed the fingers of her free hand up and down Jake's arm. "Don't you think so, Jake?"

Two deep lines burrowed across Jake's forehead and his eyes grazed Hanna's before shifting away. When he cleared his throat several times, she sensed he was stalling. He pushed away from the wall and pulled his arm free from Shelby's clutch. "If serving in Paraíso is where God wants you," he said. "But you do realize, don't you, that living here is a lot different than coming for a ten day mission trip?"

"Of course I do," Shelby replied, planting a fisted hand on her hip.

Jake slipped his hands in his pockets. "Well, okay," he said. "You just need to understand there's a lot more to being a missionary than speaking the language."

"I do," Shelby said with a pout. "That's the reason I want to come back. I'm already falling in love – with the place and the people. I'm sure I wouldn't have any trouble adapting. Besides, after all these years it would be so much fun getting to work with you." She slipped her arm back through his and batted her eyes at him. "God does work in mysterious ways, doesn't He? I know I took the long way getting here, but the more I think about it, I just can't help believing He's the one who has brought us back together."

Hanna looked over just in time to see Maleah roll her eyes. If

Shelby's words had not hit her like a fist to the gut, she would have laughed. How she wished she *could* laugh. Perhaps finding the humorous side in all this would help her let go of any notions she'd ever had of establishing a relationship with Jake, and she could get on with her life.

Unfortunately – at the moment – nothing about the situation seemed comical.

Since simply disappearing was not an option, she chose the next best thing. After slipping through the kitchen door, she almost ran to her apartment. As she plopped down on the edge of the bed, she felt her face flush red with anger, but she was so jealous she wouldn't have been surprised if it had turned green. She swatted in frustration at the uninvited tears coursing down her cheeks. Why had she allowed herself to care enough for Jake Mason that his rejection could cause her so much pain?

As for Shelby, she couldn't remember ever feeling this way toward another individual: seething irritation, aggravation, exasperation . . . bordering on hatred. As a child of God, she knew what she was feeling was wrong, but she didn't care. She pulled her legs up on the bed and crossed them Indian style. Except for the light from the patio filtering through the sitting room window, she sat in darkness, tears dripping off her chin onto the bedspread. She needed to talk to someone, but whom?

Talk to Me . . . the still small voice of her heavenly Father prodded her.

"But Father . . . I can't," she sobbed. "What I'm feeling is all so wrong."

Try Me.

Wiping her nose with the back of her hand, Hanna took a deep breath.

"Lord, I can't believe I'm feeling and acting the way I am," she whispered. "After last night, I knew today wasn't going to be easy, so this morning I tried to prepare myself; yet nothing I've done seems to have helped. Watching Jake and Shelby interact today, I have to confess – every bone in my body aches with jealousy, and every insecurity I've ever had seems to have risen up to mock me. To make matters worse, I've sulked like a five-year-old who isn't getting her way."

Hanna leaned back on her elbows, tilted her head up and stared at the ceiling fan – its blades, swirling shadows above her.

"You know I tried to pray several times today, although praying might be considered a rather loose description of what I was doing; is probably a loose description of what I'm doing now. Lord, I know, I really do – I know Your word says love is patient and kind, and is not jealous. I know Jesus said that by our love for one another the world will know that we are His disciples. I want to do it Your way – I want to love others as You love me. I want to trust You, believing that if you want Jake and me together we will be, and if not . . . it will be okay. But I'm sorry. Right now I'm so jealous I don't know what to do."

Hanna closed her eyes. Images of Shelby cozying up to Jake scrolled across the back on her eyelids. She clawed at the bedspread beneath her hands as fresh tears squeezed between her eyelashes and slid down her cheeks.

"I know Shelby is my sister in Christ, so I guess I've got to love her, but that doesn't mean I have to like her – does it?" Another sob slipped through her lips. "Lord, I really don't like her." She took another ragged breath and continued. "Oh, how I hope it's okay for me to share all this with you. You're big enough to handle it. Right? I mean, look at David in the Psalms. One time didn't he even ask You to send his enemies down to the pit of hell – alive? Well, I haven't gone that far, although I'm not going to say the thought hasn't crossed my mind."

~~~~~

Hanna's sleep was restless. Knowing she would have to face a couple more days with Shelby flaunting her victory was almost more than she could bear. Although she'd tried to give her hurt and disappointment to God, she had not been willing to let go of it completely. When the neighbor's rooster's *cock-a-doodle-dos* rattled the panes of her windows a good fifteen or twenty minutes before sunup, she considered ringing the bird's neck. Instead, she rolled on her side and faced the sitting room in anticipation of the first rays of sunlight she knew would soon dust the darkened sky. While she waited, the conversation the previous evening between Jake and Shelby replayed again and again in her thoughts. What would happen if Shelby actually got an assignment in Paraíso? Hanna shuddered at the mere possibility. She knew there was no way she could work day in and day out with the woman. She would hate to leave the Andersons, and she would miss Isabela and Giselle, but maybe it was time for her to start making plans to go somewhere else.

When Hanna arrived at the worksite several hours later, her heart felt heavier than it had the day before. Even so, with only two work days remaining, she needed to do her part. If the building was to be completed, there wasn't any time to waste on foolish relational issues.

As the day progressed, Hanna noticed Jake was more focused on his work than on Shelby, resulting in several melodramatic performances, none of which appeared to get his attention. Hanna couldn't help but derive pleasure at seeing the look of bewilderment on the woman's face. She resisted the temptation to say, "Welcome to my world."

That evening the group returned to the Andersons' for supper as usual, but Jake didn't linger afterwards. Hanna overheard him telling Conner he had a few things to finish up at the worksite. Thirty minutes later, Shelby was missing. Hanna had no doubt she'd gone after Jake. The urge to fight back rose within her faster than the countryside floods after a dam breaks. She'd allowed Shelby to intimidate her for two days – Enough was enough!

Hanna marched toward the new church building, her steps firm and confident as the coral shadows of dusk deepened to grayish blue. Latin music pulsated from a nightclub on a corner near the construction site, and a cluster of men clogged the sidewalk, forcing her into the street. When she passed a couple of men playing dominos in front of a small store, she nodded in greeting and plowed ahead, feeling almost giddy as she contemplated the look on Shelby's face after she put her in her place. Once she reached the church facility, she stood outside the concrete block structure, which was amazingly close to completion, and tried to catch her breath. Gradually the pounding of her heart settled to a normal rhythm.

Sweat dripped down the sides of her face, and she wiped it away with the tips of her fingers. She thought she heard voices coming from the back of the large, main room. With determination she feared had faded with the last rays of sunlight, she stepped inside, then . . . abruptly stopped.

A bare bulb hanging from a thin cord in the middle of the room served as the only light, but Hanna could see Jake and Shelby standing in the shadows, arms entwined and lips locked in a passionate kiss. In shock, she stood for a few seconds, her feet rooted to the floor. Did Jake and Shelby stage their exit? Had this intimate rendezvous been planned all along? With much regret, she watched as any respect she'd ever had for Jake Mason evaporated before her eyes like dew on a warm summer morning.

Propelled by her contempt for the man, Hanna began retracing her steps. She had almost succeeded in leaving unnoticed, when she tripped over a two-by-four that had been left lying on the ground. With the scraping of wood on concrete, and the clunk of her shoes against the floor, she interrupted the romantic tryst only a short distance away. Before running from the building, she glanced over her shoulder long enough to realize she'd been seen. Once outside, she walked at a clipped pace toward the Andersons'. The church facility was a half a block behind her when she heard Jake calling her name. She picked up her speed, almost knocking a woman over as she exited the corner colmado. When Hanna heard the thudding of Jake's tennis shoes echoing on the sidewalk, she broke into a run, but he was faster. His hand wrapped around her arm, stopping her mid-stride. Hanna lowered her head, gasping for breath, her chest rising and falling in painful, uneven jerks. Tears mingled with sweat dropped off her face onto the cracked pavement below.

Jake tightened his grip on her arm and leaned over as he tried to catch his breath. "Hanna, please . . . give me . . ." He gulped in air before continuing. "Please let me explain."

Hanna squeezed her eyes shut, hoping to stop the flow of tears. When she opened her mouth to speak, she hiccupped a sob. Self-loathing rose in her throat, choking off the words. How could she have made herself so vulnerable? She shook her head. As she yanked her arm loose from his grasp, rough broken blisters on the palm of his hand scraped across her skin. When she turned and began walking again, he did not follow.

Caribbean Paradise

Chapter Twenty-Seven

Hanna slipped into the house, breathing a sigh of relief when she found the living room and kitchen empty. At least she didn't have to explain the deluge pouring down her cheeks. She trudged into her apartment and threw herself on the bed, pressing her knuckles against her mouth to muffle the sobs.

She must have cried herself to sleep because she awoke with a start a while later to the sound of voices on the patio. The cobwebs were thick, and it took a few minutes to remember why she was laying on top of the covers still fully clothed. As memories of the painful encounter at the church returned, she tried to dislodge the ache in her heart, but was unsuccessful in stopping a new surge of tears. She got up and walked to the dresser, pulling tissues from a box. Getting ready to blow her nose, she stopped short as the voices drifting through the sitting room window became more distinct.

It was Jake and Conner.

Hanna knew she was developing a bad habit, but when sound carried so clearly into her apartment, it was hard not to listen. One day she might confess to Conner and Maleah, but she would add another transgression to the list before she did.

Leaving the room draped in darkness, she eased into one of the white wicker chairs just as Conner exclaimed in a loud whisper, "You did what? Please tell me you're kidding."

"I wish I could," Jake said.

"What were you thinking?"

"That's just it, I *wasn't* thinking. I know this is going to sound like a juvenile excuse, but it was like that high school kid who once cared for her moved back in and took over."

"More like that high school boy's hormones moved back in and took over." Conner's sigh was heavy. "But I'm just curious, why did you come running to me with this story?"

"Well . . . I thought . . . you see . . . " Jake cleared his throat and tried again. "Because I wanted you to hear the story from me before you heard it from someone else."

Hanna sat up straighter, pressing her lips into a thin line. Now she understood what he was doing. He wasn't remorseful. He just didn't want Conner and Maleah hearing about his little rendezvous from her.

"Who else knows about this?" Conner asked. "Surely you didn't think Shelby was going to tell me."

Jake chuckled. "Ah no . . . although I wouldn't put it past her to let it slip in a boastful sort of way."

"Ah come on. Do you think she would actually tell us the two of you met up at the church in the dark like two high school lovers meeting behind the school gym?"

"I don't know." Jake's voice sounded shaky. "Yes . . . no. One minute she seems to have gotten her life straight, and the next, she doesn't seem any different than that fifteen year old girl I dated back in high school."

"Uh-huh, well," Conner said, clearing his throat, "I hate to say this, but she could probably say the same about you. Would you mind telling me a little of your and Shelby's history?"

A chair creaked as someone shifted. "I guess not," Jake said. "What exactly did you have in mind?"

"For starters, how involved were you? I mean, was there anything in your past that might have made Shelby think you'd be interested in a more physical relationship now?"

Hanna placed both feet flat on the floor and leaned forward, being careful not to make any noise. She rested her elbows on her thighs, cupping her chin in her hands. She heard Jake take a deep breath, and then blow it out slowly. She realized she was eavesdropping on some rather personal information and braced herself for the worst. Perhaps she should get up and walk away, but as long as she stayed in her apartment, she'd be able to hear them.

She focused for a brief second on the door. She could wait it out in the kitchen or walk into the living room where they could see her, but that would mean facing Jake, which in her opinion was out of the question. She opted for staying put and concentrated on listening to his response.

"The way things ended between us, I would say no," he said. "But that's just because God used the exhortation of a pastor at a youth conference one summer to help save me from a lot of future heartache. Unfortunately, the man's advice didn't have the same effect on Shelby."

"Why do you say that?"

Hanna heard the scraping of chair legs on the brick floor of the patio. "Let me back up a little," Jake said several seconds later. "Shelby and I met the fall of my junior year – her sophomore year. She was new in town and started attending some of our church youth functions with friends. I noticed her soon after that, but when one of her friends told me she wasn't a Christian, I decided not to ask her out. A month or so later, when a youth evangelist spoke to the group one night following a hayride, Shelby made a profession of faith."

"And after that you felt it was okay to ask her out."

"Well, yeah . . . and within a couple of months we were going steady or going out – whatever you want to call it – we weren't seeing anyone else. At first Shelby appeared to be enthusiastic about her newfound faith, but over time her sense of excitement started to dwindle."

"Let me guess. By then it was too late – you thought you were in love."

Jake's laugh sounded brittle. "In love . . . in lust . . . By then my own walk with God was on the decline. I went through the motions, but it was all a show. As a starter on our basketball team, I'd begun to dream of playing college ball and perhaps eventually getting to play professionally. With Shelby as my girlfriend, I was the envy of every guy in the school. It didn't take long for all that attention to go to my head. I thought I was the big man on campus. After a while I started compromising on some of the decisions I had previously made regarding dating relationships. As a result, more often than not our dates ended with us parked somewhere on a dark street – "

"Wait a minute. I thought you said you two weren't physically involved."

"Me too," Hanna mouthed as she rolled her eyes. She wondered if Jake was squirming.

"What I said, or what I guess I meant, is we weren't physically involved when we parted ways."

"Does that mean that earlier in the relationship you *had* been?"

Hanna wasn't sure she wanted to hear the rest of this story. She sat up, pressing her back against the chair. Did she really want to know how physically involved Jake and Shelby had once been? And since Jake was confessing his "sins" to Conner and not her, maybe it was time to make her presence known. She looked at the lamp sitting beside her. If a light came on in her apartment, perhaps the men would realize she was awake and move their discussion elsewhere. Jake cleared his throat.

Then again . . . maybe she'd listen a while longer.

"Not as involved as we could have been," he said, "although those dark road make-out sessions were just temptation looking for a place to happen, and I praise God we never went too far. I thought it strange I was consistently the one who said we needed to stop and go home. Shelby never seemed to understand my convictions. I blamed it on the fact she was a young Christian.

"That summer we attended a youth camp, and one of the conferences was on saving yourself for marriage. Like I mentioned earlier, God used those sessions to remind me of the importance of not allowing myself to get into compromising situations where I might not have the willpower to say no. By the end of the week I was broken and repentant. I tried to help Shelby understand why keeping ourselves pure for our future mates was so important, but her response was always the same: We were going to get married one day, therefore it didn't matter. By then I had my doubts and wasn't sure she was the one God had chosen to be my future wife, although at the time I didn't tell her."

"What *did* you do?"

"I told her I felt it would be best if we stopped spending time alone. After that, any time we went out it was with another couple or in a social setting. She thought I'd lost my mind. We continued dating for a little over a month, but spent most of the time arguing. A week before school started that fall, I told her I didn't think our relationship was going to work."

"What happened then?" Conner asked.

"Within a matter of weeks Shelby stopped going to church. By homecoming she was dating the school quarterback. She tried for a while to use their relationship to make me jealous. Although I worried about the decisions she might make, the fact that she was dating someone else didn't bother me. I tried to talk to her one afternoon about being careful in her dating relationships. She responded by calling me a name I won't repeat, then made it clear I had no business telling her how to live her social *or* private life. By the time I graduated, we had lost touch with one another."

Hanna heard Greta let out a deep, guttural growl, followed by the sound of footsteps moving toward the low-railed fence bordering the patio. "What is it, girl?" Conner said.

"Do you see anything?" Jake asked.

"There's something rustling over by the back fence. Probably a rat."

As Hanna listened to Conner walking back across the patio, a sensation reminiscent of prickly feet against skin scurried up her spine. Where were Angel and Sugar when she needed them?

"Okay . . . " Conner's voice drifted her way. "Where were we? Oh yeah . . . Do you know where Shelby's been? What she's been doing?"

"She shared a good bit with me on the trip from the airport to Paraíso. Just as I'd feared, she made some bad choices, but ultimately the consequences led her back to church. She claims this time to have made a genuine decision for Christ."

"And do you believe her?"

"I do, but I think she's still young in the Lord. What bothers me is I don't have that as an excuse for my actions tonight."

"What would you blame your actions on?" Conner asked.

Hanna heard Jake blow out his breath. She wished she had the nerve to peek out the window so she could see what he was doing.

"I have allowed myself to wallow in self pity too long," he said. "For three years the void in my heart has been growing deeper and wider, all because I was unwilling to humble myself and take my hurt . . . my anger . . . my grief . . . to the Lord, and let Him help me deal with it." Jake's voice sounded thick with emotion. "I blamed God for my pain, so I stopped praying and reading His word. As a result, I have gone through the most spiritually dry season of my life, which ultimately led to a total lack of discernment when temptation came knocking. I take full responsibility. I can't blame Shelby – She's just a babe in Christ." Jake paused, taking a deep breath. "I've really set a fine example, haven't I?"

Hanna heard the kitchen screen door squeak open and shut. Seconds later, light from the breezeway seeped under her apartment door. It was probably Maleah. Hanna held her breath, wondering what she would say if she came in to check on her.

"Who turned on that light?" Jake asked.

Hanna imagined both men had turned their heads toward the brick wall separating the breezeway from the patio.

"Probably Maleah. I saw her walk through the living room a few minutes ago."

"Can she hear us?"

Conner chuckled. "I suppose she could if she wanted to, but I doubt she's that interested."

Hanna released her breath when the light went off and she heard the screen door open and close again. She shifted in the wicker chair, pulling her left foot underneath her. Several more seconds passed before the conversation on the patio continued.

"You still haven't told me who saw you and Shelby together," Conner said.

"Hanna." When Jake spoke her name it was barely above a whisper. If she hadn't been listening closely, she would have missed it.

"Hanna!" No chance she would have missed that. Conner lowered his voice to a loud whisper. "Jake, not Hanna."

"Oh how I wish it had not been. I wish it had been anyone but Hanna."

She almost felt sorry for him. Could it be it actually bothered him that she had seen the two of them together?

"What was Hanna doing there?" Conner asked.

"I don't know, but she was there, and I know she saw us. When she ran from the building, I followed. I caught up with her a block or so away. I tried to talk to her, but she wouldn't listen, so I went back to get Shelby."

"Where is Hanna now?" Conner asked.

Jake's voice dropped an octave. "I'm assuming she's in her apartment. When was the last time you saw her?"

"During supper I guess. The lights are off in her room. She's probably in bed."

A precarious silence throbbed at Hanna's temples. Several minutes passed before Conner spoke again. "Jake, I've got to know something. Did you and Shelby plan to meet at the church?"

"NO!"

Hanna's entire body jolted as if she'd grabbed hold of a live electrical cable.

"No!" Jake continued, his voice significantly lower. "I went over there to finish up some work, just like I said I was going to do. I hadn't been there ten or fifteen minutes when Shelby showed up. She walked around, talking about how great it was being with me again. Next thing I know she's standing in front of me, running her hand up and down my arm, then along the side of my face. Before I realized what was happening we were kissing. I guess I just . . . I don't know. What can I say? I messed up – Big time."

"You said you went back and got Shelby after Hanna refused to talk to you. What happened then?"

"I told her we needed to come back here. She started running her hand up and down my arm again and tried to convince me to stay. When I stepped away and told her I was leaving, she got all sulky. A couple of times on the walk back she tried to hold my hand, but I wouldn't let her."

"So she knows you feel what you two did was not right."

"Oh yes. I made it clear it should have never happened. I apologized and told her it wouldn't happen again."

"How did she respond?" Conner asked.

Jake grunted. "She said I had no need to apologize because she was glad it happened and wouldn't mind if it did again."

"And you said . . . "

"Whether she agreed or not, I felt I not only owed her an apology, but I also owed Hanna one. I left her here with the intentions of heading home, but ended up walking around for a while, then circling back this way. When I saw your light was still on, I decided it was time to talk."

"Hard lesson," Conner said, "but if this is what it took to wake you up and make you realize it's time to get things right with God, then I'm glad it happened. It could have been a lot worse."

Jake drew in a deep, long breath. When he let it out, the sound reminded Hanna of a flame being ignited in a hot air balloon. "You're right about that," he said to Conner. "The part I hate the most is that Hanna got hurt in the process. I don't know if she'll ever forgive me. She and I have had our ups and downs – all the downs my fault, I confess, but until Shelby arrived I really thought I was beginning to care for Hanna. Now I wonder. If my feelings for her were sincere, how could I have allowed myself to be drawn away by another woman, even briefly? And to think I gave Hanna the cold shoulder for months because I was *being true to my memories of Katie.* What a hypocrite I am."

When Hanna heard the sound of a chair being pushed away from the patio table, she stood noiselessly. Her left foot had fallen asleep. She shook it a couple of times as she hobbled over to the window and peeked through the louvered slats. Jake had his hands on the sides of his chair and was propelling himself into a standing position. "I'm sorry for keeping you up so late," he said, "but I appreciate your taking the time to listen."

"Isn't that what friends are for?" Conner said as he stood. "Now I think we need to sleep on all this, pray about it . . . I'm going to share what happened with Maleah," he glanced at Jake, "if that is alright with you." When Jake nodded, Conner continued. "Unless the Lord says *no,* I'm thinking tomorrow morning we need to have a meeting – you, Hanna, Shelby, Maleah and me."

"Whoa . . . " Jake said. "That sounds like a roast Jake session, if you ask me. But I guess I have it coming. I'm willing to do whatever you and Maleah believe God tells you we need to do."

Chapter Twenty-Eight

The following morning, Hanna played innocent when Conner informed her, Maleah, Jake and Shelby that he needed to talk to them for a few minutes, and then sent the rest of the volunteer team on ahead to the worksite. Once everyone else was gone, they assembled at the dining room table with Conner on one end and Jake on the other. Maleah sat to Conner's right and Hanna sat next to her, forcing Shelby to sit across from them. A half dozen breakfast rolls remained on a plate in the center of the table, and the faint aroma of warm sourdough bread lingered in the air. Hanna's mouth watered. She could almost taste the gooey cinnamon filling and powdered sugar icing.

After they were all seated, Conner surveyed the group, his eyes reflecting the patience and kindness Hanna had come to appreciate about the man. "I'll explain in a minute the reason I've called this impromptu meeting," he said, "but I would like to pray before we get started."

As Hanna lowered her head she caught a glimpse of Shelby fidgeting, her eyes darting from Conner to Jake. How fitting she should be the only one at the table who didn't know what was coming. She looked so disconcerted Hanna wouldn't have been surprised if she had jumped up and bolted from the room. Seeing her stripped of her confident *I'm in control* façade, she was tempted to feel sorry for her.

With her head bowed, Hanna tuned her thoughts to Conner's prayer as he asked for God's guidance, wisdom and discernment, and that the matter at hand, which he did not address by name, would be handled in a Christlike manner. After saying "amen," he cleared his throat and looked up. Small beads of perspiration dotted his forehead. Hanna admired the man for what he was getting ready to do. She imagined she was seeing an example of the type person Jesus was referring to when He said, "Blessed are the peacemakers, for they shall be called sons of God."

Conner gave a brief recounting of his conversation with Jake the previous night, leaving out the parts about Jake and Shelby's high school romance. When he finished, he turned to Hanna. "I believe Jake has something he'd like to say to you," he said.

Hanna adjusted her focus to Jake, who stared at the table where his darkly tanned forearms rested side-by-side, hands balled in fists. After a few seconds of strained silence, he lifted his eyes. They reminded Hanna of shimmering pools of aqua blue water. The pounding of her heart rapidly increased, and she blinked back tears of hurt and anger, banishing the impulse to ask him why he had to mess things up.

When he spoke, his voice sounded raspy. "Hanna, I owe you an apology." He closed his eyes and shook his head. "No, that's not true." His eyes met hers. "I owe you much more than an apology. I have acted the fool in recent months and more specifically recent days. Unfortunately, as a result of my selfish actions, you got hurt. I'm sorry. You deserve so much better."

Hanna detected movement on the other side of the table. She glanced at Shelby, who was shoved back in her chair with arms folded across her midsection. She had Jake pinned in a seething glare. Hanna flinched when the woman uttered a curse.

"You know, Jake, this isn't my fault." The words came out of Shelby's mouth like spit. "You led me on. I'm not sure what all you told Conner or your little friend here," she darted her eyes at Hanna. "But – it takes two to tango. Don't you dare put this off on me."

Hanna felt her blood start to boil. Amazingly, Jake seemed unperturbed by the woman's outburst.

"Shelby, I also owe *you* an apology," he said, his voice holding steady. "Trust me, I'm not trying to put anything off on you. I take full responsibility for my actions, and . . . I'm sorry."

Shelby huffed, drew her arms tighter across her stomach and muttered another curse. The tension in the room was thick, the Dominican morning hot and muggy. Hanna felt sweat trickling down the back of her neck and lifted her ponytail. She caught Jake watching as she wiped the moisture away with her hand. The corners of his mouth lifted. Before she realized what she was doing, she smiled.

"I'm sorry," he mouthed. Hanna felt her face flush. Why did he continue to have this kind of effect on her? She knew she had no choice but to forgive him, yet she feared she'd never be able to trust him again. If they were to start dating, she was afraid what happened with Shelby would continue to haunt her and she would live in fear of someone else catching his eye and drawing him away.

"I accept your apology and I forgive you." She drew a ragged breath and studied her hands.

"But . . . " Jake said.

Hanna felt her eyes fill. Several tears spilled over and ran down her cheeks. She brushed them away in frustration. Jake reached a hand in her direction, but she pulled away before he could touch her. Watching him from beneath tear-laden lashes, her heart constricted at the hurt in his eyes, but she had to maintain her resolve not to allow herself to get pulled back in too quickly. She raised her head, moistening her lips before speaking. "I keep thinking about something my mother often told me. Trust, once broken, is hard to regain. Life has taught me she was right. Jake, I really do forgive you, but I'm afraid it may take me a long time to trust you again." She heaved a ragged sigh. "And that . . . breaks my heart."

"Oh, *please*!" Shelby said as she thrust her chair back, knocking it to the floor as she stood.

Hanna looked up. "Shelby, wait." Her breath caught at the piercing scowl the woman fastened on her, but she needed to finish before she lost her nerve. "Listen, *I* owe you an apology."

"Me?" Shelby loosed a mirthless laugh. "Whatever are you talking about?"

"I've been jealous of you since the night you arrived, and I've not treated you as I should. I've asked God to forgive me for my unChristlike behavior, but I need to ask for your forgiveness as well."

"You're serious, aren't you?" Shelby asked.

"I am."

Maleah's chair creaked as she leaned forward, forearms on the table. "That goes for me too," she said. "Shelby, my attitude toward you, and many times my actions, have been all wrong. Would you please forgive me?"

Shelby's eyes burned like two emerald fires. "You're all crazy. You know that, don't you?" Before anyone could respond, she spun around and stormed through the double doors leading onto the patio.

Jake pushed his chair back and started to stand. "Jake, no," Conner said, shaking his head. "That's probably exactly what she wants. My guess is she's trying to lure you away from the rest of us."

Maleah rose from the table. "I'll go talk to her," she said as she slipped past her husband and headed toward the patio.

"Now what?" Jake asked.

"We wait," Conner said.

Hanna folded her hands in her lap and kept her eyes lowered. She could hear Maleah's and Shelby's voices rising and falling as if they were either arguing, or at the least, engaged in a heavy debate, but their words were unintelligible. A grin inched up her face at the thought of asking Jake and Conner if they would be interested in relocating to her apartment where they would be able to hear everything that was being said.

"What's so funny?" Jake asked, startling her.

She raised her eyes to meet his. "Nothing." It was all she could do to keep a straight face.

Jake lifted an eyebrow. "Why don't I believe you?"

Hanna bit her lower lip. "Maybe I'll tell you someday, but not today."

Conner chuckled. "Listen you two . . . once Maleah comes back in with Shelby, I'm going to suggest they walk on over to the church while the three of us stay behind a few minutes longer. I've got something I want to share with both of you, but would rather wait until Shelby is out of hearing range."

Hanna and Jake exchanged looks. "Okay with me," Jake

said.

Hanna nodded. "Me too."

Minutes later, Maleah walked into the room with a more subdued Shelby at her side. "I believe Shelby has something she'd like to say," she said.

Shelby's eyes started with Jake, moved to Hanna, then Conner, before settling on a spot somewhere in between. "I'm sorry, you guys. I'm new at all this," she said, her voice cracking. "I've only been a Christian for a little over a year. Sadly, I often find myself falling back into old patterns of behavior." She cut her eyes at Maleah, then, circled the table again. "Jake, Hanna . . . I accept your apologies, and I'm also asking for your forgiveness."

Maleah slid her arm around Shelby's waist. Hanna prayed for strength as she rose from her seat and made her way to where the two ladies stood. Maleah reached out her arm, drawing her in.

When Conner announced his plan for Maleah and Shelby to go on ahead to the construction site while he, Jake and Hanna stayed behind for a few minutes, Shelby didn't say anything; but Hanna saw her flash a look in their direction, mistrust written all over her face. When Maleah slipped her arm in hers, she turned around, and the two walked out the door together. Even so, it was obvious Shelby wasn't pleased with the arrangement.

Conner scraped his chair back and stood. "Let's move to the living room," he said, "where it's more comfortable." He waved his hand toward the sofa. "Why don't the two of you sit over there?"

Hanna sat on one end of the couch with both feet planted on the floor. Looking straight ahead while Conner pulled a wing back chair toward her, she idly ran her hand across the couch's chenille tapestry. She saw amusement in his coffee-colored eyes as he settled on the cushioned burgundy and beige striped seat. When Conner started laughing, she turned her eyes toward Jake. He was snuggled up to the other end of the sofa, knees together, feet facing forward, hands uncharacteristically folded in his lap. His posture reminded her of scenes from TV shows where a teenage boy is forced to sit alone in the living room with his date's father while he waits for the young lady to finish getting ready. No wonder Conner was laughing.

"What?" Jake asked, his eyes flickering from Conner to

Hanna.

"You two look so uncomfortable," Conner said, "like you're both afraid the other one's going to bite."

Jake's downcast eyes rested on Hanna. "Well, I know *she* doesn't bite, but chances are she thinks *I* do," he said.

A laugh gurgled up from Hanna's stomach; she couldn't hold it in. She picked up a pillow and threw it at him. "You're pathetic," she said.

Although she was laughing, she wanted to scream. Why did she let him get to her so easily? She needed to be careful. She couldn't let him charm her into trusting him again. He needed to realize a few impish grins did not cancel out what he'd done. If he wanted her respect, he was going to have to earn it.

Jake nestled his body at an angle into the corner of the sofa, rested his left arm on the rounded side and crossed his right ankle over the knee of his left leg. Hanna shifted slightly in his direction, pulling her left foot up underneath her.

"That's better," Conner said, still snickering. "Now for the reason I called this meeting. Maleah and I talked and prayed about this last night, then again this morning. We have some concerns about Shelby we feel need to be addressed." His countenance grew somber as he focused for a moment on Jake. "While this is something we believe you especially need to be made aware of," he shifted his eyes to Hanna before continuing, "we felt it might be helpful if Hanna knew about our concerns as well."

Hanna looked at Jake. He lifted his shoulders. "Okay," he said as he placed both feet on the floor and leaned forward, resting his forearms on his thighs. "You've got my curiosity up. Let's hear it."

"Have either of you ever heard of a Jezebel spirit?" Conner asked.

Hanna shook her head.

"A Jezebel spirit . . . " Jake repeated the words slowly, his eyebrows drawn together in thought. "I've heard of it, but can't say I know anything about it."

"Wasn't Jezebel the wife of King Ahab," Hanna asked, "and didn't she threaten the prophet Elijah?"

"She was and she did," Conner said. "There's also a reference in the second chapter of Revelation to a woman named Jezebel who called herself a prophetess. In both cases the women were schemers – controlling, manipulative and seductive."

"Where are you going with this?" Jake asked.

"Some believe a person can be influenced by what is called a Jezebel spirit. They claim whenever this happens, the person – most times a woman – will often act out in the ways I just described."

Jake narrowed his eyes. "I see . . . and do you think this is what has happened with Shelby?"

"Quite possibly, although I can't say for sure. Neither Maleah nor I know enough about it to make a definite call. But whatever the cause, we fear Shelby's past lifestyle is still more often than not dominating her actions. Bottom line – there appears to be some junk she picked up along the way that she has yet to shed in terms of influence when it comes to her behavior. If you recall, Shelby admitted as much a little earlier."

Jake leaned against the padded back of the sofa, resting one arm along the top and the other one on the armrest. A shadow of concern drifted across his face. "Yeah she did, and I see what you're saying," he said. "But if a past lifestyle is what's influencing her behavior, what's *my* excuse?"

Hanna placed her hand over her mouth and stifled a laugh. Jake cut his eyes at her. "No comments from the peanut gallery," he said. "Something tells me this is serious stuff we're talking about here." Although she could tell he was trying to maintain a stern expression, laughter danced in his eyes.

She lifted her hands and shrugged. "I didn't say a word."

"You didn't have to. What you are wanting to say is written all over your face."

"Okay, you two. Let me finish," Conner said, looking at Jake. "Your excuse, my friend, is the admonition Jesus made to the church in Ephesus, also found in chapter two of Revelation – You left your first love."

Contrition replaced the laughter in Jake's eyes. "You're right," he said, nodding, "absolutely right. Although outwardly I was doing all the right things, inwardly my heart toward God had become as dry as the road leading into Anse-a-Pitres."

"Making you easy prey when temptation came knocking," Conner said.

Jake studied the floor. "That's all getting ready to change," he said. "I've accumulated a lot of unresolved junk so it may take me a while, but starting today I'm going to begin the process of getting my heart right with God."

"In the meanwhile, you need to keep your distance from Shelby," Conner said. "Under no circumstances should you allow yourself, even for a moment, to be alone with her. Furthermore, when we take the team back to Santo Domingo tomorrow, she's going to be riding with me."

"I'm in full agreement," Jake said, "but I've got something that's really been eating at me."

"What's that?" Conner asked.

"Remember the other night when Shelby asked about sharing her testimony with some of the people from the church?"

"I do."

"Well, I've been feeling bad about that. I *was* the one who suggested she might have the opportunity to share. I even told her I thought God could use her past in order to help others."

Conner gazed toward the patio. "Under different circumstances, I believe that may have been a possibility," he said, looking back at Jake. "But the timing wasn't right, and I don't think Shelby is ready. It appears she's still got an awful lot of her own baggage to deal with first."

"I understand and agree. I just feel bad because I prematurely encouraged her to consider doing something God may one day have her do – not here, but maybe somewhere else."

"Perhaps that should be another lesson learned, a reminder to be careful not to make plans without checking with God first," Conner said. "But for now, you'll need to let it go and trust God to work it out in His time."

"Let go and trust God – I'm beginning to realize that's something I haven't been willing to do in a long time," Jake said.

Hanna cleared her throat. Jake and Conner both looked at her. "I have a concern I would like to voice."

"Go ahead," Conner said.

She studied the floral pattern in the rug, her hands entwined in her lap. "Speaking of trust . . . I guess . . . truth is . . . I don't trust Shelby." She looked at Conner. "I don't mean for today or tomorrow. I mean in the long run."

Conner's brow wrinkled. "I'm not sure I'm following you."

"I think I know what she means," Jake said.

Hanna narrowed her eyes as she turned to look at him. "You do?"

"Uh-huh, I do. You're afraid she won't stay out of the picture once she's gone," he said.

"That's it. I know she was apologetic this morning, and I'm certainly not saying she wasn't sincere – "

"I think I hear one of those buts . . . coming," Jake said.

"But . . . " Hanna said, eyeing him with mocked irritation, "I believe if she were to have her way, she'd still like to see something happen between the two of you. As for me, she probably would prefer I was non-existent. Maybe I'm wrong, but . . . "

Conner threw his head back and laughed. "But . . . " he said. "I love it."

Jake's grin slowly dissolved. "Truth is, I think she's right."

"Oh, I agree," Conner said. "So what do you think needs to be done?"

"After we left the worksite last night, I tried to make it clear a relationship between us wasn't going to work, but . . . " Jake shook his head and laughed. "Now I'm doing it. But . . . I don't think she was listening."

"In that case, I believe Maleah and I need to sit down and talk to her," Conner said. "We'll do it tonight. While we're at it, I'd like to encourage her to get some solid, biblical counseling. Maybe we can help her understand that many times even Christians need a little help overcoming past influences in our lives."

"Do you think she'll listen?" Hanna asked.

"Don't know," Conner said. "She's obviously a very strong-willed woman. We can hope and pray once she leaves this will all be behind us. In the long run, only time will tell."

Hanna sighed. "I sincerely hope she'll listen to you and get some counseling, but something tells me in terms of her desire to return to Paraíso, she's not going to give up that easily. Jake's not the only one who needs to let go and trust God, but this is hard. I really don't want her coming back."

Chapter Twenty-Nine

The next day, as Jake followed Conner on the four and a half hour drive back to Paraíso, he had a lot of time to think and, more importantly, pray. It was passed time for him to make things right with God. He knew he had allowed himself to wallow in self-pity far too long. His own stubborn pride had almost resulted in a relational catastrophe.

The last twenty-four hours with Shelby had been tense, but manageable. He could tell she was not pleased when he kept his distance from her. She appeared even less pleased when Conner informed her she would be riding with him on the trip to Santo Domingo. At the airport, she'd tried to pull Jake aside to say good-bye, but he'd been adamant they stay with the group. When she attempted to hug him, he extended his hand, keeping her at arm's length. After shaking his hand, she smiled what he would have best described as a smirk, kissed her index and middle fingers, and then placed them on his lips.

"You're going to miss me when I'm gone," she said. "That's okay, though. It'll make it that much sweeter when I come back." She turned and walked away before he could respond.

Jake prayed she would get the emotional and spiritual counseling she needed, but also asked God to thwart any plans she might try to make to return to Paraíso.

When Maleah invited him and Isabela to stay for dinner that evening, he readily accepted. After finishing off a delicious slice of Maleah's apple pie, he idly wiped his hands on a napkin, debating on whether he should share with the others the progress he'd made since they had talked the day before. Laying the napkin on the table, he accidently knocked his fork against the empty dessert plate. It clanked in protest, disrupting the silence created by a lull in the conversation. When the others looked at him, he cocked one side of his mouth, offering them what he knew was a self-conscious grin. He guessed now was as good an opportunity as any to say something. "If you guys don't mind," he said, "I'd like to share a little of the journey I've been on today."

"Why certainly," Maleah said. "What's been going on?"

Jake looked at Hanna. She'd been quiet all evening. She lifted an eyebrow and gave him an unenthusiastic nod, her dark green eyes daring him to prove he wasn't the rogue his actions in recent days insinuated he was. The day before she'd said he'd lost her trust, but he knew he'd also lost her respect. He ran his fingers through his hair. His throat suddenly felt like someone had stuffed it full of cotton. When he tried to clear it, it didn't do much good. He shifted his gaze to Maleah, hoping that would help.

"For starters," he said, "I've probably prayed more in the last twenty-four hours than I have since Katie died. What happened with Shelby helped me realize how foolishly I've been acting. I've allowed Satan to gain a lot of ground in my life, all because I wasn't willing to let God help me work through the grief I've experienced since losing my wife."

"So what are you planning on doing now?" Conner asked.

"I've already asked God to forgive me for being so stubborn, and I know He has because of the peace I've felt today. The question I keep asking myself is why I allowed all the junk to keep me from this kind of peace over the past three years."

Maleah nodded, understanding reflecting in her eyes. "Maybe you need to let this be a reminder the next time you are tempted to push God away instead of trusting Him to help you work through something – no matter how painful it may be."

"I know certain aspects of what I still need to work through are going to be painful," Jake said, "but I'm tired of fighting this battle. I told God earlier today I'm ready to let Him bring some much needed emotional healing in my life." He looked down as his throat choked with tears.

"We'll be praying for you," Conner said.

"We sure will," Maleah added. "If there's anything else we can do, let us know."

Jake looked up. "Actually, I would like to get away for a few days – alone. There's a place I've heard about . . . a retreat facility near Constanza. I was thinking it might be easier if Isabela wasn't around – "

"We'd be glad to keep her for you," Maleah interjected.

"Jake . . . " Hanna leaned toward him as she said his name. It was the first time she had spoken directly to him all evening. Was that compassion he saw on her face? "If it would help, I could stay with her at your house."

He glanced at Maleah.

"It's whatever you think would be best," she said. "You know we don't mind keeping her here, but if you think she'd do better in her own home, we certainly understand."

"I'm sure she'd love to have a three or four day slumber party with Sophie," Jake said, "but everyone else might rest better if Isabela was in her own bed at night."

"Then let me keep her. I may not be Sophie, but . . . " Hanna hesitated as a soft giggle slipped through her lips.

Jake lifted his eyebrows. "But . . . what?" he asked.

"She and I could have our own little slumber party. It'll be fun."

"I'm sure it will be," he said.

"So it's settled?"

Jake heard the question in Hanna's voice. "Sounds great," he said.

If it sounded so great, why did he feel like a boa constrictor was squeezing the breath out of him? Hanna's offer to keep Isabela should have been a welcome relief from the distrust he'd felt emitting from her all evening.

"When did you plan on leaving?" Conner asked.

Absently, Jake answered. "I thought I'd rest for a few days, then head out." Emotions he thought he'd put to rest rolled over him like the turbulent waves of the Caribbean during a tropical storm.

"Just let me know when you need me," Hanna said.

He pasted on a neutral smile in an effort to mask his uneasiness. "I will."

Hanna's whole attitude appeared to have changed. Strangely, so had his. What would "playing house" with Hanna for three or four days do to Isabela's notion that God had sent her to be her new mommy? Was this how a mama grizzly felt whenever she feared one of her cubs was in danger? Jake still wasn't ready for anyone to take Katie's place in his daughter's heart, not even Hanna. Maybe this wasn't such a good idea after all.

~~~~~

Three days later Hanna arrived at Jake and Isabela's house a few minutes before six in the morning. The sky above the mountains blushed a delicate apricot, and the air was refreshingly pleasant. She closed her eyes, savoring the moment. By noon the sun would be blistering hot, and the streets of Paraíso sizzling like bacon in a frying pan.

She tapped lightly on the front door. It squeaked as Jake pulled it open. His eyes looked soft and sleepy. He was wearing a pair of faded blue jeans and a white knit shirt, accenting his deeply tanned face and arms. Combing his short, dark hair with his fingers, he quietly greeted her. "Good morning."

"Good morning." She felt her heart do a little ka-thump.

"Come in." He took the small suitcase she carried. "I'll put this in my bedroom," he said. "Make yourself comfortable."

He walked away, leaving behind the fresh smell of soap mingled with the masculine scent of the now familiar cologne. He had told Hanna she could sleep in his room while he was gone, but she would probably make her stay a real slumber party, opting instead to stay with Isabela in her room. Although silly, the idea of sleeping in Jake's bed seemed inappropriate.

She had taken only a couple of hesitant steps toward the living room when he returned. He smiled, but the effort appeared obligatory. She could tell something was bothering him. Clasping her hands behind her back, she looked around. "I'm assuming Isabela is still asleep," she said, trying to make conversation.

He stuffed his own hands in the pockets of his jeans. "She is. We were up late, so I wouldn't be surprised if she sleeps until eight or eight-thirty. Rosalinda should be here around nine. Once she gets here, if there are other things you need to do, you can leave Isabela with her."

Hanna swallowed around the lump rising in her throat. Jake's blue eyes appeared to be challenging her, and emotionally he seemed detached. For the first time since the trip to Pedernales, it felt as if the Jake from her earlier days in the country had returned.

"Okay, but don't worry about things here," she said. "We'll be fine."

A tumultuous silence hung between them.

"I guess I'd better get on the road," he finally said, after what seemed to Hanna like an eternity.

She followed him to the door. "I'll be praying for you," she said.

He turned, his countenance a little warmer. "Thanks. When Isabela wakes up give her a kiss for me . . . " His eyes glistened with tears.

Hanna placed her hand on the side of his arm. "Jake, we're going to be okay."

He shook his head. "I know . . . It's not that . . . " He shifted his gaze to a spot somewhere over her shoulder. She resisted the urge to turn around, but realized he wasn't looking at anything in particular.

"Then . . . what?" she asked.

Slowly he brought his eyes back to hers. "The memories are fading," he whispered. "In the beginning I thought they'd live on . . . fresh, crisp – forever . . . " His voice cracked.

She moved her hand to the side of his face. He covered it with his. His whole body lifted and fell as he sighed. "I don't want Isabela to forget her mother," he said.

Hanna laid her other hand on his face and, like a mother determined to get her child's attention, forced him to look at her. "Is that what this is all about?" she asked. "Are you afraid if Isabela spends too much time with me she'll forget Katie?"

The stubble on his cheeks tickled her palms as he nodded.

She almost laughed and repositioned her hands, placing them on his shoulders. "If it will make you feel better, we'll spend all our time talking about Katie," she said. "We'll look at pictures. I'll get Isabela to tell me stories. Whatever you want us to do."

He blew out his breath. "I want you to do whatever you guys want. In the meanwhile, I think it is way past time I get to the bottom of my grief and let God bring healing to this wounded heart. Please just pray for me. I know it's not going to be easy."

~~~~~

While Jake was away, the small congregation met for the first time in the new church facility. Sitting on one of the rough, backless pews, sandwiched between Isabela and Giselle, the two overhead fans doing nothing but stirring the suffocating heat, Hanna was reminded once again of the contrast between life in the Dominican Republic and the United States. As the service wore on, and the temperature rose, a dull ache settled above her eyes. Her stomach threatened mutiny as the essence of fresh paint and stain simmered with the stench of garbage rotting in the streets. The distinct *aroma* of seafood being sold at the Sunday market only a couple of blocks away didn't help. Latin music bellowing through open doors mingled with the unrestrained rumble of motoconchos, adding to the local ambiance as well as Hanna's headache. She tried to focus on Conner's sermon, but the meaning of his words evaporated before they passed from her ears to her brain. It was one of the many days she had to pray for an extra measure of grace. Such days were less frequent than they were when she first arrived in the country, but still surfaced from time to time.

Two days later Jake returned. The change was evident the moment Hanna saw him walk in the door. His whole countenance had been transformed. His eyes sparkled, and his good looks radiated from the inside out. For the first time since the incident at the church worksite she was hopeful the respect she once had for him was going to be restored.

A week later, summer drew to a close and she finally began teaching her four students. They met each weekday morning and afternoon in a classroom at the Community Center, taking a two-hour break for lunch and a siesta – according to Dominican custom.

On Friday afternoon of the fourth week of classes, Jake dropped by as Hanna finished up the day's lessons. He leaned against the wall just inside the door and listened as she gave the children homework for the weekend. He was wearing khaki shorts, a navy blue T-shirt and a pair of rubber soled flip-flops. She puzzled over his choice of attire. When she realized he was watching her every move, her heart fluttered as if a family of butterflies had suddenly taken up residence in her chest. She gave the children last minute instructions for the day, then dismissed them, hoping her voice didn't sound as rattled as she felt. She began straightening books and papers on her desk while keeping an eye on Isabela as she made a mad dash for her daddy. Jake swept the little girl up in his arms and gave her a big bear hug. When he nuzzled his five o'clock shadow against her cheek, Isabela squealed in delight. An affectionate smile voluntarily lifted the corners of Hanna's mouth.

"What'ya doing here, Daddy?" Isabela asked.

"I came to talk with Aunt Hanna for a minute. Is that okay with you?

"Sure. What'ya gonna talk about?"

"Nosy, aren't we?" he said, still holding the child in his arms.

"No. I just wanted to make sure it wasn't about me. I've been trying to be good in school."

Jake's laughter filled the room. "Have you done something you don't want me to know about?"

Isabela turned. From beneath thick black lashes she gave Hanna a sad puppy dog look. "I don't think so . . . "

Hanna shook her head and smiled. "You've been doing very well, Isabela. You don't need to worry."

"Good!" A giant grin stretched across the little girl's face.

"Well, then," Jake said as he lowered the child to the ground, "since this meeting is obviously not about you, why don't you go on home with Sophie. I'll come by and pick you up in a little while. Celia is waiting outside to walk you guys home."

"Okay," Isabela said.

Sophie stood at Isabela's side, having watched with quiet, wide eyes the interaction between her and Jake. "Come on, Sophie," Isabela said as she reached out to take her hand. "Let's go."

Hanna restacked the books and papers on her desk while Jake watched Isabela and Sophie as they joined Celia out front. When his gaze came to rest on her again, she offered him a timid smile.

"How's our little missionary school going?" he asked as he walked in her direction.

"With almost a month behind us, I'd say it's going well. Why? Are you here as a representative of the school board or something?"

He tilted his head back and chuckled. "First Isabela, now you. Trust me, my visit has nothing to do with school." He paused for a moment. "But you know . . . I don't think this school has a board. Maybe I need to look into that."

Hanna studied him for a moment, and then slapped his arm when she realized he was teasing. "You're bad, you know."

"I know," he said, rubbing the spot where she'd hit him, a pained expression on his face. "But I'm trying hard to reform."

"If you say so." She leaned against the desk, gripping the edge with her fingers. "If this isn't about school, why are you here?"

"Well . . ." he said, his eyes roaming around the room. "I was wondering if you might be interested in going to the watering hole at Los Patos with me." His eyes came to rest on her. "We could pick up a bite to eat from one of the vendors, then sit and talk for a while."

"Talk? Is this business or pleasure?"

"Pure pleasure, I assure you Miss Truly." He narrowed his lips in a smirk as his eyebrows arched in amusement.

She glanced at the knee-length skirt she was wearing, hoping the warm flush on her face would cool before she looked back up. "I'm not exactly dressed for the beach," she said.

"Actually, I was thinking mostly of sitting and enjoying the view, but we might do a little wading, so you would probably be more comfortable in shorts. We could run by the house and let you change."

"That should work," she said. "By the way, is this a date?" She hoped the question was not out of line.

His eyes lingered on her face for a moment. "Yeah, I guess it is. It's been a long time since I asked a young woman out. You might say I'm a little rusty. So what do you say?"

She was tempted to dance and shout, even throw her arms around his neck and squeal in delight, but deciding he might think that was overkill, she willed herself to respond a little more calmly. "Yes . . . I accept your invitation."

Jake expelled his breath, and Hanna realized he'd been holding it as he waited for her answer. She almost giggled.

"Good. Then why don't we get going," he said.

Chapter Thirty

It was close to five o'clock when Hanna and Jake arrived at the Los Patos watering hole, where pastel-painted clapboard shanties and pavilion-like huts with thatched roofs sat along the edge of the water. Hanna had not been back to the balneario since the García family was baptized. Despite the heat of the day, when Jake slipped his hand in hers as they walked over white pebbles toward the shallow lagoon, chills ran up her spine.

"Are you hungry?" he asked.

She eyed the shacks with suspicion. "I guess so. Is the food safe?"

"As safe as anything else you're going to get around here, with the exception of Maleah's kitchen."

"In that case, maybe we should have fixed sandwiches and brought them with us."

"No, it's okay. The food is usually quite good."

Still skeptical, Hanna fell in step beside Jake as he moved toward one of the wood-frame buildings painted a weathered turquoise-blue, with an opening cut into the top of one wall, and a serving counter built along the bottom half. Bags of chips and packages of cookies lined the rough interior walls.

"How about an empanada?" Jake asked.

"Okay," she responded. Since arriving in the Dominican Republic, she had on a couple of occasions eaten the deep fried meat or cheese-filled pastry shells called empanadas. She'd liked them.

A young Dominican man greeted them as they approached his makeshift restaurant. "Bueno día. ¿Cómo puedo ayudarle?"

Jake ordered two Cokes, two meat empanadas, and three fruit-filled pastelitos, similar to an empanada, only smaller, for dessert. Food and drinks in hand, he nodded toward a row of tables sitting on the river's edge. "Do you want to sit at a table?" he asked. Several were covered in red and white tablecloths and flanked by plastic chairs in red, yellow or blue. A mangrove forest served as a natural canopy.

"Sure."

While they ate, Hanna savored the quaint feel of their outdoor *cafe*. She could hear the sound of water trickling down the mountainside a short distance away, soothing her senses like a lullaby. She could almost see the mountain stream as it elbowed its way through lush green foliage before spilling over the edge. "I feel like we're being featured in a travel brochure for a tropical island paradise," she said.

Jake took a swig of his bottled Coke and nodded. "Why not? We do live in Paradise, you know."

She laughed. "That's right, I keep forgetting – Paraíso means paradise."

"What do you *mean* you keep forgetting?" He lifted his chin, appraising their surroundings with his eyes. "Haven't you noticed how much our charming mountain village resembles what you've always imagined paradise would be like?"

Hanna almost choked on a bite of empanada.

One side of Jake's mouth lifted. "Was that a yes or a no?"

She swallowed. "Let's just say for the moment this looks and feels like I might would imagine paradise to be like."

"For the moment . . . By tomorrow this whole area will be crowded and noisy. On weekends the locals hit the balnearios in mass." He turned and looked at her. "Have you ever poked an ant bed with a stick?"

"I have."

"What happened?"

"The ants swarmed like crazy."

"That's what it'll be like. Every inch of the place will be crawling with people."

Hanna shuddered as she envisioned the beach and balneario

overrun with people; the solitude shattered by radios bellowing the ever popular merengue with its trademark accordions, or the bachata with its twangy crooners singing about unrequited love, reminiscent of country music back home. She closed her eyes, thankful for the peace and quiet. Although laughter drifted across the lagoon as a group of children played in the water, and she could hear the faint drone of a radio escaping from one of the nearby shanties, the overall mood was calming.

Jake wadded up the wrappers from his empanada and pastelitos. "Why don't we go wading?" he said.

She handed him her empty wrappers and stood, wiping crumbs off her red shorts. Moments later, he held her hand tightly as they stepped into the clear pool of fresh water. It seemed ironic that not more than a stone's throw away the salty Caribbean splashed against the shore. Treading gingerly, she could feel the small white stones pushing against the bottoms of her flip-flops. Once they were knee deep, Jake ran his free hand through the water, showering her face with a refreshing spray. She reached down to return the favor, but was stopped short when he slipped his arm around her waist and pulled her to him.

"Oh no you don't," he said, his face only inches from hers. Hanna's heart hammered in her chest as his eyes drew her close, his smile spreading warmth all the way to her toes. "I could dunk you *so* easy right now. You know that, don't you?"

"I wouldn't go down without a fight," she said.

"What exactly does that mean?" His breath lightly caressed her lips.

"I'd take you with me."

He took a step back. "You talk big, but you don't scare me."

"Then why did you back up?"

He only grinned and nodded toward a mangrove swamp several yards away. "Why don't we go sit on one of those rocks over there."

As they sat with their feet dangling in the water, Hanna assessed the opposite shoreline. Dozens of palm trees adorned the tropical setting. Some stood tall, while others leaned at various angles away from the ocean; many were bent and knobby like an old woman's knees. She laughed out loud at the thought.

"What?" Jake asked.

"Those palm trees. Don't some of them remind you of old, knobby knees?

He leaned forward, resting his forearms on his legs. "Now that you mention it, they do. What about the roots in that mangrove swamp? Can you see the gnarled and arthritic fingers?"

She shifted her gaze to the braided channels of the swamp with its roots climbing in and out of the water, providing protection to a variety of bird and marine life. Through the gnarled limbs, a shaft of light reached upward. "I can," she said, tilting her head to one side as she studied the contours of the swamp, its foliage modeling varying shades of green. "You know, I believe God's favorite color is blue," she said, "but I think just maybe His second favorite is green."

As Jake straightened, Hanna felt his fingers brush lightly across the top of her hand before intertwining with hers. "My favorite color is green," he said.

"Why?" she asked as she idly ran her right foot through the water, letting it trickle between her toes as her foot broke the surface.

"Because that's the color of your eyes."

She stifled a laugh and looked at him. "Now that's as good a pick-up line as I've ever heard." She noticed his five o-clock shadow was heavier than usual.

Was he growing a beard?

"What are you thinking?" he asked, interrupting her speculations.

She shrugged. "Oh, I don't know . . . "

"You don't know, huh? You sure were giving me the once over."

She'd been caught. Warmth scampered across her cheeks. She hadn't realized she'd been so obvious. "Actually, I was wondering if you were growing a beard."

He ran his free hand along the side of his face and chin. "I haven't shaved in two or three days. Being lazy I guess. What do you think? Should I let it grow?"

"I like it. A close beard would be nice. Not much more than

what you have now."

His face brightened. "I'll do it. But if you decide you don't like it, let me know and I'll shave." He squeezed her hand.

Hanna's old fears resurfaced without warning. Panic inched its way up her back, and she felt sweat breaking out across her upper lip. Although she had begun to believe the *new* Jake was someone she could trust, waves of insecurity rolled over her. Was she ready to move forward in their relationship, if indeed that was where this was headed? Was she fully convinced he was trustworthy? She lifted her free hand, bracing the knuckle of her forefinger against her teeth as she wrestled with what she should do.

"Is everything okay?" Jake asked, removing his hand.

She couldn't say anything. It felt as if her throat were closing in, suffocating her words. She turned toward him. He looked crestfallen, his eyes searching hers as he waited for a reply. She took a deep breath and tried again to speak. "I need to be honest with you," she said. "I'm fighting a bit of a battle. After what happened with Shelby, I lost a lot of trust in you. In recent weeks there's been a significant change – I can't argue with that fact. Even so, I'm afraid of letting go and allowing myself to trust you again."

When he opened his mouth to say something, she reached out her hand and stopped him. "No, wait. Please let me finish." Now that she was talking, she needed to get it all out before she changed her mind. "I was deeply hurt once in a relationship. It wasn't anything like what you've been through in terms of losing a spouse, but my heart was broken. I was betrayed by someone I trusted, someone who proved not to be the person he'd originally led me to believe he was. The night I saw you with Shelby, memories of the heartache I suffered in that season of my life arose to taunt me. I care for you a lot, Jake. I want to trust you. Believe me . . . I really do. I'm just afraid of getting hurt again."

For several long minutes he didn't say anything. Hanna fidgeted, lifting and lowering her feet in the water, watching as cool, clear droplets escaped through her toes and returned to the safety of home. When she heard him draw a ragged breath, she dared to look his way. Tears shimmered in his eyes, reflecting the blue-tinged water below. A lone tear spilled over his eyelid, and she reached up and wiped the moisture from his cheek. He covered her hand with his, holding it to his face for a brief moment before tenderly kissing her fingertips.

When he spoke, the words sounded laborious, but clear. "Hanna, I don't know what to say . . . " He stopped to clear his throat. "I have prayed and prayed over the last couple weeks, asking God to make His will for our relationship evident. I understand your struggles. I'm so sorry that out of my own self-centeredness and rebellion I caused you pain. I didn't know about the previous relationship. I don't blame you for wanting to be cautious. Although our circumstances are different, the fear of getting hurt again is the reason I have fought so hard against the feelings I've had for you . . . almost from the moment I first saw you standing in the airport looking like a lost, scared kitten."

Hanna smiled as she remembered how lost and frightened she'd felt that night. "You're kidding? Honestly, those first weeks –" She pursed her lips and arched her eyebrows. "Well . . . actually – months, I thought you practically loathed the sight of me."

His laugh rumbled up, sounding deep and throaty. "Oh . . . I tried so hard to loathe you, so hard to find reasons not to like you. Dealing with Katie's death has been by far the hardest thing I've ever done. When I realized I might be attracted to you, my greatest fear was in knowing if I allowed myself to love again, I would be running the risk of losing again. Like I said, our fears are much the same."

"They are, aren't they?" she said, her eyes meeting his.

He caressed the side of her face with the tips of his fingers, pushing a wispy strand of hair behind her ear before resting his hand on her shoulder. His eyes, which had not left her face, fell on her lips. Lifting his hand again, he brushed one finger across her bottom lip then cupped her cheek. Leaning close, he kissed her. Warmth rushed from the pit of Hanna's stomach to her face. Could she trust this man? If she didn't decide soon, her heart would decide for her.

"I've waited until I knew for sure before telling you this," he said, "but I believe one of the reasons God brought you here was to fill a void in mine and Isabela's lives." He paused, a pregnant silence filling the space between them before he continued. "Hanna, I love you."

She gulped. Had he just said what she thought he said? Was it actually possible Jake Mason loved her? And what about her feelings for him? Two months ago she was convinced she was falling in love, but after the incident with Shelby, she'd been working overtime to protect her heart. What *did* she feel for him? Could she honestly say she loved him? When she looked into his eyes, searching for an answer, she noticed all the color had drained from his face.

"I think this is where you're supposed to say, *I love you too*," he said.

Her eyes flooded with tears. When she spoke, her voice barely produced a raspy whisper. "Jake, I . . . I do love you . . ." As the words came out of her mouth, he pulled her to him, pressing her head against his chest. She knew she could get used to being held in his arms. "I'm just scared," she said, hiccupping a sob. "I don't want to get hurt again."

As he drew her tighter, she heard an almost inaudible laugh fluttering in his chest. "I guess we'll have to battle our fears together," he said. "I'm probably as scared as you are, but I'm tired of fighting against the feelings I know I have for you." He grasped her shoulders and pushed her away from him. "You know, if this is God, why are we afraid of getting hurt again? It's really not about me trusting you or you trusting me. The question we need to be asking ourselves is whether we are willing to trust Him."

Hanna nodded. She knew he was right.

"What do you say?" he asked, once again caressing the side of her face with his fingertips.

"I agree," she whispered.

"Good." His lips met hers, lingering a moment longer than before. "Guess we'd better be heading home," he said, his mouth barely a breath away.

They were almost to the van when Jake raised his head and looked toward the ocean, ridges forming across his forehead. As the wind rustled their hair, dread crawled up Hanna's back. Was there reason to feel alarmed? She followed his gaze. Had he seen or heard something?

"What's wrong?" she asked, keeping her voice low.

He held out his hand. "Let's walk down to the beach for a moment."

As they approached the water's edge, a gusty breeze teased loose tendrils of hair that had fallen loose from Hanna's ponytail. Several fishing boats sat on the white-pebbled beach. Like everything else in the area, they were painted varying hues of blue, green, red or yellow and served as reminders that Los Patos was nothing more than a tiny fishing village boasting a breathtaking beach along the southwest coastal highway. As she watched the white-capped waves tumble toward the shore, a fine mist blew across her face. She ran her tongue over her lips – they tasted salty. When Jake turned and gazed inland, she revolved with him. Trees danced gracefully in the breeze. The setting whispered an alluring welcome, but she sensed all was not as it seemed.

Jake placed his hand on the small of her back, guiding her toward the van. Her heart pulsated in her ears, sounding like a woodpecker excavating a hole in a hollowed out tree. "Are you going to tell me what's wrong?"

He lifted his chin, his eyes darting from tree to tree. "You see those trees – the swirling dance they're doing. I'd feel better if they were just swaying."

She cut her eyes upward. "What does it mean when they're swirling instead of swaying?"

"I'm no weatherman," he said, glancing over his shoulder toward the ocean, "but . . . my guess is there's a storm headed this way."

From the direction of the watering hole Hanna heard a radio blaring. Some of the weekenders must have arrived while they were out on the beach. When it came to music, Dominicans were worse than teenagers back in the States. It seemed their motto was: The louder the better. Her eyes followed the sound to a group of men playing dominoes under one of the thatched-roof pavilions. The music switched to a news broadcast as Jake reached over to open the van door for her. He placed a finger to his lips.

When the music resumed, he called out in Spanish to the four domino players. "Are we under a hurricane watch?"

"Si, senor," one of the men answered. "Hay un huracán . . . tal vez viene aquí – in dos o tres días."

"Es tan fuerte," said one of the other men.

"Gracias," Jake said as he turned to help Hanna into the van.

"Is there really a hurricane headed this way?" she asked when he climbed in on the driver's side.

"That's what they said," he answered, concern etched across his face. "Doesn't sound good. When we get back to the house we'll see what we can find out."

Chapter Thirty-One

The next two days were spent in preparation for the approaching hurricane, which if it continued on its projected path would hit somewhere between Barahona and Perdernales. Hanna didn't need a geography lesson to realize that meant Paraíso was likely to take a direct hit. There were whispered concerns expressed among the adults – questions of whether they should try to go somewhere inland or remain in Paraíso. Ultimately it was decided they would probably be as safe at home as they would be riding the storm out in a hotel farther inland. Jake and Conner made a trip to Barahona to buy supplies: food as well as materials to hopefully help make their homes, the Community Center and the church building more secure.

Thirty-six hours before the storm was expected to make landfall it was upgraded to a category four, then downgraded to a strong three twelve hours later. With maximum sustained winds pushing 125 miles per hour and possible storm surges as high as ten feet or more, significant damage was expected. Unless it decided to jog to the east or the west, the eye of the storm would pass over Paraíso sometime during the late night, early morning hours.

Having grown up along the Gulf of Mexico, Hanna was no stranger to hurricanes. She and her family had evacuated their home in Daphne, Alabama on several occasions as hurricanes moved into the Gulf and threatened landfall nearby. She could remember the impact of two hurricanes in particular that significantly damaged much of the beachfront property of Alabama as well as the panhandle of neighboring Florida. Only once was their home damaged, and then nothing major. Even so, she was very much aware of the devastation a hurricane the size of the one now bearing down on the island could cause.

While familiar with hurricanes, Hanna had never had to ride one out. There had always been time and opportunity to evacuate. Her anxiety level rose steadily as the storm drew closer to the southern coast of the Dominican Republic and Haiti. It was one thing to be living along the coast of the United States as a hurricane approached, but a whole different story to be living on an island in the middle of the ocean. She couldn't help but feel the sheer vulnerability of the situation. Even if they wanted to evacuate, the best they could do was travel a couple hours inland. Realizing there was no place where they could go in order to avoid the storm altogether made her feel small and defenseless.

When the hurricane was about twelve hours out, Hanna helped Maleah transfer bottled water and non-perishable snacks from the kitchen to the hallway where they planned to take cover during the worst of the storm.

"You've been through a hurricane since coming to the DR, haven't you?" Hanna asked as she placed a case of water on the floor.

Maleah nodded. "Three years ago. It was a little over a month before Katie died. The storms in the Atlantic and Caribbean were unusually bad that year. We were fortunate only one passed over the island."

"What was it like?"

Maleah opened the doors to the hall closet, pulled out several pillows and handed them to Hanna. "It hit farther west than this one appears to be headed. It caused a lot of flooding and mudslides in Haiti. Jake and Katie were closer to the eye than we were."

Hanna laid the pillows on the floor before taking the armful of blankets Maleah was holding out to her. "Is this part of the country prone to flooding and mudslides?" she asked.

Maleah closed the closet doors and leaned against them, her arms folded across her chest. "Depending on the circumstances, it can be," she said, "but nothing like Haiti. The land there has been so badly stripped, it is extremely susceptible to erosion and, in the case of heavy rain, mudslides."

"What about structural damage – like to houses and buildings?"

"We're blessed because our homes are made of concrete blocks and built on solid foundations. For so many, the flimsy structures they call houses don't have a chance."

"I was wondering about that," Hanna said as she followed Maleah into the living room. "Is there someplace for those people to go?"

"What people?"

Hanna almost came out of her skin at the sound of Jake's voice. When she turned around, he was standing in front of her, a cot size mattress in his arms. His lips curled into a smile. "Did I scare you?" he asked.

She shook her head. He deserved a beating. "I was wondering about the people whose homes aren't sturdy enough to survive a storm like this," she said.

"I'll let Jake answer your question," Maleah said as she walked away. "I have a few more things I need to get done in the kitchen."

Jake tilted his head toward the hallway. "Come with me," he said as he shifted his grip on the cot mattress. "Let me get this thing where it needs to go." He continued talking as Hanna followed him into the hall. "Those from around here can go to the Community Center and church. Conner and I were there only minutes ago making sure everything was secure. A few families have shown up already. I'm sure more will be arriving as the afternoon and evening progress."

"But they'll probably loose their homes, won't they?"

"Many will," he said, the light in his eyes darkening. "I've been thinking a lot today about the people in Haiti. The destruction Katie and I saw when we went to help following the hurricane three years ago was far worse than anything I've ever seen. Flooding and mudslides had washed out entire villages in the mountains above Anse-a-Pitres. Hundreds of people lost their lives."

Hanna felt her gut constrict at the implications of what he'd said. "Entire villages?"

He stared past her for a moment, apparently lost in thought. "They were just gone," he finally said. "Not that there had been much to begin with, but what little there had been was gone. For those who survived, there was nothing left for them to return to. The bare essentials they had once owned were buried under thick, life-sucking mud." Tears shimmered in his eyes. "Until you've actually seen it for yourself, you can't begin to imagine the sheer horror and shock of it all. The fact they had no means to even try and start over adds a whole new meaning to the definition of *homeless*."

~~~~~

A couple of hours later Hanna walked across the street to check on the Garcías. She was shocked to discover the shelves of the colmado were almost completely empty.

Señora García greeted her from the doorway leading into the kitchen of the family's home. "Bueno Día."

Hanna leaned down and kissed the woman on the cheek. "Bueno día. ¿Cómo está?"

"Bien, bien," she answered, a cheerful smile brightening her round face.

With the wave of her hand, Hanna motioned toward the empty shelves. "Did you save anything for your family?" she asked in Spanish.

"Sí, tenemos suficiente."

Hanna hoped they really had kept enough for themselves. Knowing the generosity of the kind Dominican family, she wouldn't have been surprised if they had given most of it away to those they felt were more needy than they were.

When Señora García asked if she was apprehensive about the storm, Hanna confessed her fears to the tenderhearted, older woman whom she often referred to as her Dominican mother. Señora García invited her into the kitchen, where she poured them both a cup of coffee. As they sat at the family table sipping coffee, the woman recounted anecdotes of major hurricanes she'd lived through in her lifetime.

Señora García shook her head and laughed. "Even when we

did not know Him as Savior, our heavenly Father still watched over us. I have no reason to be afraid. I'm sure He'll protect us this time as well."

It humbled Hanna to realize this sweet lady, who had only recently given her life to Christ, was experiencing a greater peace than she was. She could learn a lesson or two from such confident, childlike faith.

~~~~~

As Hanna stood with Jake in the breezeway outside of her apartment later that evening, she stopped and listened to the howling wind as it whipped through the metal bars that hemmed the area in on one side. The children were all in bed, and Maleah and Conner had only minutes earlier retreated to their bedroom. The hurricane wasn't expected to make landfall for another five or six hours. Maleah had suggested they all try and get a little sleep.

"The wind is really picking up," Hanna whispered, as if speaking quietly would hold the storm at bay.

"I know you're going to think I'm crazy, but I like the sound of a good storm," Jake said.

She fixed her eyes on him. "You *are* crazy. You sound like those guys who like to chase tornadoes."

"Now that you mention it, I *have* chased a tornado or two."

"You're not serious, are you?"

His mouth lifted in a lopsided grin. "I am. Remember . . . I grew up in tornado alley."

"Like that explains it," she said. "Where I grew up isn't exactly immune to tornadoes, but I never had a desire to chase one."

"Don't you like adventure?"

Hanna shook her head as she opened the door leading into her apartment. "That all depends," she said. "I guess I never considered testing my skills against the powerful side of nature an adventure." After stepping inside, she turned and looked at him. "I guess you just might have to be brave enough for both of us."

Cupping her cheeks with his hands, he leaned forward until his face was only inches from hers. "For you my fair maiden, I will

Caribbean Paradise

be brave. I won't let the fiery dragon get you."

A soft laugh escaped her throat as his nearness caused the inevitable heat to rise to her face. She was certain he could feel her cheeks burning hot beneath his hands as he lightly brushed her lips with his before wrapping his arms around her waist and drawing her to him. She snuggled into his embrace. Although the wind continued to howl only a few feet away, she felt amazingly safe in his arms.

"I could stay here like this for the rest of the night," he said, "but it might not be a good idea."

She lifted her head, and he rested his hands on her shoulders, kissing her again. "You try to get some sleep. If you need me, I'll be right in there," he said, pointing toward the Andersons' living room where the sofa had been turned into a temporary bed.

She nodded like an obedient little girl. "Okay."

Sleep must have come easier than she expected, because the next thing Hanna knew she was awakened by a loud knock on the door. She opened her eyes to a room cloaked in darkness as black as coal. The wind shrieked, reminding her of a bobcat she once heard while on a camping trip with her parents, and a thunderous rain pelted the roof. She wondered how she'd ever slept through it. She sat up as the door to her apartment opened.

"You decent?" Jake asked.

Although she couldn't see his face, she was certain he was grinning. "I am," she said. "Do I need to get up?" She blinked when he switched on the light, chasing the sooty shadows away. "That wasn't nice," she said.

"I just wanted to help you wake up."

Hanna swung her legs around and sat on the side of the bed. "Thanks a lot." She tilted her head from side to side, trying to loosen the kinks and disengage the cobwebs. Through drowsy eyes she looked at him. "Guess I went to sleep."

"Looks that way," he said. She could see his devious grin now.

After slipping her feet into flip-flops she'd left sitting beside the bed, she stood. "What time is it?"

He glanced at the watch on his wrist. "Eight minutes after two."

"What's the latest on the hurricane?"

"Praise the Lord, about forty-five minutes ago it was downgraded to a weak category three. The last weather report said it could be downgraded again by the time it makes landfall, which is expected a little over an hour from now. Unfortunately, it appears we will still take a direct hit. It's a large storm. They're predicting the outer rings will impact the island as far east as Santo Domingo and west as Jacmel, Haiti, and then cause further damage inland as it moves north across the island."

"Is that concern I hear in your voice?" she asked, walking toward the dresser. "What happened to your adventuresome spirit?" She pulled the scrunchie from her hair and shook the dark tresses loose.

"It's still there," he said as he stepped up behind her. "But as the storm draws closer, my more cautious side recognizes the seriousness of our situation."

She picked up a brush and pulled it through her thick hair. She could see Jake's reflection in the mirror. "Don't go and get too serious on me. The brave knight in shining armor I was talking to earlier helped me feel a little less anxious."

He placed his hands on the sides of her arms and peered over her shoulder. "In that case, my fair maiden . . . there's no reason to fear." He ran his right hand through her hair, sending shivers up her spine. "Leave it down," he whispered.

She laid the brush on the dresser and leaned back against his chest as he slipped his arms around her waist. Right now she needed to feel he was indeed her knight in shining armor whose sole responsibility was to keep her safe.

Caribbean Paradise

Chapter Thirty-Two

By two-thirty the four children had been bedded down on pallets in the hallway, and their giggles could be heard above the sound of the storm as it drew closer. Conner and Maleah sat on one side of the giggling foursome, while Hanna sat next to Jake on the other. She shifted restlessly, trying to find a comfortable position.

"You're worse than Isabela," Jake said, laughing.

Hanna scrunched her nose. "What exactly does that mean?"

"Constant motion."

"Guess I'm just feeling a little apprehensive."

"Can't imagine why," Maleah said.

Jake draped his arm over Hanna's shoulders and drew her close. She nestled under his protective embrace. "That's better," she said as she closed her eyes.

The fierce rattling of the windows jerked her back to reality a short time later, awakening her from a light slumber. It sounded as if the roof were being ripped away, shingle by shingle. She'd only been awake a few minutes when the lights went out.

"Se fue la luz," Maleah said.

There go the lights Hanna had learned soon after arriving in Paraíso was a good translation of the frequently used Spanish phrase. She blinked her eyes, wondering how long it would take them to adjust to the intense darkness.

"I'm surprised we've had electricity this long," Jake said as he pulled her closer.

"Unfortunately, now that it's gone, we may go weeks before it's restored," Conner said.

Although she certainly took no pleasure in the frequent power outages, Hanna felt she had adapted. But weeks . . . What was it going to be like to go that long without electricity? No water to take a shower, power to keep food cold in the refrigerator, or fans to provide relief from the heat. It wasn't like they had somewhere they could stay until everything was back to normal. A sense of foreboding enveloped her like a thick mist. She rested her head on Jake's shoulder and closed her eyes, but this time sleep eluded her.

Some time later the wind abruptly stopped howling, and the rain no longer pounded the roof or pelted the windows. Hanna shuddered involuntarily at the eerie silence. Jake's arm tightened around her shoulders. "What's wrong?" he asked. "Surely you're not cold."

Another tremor ran through her body. "It's just so quiet. Kind of creepy after all the noise."

"Strange, isn't it, that the eye of a hurricane is almost peaceful?" Maleah's voice drifted across the sleeping children.

"Deceptive is what it is," Conner said. "About the time you think it's all over, it starts up again."

As Conner had predicted, the winds returned, at times appearing angrier than before. Carried along by screeching gales, the rain battered the outside walls with such unrelenting determination Hanna thought surely the big bad wolf only needed to huff and puff a few more times before he succeeded in blowing the house down. As the explosion of snapping tree limbs pierced the darkness, and flying debris thrashed the concrete dwelling from all sides with deafening thuds and smacks, Hanna bit her lower lip in an effort to keep from screaming and demanding that it all stop. Jake must have sensed the tension surging through her body, because he lifted his hand from her shoulder and placed it on the side of her face, pushing her head down upon his chest. She pressed her ear tight against the softness of his knit shirt, hoping to drown out the terrifying growl of the hurricane. Gently he began rocking as if she were a small child. She felt tears welling in her eyes as the tenderness of his actions deepened the love she had for him – her knight in shining armor.

When the sound of Maleah's alto voice rose in song above the fierce screams of the storm, Hanna smiled. The words of praise, familiar and comforting, served as a subtle reminder that although she might call Jake her knight in shining armor, ultimately God was her King and the only one powerful enough to safeguard them all. She had no doubt Jake would do anything he could to keep her and Isabela safe, but he was only flesh and blood. If he were to succeed in sheltering them from harm, God was the one who would provide the means by which he would offer protection.

While Jake rocked and Maleah sang, the peace of their heavenly Father settled over Hanna's fearful heart. Taut muscles throughout her body relaxed as the promise of God's word covered her like a warm blanket on a cold winter's night. Soon she was humming softly as Maleah's song, taken from Psalm 91, filled the darkness with the light of God's protective presence.

He who dwells in the shelter of the Most High will abide in the shadow of the Almighty. I will say to the Lord, 'My refuge and my fortress. My God, in whom I trust!' For it is He who delivers you from the snare of the trapper and from the deadly pestilence. He will cover you with His pinions, and under His wings you may seek refuge. His faithfulness is a shield and bulwark. You will not be afraid of the terror by night, or of the arrow that flies by day; of the pestilence that stalks in darkness, or of the destruction that lays waste at noon. A thousand may fall at your side, and ten thousand at your right hand, but it shall not approach you. For you have made the Lord your refuge, even the Most High, your dwelling place. No evil will befall you, nor will any plague come near your tent. For He will give His angels charge concerning you, to guard you in all your ways.

~~~~~

Hanna had never seen anything like the destruction and devastation left behind by the storm as it swept through the small fishing village of Paraíso. The flimsy structures so many had called home were totally destroyed. Downed trees, electrical cables, and phone lines littered the landscape. Debris jammed the streets, cluttered the yards and hung like Spanish moss from rooftops and battered trees.

For the next several weeks Hanna worked with Jake, Maleah and Conner day and night, doing what they could to help those hardest hit by the hurricane. The García family labored faithfully alongside the missionaries as they sought to offer hope to those who had literally lost everything but the clothes on their backs. Although a number of the church members lost their homes, no one was killed or even seriously injured. Loss of life in Paraíso miraculously had been minimal. News from other places up and down the southwest portion of the island was not as good. More than three hundred people were missing, many feared dead, in a small community east of town. Jake said it would probably be weeks, maybe months, if ever, before the truth of what happened to some would be known.

More than four weeks passed before power was restored. Once their own lives started showing signs of normalcy, Jake and Conner began making plans for a trip to Pedernales and Anse-a-Pitres. The fact that a small tropical storm had reportedly nested over that part of the island for several days only a couple of weeks after the hurricane hit was concerning. They had not heard from anyone in the area and were anxious to find out how the two towns had fared. Hanna was more than pleased when Jake asked if she would like to go with them.

The afternoon before they were scheduled to leave, she walked down to Jake's house to pick up a few items Conner needed to pack in a footlocker of supplies they were taking with them. The front door, as usual, was open. She tapped lightly on the doorframe and was getting ready to say, "Anybody home?" when she heard the sound of Jake's voice coming from the living room. Hesitantly, she stepped inside. He stood with his back to her, looking out the double patio doors while talking on the telephone. As if caught on a morning breeze, his words drifted clearly in her direction.

"Yeah, Shelby . . . listen I understand. No, no . . . I appreciate your offer to help."

A sick knot twisted in Hanna's stomach, and she feared she was going to loose her breakfast. When she opened her mouth to make her presence known, nothing came out.

"I agree," he said. "You're right." She could see him nodding as he listened. Several times he mumbled an "uh-huh" or a "yeah . . ."

Taking slow, deliberate steps, she backed up, but could still hear him as he brought the conversation to an end. "Once again, Shelby, I appreciate your offer to help. Yeah, it's been good talking to you too. Okay, you too. Good . . . Uh-huh . . ."

Hanna practically ran down the driveway toward the street. She wanted to get away before Jake saw her. She was halfway to the Andersons' when she heard footsteps approaching from behind. Feeling certain it was Jake, she accelerated her pace. She was in no mood to talk to him. But no matter how fast she walked, it was evident he was determined to catch up. Just as unwanted tears began splashing down her cheeks, she felt a hand clamp around her arm. She turned her face away and tried to jerk free.

"Hanna, hold up," he said.

She tried again to free her arm, but to no avail. Instead of letting go, Jake reached around and grabbed her other arm, forcing her to stop and turn in his direction. Looking down at the street, she refused to make eye contact.

"What'ya want?" she asked, spitting the words out in frustration.

He placed his fingers under her chin and gently lifted her face. With his thumb, he began wiping away the tears. "How long had you been standing at my door," he asked.

"Long enough," she answered, sniffing as she tried to stop the flow of tears.

When he grinned, she balled her hand in a fist, resisting with every fiber of her being the desire to slap him. "It's not funny," she said through gritted teeth. She glared at him from beneath lashes heavy with tears. She could tell he was trying not to smile. She wanted so badly to stomp her feet in the graveled street and yell at him. "How *dare* you think this is humorous!" she finally said.

"I know, I know," he said. "But what you think was long enough obviously wasn't."

Hanna felt the warmth of one lone tear slide down her left cheek. "Say that again."

Jake's smile gave way to laughter. "If you really had been standing there long enough, you would know there is no reason to be upset."

"You were talking to Shelby, right?"

"I was."

"Just how often do you two talk?"

"Oh, let's see . . ." His eyebrows slanted in a thoughtful frown. "This was the third time since she left."

Hanna fastened her eyes on him. "And what is it y'all have to talk about?"

"First of all, I want to make it clear that not once have I called her," he said, meeting her unrelenting gaze. "Have you got that?"

She nodded slowly.

"Okay, then. As long as you understand."

"I do."

"The first time she called wanting to apologize again for the way she'd acted while she was here. And . . ." He took a deep breath. "You do want me to be completely honest, don't you?"

"Yes," she replied as the knot in her stomach twisted tighter.

"She asked if there was any chance things might work out between us one day."

Hanna beat a fisted hand against the side of her leg. "What did you tell her?"

"I told her no." As he shifted positions, broken asphalt crunched beneath his feet. "I was nice, but I said I didn't feel it was God's will for the two of us to be together. She seemed a little hurt, but said she understood."

"So . . . why did she call the second time?"

"Remember," he said, wiping sweat from his brow, "I'm being upfront with you."

"Okay . . ."

"She called to tell me she was investigating the possibility of coming back to Paraíso on a short term missionary assignment."

Once more Hanna's breakfast inched its way up her throat. "Is she coming back?"

"No," Jake said, shaking his head. "I told her I didn't think it was a good idea. I also told her about us."

"How did she respond?"

Caribbean Paradise

"She said she was pleased for us," he replied with a shrug. "But who knows what she really thinks."

"So why did she call this time?"

"She said she'd heard about the damage the hurricane had caused and she'd been worried sick about all of us when she couldn't get through." He sighed. "She wanted to see if there was anything we needed. She offered to come down as soon as possible to bring supplies, help with clean-up . . . whatever we needed."

"And you said?" Hanna asked, scuffing the toe of her sandal in the gravel.

"I told her how much I appreciated the offer, but once again strongly emphasized I didn't think it was a good idea for her to come back – even if it was only for a few days."

Hanna took a deep breath, releasing it with a puff of annoyance. "Jake, why *do* you feel so strongly it would not be a good idea for her to come back? Are you afraid to see her again? Afraid you might still be attracted to her?"

"No," he said, touching her cheek. "The reason is exactly what I told her. I don't think this is where God wants her. I didn't tell *her* this, but I'm convinced her motive for wanting to be here is all wrong."

"Her motive being you – Right?"

He dropped his hand to his side. "Yeah. I'm afraid she's gotten some idealistic notion in her head that if we worked together for a while, I'd come around to seeing things her way, and we'd end up together."

"How is it that you're so confident that's not true?"

Jake chuckled.

"Stop laughing," she said, stomping her foot. "I'm being serious."

"I know," he said as he took her face in his hands. "I'm confident it's not true because I'm convinced I'm in love with you." The corners of his mouth twitched. "Hey, that rhymes. Pretty good, huh?"

Hanna's chin quivered as fresh tears pooled in her eyes. She wanted to believe him, to trust that he loved her and would never hurt her; but just hearing him speak Shelby's name had caused a legion of insecurities to resurface. How could she know for sure he was telling her the truth? How could she be certain Shelby wasn't going to show up one day and take him away from her? What was she supposed to do with the fears still loitering in her mind and heart? Several tears escaped and ran down her cheeks. Still holding her face in his hands, Jake used his thumbs to wipe them away.

"It wasn't that bad, was it?" he asked.

"What?"

"My rhyme."

"No. It's not that." She didn't feel like being funny. "I'm afraid. That's all."

Jake leaned closer. "I don't know how I'm going to do it, but one day I'm going to have you completely convinced I love you and that you have no reason to fear I will ever give my heart to someone else. Do you hear me?" He tilted her face toward him and briefly lowered his lips to hers. Then keeping the palms of his hands flush against her cheeks, he continued speaking. "Hanna, I love you. You are the one God brought to Paraíso for me, not Shelby. If I can help it, she won't be coming back. I'm not saying God doesn't have plans for her, maybe even plans to use her on the mission field somewhere, but I don't believe it's here. Comprende?"

Another tear slipped down Hanna's cheek. "Comprendo."

Chapter Thirty-Three

A few minutes before nine the following morning, Hanna left with Jake and Conner for Pedernales. They hadn't been on the road long when they realized the trip would probably take several hours longer than planned. While it was evident efforts had been made to clear the highway between Paraíso and Pedernales, there were sections that still had to be maneuvered slowly, with occasional detours along the way. It was a little after two o'clock before they pulled into the parking lot of the small motel where they had stayed several months earlier. Hanna was relieved to see the quaint "mom and pop" establishment appeared to have suffered little damage, and it was evident the owners were pleased to have their business.

After leaving their bags in the rooms they had rented for the night, Hanna joined Jake and Conner as they went in search of Jeremías, the pastor of the Pedernales congregation. Upon finding him, Jake asked about Pastor Hennrick. The young man said he had not heard anything from Hennrick or anyone else in the Anse-a-Pitres church since the storms.

As they walked back to the van, Jake clutched Hanna's hand with such fervor she had to bite her bottom lip to keep from wincing. Deeply furrowed forehead, eyes at half-mast, lips drawn into a narrow line – his face showed signs of the tension she could feel in his grip.

"I want to make a trip across the border this afternoon," he said once they were seated in the van.

Conner checked his watch. "It's almost three o'clock. I don't think we have time."

"We'll make it quick. We can go straight to Pastor Hennrick's house, then head back. I just want to make sure everyone is alright."

"I don't think it's a good idea," Conner said, shaking his head. "I understand your concerns, but one more night isn't going to make that much difference. We'll head out first thing tomorrow morning."

Jake's jaw tightened. "You can stay here if you like, but I'm going."

"What about Hanna?"

"What do you want to do?" Jake asked, looking in her direction.

"I guess I'll do whatever you do," she said with a shrug.

He glanced over his shoulder at Conner. "You staying or going?"

"I guess I'm going." Conner's heavy sigh told Hanna he still wasn't pleased with the idea.

~~~~~

The stench of the remote Haitian village sweltering in the mid-afternoon heat assaulted Hanna's nostrils while they were still some distance away. She almost choked on the bile that rose in her throat.

When they reached the outskirts of town, it was evident the area had suffered significant damage, but shock didn't set in until they arrived at the empty lot where Pastor Hennrick's house once stood. Nothing remained but a few splinters of wood and broken remnants of what little furniture the family had owned. Asking neighbors about their whereabouts was not an option. They, along with their homes, were also gone. An emaciated dog lapped thirstily from an old metal drum full of stagnant water swarming with mosquitoes. The din of the hungry insects buzzed in Hanna's ears, and the noxious air smelled like death.

Deep crevices formed along Jake's brow as he stood on the fragments of what had been the flimsy foundation of Pastor Hennrick's home. Raking his hand through his hair, he stared in what appeared to be stunned silence at the deserted, crumpled landscape. Hanna slapped at carnivorous mosquitoes munching on her bare legs and fixed her eyes on Conner, pleading with him to say something. She considered slapping *him* when he only shrugged. Her heart pounded in her ears as the foreboding quietness surrounded them. When she didn't think she could endure it any longer, she gently placed her hand on Jake's arm.

"Don't you think we should be heading back?" she asked.

He continued his silent vigil. She thought perhaps he had not heard her and was considering asking again when he slowly nodded. "I guess so," he said, "but first I want to see if we can find someone who knows what happened to Pastor Hennrick and his family."

"Jake, we don't have much time," Conner said.

The muscles in Jake's jaw twitched. "I'm not leaving until I find out where they are."

For thirty minutes Hanna walked beside Conner as they followed Jake up and down the streets of Anse-a-Pitres looking for someone who knew something about Pastor Hennrick. A number of people knew the family, but didn't know where they were or if they'd been injured in either of the storms. When Conner insisted it was time to head back, Jake reluctantly agreed. Nothing was said until they reached the border, which to their dismay had already been closed for the day.

Conner scanned the area as he turned in a circle. "Now what?" he asked, lifting his hands.

Jake stared unblinking at the locked gate. "I guess we could walk down the riverbed and try to get across, but . . . no, that won't work. It's too great a risk. I don't want to end up in the Pedernales jail."

"What other options do we have?" Conner asked.

Jake looked over his shoulder. "Maybe if we return to Anse-a-Pitres and try a while longer we'll find Pastor Hennrick or someone from his congregation, and we could stay with them."

Hanna brushed her hands together, trying to remove some of the grit, while glancing toward Anse-a-Pitres. Panic rippled up her spine at the thought of spending the night in a smelly, rat infested Haitian shanty with no electricity, running water or bathroom facilities. It was hard to imagine that would be better than staying over night in the Pedernales Jail.

"Jake, are you sure?" she asked, swallowing around the sickening lump in her throat.

"Sure about what?"

"That we'd be better off trying to find a place to stay in Anse-a-Pitres."

"Do you have any idea what kind of people you would be forced to spend the night with in a Dominican jail?" His chin had turned to steel. "And don't think for one minute they would let you stay with Conner and me."

"But I thought you said the border guards know you," she said, gulping back tears.

Jake scoffed. "Some do, but they wouldn't risk getting caught letting us back across unless there was a significant bribe involved."

Sweat trickled down the side of Hanna's cheek and crawled under her chin. "And you really think they would put us in jail?" she asked.

"I'm certain they would threaten in hopes of getting some money, but we don't have enough cash on us to make what they would consider a decent offer. If it were just Conner and I, I'd risk it – try and call their bluff. But having you with us would increase the probability of them attempting to make us pay up. I'm not willing to take that chance."

Tentacles of fear spread through Hanna's body. "Do you think they might hurt me? I mean, you don't actually think someone might . . . " Bile burned her throat. She closed her eyes against the whirling, nauseous thoughts.

"Hanna." Conner laid his hand on her arm. She opened her eyes and looked at him. "Honestly, I don't think anyone would harm you," he said, casting a warning glance Jake's way. "I would hope knowing you are an American citizen would help . . . but, I don't know. It's probably not a risk we want to take."

Jake pulled a bandana out of his back pocket and mopped the sweat from the sides of his face. "Exactly my point," he said, the intensity of his gaze meeting Hanna's. "Most Dominican men talk a big talk, but rarely follow through. Even so . . . " he shook his head, "the risk is too great." He turned around. "We're going back."

For more than an hour they walked the streets of Anse-a-Pitres hoping to find someone Jake knew, or at least somebody who knew Pastor Hennrick. While they searched, the sun descended along the horizon, painting the sky with broad strokes of orange and brick red, then washing it slate gray before leaving the land covered in syrupy darkness, at which point Jake suggested they try to find a deserted shack or lean-to where they could spend the night. Earlier he had led them to a small cinder block building he said once served as a hotel, but it appeared to have suffered significant damage from one or both of the storms and was no longer in operation. As they turned a corner a couple of streets from where Pastor Hennrick's house once stood, a deafening yell pierced the oppressive night air. Hanna stifled a scream. Conner shone his flashlight on a man dressed in a tattered uniform. The Haitian's ebony hands shook as he held a gun within inches of Jake's face.

Jake raised his hands and calmly spoke to the man in what Hanna assumed was Creole. Beads of sweat broke loose from her brow and slithered past her right eye. Her legs felt like mush. Tears blurred her vision while a few spilled down her cheeks. She would have wiped them away, but was afraid any movement might startle the man who now pointed his gun at Jake's chest. Jake continued talking as if the two of them were enjoying a friendly conversation. Hanna thought she heard him mention Pastor Hennrick, but otherwise understood nothing that was being said. When the man lowered his gun, she gave herself permission to breathe again.

"This young man is with the Anse-a-Pitres police," Jake said, a weary smile lifting the corners of his mouth. "He's also a member of Pastor Hennrick's church."

Hanna didn't know whether to laugh or cry. Conner whispered, "Thank you, Lord."

"Amen," Jake said. "He told me that after losing everything in the hurricane, Pastor Hennrick and his family returned to Thiotte – the village where they lived before coming here."

"That's good news," Conner said. "At least now we know they're okay."

Jake nodded. "You don't know how much better that makes me feel. Pastor Hennrick and Madame Hennrick are like family to me."

"I guess this means we're not going to be arrested," Conner said.

"No, we're not. But when I explained our situation to our friend here, he said he could let us stay in one of the buildings they sometimes use as a jail cell. There's no one there right now."

Hanna shook her head at the irony of it all. They had come back to Anse-a-Pitres hoping to avoid being arrested, only to be offered a room at the local jailhouse inn. "Would we be able to stay together?" she asked, her voice quivering as the words slipped through her lips.

Jake slid his hand in hers. "Yes," he said. "My guess is there's only one room."

Chapter Thirty-Four

True to Jake's prediction, the facility consisted of one small room Hanna guessed was at best eight feet by eight feet. The walls were made of concrete, the floor – dirt, and the roof – corrugated metal. There was no electricity, running water, toilet or sink – not even a bucket of water, although it probably wouldn't have been clean if there had been. The only light was the flashlight Conner had fished out of his backpack minutes before their initial encounter with the young Haitian policeman. As Conner shone its illuminating beam around the jail cell, Hanna almost wished he hadn't. Her nose already told her it'd been a long time since the tiny cubicle had been cleaned, but seeing what it looked like only made it worse.

Stepping carefully, the three of them made their way to the far side of the room where Jake removed a T-shirt from his backpack. When Hanna raised her eyebrows, he shrugged. "You never know when you might need a clean T-shirt," he said.

"And what are you planning on doing with it now?" she asked.

He grinned. "It's going to serve as a mat upon which my fair maiden is going to sit."

"Oh, please . . . " Conner said as he slid down the concrete wall and sat cross-legged on the floor with the flashlight wedged between his legs, shining its solitary beam upwards and causing eerie shadows to dance upon the ceiling and scamper along the dank walls.

"The fair maiden thanks you," Hanna said, glancing around the room. "However, before settling in for the night I have a need I don't think can wait until morning. I'm almost afraid to speak it for fear I won't like the answer."

"What is it?" Jake asked.

"I haven't used the restroom since we left Pedernales earlier today. I don't guess there's a ladies' room hidden away somewhere in this fine establishment?"

"Yeah, well . . . " Jake said, looking around. "From the smell of things, I fear others who have stayed here in the past thought there were facilities on the place, but I'm afraid there are not. So . . . let's see . . . "

He stepped outside and spoke for a few minutes with the young police officer now standing guard in front of the jail cell.

"What did he say?" Hanna asked when Jake returned.

He cleared his throat. "Uh . . . there's a bucket out back you can use."

Conner laughed.

"I was afraid of that," Hanna said. "You know . . . I really should be mad at you about now."

"Why is that?" Jake asked.

"If you had listened to Conner and waited until tomorrow, we wouldn't be in this predicament."

Conner grunted. "I'll second that, my friend."

"I know," Jake said. "Don't think I haven't thought the same thing more than once in the last hour. I'm sorry . . . really I am. Thank you for taking it so well."

"Don't thank me until we're out of here," Conner said. "I'm not promising what my attitude will be a few hours from now."

"That makes two of us," Hanna said. "My attitude may turn sour momentarily. Where did you say this not-so-private bathroom is located?"

"Out back. Do you want some company? I know how you women are – never wanting to go to the ladies' room alone."

Hanna placed a fisted hand on her hip. "That wasn't very smart, you know."

"What do you mean?"

"Getting cute with me right now probably isn't such a good idea."

"I see . . ." Jake's lips morphed into a smirk. "Does that

mean you want to go alone?"

Hanna looked toward the door leading into the dark street. "Under normal circumstances I would refuse the offer, but at the moment I'm tempted to accept." She placed her other hand on her hip. "You *will* keep your back turned."

"I promise to be the perfect gentleman."

"Are you actually going to use the bucket?" Conner asked.

"Probably doesn't matter," Hanna said, stopping at the door. "But I do think I'll step around back. I'm assuming it will be a little more private than out front."

Jake escorted her to the backside of the building. The darkness was so thick there was no need to worry about being seen. He positioned himself at the corner of the concrete structure, while she ventured several feet away on her own. "You know," she said as she hiked up her skirt, "this is one of those rare occasions when I wish I was a man. I guess I can at least be thankful I don't have on blue jeans or slacks."

"Personally, I'm glad you're not a man," Jake said between chuckles.

"That may be, but right now it would make my life a lot easier."

Back in their *hotel* room, Hanna was thankful to have Jake's clean T-shirt to sit on. Not that it made the room smell any better, but at least she didn't have to sit on whatever it was that smelled so putrid or . . . would that be rancid? Whatever it was . . . it stunk. Unfortunately, she knew she didn't smell much better. Her body reeked of salty sweat and sun-baked skin. Her face, arms and legs were coated with grit; and sand crunched between her teeth. Damp tendrils of hair hung loosely around her face – now free from the ponytail she'd brushed into place hours ago. Her stomach growled, reminding her she hadn't had anything to eat since noon.

As weariness from the day's adventures overtook her, she rested her head on Jake's shoulder and closed her eyes. She awoke a while later to the sound of Jake snoring lightly on her left and Conner not so quietly on her right. Amazing – They all three had fallen asleep sitting upright in a hot, foul-smelling jail cell on the backside of nowhere. That's what you call exhaustion.

She raised her eyes toward where she'd earlier seen a small window positioned high on the opposite wall and wondered what time it was. There was not even a hint of light. Realizing she couldn't go back to sleep, she slowly lifted her head, being careful not to wake Jake. As she scratched the welts that had arisen on her calves, she was reminded of the warm welcome she'd received from a family of mammoth mosquitoes inhabiting the ladies' room out back. She could hear a critter – probably a rat – munching on something in the corner. She hoped it was true what people said – that rats were more afraid of humans than they were of them – but she sincerely doubted it. She puzzled over the fact that so many of the people in Anse-a-Pitres were painfully thin and malnourished while the rats she'd seen around town were plump and well fed. How was it possible the rodents were able to find food sources the people somehow were missing?

Hanna jumped when Conner snorted and cried out in his sleep.

"What the . . . " Jake said as he jerked his head up, hitting it on the wall. "Was that an earthquake?" His voice sounded thick. Hanna could tell he was not yet fully awake.

"Probably," she said, pressing her fingers to her lips in an effort to keep from laughing. "My guess is it registered at least 6.0 on the Richter scale."

"Are you serious?" Jake sat up straighter.

"Serious about what?" Conner asked, his words slurred.

"About the earthquake," Jake said.

"You know what this reminds me of?" Hanna asked before Conner could comment.

"What," the two men asked in unison.

"The story of Paul and Silas. Remember . . . they were in jail once during an earthquake. Only difference is you guys were snoring, not singing." She tapped her fingers on her knee. "Now that I think about it," she said, "that's what it was. It was the two of you snoring that rattled the walls."

"Hey, not me," Conner said. "I don't snore."

"Don't blame me," Jake said. "I *know* I don't snore."

"Well, I would beg to differ," Hanna said. "And I have a

witness, although I think he skedaddled when the walls started shaking."

"Who?" Jake asked. "The police officer?"

"No. I think he's still out front," she answered. "I'm talking about Templeton."

"I think the smell in this place is getting to her," Conner said. "*Who* is Templeton?"

"The rat in *Charlotte's Web*."

"There was a rat in here?" Jake asked.

"I can't say for sure because I couldn't see in the dark. But in between listening to the two of you . . . ah . . . snoring . . . I could hear something over there." She pointed toward the corner where she'd heard their visitor snacking, but then realized neither of the men could see what she was doing.

"I guess that means our guard is in trouble," Jake said.

"How's that?" Conner asked.

"Just going back to Paul and Silas in the Philippian jail. Remember? Although the doors of the jail were shaken loose, none of the prisoners escaped. In this case it sounds like one may have gotten away."

"I'm glad he's gone," Hanna said as she slipped her arm through Jake's. "By the way, what time is it?"

Conner turned on the flashlight and looked at his watch. "Almost five-thirty," he said.

"So what do you guys want to do now?" Jake asked.

"We could sing," Hanna suggested.

"Hum . . . I think not," Conner said. "What I mean is – you can sing, but I don't think you really want me to."

Jake laughed. "He's right. You don't want to hear him sing. Come to think of it, you probably don't want to hear me sing either. Are you up for a solo?"

"Not really," Hanna said, snuggling closer to his side. She felt his shoulder rise and fall. "What was that about?" she asked.

"Just thinking . . ."

"Care to share?"

"Good thoughts, actually. I was thinking about how far God has brought me in recent months. Since returning to the DR, I've made the trips to Anse-a-Pitres out of a sense of duty, not because I wanted to. Too many unhealed memories . . . I was bitter toward the people here. Although I knew it wasn't their fault, I still wanted to blame them for Katie's death."

"Really?" Conner said. "I never realized you blamed the Haitians for what happened."

"It wasn't something I wanted to admit. But every time we made a trip to Anse-a-Pitres, I knew the anger was there."

"And now?" Hanna asked.

"The anger, the bitterness, the blame – It's all gone. How ironic. Here I sit sweltering in a stinky jail cell, but I haven't felt this good about this place since before Katie died. I'm sorry you guys are having to go through this with me, but I think God knew I needed time to sit for a while . . . in dark, hot, smelly Anse-a-Pitres, so I could more clearly see the work He's been doing in my life."

"In that case, I'm glad to be here," Conner said.

"Me, too," Hanna said as she squeezed Jake's arm. "In fact, I think I needed this time as well. Being here has reminded me of something I told the Lord the first time I visited Haiti."

"You mean when you came with us several months ago?" Jake asked.

"No. When I came with my mother twelve years ago."

"You were in Haiti when you were . . . ah . . . " Jake stopped to think. "Sixteen? Why did I not know that?"

"I guess because I've never told you."

"And why not?"

"You want the truth?"

"I think so . . . "

Hanna sat up straight and shifted on her T-shirt pallet. "I was afraid you would make fun of me because the first time I came to Haiti was as a tourist."

"Why did you think I would do that?"

"I believe I know," Conner said. "It's probably because for a while you were looking for any excuse – no matter how trivial – not to like her."

"Was it really that bad?" Jake asked. "Never mind, don't answer that question. Hanna, have I told you lately how sorry I am for the way I treated you when you first arrived?"

She squeezed his arm. "Yes you have – more than once. It's okay."

"Good," he said, exhaling. "So what was it you told God on your first trip to Haiti?"

"I told Him I wanted to come back one day, not as a tourist, but as a missionary."

"Really? What prompted that?"

"It was the people. While I tried desperately not to stare, the immense suffering I saw in their faces haunted me. They reminded me of the starving children in those commercials soliciting help. Only problem, there was no remote and no way to change channels. While most of those traveling with us didn't seem to notice, God wouldn't let me forget."

"Did you ever dream twelve years later you would be back in Haiti sitting in a jail cell with the likes of the two of us?" Jake asked.

"Can't say that I did," Hanna replied as a grin tickled the corners of her lips. "I don't know that if I knew then what I know now I would have told God I wanted to come back. I'm beginning to think that's how He gets us on the mission field. He lets us run for a while wearing rose-colored glasses, then by the time we realize how hard this journey we signed up for really is, we've already fallen in love with the people and the work He's called us to do."

"It's kind of like having children," Conner added. "By the time you realize that sweet, cuddly baby is going to grow up to be a smart-mouthed kid, you've already committed and it's too late to turn back."

"So . . . " Jake said, inhaling deeply, "do you feel your original call was actually to Haiti?"

"Good question." Hanna tented her hands, pressing her forefingers against her chin. "One I've asked myself a number of times, especially after coming here with the two of you that first time. To be honest, I hadn't really given it much thought until then. But since that time, I've wondered if one of the reasons God brought me to the Dominican Republic was in order that I might also have the opportunity to work with Haitians."

"Hum..."

Hanna thought Jake was getting ready to say something, but then didn't. "What?" she asked.

"I don't know..." he said, pressing his back against the wall and lightly tapping his head on the concrete. "I just don't know."

"Me either," Conner said. "Whatever it is... I don't know either."

"Aw... come on," Hanna said, punching Jake in the arm. "What is it you don't know?"

"Let me ask you a question," he said, leaning forward. "Give it some thought before answering. Okay?"

"Okay..."

"Do you feel it is possible God has been preparing you to work directly with the Haitian people?"

"As in... live in Haiti?"

"Not necessarily. Maybe live in Pedernales, but with the primary assignment being to work in Anse-a-Pitres?"

Hanna gulped. "Are you serious?"

"Well, yeah..."

"Could that actually be a possibility?"

Jake laughed. "It might be."

"Then I don't have to give it a whole lot of thought. I've been asking God to make a way for me to do just that. If you were to tell me it could happen, I would have to believe it was an answer to my prayers."

"Whoa..." Jake said. "Double whoa..."

Conner started laughing. Hanna turned her head toward him. "Why are you laughing?" she asked.

"I love it when I get to see such a clear example of God at work," he said.

"What are you talking about?"

"I need to let Jake answer that question," he replied.

She looked at Jake. "Okay, so tell me. What's he talking about?"

The sound of Jake's laughter echoed off the walls of the small jail cell. "I don't think this is how I imagined this was going to happen, but here goes... Hanna, will you marry me?"

Hanna felt sure her heart skipped a beat. Did he say what she thought he said? And if so, was he serious? Surely this wasn't some kind of cruel joke, but why here? Why now? Before she could say anything, Jake moved from where he'd been sitting and knelt on one knee in front of her.

"You don't have to get up," he said, "but at least I'll try to do this from the proper position. Let me ask you again. Hanna Truly, will you be my wife?"

She gasped. "You're serious!"

"As serious as I've ever been," he said, taking her hand in his.

"But . . . What does this have to do with me asking God to open up an opportunity for me to work in Pedernales?"

"Oh, good grief," Conner said. "Would you give the poor man an answer? The suspense is killing me."

A rooster crowed in the distance as Hanna glanced around the musty jail cell where rose-colored fingers now reached through the small window and danced along the walls. She tried to keep a straight face, but burst out laughing instead.

"Please," Jake said, "as bad as this floor is to sit on, it's even more uncomfortable kneeling. Would you give me an answer? We can laugh later."

She clamped her bottom lip with her teeth, but laughter rumbled up from deep inside until tears rolled down her cheeks. Jake gave up and sat on the floor in front of her.

"I'm sorry," she managed to say between stifled giggles. "Okay. I know." She glanced up at the ceiling, willing herself to stop laughing. "It's just, do you have any idea how . . . Oh, I don't know. Yes! Yes! This is crazy, but yes – I will marry you!"

Conner rested his head against the wall and laughed. Jake leaned forward, placed both hands on the sides of Hanna's face and kissed her. As he sat back down, his laughter joined with Conner's so that the whole room was filled with the sound of joyful celebration. A few minutes later the young Haitian police officer stepped into the room, white teeth shining in his black satin face. Hanna knew there was no way he understood what had just happened.

She guessed it was true what they say – Laughter is contagious.

Caribbean Paradise

Chapter Thirty-Five

As they began the long, dusty walk toward the border, Hanna twisted the top off a bottle of water Conner had handed her seconds earlier and took a swig. Although warm, it was refreshingly wet. She squinted in the bright light as the sun, now a shimmering yellow ball, climbed the sky in front of them. With her free hand she pulled the scrunchie from her hair. It fell across her shoulders and down her back in a tangled mass. As for her skirt and blouse – dirt and wrinkles competed for first place. They looked slept in. She grinned. Maybe because they were. Several layers of grime encrusted her arms and the calves of her legs. She could only imagine what her face looked like. She ran her tongue over her teeth and shuddered. They were covered with a gritty scum. Her breath had to be foul.

Now that he could see her in the light of day, she wondered if Jake still wanted to marry her. Granted, he needed a shower as much as she did, but with his mussed up hair and tanned, bearded face covered in dirty sweat, he looked handsomely rugged, not nasty like she felt.

"What'ya thinking?" he asked, breaking into her thoughts.

Might as well be honest. "Just wondering if you still want to marry me?"

"Some reason I shouldn't?"

"Look at me," she said, fanning her arms out.

He nodded. "I see what you mean."

"Does that mean you take back your proposal?"

He cocked his head to the side. "Can't do that."

"Why not?"

"Don't want to disobey God."

"That reminds me. You never explained why you suddenly asked me to marry you after I told you I'd been asking God for an opportunity to work with the Haitians."

He finished off his bottle of water. "Because God's answer to your prayer was an answer to mine," he said.

"I'm sure you think I can fill in the blanks, but I need a little more information than that."

"Long version or short?"

"Long."

Jake wiped the sweat from his forehead, then looked at his filthy hand and laughed. "Okay, let's see . . . The day before the hurricane made landfall, a representative from the mission board called to see how we were doing, whether we were going to ride out the storm or evacuate – General procedure. While we were talking, he asked if I would pray about accepting another assignment, which would require a move back to Pedernales. They are exploring the possibility of beginning work in Anse-a-Pitres and thought I might be interested."

Hanna's eyes widened. "Are you serious?"

He nodded. "Truth is . . . I'd already been feeling pulled in that direction, so the request was a great confirmation. Only problem, I wasn't ready to put that kind of distance between you and me. I knew if God wanted me in Pedernales I couldn't let our relationship stand in the way, but I kept sensing there was more to His plan than I could see. A couple of weeks ago I shared all this with Conner and Maleah and asked them to pray with me about it. That's one of the reasons Conner and I asked you to make this trip with us again." He smiled. "That and the fact you're a lot nicer to look at than Conner."

"How can you say that?" Conner asked, giving them a toothy grin as he ran his hand over the red stubble along his jaw. Hanna thought the brownish-red sand coating his face and arms blended well with his hair.

"The way I look this morning," she said, "he's probably wondering where in the world he ever got the idea I was better looking than you."

Jake glanced at her, then Conner, then back at her. "I have to admit it's close, but I still think you win."

As his brow furrowed, Conner tilted his head up at an angle. "Ooh, you are probably in trouble now," he said.

Hanna thrust her lower lip forward and nodded. "If we were already married, he'd be sleeping on the sofa tonight," she said. "Better yet, I think I'd be sending him back to spend another night with Templeton in the Anse-a-Pitres jail."

Jake slipped his hand in hers. "I apologize," he said. "I think you look absolutely beautiful."

"Now you're plain out lying." She glared at him, willing herself not to smile. "Why don't you finish your story before you make matters worse."

"Uh-huh, well . . . let's see, where was I?" He cleared his throat. "Oh yeah . . . I wanted to ask you to come on this trip because you're so pretty." When he glanced at her and smiled, Hanna rolled her eyes. "Don't believe me, huh?" he said, squeezing her hand.

"Just finish your story."

"Okay . . . If you insist. The plan was that I would drop a few hints, asking what you thought about Pedernales, if you thought you might be willing to live here one day, what you thought about Anse-a-Pitres, the Haitian people, etc . . . "

"What if you had asked me those questions and my responses had been negative?"

"I wasn't even willing to go there. I have felt so strongly that God brought us together, I just knew somehow, someway, He was going to work it out. And He did!"

Before Hanna knew what had happened, Jake lifted her off her feet and swung her around. "I think this is one of the happiest days of my life," he said.

~~~~~

That evening, after the traveling threesome shared with Maleah about their adventure in Anse-a-Pitres, Jake told Isabela he'd asked Hanna to marry him. The child could hardly be restrained as she danced around the Andersons' living room and then pounced upon Hanna while exclaiming, "You're going to be my new mommy!"

With tears running down her cheeks, Hanna encircled the little girl with her arms. "That's right, sweetheart. And what an honor and privilege that will be."

The following day, which was a Wednesday, Hanna and the children returned to the schoolroom at the Community Center for the first time since the hurricane hit the small hamlet of Paraíso. After finishing their lessons Friday afternoon, Hanna locked the classroom door and pocketed the key in her skirt. As she stepped onto the sidewalk, the late afternoon sun brutally attacked her eyes. She'd been battling a headache all day. Now her whole body ached.

While making their way back to the Andersons', she kept a close eye on the children as they playfully tussled only a few feet ahead of her. Oh to have that much energy. Passing a fruit and vegetable stand, she nodded in greeting at the older gentleman standing behind the crude structure, which looked as if it had been constructed of wood and scrap metal gathered after the storm. When she lifted her head, a throbbing pain pulsated from the back to the front, washing her in nausea. She stopped for a moment and leaned against the concrete wall of a local hardware store, praying the sidewalk would stop swaying and her stomach would settle. She'd never had a migraine, but from what she'd heard, this had the makings of good one.

"Aunt Hanna, are you okay?" Isabela's voice broke through the painful fog.

Hanna took a deep, shaky breath and pushed away from the wall. "I'm fine, sweetheart," she said. "Just a little tired." She looked up to find four pair of curious eyes fixated on her. Isabela slipped her hand in hers. Hanna held her other hand out to Sophie.

"Caleb and I could run home and get Momma to bring the car back and pick you up if you don't feel like walking," Daniel said.

She started to shake her head but stopped when the slight movement threatened to bring on another round of nausea. "No, that's okay," she said, hoping her smile looked reassuring.

By the time they arrived at the house, Hanna had managed to convince the children she was fine. They ran in ahead of her and disappeared before she had time to make it to the living room. As she headed for the kitchen, she saw Maleah sitting in the dining room, a collection of sheet music spread across the surface of the table.

"Hi there," Hanna said. Her voice sounded anemic even to herself.

Maleah glanced up. "Oh, hi." She looked down and then immediately back up. "Are you okay?" she asked.

"Yeah, I'm just tired. I probably need to get to bed early, that's all. My body's still trying to recover from all the fun I had Monday night." She felt her chin tremble as she made a feeble attempt at smiling.

"Are you sure?" Two deep lines appeared across Maleah's forehead. "You look a little flushed. You don't have fever, do you?"

Hanna ran her hand across her own forehead, which she admitted felt warm. "I don't know . . . It's probably just the heat."

Maleah rose from the table and walked toward her. "Do you have any other symptoms?"

"Symptoms?" Hanna closed her eyes, hoping to ease the pain. "You make it sound like I've got something."

"Maybe you do." Maleah placed the backs of her fingers on Hanna's cheek and then moved her hand to her forehead. "You're burning up."

"I'm sure it's not that bad. I just think I'm worn out."

"You didn't answer my question a few minutes ago." The look of concern on Maleah's face was disquieting.

"I don't know . . . I have a headache and feel a little achy. Maybe I've got the flu or something."

"Or something . . . Come on, let's get you in bed."

Hanna let Maleah lead her through the kitchen to her apartment where she undressed and put on a pair of lightweight pajamas – soft yellow cotton shorts and a matching T-shirt. Maleah plumped the pillows and helped her get in bed. Hanna laid her head back and closed her eyes.

"Is that ceiling fan on too high?" Maleah asked.

"No, it's fine."

When Maleah returned a few minutes later with a thermometer, glass of water and bottle of ibuprofen, Hanna opened her eyes, wincing at the pain. Obediently she opened her mouth so

Maleah could insert the thermometer. A minute later it beeped. The expression on Maleah's face when she read the results was not encouraging.

"So, what's my temp?" she asked, holding out her hand to take the glass of water.

Maleah cleared her throat. "103.7."

Hanna stared at her for a moment. "Are you sure that thing is working? Isn't that high for someone my age?"

Maleah walked toward the tiny bathroom and pulled out a washcloth from the cabinet below the sink. "I have no reason to think the thermometer isn't registering correctly," she said. After running water over the dark green bath cloth, she returned to Hanna's side. "And yes . . . that is a high temp for an adult."

Hanna closed her eyes as Maleah gently rubbed the cool cloth over her face. She wouldn't have been surprised if it had sizzled. The familiar gesture reminded her of her mother and the discussion she'd had with Isabela when the child had been sick a while back. Several minutes later, Maleah returned to the sink and soaked the washcloth again. "You try to get some rest," she said as she laid the wet cloth on Hanna's forehead. "I'll check on you in a little while."

Chapter Thirty-Six

Hanna awoke a while later, but opening her eyes seemed too painful an endeavor. If she'd been beaten with a baseball bat, she didn't think her body would ache any worse. Someone held her hand, rubbing the back with what felt like a thumb. Drawing a deep breath, she detected a trace of Jake's cologne.

"You awake?" he asked, his voice barely above a whisper.

Hanna still didn't open her eyes. "Uh-huh," she said. "How long have you been here?"

"An hour or so. Maleah sent Celia to get me."

He let go of her hand. She heard a chair scraping against the floor and then felt something cool against her lips. "Let me slip this thermometer in your mouth so we can see what your temp is now," he said.

She opened her mouth. When the thermometer beeped, he pulled it back out.

"So?" she asked.

"103.3."

"Down a little from earlier."

"A little," he agreed, sounding tired.

Hanna heard his shoes squeaking on the terrazzo floor as he walked toward the bathroom, followed by the sound of running water in the sink. She wasn't surprised when he returned and placed a wet washcloth on her forehead. Lifting her left hand, he wiped another wet cloth across her wrist and then repeated the action with her other arm. While the cool, damp cloth felt good against her hot skin, every move she made hurt. A low moan slipped through her lips.

A chair creaked. "Where do you hurt?" he asked.

"Everywhere. Even my hair follicles and little toenails."

She had hoped to get a chuckle out of him, but all she heard was a pronounced sigh. She forced her eyes open. He sat next to the bed gazing toward the back of the apartment, a lone tear snaking down his left cheek. Gritting her teeth against the pain, Hanna reached over and took one of his hands. "It's really not that bad. Just the flu. Give me a few days and I'll be okay."

Wiping the tear from his face with his free hand, he looked at her. The alarm she saw in his eyes was unsettling. She couldn't help but wonder what he knew that she didn't. Fear mingled with the physical pain she was already battling.

He cleared his throat, but when he spoke it still sounded thick. "Do you have any mosquito bites?" he asked.

"Mosquito bites?" She closed her eyes, her thoughts swirling in a cyclone of confusion and pain. "I think so . . . Seems like I've had at least one or two since the day I arrived. I try to keep my arms and legs covered with insect repellent, but . . . " She was too tired to finish.

Jake rubbed the top of her hand again with his thumb. "Do you remember if you got any new bites while we were in Anse-a-Pitres?"

Another moan escaped through Hanna's closed lips. She was thirsty – some cold water sounded good – but she wasn't sure she wanted to fight the pain involved in sitting up to drink. Jake gave her hand a gentle squeeze, interrupting her feverish debate.

"Hanna, did you hear what I just asked you?" he said.

She forced herself to focus. "Ah . . . yes, I did. When I visited the ladies' room behind our luxury hotel suite. Don't you remember me fussing and swatting at the mosquitoes?"

"You were fussing about so many things, I don't think any one in particular registered with me."

"Well . . . I remember a while later realizing I had a half dozen or so new bites on my legs."

"Is there any chance you were bitten earlier, sometime during the day?"

A dense fog blanketed Hanna's brain making it difficult to concentrate. "Does it matter?"

"Yes." Jake squeezed her hand again. "If it wasn't important I'd leave you alone."

She thought for a moment, dredging up memories from what felt like a deep, dark abyss. "I *was* bitten earlier that afternoon. There were mosquitoes in that nasty water near where Pastor Hennrick's house used to be, but I don't understand what difference it makes."

The chair creaked, and she heard him sniff. Was he crying? She barely opened her eyes, watching through slits as he wiped a few more tears from his cheeks. She entwined her fingers in his. "What do you think is wrong with me?" she asked.

He shook his head. Glistening tears pooled in the bottom of his eyes. The cobwebs were thick, but she had to stay focused. Why in the world was he so upset? *Mosquito bites . . . Anse-a-Pitres . . .* They were like puzzle pieces. The truth struck her with such shattering force, without thinking, she spoke the words out loud. "Oh, no – Katie – dengue fever."

Jake placed his face in his hands. Hanna pushed herself up while biting her lower lip in an effort to keep from crying out in pain. Slowly she moved her legs until they hung over the side of the bed. She gripped his shoulders and pulled him to her, then gently rubbed her hand up and down his back. She could feel his wet face against her neck. "It's going to be okay," she said.

"I can't do it again," he sobbed. "Oh Lord, I can't go through that kind of heartache again."

"Shh . . . I'm going to be okay." She choked on her own tears. "Come on . . . listen . . . even if I have dengue fever, I'm going to be okay. What happened with Katie won't happen again."

His body relaxed, but he clung to her like a little boy. She ran her fingers through his hair. It felt amazingly soft; she'd expected it to be coarse. A few minutes later, he sat up straight. As she wiped the dampness from his cheek, he grasped her hand, leaned over and kissed her tenderly. As bad as she felt, the taste of his lips on hers still sent chills up and down her spine.

"I hope whatever I have isn't contagious," she whispered.

He offered her a fragile smile. "I'm sorry," he said, looking down at her hands now clasped tightly in his. "You can't imagine the pain . . . " His voice broke. "After I lost Katie, I never dreamed I could love that way again. For a long time I didn't want to. Then God brought you into my life." He moistened his lips with his tongue as he placed his hands on either side of her face. Leaning in, he kissed her again. "It's not contagious," he said, his mouth only inches from hers.

After helping her get settled back in bed, he took her hand in his once again.

"Do you think I have dengue fever?" she asked as she closed her eyes.

"I do."

"Do you think I'm going to die?"

His laugh sounded shaky. "No. For a while you may think you're going to, but I'm sure in a week or two you'll be fine."

"But Katie died."

"She developed hemorrhagic fever. Once that happens, chances of survival decrease, especially if it's not detected and treated early. I didn't know the difference. Until she went into shock, I thought it was a simple matter of treating the symptoms. By the time I realized something was terribly wrong and managed to get her to a hospital in Santo Domingo, it was too late."

Hanna opened her eyes, turning her head to look at him. "I thought she'd died from complications of dengue."

"I guess you might say that's what dengue hemorrhagic fever is, but it's very rare and happens more frequently with children or people who've had dengue fever before."

"Why were you wanting to know if I had been bitten by mosquitoes earlier in the day?"

Jake leaned a little closer. "Because . . . mosquitoes that carry dengue usually bite during the day, not at night. Mosquitoes that carry malaria generally start biting around dusk."

Hanna closed her eyes again. They felt like they were on fire. "Since I was bitten during the daytime *and* at night, how do you know I don't have malaria?"

He chuckled. "So many questions. You sound like Isabela."

"But *how* do you know?"

Another chuckle. "*Be . . . cause* symptoms are different. Plus it's a little too early for you to be showing signs of malaria."

"Oh."

"What? No more questions?"

"Well . . . maybe one more. How do you know I won't have complications?"

"Like I said earlier, it's rare for the disease to progress to the hemorrhagic stage – especially if you've never had dengue."

She thought she heard a tinge of doubt in his voice. "You aren't 100% sure, are you?"

"I'm sure," he said, releasing a sluggish sigh. "It's just a part of me says, *what if?*"

"I had a discussion one time with a friend about the *what ifs*. You know what she told me?"

"What?" Jake asked as he rubbed his thumb up and down the back of her hand again.

"The *what ifs* are of the devil. He uses them to rob us of our joy in the Lord."

"I think your friend was right. The enemy wants to use this to take away the newfound joy I have in the Lord and in my relationship with you. Well . . . I'm not going to let him"

"Me, either . . . " Hanna whispered.

Chapter Thirty-Seven

Hanna suffered through a restless night. One minute she would feel chilled and shake until her teeth chattered, and the next – she wouldn't have been surprised if someone told her she was sleeping on top of a hot furnace. Every muscle throbbed and each individual joint ached. Whenever she shifted positions in bed she had to stifle the natural reflex to cry out in pain. Her eyes burned even behind closed lids. She was vaguely aware of the coming and going of a handful of people: Maleah, Conner, Giselle and Señora García. As far as she knew, Jake never left her apartment. Once during the night she heard him snoring. Opening her eyes, she found him sleeping in one of the chairs in her sitting room. With his head resting against the wall, long legs stretched out in front and arms folded across his chest, she guessed he had to have been terribly uncomfortable.

She awoke the following morning to the sound of Jake and Isabela talking in hushed tones near the door.

"But Daddy, I'll be real quiet. I promise."

"Darling, I know, but Aunt Hanna doesn't feel well. She'll be better in a few days, then you can see her."

"But I colored this picture for her." Isabela's voice trembled. "I'll just give it to her and then leave."

"Maybe later. Let's see how she's feeling this afternoon."

"But Daddy . . . "

Hanna opened her eyes and lifted her hand, trying to get Jake's attention. He glanced in her direction. From where Isabela stood on the other side of the half opened door, the child couldn't see her. "Jake, it's okay," she said, her words a raspy whisper. "Let her come in."

He shook his head. She could hear Isabela crying.

"Really. It's okay," Hanna said.

Shaking his head again, this time in disapproving compromise, Jake pushed the door open wider. "You can stop crying now. Aunt Hanna said it's okay, but you can only stay a minute."

Hanna coerced her lips into a shaky smile and reached her hand toward the child. "Hi sugar. How are you doing this morning?"

Isabela sniffed and wiped the tears from her cheeks with the back of her hand. "Fine." She held out a piece of paper. "I drew this for you."

Hanna waved her over. "Let me see."

The child inched her way toward the bed and handed her the picture. It was a drawing of a turquoise house with three people standing in the front yard. At the top of the page a big, yellow sun filled the blue sky.

"It's beautiful."

"That's you and me and Daddy."

Hanna laid the picture on the bed and then wrapped her arm around the child, pulling her close. "I love it. Thank you for coming to see me." Isabela nodded and offered her a shy, dimpled smile before glancing up at Jake. Hanna had never known her to be so quiet. She drew her tighter, resisting the urge to cry out when pain radiated through her arm and shoulder. "I love you," she said.

"I love you too," Isabela replied.

The child's bottom lip quivered, and a tear slid down her cheek. Hanna wiped it away. "What's wrong, sweetheart?"

Isabela's blue eyes flooded. "You're not going to die, are you?"

Jake knelt beside her. "You and I already talked about this – Remember? Aunt Hanna is going to be fine."

Isabela snubbed as tears clumped her thick bottom lashes.

Hanna took her hand. "Sweetie, I really am going to be okay. You remember when you were sick and how bad you felt, but after a little while you felt better, didn't you?"

The child's dark ringlets bounced as she nodded.

"It's going to be the same with me," Hanna said.

"Do you want me to get Celia to make you some chicken soup?"

"I would love to have some of Celia's chicken soup. I'll even let you feed it to me if you'd like."

Isabela's trembling lips curled into a smile. "Okay, maybe for lunch or dinner."

"That sounds good."

After Jake escorted the child back into the main house, he returned to his post beside Hanna. He pushed her hair away from her face, his fingers caressing her cheek as he withdrew his hand. "Sorry about that," he said.

"No problem. It was probably a good idea to let her see that I'm okay."

"So are you?"

"What? Okay?"

He nodded as he took her hand.

"I suppose. Okay is a relative term," she said.

He leaned closer. "Meaning you're really not okay."

"I feel like someone beat me with a sledge hammer," she said, closing her eyes, "but other than that . . . "

"You moaned off and on all night."

"And *you* snored."

"I don't snore."

Hanna looked at him through narrowed eyes as a grin teased the corners of her mouth. "I know . . . you just breathe heavily."

His offended expression dissolved into a smile as he rubbed his thumb along the back of her hand. A tingling sensation crept up her arm spreading fingers of warmth from the top of her head to the ends of her toes. How could she feel so bad and yet so good all at the same time?

~~~~~

For two more days Hanna battled a high fever along with the aches and pains associated with dengue fever. Jake hovered anxiously over her day and night. He had spoken with a doctor at the small hospital in Paraíso, who assured him – considering Hanna's symptoms – there was nothing to worry about, and the fever would simply have to run its course. Even so, Jake wore his concern like a heavy wool coat, which in the tropical climate of Paraíso was hard to miss. What little sleep he got was on a cot Conner set up in the sitting area of Hanna's apartment. She tried to get him to go home where he could get a good night's rest in a real bed, but he wouldn't hear of it.

Isabela returned twice, both times bringing Sophie and a bowl of chicken soup, which between giggles they spoon-fed her. Maleah checked on her like clockwork. When Giselle stopped by Monday morning, Jake told Hanna he was going home to take a quick shower and then check on a few items of business at the Community Center.

After he left, Giselle sat down in the chair beside Hanna's bed. "For you I pray. We all pray," she said, practicing her English.

"Thank you. I appreciate it. How was church yesterday?"

"Bien. We miss you."

"I missed being there. Hopefully I will be back next Sunday."

Giselle shook her head. "I hope. Tal vez no. Dengue – you sick más."

"Have you ever had dengue fever?"

"No. My sister. Sick dos weeks."

Hanna nodded. "Then maybe in two Sundays I'll be back."

Giselle smiled and nodded. "I pray más. Mi familia pray too."

~~~~

Sometime during the early morning hours the next day, Hanna awoke feeling as though she'd stepped out of the shower soaking wet and gotten in bed without drying off. Her pajamas and sheets were drenched in sweat and she felt much cooler. The pain was also significantly less. She sent Jake to get fresh sheets from Maleah while she slipped into the bathroom to change into a dry pair of pajamas. Once Jake and Maleah had her comfortably settled back in bed, Maleah returned to the kitchen to start breakfast. Jake pulled the chair back over beside the bed and sat down.

"I feel a lot better," Hanna said.

He only nodded.

"I thought you would be relieved."

"I am," he replied, offering her an unconvincing smile.

She arched an eyebrow. "Why do I sense there's a *but* in there somewhere?"

He ran his index finger down her nose. "Because there is."

Hanna sighed. Was she going to have to drag it out of him? "Okay, what is it?"

"You're not well yet."

"How do you know?"

He glanced toward the back of the apartment. "I just know dengue fever. This is kind of like the eye of a hurricane."

Staring at him, she repeated what he'd said. "Like the eye of a hurricane . . ." Her eyes widened as the truth registered. "Are you saying I'm going to have to go through what I just went through – *again*?"

Jake focused his eyes on her. "I'm afraid so. Maybe not as bad, but the fever and the pain will return, along with a rash."

"A rash?" She pulled the sheet back. "Like this?" she asked, pointing to her measles-covered legs.

"Like that."

Less than twenty-four hours later the fever returned, along with the all too familiar aches and pains. Hanna was tired of hurting. The following morning she noticed her throat was sore and she felt a little nauseated. By early afternoon waves of nausea rolled over her frequently. She had only picked at the sandwich Maleah brought earlier; she wished she hadn't eaten what little she had. The food lodged in her throat, threatening at any moment to come back up. She tried to relax, but the nausea refused to go away.

Jake sat in one of the wicker chairs in the sitting area of her apartment, reading a book. She'd already consumed enough of his time lately; she hated to disturb him. Except for a few hours the previous day when she felt better, he had only left her side for short periods of time, usually just long enough to run home, take a shower and change clothes. If she had doubted his love before, she certainly didn't any longer. While she'd been ecstatic when he'd asked her to marry him, she knew the truth: In the days immediately following his proposal, she'd cried out to God more than once for the peace she knew she had to have before she'd be able to follow through on their plans to get married. Although she felt certain God had brought them together, up until a couple of days ago she had continued to struggle with fears of rejection. When she got well she was going to celebrate the fact she was finally convinced she could trust the man she loved.

Moments later her lunch rose in her throat, and she realized she was fighting a losing battle. "Jake," she whispered as she sat up. She gripped the side of the bed as the room starting spinning around her. She closed her eyes, hoping it would stop.

Jake rushed to her side. "What are you trying to do?" he asked as he encouraged her to lie back down.

"I think I'm going to be sick. I need you to help me get to the bathroom."

He glanced around. "Is there a trash can over here somewhere?"

She dared to shake her head.

He slipped his arm around her waist and helped her to her feet. The room swayed, and her wobbly legs gave way. In one smooth motion he scooped her up in his arms and carried her to the bathroom.

After heaving her lunch and flushing it away, Hanna sat on the bathroom floor resting her head on the rim of the white porcelain toilet. Jake ran a cool, wet washcloth over her forehead before cupping his hand under her chin and lifting her face so he could wipe her mouth.

She blinked back tears. "This has been the ultimate test. You really do love me, don't you?" she said.

He leaned over and kissed the top of her head. "I really do. Are you ready to go back to bed or do you still need a minute?"

She could feel and hear her stomach rumbling, but the nausea was gone. "I think I'm ready to go back to bed now."

Jake picked her up with what seemed to be no more effort than he would have needed had she been a small child. When she nestled her face into his neck, his beard tickled her cheek. He sat on the bed, still holding her in his arms. She pressed her head against his shoulder.

"When did you start feeling nauseated?" he asked.

"Sometime earlier today. It's been coming and going for several hours."

"Any other new symptoms?"

She swallowed. "My throat is a little sore and I've felt real clammy . . . Guess that goes with the nausea."

He stood and gently lowered her onto the bed. Taking one of her hands in his, he examined the rash on her arm. "Let's take your temp again," he said a few seconds later.

The thermometer beeped. After taking it out of her mouth, he looked at it and shook his head. "104.1." His forehead creased in thought as he gazed toward the sitting room window.

Exhausted, Hanna closed her eyes. "What are you thinking?" she asked.

"I think . . . "

When he didn't say anything more, she barely lifted one eyelid. He was nodding as if to add emphasis to what he was getting ready to say. "I think it's time you and I made a trip to Santo Domingo," he finally said.

Her eyes flew open. "Santo Domingo. Why?"

"I want a doctor I know there to look at you. I waited too long once before. I'm not going to do it again."

A torrent of tears overflowed Hanna's eyes, cascading down her cheeks. Jake sat on the side of the bed and pulled her to him. She snuggled against his chest. "But you told me it was only dengue fever," she said between muffled sobs.

"I still think that's all it is, but these new symptoms have me concerned." His voice sounded thick. "If something happened, I could never forgive myself. I've only recently gotten over the guilt of knowing I allowed Katie to die. I'm not going to do it again."

Hanna pulled back, looking at him through watery eyes. "It's not your fault Katie died," she said, the words intermingled with hiccups and sniffles.

He sighed. "In some ways it was. If I'd gotten her to the

hospital sooner . . . " A anguished moan escaped his throat.

"No Jake – it wasn't your fault."

~~~~~

Hanna could barely endure the pain of getting up and down to go to the bathroom, she was afraid to imagine the impact four or five hours on bumpy roads was going to have on her tired achy body, not to mention the additional nausea weaving up, down and around mountain roads would generate. Jake promised to drive slowly. She knew he would try, but doubted it would make much difference.

Maleah made the trip with them. By the time they arrived in Santo Domingo Hanna's pain level was a ten and still rising. She had been battling dry heaves for several hours and no longer had the strength to open her eyes. She had given up on trying to talk. Drifting in and out of consciousness, she heard Jake and Maleah fussing over her, and then felt herself being lifted onto a gurney and wheeled into what she later learned was one of the better hospitals in Santo Domingo. Once inside she was cognizant of medical personnel working on her, hooking her up to an IV, taking her blood pressure, listening to her heart, but through it all she never regained enough strength to respond; even the effort it took to move her hands or feet seemed more than she could manage. She knew her lack of responsiveness would probably propel Jake into a state of panic, but she was too tired to continue fighting. She drifted off, praying God would comfort him and fill his heart with His peace.

~~~~~

Waiting in the hallway while the doctor and two nurses worked on Hanna, Jake paced the floor for a few minutes before resting his weary body against the wall and sliding to the white tiled floor. The smell of disinfectants hung in the air, dredging up painful memories he wanted to forget. Leaning forward, he placed his face in his hands. Maleah settled in beside him, the touch of her hand warm on his arm. He didn't look up. "Wasn't once enough?" he asked. "Why do I have to do this again?"

Her voice was soft, but firm. "Jake Mason, you listen to me. This isn't going to end the way it did the last time. Don't *you* give up!" She gripped his arm. "Do you hear me?"

He shook his head. Giving way to self-pity seemed fitting. "I tried holding on in faith last time. What good did it do me?"

Maleah sighed, and then he heard her quietly praying. He was glad someone could because he knew he couldn't – not after he'd finally let go and trusted God again, only to have Him betray his trust – just like He'd done three years before.

An older Dominican nurse with dark, weathered skin stepped from the room where they had taken Hanna. "You may come in now," she said in Spanish.

Jake rose and helped Maleah to her feet, and then followed her into the room. The doctor and one of the nurses still worked on getting Hanna settled. An IV dripped rehydrating fluids into her body, while another machine monitored her heart rate and blood pressure. Other than the steady rise and fall of her chest, she lay perfectly still.

The doctor turned and spoke to them Spanish. "We've gotten her stabilized, but I can't promise she's completely out of the woods yet. She's a very sick young woman."

Jake bit his lower lip in an effort to hold back the scream that had risen in his throat. Weren't those the exact words this same doctor said to him the night he brought Katie in? What kind of sick joke was this?

"Doctor, is there anyway you can tell if she has hemorrhagic fever?" Maleah asked.

The doctor's eyes rested on Jake for a few seconds before settling on Maleah. "My first inclination is to say it's just a serious case of dengue. There doesn't appear to be any of the typical bleeding symptoms of hemorrhagic fever. And while I'm sure she's given you a good scare, I don't think she's gone into hemorrhagic shock. She appears to be sleeping or has possibly fainted due to the pain. She's also severely dehydrated. Once we get fluids in her, along with some pain medication, I'm hopeful she'll come back around. Of course that may take a few hours. We'll keep a close eye on her."

"So are you saying she's in no danger of dying?" Maleah asked.

"As long as there are no further complications . . ." he said, patting Jake on the arm as he walked toward the door.

Jake stepped to the side of Hanna's bed. After brushing strands of dark hair away from her face, he leaned down and kissed her on the forehead. Large tears spilled over and splattered on the pillow. Maleah came and stood beside him. "I'm sorry for getting so upset," he said between sobs. "I just don't understand why God would let this happen again."

"I know." She sniffed away her own tears. "I certainly won't pretend to understand. But I'm not giving up hope, and neither are you."

"I haven't," he said. Picking up Hanna's limp hand, he closed his eyes and began to pray. "Father, I don't understand why Hanna had to get sick, but I've got to trust that none of this has taken You by surprise. Please forgive me for my anger and lack of faith. It's just hard to watch her suffer and then feel so helpless to do anything about it. Maybe that's the point – You want me to know You're the One I am to be trusting to take care of the ones I love. So Lord, I'm asking You to hide us in the shadow of Your hand."

His voice broke and a few more tears rolled down his cheeks. He drew a shaky breath before continuing. "Lord, I love her, but I know You love her even more than I do. Ultimately I know I've got to trust You, but I want her to be my wife, and Isabela is so excited about having her as her new mommy. So Father, would You please touch and heal her body?"

Once he'd finished praying, Maleah started to sing. Jake recognized the song as the one she had sung during the early morning hours while they sat in the hall waiting for the hurricane to pass. A soothing peace he could not explain settled upon his troubled heart, and he knew they were not alone. His tears splashed on the hospital blanket like raindrops on a sidewalk during a spring shower.

~~~~~

The night hours tarried, and it seemed the morning delayed

her arrival. While Hanna did not grow worse, neither did she show any drastic signs of improvement. Sitting beside the hospital bed, Jake kept a silent watch, while Maleah slept on a small sofa under the window.

A thin rose-colored streak was forcing its way through a slit between the thick curtains when the doctor walked in, Hanna's chart in his hand. "Her vital signs are stable." He flipped to a second page and his forehead furrowed. "I have to admit I'm puzzled over the fact she's still unresponsive. I was hopeful she was just dehydrated and would come around once we got some fluids in her. Have you noticed any movements – hands, feet, eyelids – anything?"

"Nothing I could see," Jake answered.

"Has she made any sounds? Any moaning or groaning – like she's in pain?"

Jake shook his head. "Nothing."

"Most puzzling," the doctor said as he picked up her hand and examined the rash on her arm before pulling her eyelids back and checking her eyes. "I still don't see any indications this might be hemorrhagic fever. We've had cases . . . " he stopped and cleared his throat, looking for a moment at Jake, "as you well know . . . when a patient with dengue hemorrhagic fever goes into shock and then a coma, but . . . let's give her a few more hours. In the meanwhile, why don't you two talk to her, see if you can get some kind of reaction from her."

Caribbean Paradise

Chapter Thirty-Eight

Hanna could hear voices – talking over her, talking about her – but any attempt to open her eyes or move her lips to speak seemed an unattainable task. Her hands and feet felt like lead. She'd awakened earlier and heard Maleah singing the song she sang the night of the hurricane. She'd also heard Jake praying. But lacking the strength to say anything, she'd soon drifted back to sleep. Now that she was awake again she was determined to say or do something. Someone stroked the back of her hand; she felt certain it was Jake, his thumb rubbing up and down. The tender expression of his love brought a smile to her lips.

"Look," she heard Maleah say. "Jake, look – she's smiling!"

Hanna felt Jake grip her hand. His voice penetrated through the fog. "Hanna, sweetheart, are you awake? If so, move your hand."

She fought against the grogginess that seemed determined to keep her imprisoned in a black hole. *You can do it,* she told herself as she labored in her efforts to obey his command.

"Good," he said. "Maleah, she squeezed my hand."

Another smile lifted the corners of Hanna's mouth. Jake sounded so pleased she couldn't help herself. A second later she felt someone's breath near her face. She breathed in the subtle scent of Jake's cologne just before his lips touched hers. Mustering enough strength to speak, she whispered, "I love you."

A full-blown celebration erupted around her. She wanted to open her eyes, but her lids felt as if someone had injected them with a numbing agent. Once again, she fell into a deep slumber.

She awoke a while later to the sound of a male voice

speaking Spanish. Still battling grogginess, she opened her eyes to blurry and unfamiliar surroundings. A man wearing a white medical jacket – she guessed he was a doctor – stood on her right. She turned to look at Jake, sitting in a chair drawn up close to the other side of the bed. His smile was broader than any she'd seen on his face in recent days.

"Hey, sweetheart," he said.

"Hey to you too," she said. She wouldn't have thought it possible, but Jake's smile got even bigger. She could hear Maleah laughing behind him.

"How do you feel?" he asked.

Hanna surveyed the room. She blinked several times, hoping to chase away the cobwebs. Her eyelids still felt heavy. What was it Jake had asked her? She couldn't remember.

"Where am I?" she asked.

"In a hospital in Santo Domingo," he answered.

She nodded. Her tongue felt thick. "I have dengue fever."

"That's right. You got dehydrated, so the doctor admitted you to the hospital and put you on an IV for fluids."

Trying to think was akin to fighting her way through dense, murky water. Why was she so groggy? "Am I on any kind of medication for pain?" she asked.

"Ah, yeah . . . you are." Jake looked at the doctor and asked in Spanish what they were giving her.

"That's what wrong," Hanna said before the man could respond.

"What's that?" Jake asked.

"The pain medication – whatever it is – a little bit goes a long way with me. If he put me on a normal dosage, it's too much." Her words sounded slurred even to her own ears.

"Do you want me to ask him to lower the dosage?"

"Ask him to take me off of it all together. If I'm still dehydrated and need the fluids, that's fine, but I'd rather not have any more pain medication."

Jake arched an eyebrow. "Are you sure?"

She nodded. "I don't like this drugged feeling. I'd rather be in pain."

While the nurse worked on removing the bag containing medication for pain, Hanna closed her eyes and drifted back to sleep. When she awoke a while later, all was quiet. She turned her head to the left and could see Maleah curled up on a small sofa positioned along the far wall. Jake sat in a chair beside her, his arms and head resting on the hospital bed. The soft, rhythmic sound of his breathing told her he was asleep. Tears of joy filled her eyes as she realized how much she loved him. She raised her hand, which already felt much lighter, and laced her fingers through his hair. As before, she was surprised at how soft it felt. He stirred, but did not awaken.

~~~~~

Two weeks passed before Hanna felt she was finally regaining her strength and feeling more like herself. It was time to return to the classroom. She could only imagine how far behind the children were in their studies. If it were not for her relationship with Jake, she would have probably been dismissed months ago. She'd been in the country almost eight months and had spent only a little over a month of that time doing what she'd come to do. Since returning from the hospital, she'd prayed repeatedly that God would keep her from slipping into a pit of shame over this grim reality.

"I'm hoping to start classes again soon," she said to Maleah one evening as they prepared supper.

Maleah nodded while continuing to brown the hamburger meat she had in a skillet on the stove. "Sounds good to me, as long as you feel you're ready."

"I'm still a little weak, but I'm sure I'll be fine. I just feel bad because the children have already missed so much."

"It's not your fault."

Hanna pulled tomatoes and lettuce from the refrigerator. "I feel like it is."

"No big deal. They're fine." Maleah's back looked rigid. "I've been working with them while you recuperated," she said.

Hanna drew a deep breath as she chose a knife from a nearby drawer. Was it her imagination or did Maleah sound a bit put out? "That's another reason I'm feeling bad about all of this," she said as she began chopping the tomatoes she'd placed on a cutting board next to where Maleah was cooking. "I'm supposed to be relieving you from that responsibility so you can be more involved in the work with Conner."

Maleah walked to the sink and drained grease from the skillet. Returning to the stove, she looked at Hanna. "You do realize, don't you, that once you and Jake get married and move to Pedernales, I'm going to be teaching my children again anyway? Your classroom is going to shrink significantly."

Hanna continued chopping tomatoes. "I guess you're right. This isn't exactly what you bargained for when you requested a teacher, is it?"

"Can't say that it is, but I'm trying hard not to complain. Although I thought God was bringing you here to teach our children, He obviously had other plans."

Sensing disappointment in her friend's voice, tears smarted Hanna's eyes. "I'm sorry it hasn't worked out," she said.

Maleah stirred tomato sauce into the browned hamburger meat, and then added chopped onions and garlic. "Me too," she finally said, wiping her hands on a kitchen towel. "I'm going to miss you."

"You're not upset because the children have missed so much school?"

"Gracious no." Maleah slipped her arm around Hanna's waist and hugged her. "I'm just already anticipating how lonely I'm going to be once you're gone. I know we'll be close enough to visit, but it won't be the same."

"I'm going to miss you too," Hanna said. "I've really come to count on your friendship."

"I keep telling myself it'll be okay," Maleah said, her voice choked with tears. "I know things are turning out according to God's plans, so we have to trust Him."

"Yeah, you're right. I continue to be amazed at how God works. All through seminary and the two years I spent teaching in Alabama, I kept asking Him to bring a godly man into my life who also felt called to missions." A small chuckle rose in Hanna's throat. "I had these idealistic visions of us skipping off into the sunset of blissful missionary service."

The cheerful sound of Maleah's laughter was a welcome relief compared to the tension a few minutes earlier.

"I guess lesson #1 is that life is not a fairy tale," Hanna said.

"That's for sure. What happened when Prince Charming never showed?"

"I tried to reconcile myself to the possibility that marriage was not in God's plan for me."

"I bet that was hard to do."

"Extremely." Hanna dropped torn pieces of lettuce into a bowl before turning to look at Maleah. "I've dreamed of being a wife and mother since I was a little girl. I'll never forget the night I finally laid it all down on the altar before the Lord. Surrendering those precious hopes and dreams was one of the hardest things I've ever done, but I knew I was at a crossroads in my relationship with God. Either I sacrificed it all to Him or I ran the risk of moving outside of His will for my life."

"At any time did you feel God was calling you to remain single for the rest of your life?" Maleah asked, giving the spaghetti sauce a stir.

"I didn't know for sure, but I felt He wanted me to be willing if that was His plan. I certainly never dreamed He had my future husband waiting for me in the Dominican Republic."

Maleah grinned. "Literally . . . Waiting at the airport to pick you up."

Hanna threw her head back and laughed. "I don't think Jake had asking me to marry him on his mind that night."

"Probably not." Maleah hesitated a moment before continuing. "I know the saying may be overused at times, but God really does work in mysterious ways. Just think, while you were surrendering your dreams of marriage and motherhood, Conner and I were praying for a wife and mother for Jake and Isabela. We even prayed she'd be someone who wanted to serve in the Dominican Republic. The thought never crossed my mind the person God sent to teach our children was going to be the answer to our prayers."

~~~~~

"You want to go to the watering hole at Los Patos?" Jake asked Hanna the following morning when he stopped by for a visit. "If we go now we can avoid the weekend crowd."

Reddish gray circles beneath his eyes made her wonder if he had been having trouble sleeping. Her stomach knotted up. "Well, sure," she said. "Is everything okay?"

"What wouldn't be okay?"

He hadn't exactly answered her question. Hanna still sensed something was bothering him. The sick feeling in the pit of her stomach was not going to easily be dispelled. "You look tired, that's all."

He closed his eyes and rubbed the corners with the knuckles of his index fingers. "I guess I am. I've had a lot of catching up to do at the Community Center."

He hadn't said it, but she knew it was her fault he was behind in his work.

~~~~~

Hanna settled in beside Jake on the same boulder at Los Patos where they had sat only days before the hurricane hit. She dangled her bare feet in the sparkling clear water. It was cooler than it had been two months earlier; even so, it was hard to believe autumn was well underway back home and her mother would soon be planning Thanksgiving dinner. Fall in the tropics simply meant it wasn't as humid, but for that blessing Hanna was thankful. Jake stared straight ahead and appeared to be deep in thought. She fought the temptation to give way to fears, which had been lurking just below the surface for the last forty-five minutes. She waved a hand in front of his eyes. When he looked at her, she forced her lips into a smile. "What's up?" she asked, more lightheartedly than she felt.

He shrugged. "I've been thinking about this assignment in Pedernales."

"And . . ."

He took a deep breath. "I'm not sure that's where we need to be."

"So everything's okay between you and me?"

His brow creased in a puzzled frown. "Is there some reason why it wouldn't be?"

She shook her head, not trusting her voice. She feared she might break into tears if she tried to speak. He put his arm around her shoulders and pulled her to him. She laid the side of her face against his chest. "You and I are fine," he said. "I've just been thinking about turning down the assignment in Pedernales and telling the board we've decided to stay in Paraíso."

"Why would you do that?" she asked, sitting up straight and looking at him. "A few weeks ago you were totally convinced God wanted us to work in Pedernales and Anse-a-Pitres. Why the sudden change of heart?"

Jake stared at the water. "I don't know . . . The work in Paraíso is going well. Isabela has settled in and made friends here. You have Maleah and Giselle. I have Conner." He lifted his shoulders. "I was thinking it would be easier not to uproot everyone right now."

"Jake Mason!" Hanna said as exasperation replaced the fear she'd been battling earlier. "When did what we're doing become a matter of what's easier?"

He darted his eyes at her, then looked away. "I'm not sure I'm ready to take you and Isabela to Pedernales. I know life isn't easy here, but it's even harder there."

She couldn't believe what she was hearing. "You think I don't know that?" she said. "But if that's where God wants us, we can't just decide to take the easy way out. "

"Yeah, I know . . . "

Hanna gazed across the fresh water pool toward the gnarled mangrove swamp, which although rearranged by the hurricane, had amazingly remained intact. All the original clapboard eateries were gone, but several new wood structures stood beneath the palm trees. "Come on Jake, talk to me," she said when she realized he wasn't going to say anything else. When he turned to look at her, she ran the back of her fingers along his bearded jaw. "Are you going to tell me what's bothering you or am I going to have to guess?" she asked.

He placed his hand on top of hers and held it tight against his face. "I thought I was going to lose you."

Hanna blinked. "I know, but you didn't. Is that what this is all about?"

He lowered their hands to his lap and entwined his fingers in hers. "I've been weighing the health dangers of living on the border with those of living here . . . that's all."

"But I could have gotten dengue fever in Paraíso or most anywhere else in the Dominican Republic. That's not a Haiti bound disease. You said so yourself."

"I know."

"So what's the problem? I know you're not a coward. Don't you let Satan win this one."

"But isn't it my responsibility to make decisions based on what I know will be best for you and Isabela?" His eyes pleaded with her to agree with him.

She leaned over and kissed him lightly on the lips, then pulled away, locking her eyes with his. "I know you already know this, but I'm going to tell you anyway," she said. "Ultimately, God is in charge of protecting us. Your responsibility as the spiritual leader of our home is to make sure we're all in the center of His will. No matter how hard you try, you cannot always be there to keep Isabela or me from harm. Only God can do that. And if God wants us living in Pedernales . . . if He wants us working in Anse-a-Pitres . . . then there is no safer place on earth for us to be."

Jake's jaw tensed. "I know . . . I know everything you just said is true, but I'm still struggling. I'm trying to figure out why God let you get sick in the first place. What was the point, especially when it brought up such painful memories for me?" The rigid muscles in his face relaxed and his chin trembled.

"First of all," Hanna said, praying for wisdom, "I don't believe God is ever obligated to tell us why He does what He does, although on occasion He will. Other times we simply have to trust Him. As for this particular situation, I feel what happened was mostly an attack of the devil. He doesn't want us working in Anse-a-Pitres or anywhere else in Haiti for that matter. For centuries he's had so many Haitian people blinded by voodoo, we'd be foolish to think he was going to easily give up any of the hold he has in that country."

"I agree, but – "

She reached out her hand. "Wait a minute, let me finish," she said. "I also believe Satan knew one of the quickest ways he could defeat you was for me to contract the same illness that had taken Katie. You were well on your way to being healed from the pain you suffered as a result of her death. We need to always remember – the enemy doesn't want you or me or anyone else to be set free from the bondage of past heartaches and disappointments." She took a deep breath. "Last of all . . . I know the good that God has brought about as a result of my illness."

Jake's eyes widened. "This I need to hear."

"Although I'd accepted your marriage proposal, I was wrestling with doubts," Hanna said, forcing the words through the thickness in her throat. "Satan was bombarding me with feelings of insecurity and fears of rejection. In the back of my mind I still wasn't convinced you wouldn't one day break my heart. I wanted to be your wife, but I was scared. I knew something was going to have to happen before I could follow through on our plans to get married."

Jake's mouth lifted in a shaky smile. "I'm trusting this is going to get better."

"It is . . . For you see, God used the way in which you faithfully stayed by my side and lovingly cared for me to finally convince me your love is real and genuine. Before I got sick, I was afraid to marry you. Now . . . I can't wait to be your wife."

"And you're not afraid to go back to Anse-a-Pitres?"

"Is that part of what's been bothering you? Did you think I wouldn't want to go back?"

"In part."

Hanna extracted her right foot from the water with such force droplets caught on a passing breeze, spraying them with a cool mist. "You need to silence that lie of the enemy right now," she said. "I'm not saying I don't have any fear or feelings of anxiousness about going, but I'm so convinced that is where God wants us, I'm willing to take the risk."

"And you're sure you want to marry me?"

She grinned. "I was waiting for that."

Jake lifted her chin with the tips of his fingers and gently stroked her cheek with his thumb. "Well . . . "

Shivers ran up her spine. "What did I tell you a few minutes ago?"

He brushed her lips with his. "I'd like to hear you say it again."

"I said . . . Now I can't wait to be your wife."

Praying Effectively for International Missionaries

1. Communication in another language: Hanna's fear of not being able to communicate in the language of her host country is a common concern among new missionaries.
Making it personal: Consider for a moment how you would feel if you had to function in a language other than English.
Pray . . .
*missionaries will be patient with themselves and one another, realizing that learning another language takes time.
*missionaries will be reminded that communicating the love of Christ is more important than being able to speak the language fluently.
"If I speak in the tongues of men and of angels, but have not love, I am only a resounding gong or a clanging cymbal." I Corinthians 13:1

2. Adjustments to the unique living conditions of their host country: Hanna quickly discovered that dealing with the living conditions in Paraíso was a lot more difficult than what she thought it would be when she had read about them.
Making it personal: How do you think you would handle frequent power outages or oppressive heat and humidity if you did not have air-conditioning?
Pray . . .
*God will give missionaries an extra measure of grace in order to make adjustments quickly.
*missionaries will be able to say with the Apostle Paul: *"I have learned to be content whatever the circumstances. I know what it is to be in need, and I know what it is to have plenty. I have learned the secret of being content in any and every situation . . . I can do everything through Christ who gives me strength."* Philippians 4:11-13

3. Separation from family and friends: On a number of occasions Maleah addressed the issue of loneliness. The truth is – missionaries often feel lonely.

Making it personal: Have you ever moved away from home – to another city, state or country? Do you know what it feels like to leave family and friends in order to go to school or work somewhere far away from home? Now imagine you are separated by an ocean. You cannot simply hop in the car and go see the ones you love and miss. If you were to fly, it would be expensive and could take as long as a day or two to make the trip. Spending holidays with your family would be out of the question. Even making a yearly trip back to the States might not be a reality.

Pray . . .

*for missionaries to experience a sense of "family" with other missionaries serving in the same city, mission, or country.

*for missionaries to be able to establish close friendships with some of the nationals in their host country.

*that missionaries will experience the promise Jesus made His disciples in Luke 18:28-30: *"Peter said to Him, 'We have left all we had to follow You!' 'I tell you the truth,' Jesus said, 'No one who has left home or wife or brothers or parents or children for the sake of the kingdom of God will fail to receive many times as much in this age and, in the age to come, eternal life.'"*

4. Health concerns: Jake experienced firsthand the heartache of losing a loved one to complications of a disease many in the States have never even heard of, much less had. Later he expressed a reluctance to return to Pedernales based on health risks involved.

Fact:

*Diseases rarely, if ever, seen in the United States are still common in many foreign countries. These include: malaria, cholera, typhoid, dengue fever, hepatitis, and intestinal problems caused by amebas and parasites.

*Most fruits and vegetables are not safe to consume without first disinfecting with bleach or iodine.

*Drinking tap water is to be avoided at all times, even when brushing teeth.

*If a missionary or a family member becomes ill, good or even adequate medical personnel and/or facilities are often not available.

*Communication when receiving medical care will generally be in the language of the host country.
Making it personal: Have you, your spouse, one of your children or another family member been sick lately? Gone to the doctor? Been hospitalized? What were your fears and concerns?
Pray...
*that God will protect missionaries and their families from sickness and disease.
"Beloved, I pray that in all respects you may prosper and be in good health, just as your soul prospers." III John 2

5. Safety concerns while at home and on the road: Maleah told Hanna she hoped if someone were to ever try and enter their property from the backyard, Greta – the family's pet Boxer – would give them a real scare. While visiting Santo Domingo, Hanna and Maleah both expressed a fear of driving in the nightmare they called traffic.
Fact:
*Petty theft and home break-ins are common in many foreign countries – terrorism is present in some.
*Driving in most foreign countries is like driving in the Indy 500.
Making it personal: Do you feel safe living in the area where you live? Has your home ever been broken into? Have you ever had anything stolen? Are you on the road much? Do you like to travel? What are your safety concerns when it comes to home and travel?
Pray...
*God will give His angels charge concerning missionaries and their families, to guard them in all their ways. Psalm 91:11
*at home and on the road, missionaries will dwell in the shelter of the Most High and abide in the shadow of the Almighty. Psalm 91:1

7. Spiritual warfare: Using an arsenal of lies and false accusations, Satan attacked Hanna her first night in Paraíso and then again on a number of other occasions. Later, Jake's failure to allow God to heal his broken heart served as an open invitation for an attack by the enemy. While visiting Anse-a-Pitres, Jake and Conner both noted the part voodoo plays in the spiritual darkness found on the island of

Hispaniola.
Fact:
*Missionaries all over the world daily seek to be a light in the darkness of false gods and religions such as Buddhism, Hinduism, Islam, voodoo, ancestor or tribal worship.
Pray . . .
*missionaries will daily be reminded that their *"struggle is not against flesh and blood, but against the rulers, against the authorities, against the powers of this dark world and against the spiritual forces of evil in the heavenly realms, therefore, they must be strong in the Lord and in the strength of His might, putting on the full armor of God, so that they will be able to stand firm against the schemes of the devil."* Ephesians 6:10-12

About the Author

Teri Metts is a pastor's wife and former missionary to the Dominican Republic. Over the past twenty-five years she has written Sunday School literature as well as numerous Bible studies, including two twelve-week studies, which have been used by God to help both men and women receive healing from past and present life hurts and begin the journey toward faithful, Christ-centered discipleship. Teri and her husband, Joe, live in Mississippi. They have three grown children and three grandchildren. In 2006, Teri and Joe bought their dream home – a 100-year-old bungalow. Be sure and check out Teri's Christian-based website at: www.bungalowretreat.com.

Made in the USA
Charleston, SC
27 September 2010